Paper Planes

LAURA CHACÓN
FOUNDER

MARK LONDON
CEO AND CHIEF CREATIVE
OFFICER

MARK IRWIN
SENIOR VICE PRESIDENT

MIKE MARTS
EVP AND EDITOR-IN-CHIEF

CHRIS FERNANDEZ
PUBLISHER

LAUREN HITZHUSEN
SENIOR EDITOR

GIOVANNA T. OROZCO
PRODUCTION MANAGER

MIGUEL A. ZAPATA
DESIGN DIRECTOR

DIANA BERMÚDEZ
GRAPHIC DESIGNER

DAVID REYES
GRAPHIC DESIGNER

SEBASTIAN RAMIREZ
GRAPHIC DESIGNER

ADRIANA T. OROZCO
INTERACTIVE MEDIA DESIGNER

NICOLÁS ZEA ARIAS
AUDIOVISUAL PRODUCTION

CECILIA MEDINA
CHIEF FINANCIAL OFFICER

STARLIN GONZALEZ
ACCOUNTING DIRECTOR

KURT NELSON
DIRECTOR OF SALES

ALLISON POND
MARKETING DIRECTOR

MAYA LOPEZ
MARKETING MANAGER

JAMES FACCINTO
PUBLICIST

GEOFFREY LAPID
SALES & MARKETING SPECIALIST

SPENSER NELLIS
MARKETING COORDINATOR

CHRIS LA TORRE
RETAIL RELATIONS MANAGER

CHRISTINA HARRINGTON
DIRECT MARKET SALES COORDINATOR

PEDRO HERRERA
RETAIL ASSOCIATE

FRANK SILVA
EXECUTIVE ASSISTANT

STEPHANIE HIDALGO
OFFICE MANAGER

MAVERICK

FOR MAD CAVE COMICS, INC.
Paper Planes™ Published by Mad Cave Studios, Inc. 8838 SW 129th St. Miami, FL 33176 ©
2023 Mad Cave Studios, Inc. All rights reserved.

Printed in India
ISBN: 978-1-952303-54-8

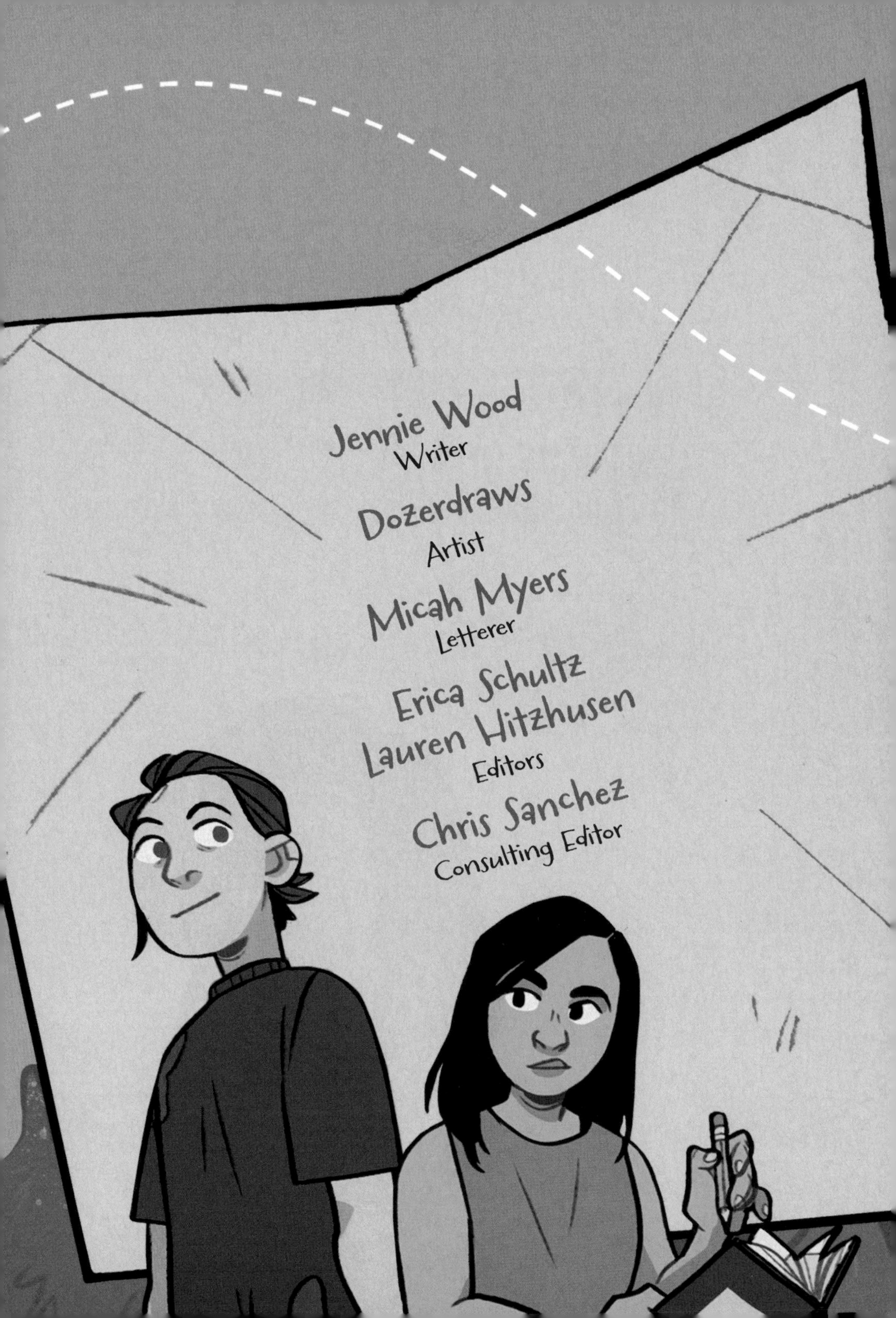
Jennie Wood
Writer
Dozerdraws
Artist
Micah Myers
Letterer
Erica Schultz
Lauren Hitzhusen
Editors
Chris Sanchez
Consulting Editor

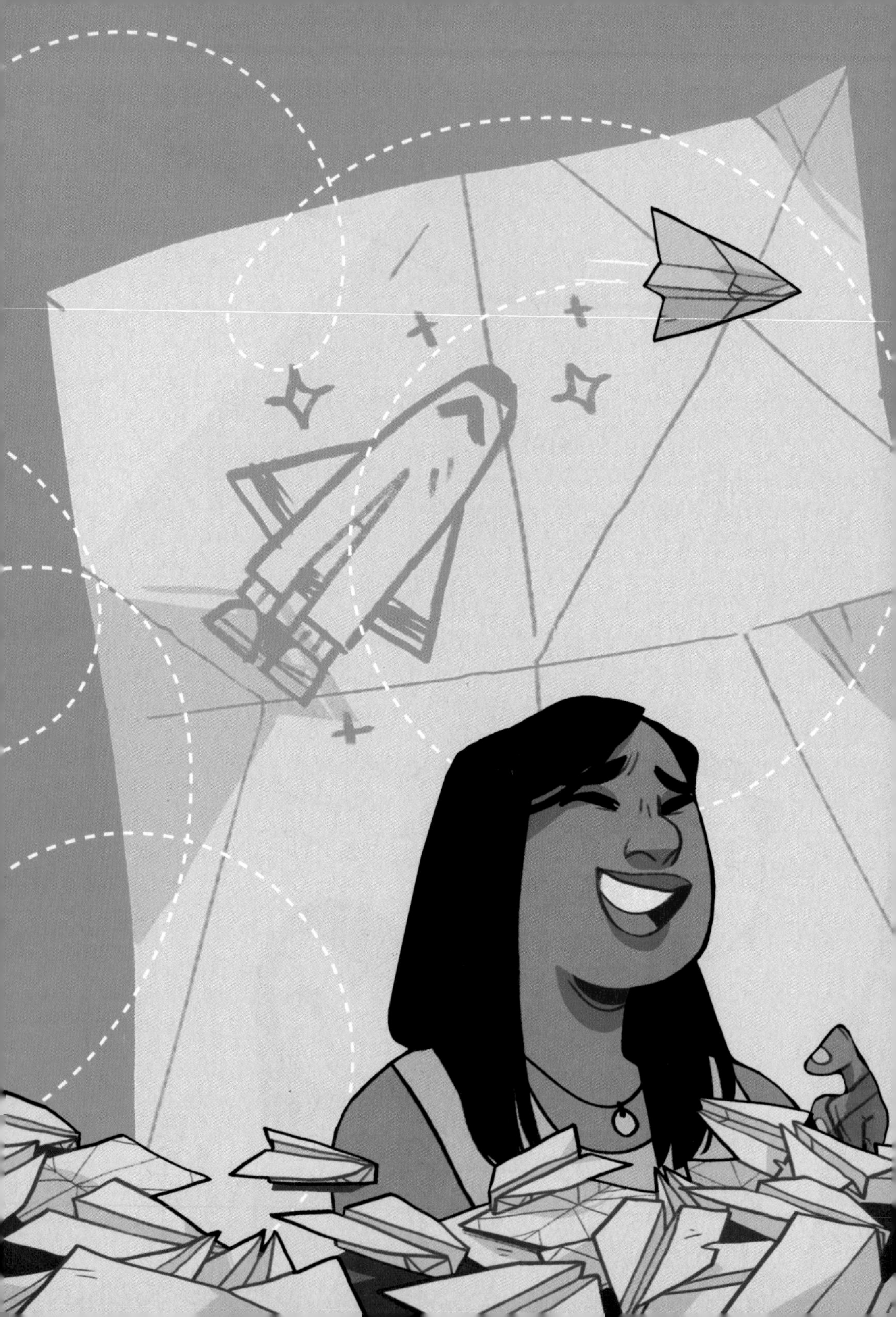

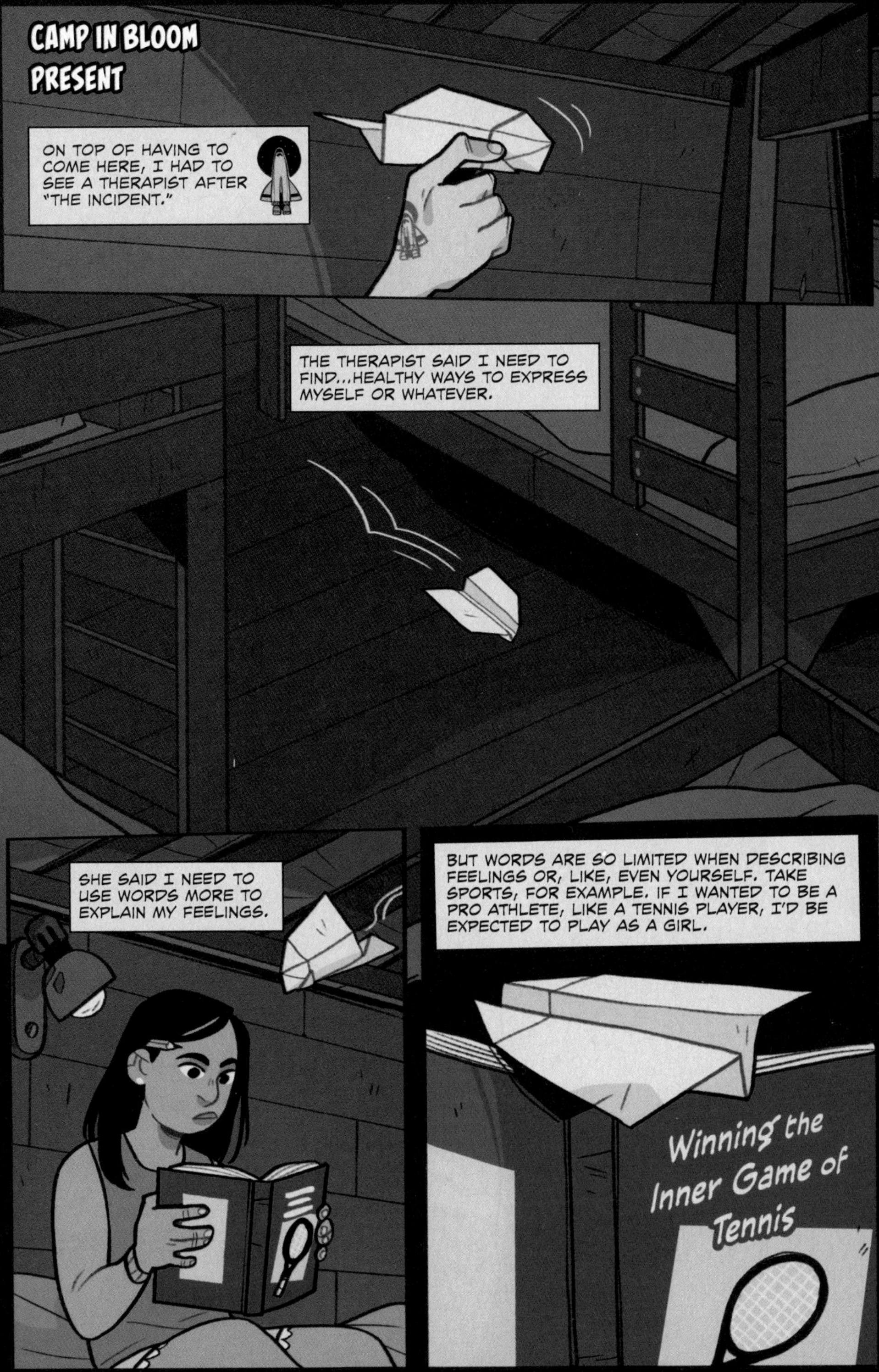
CAMP IN BLOOM
PRESENT
ON TOP OF HAVING TO COME HERE, I HAD TO SEE A THERAPIST AFTER "THE INCIDENT."
THE THERAPIST SAID I NEED TO FIND...HEALTHY WAYS TO EXPRESS MYSELF OR WHATEVER.
SHE SAID I NEED TO USE WORDS MORE TO EXPLAIN MY FEELINGS.
BUT WORDS ARE SO LIMITED WHEN DESCRIBING FEELINGS OR, LIKE, EVEN YOURSELF. TAKE SPORTS, FOR EXAMPLE. IF I WANTED TO BE A PRO ATHLETE, LIKE A TENNIS PLAYER, I'D BE EXPECTED TO PLAY AS A GIRL.
Winning the Inner Game of Tennis

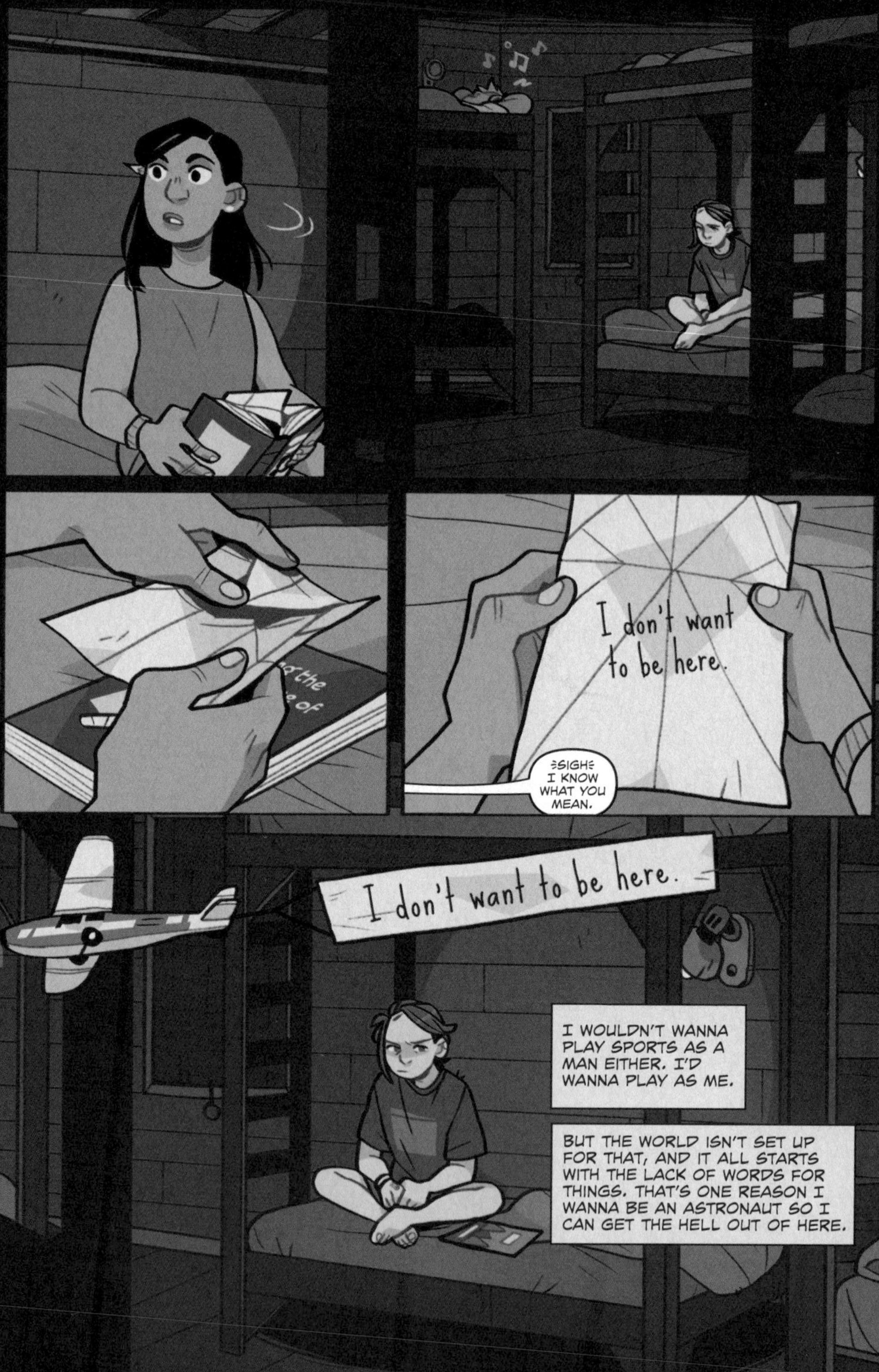
I don't want to be here.
=SIGH= I KNOW WHAT YOU MEAN.
I don't want to be here.
I WOULDN'T WANNA PLAY SPORTS AS A MAN EITHER. I'D WANNA PLAY AS ME.
BUT THE WORLD ISN'T SET UP FOR THAT, AND IT ALL STARTS WITH THE LACK OF WORDS FOR THINGS. THAT'S ONE REASON I WANNA BE AN ASTRONAUT SO I CAN GET THE HELL OUT OF HERE.

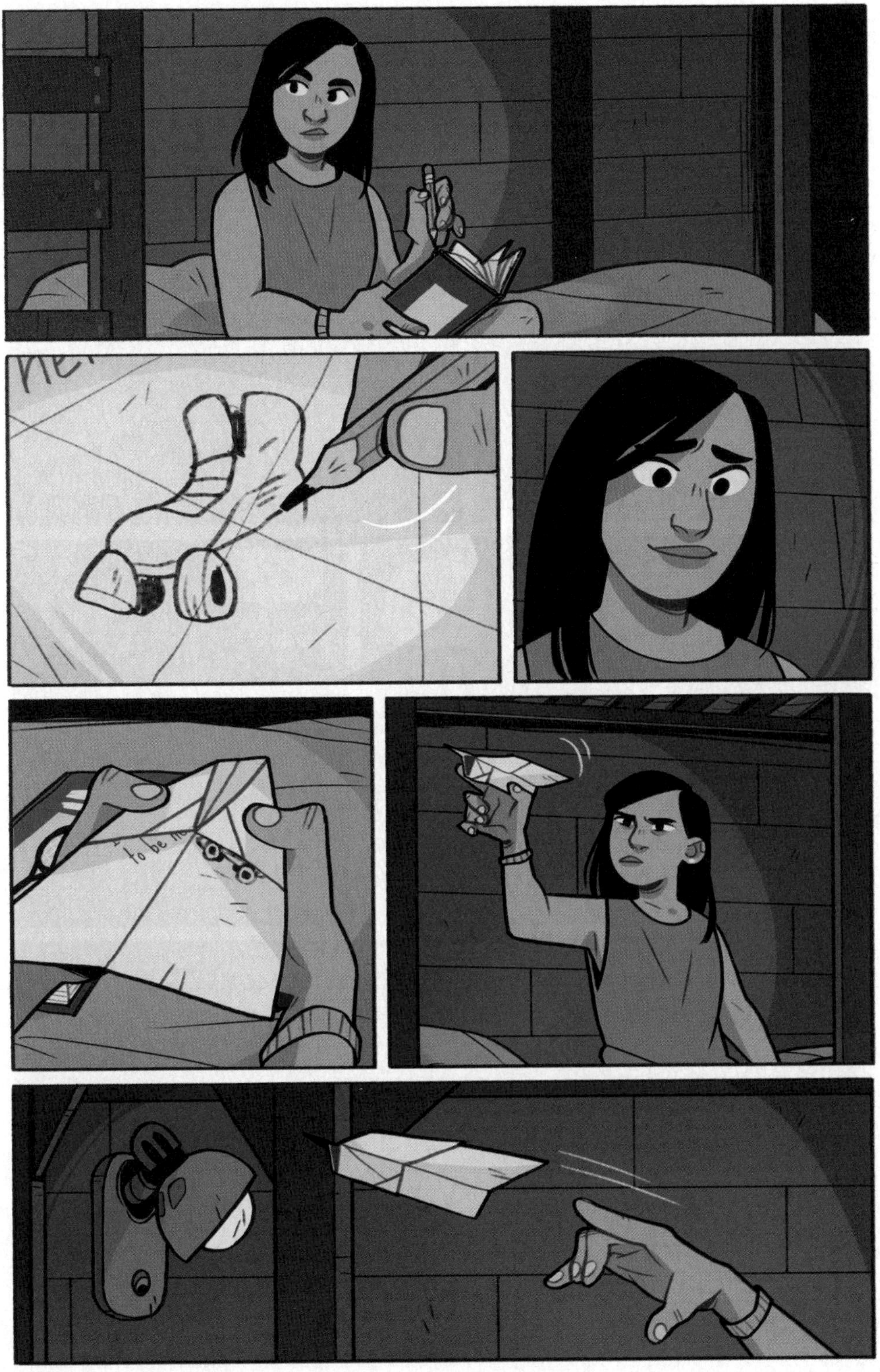

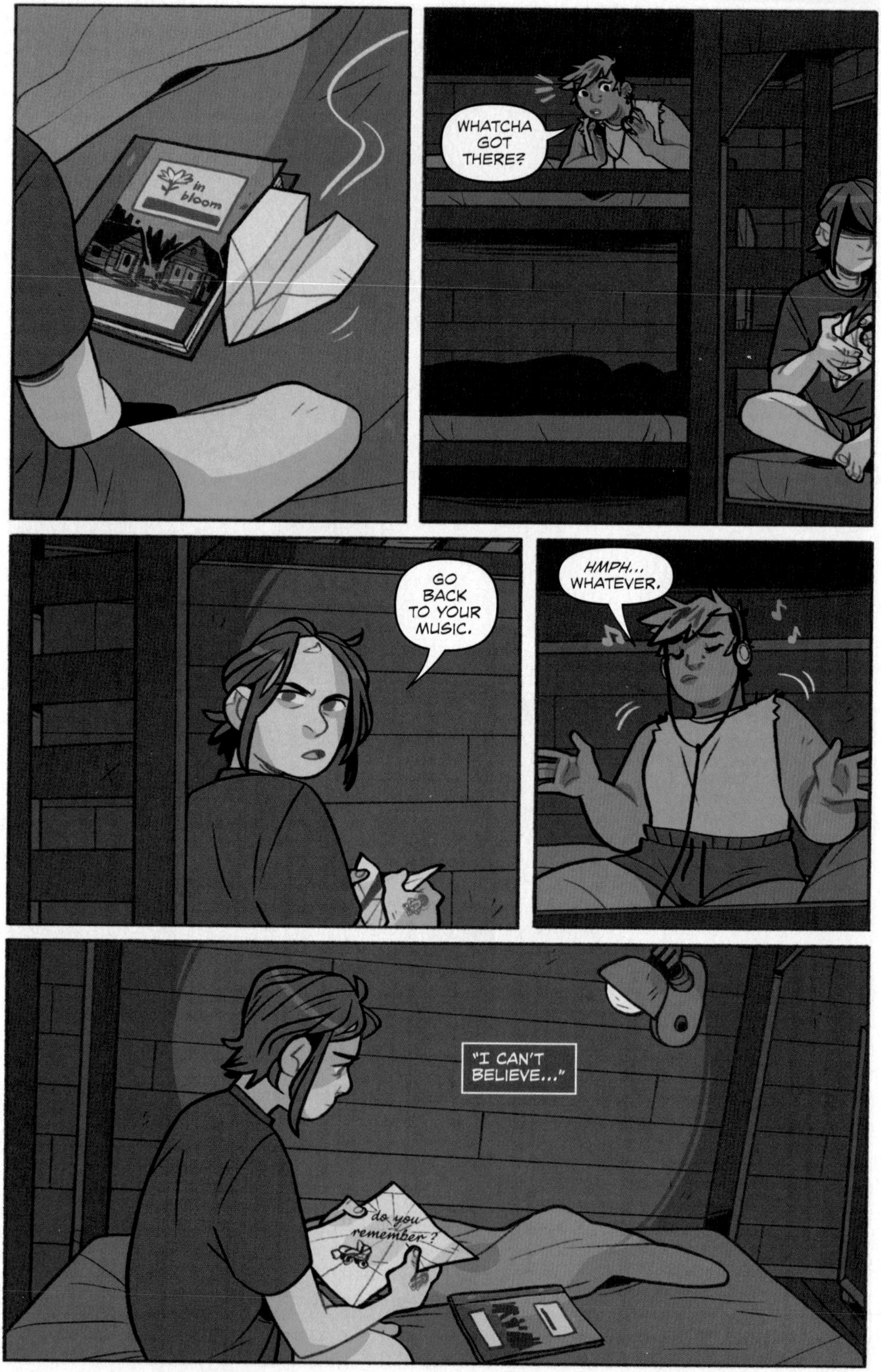
in bloom
WHATCHA GOT THERE?
GO BACK TO YOUR MUSIC.
HMPH... WHATEVER.
"I CAN'T BELIEVE..."
do you remember?

STAR FLYER ROLLER RINK, CENTRAL FLORIDA
FIVE YEARS AGO
HAPPY BIRTHDAY Leighton
...MY LITTLE LEIGHTON IS TURNING NINE!
NOW, IT'S TIME TO WELCOME YOUR GUESTS. MAKE SURE TO SMILE, SWEETIE.

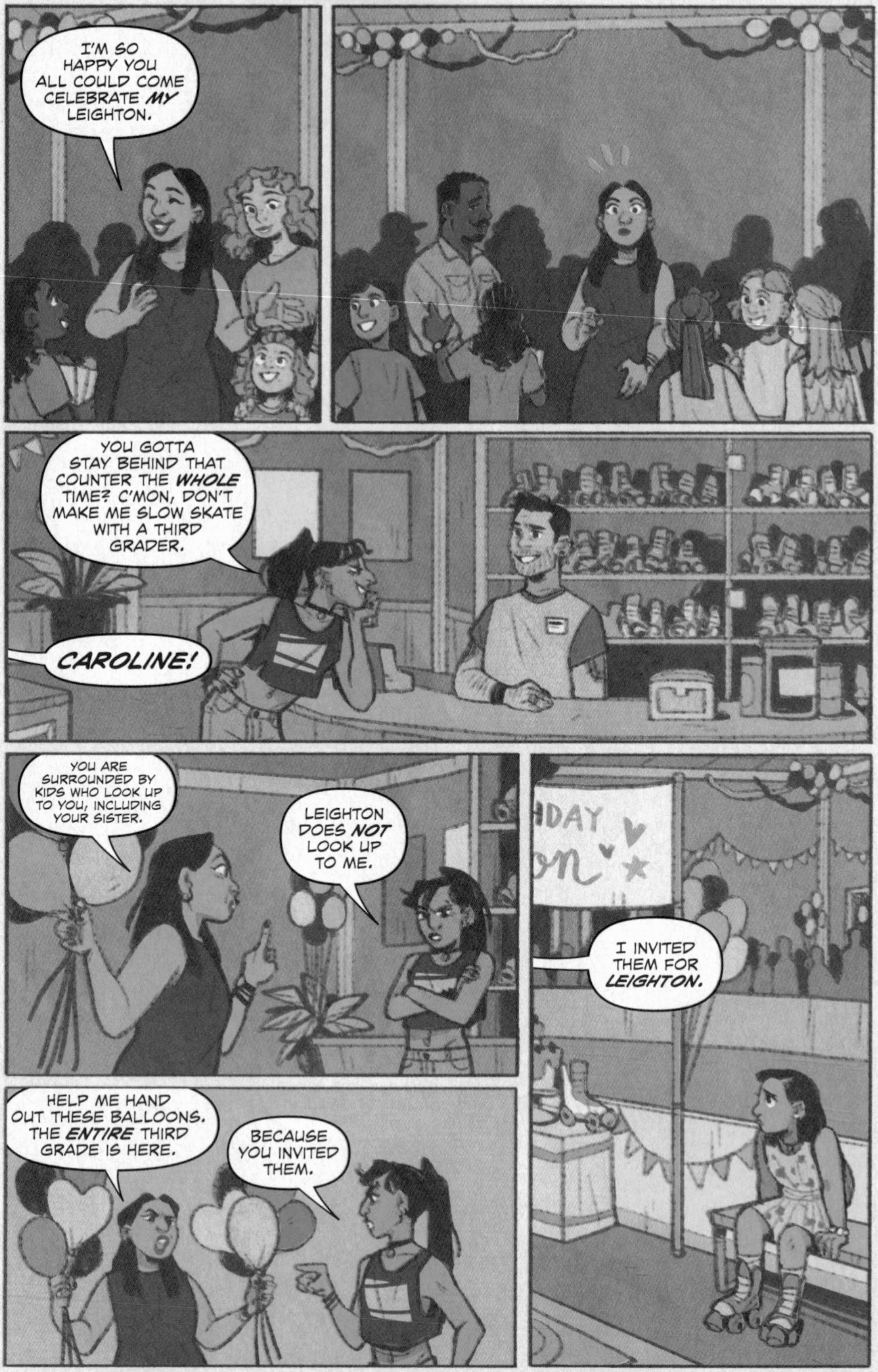
I'M SO HAPPY YOU ALL COULD COME CELEBRATE *MY* LEIGHTON.
YOU GOTTA STAY BEHIND THAT COUNTER THE *WHOLE* TIME? C'MON, DON'T MAKE ME SLOW SKATE WITH A THIRD GRADER.
CAROLINE!
YOU ARE SURROUNDED BY KIDS WHO LOOK UP TO YOU, INCLUDING YOUR SISTER.
LEIGHTON DOES *NOT* LOOK UP TO ME.
HELP ME HAND OUT THESE BALLOONS. THE *ENTIRE* THIRD GRADE IS HERE.
BECAUSE YOU INVITED THEM.
I INVITED THEM FOR *LEIGHTON.*

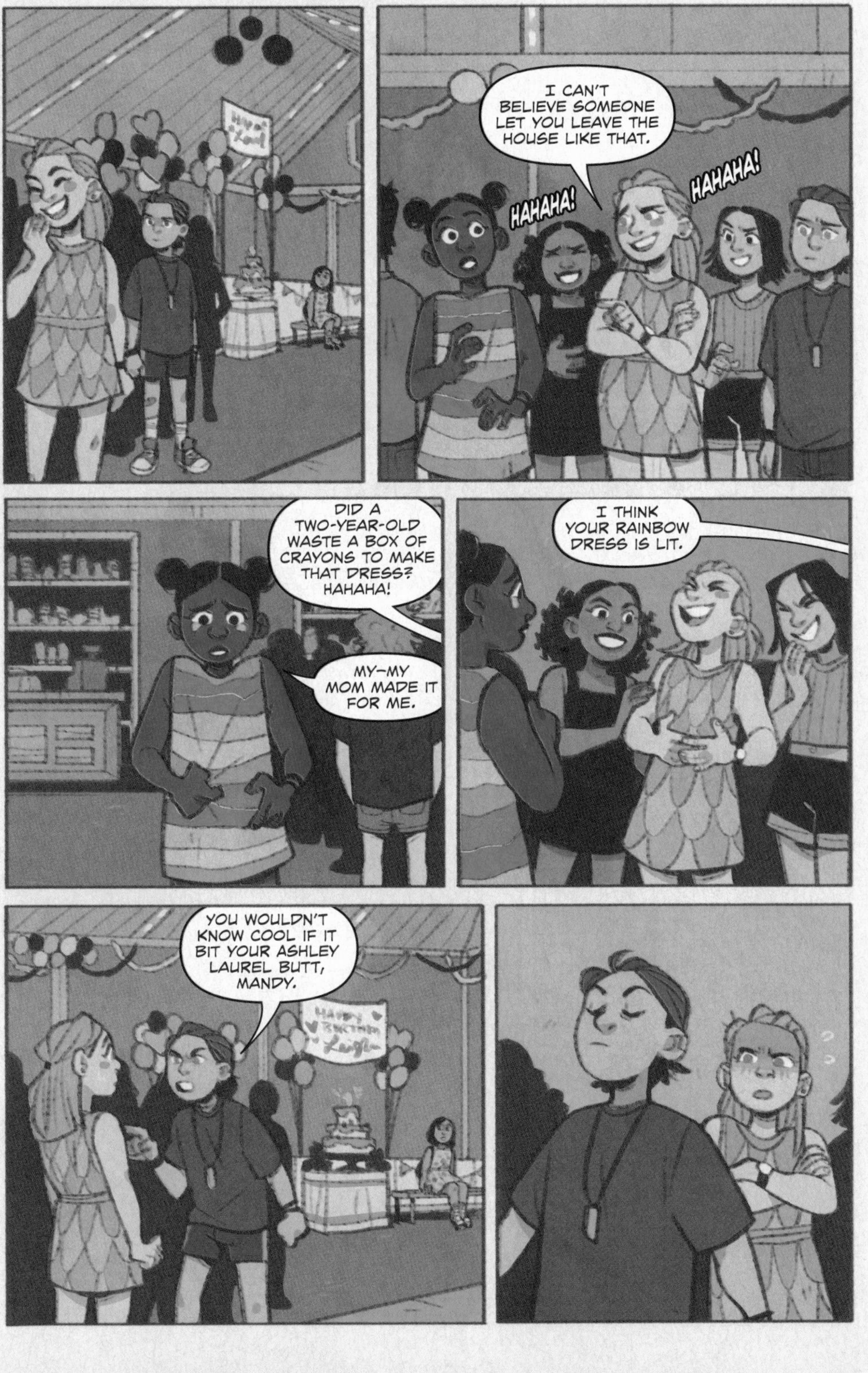
I CAN'T BELIEVE SOMEONE LET YOU LEAVE THE HOUSE LIKE THAT.
HAHAHA!
HAHAHA!
DID A TWO-YEAR-OLD WASTE A BOX OF CRAYONS TO MAKE THAT DRESS? HAHAHA!
MY—MY MOM MADE IT FOR ME.
I THINK YOUR RAINBOW DRESS IS LIT.
YOU WOULDN'T KNOW COOL IF IT BIT YOUR ASHLEY LAUREL BUTT, MANDY.

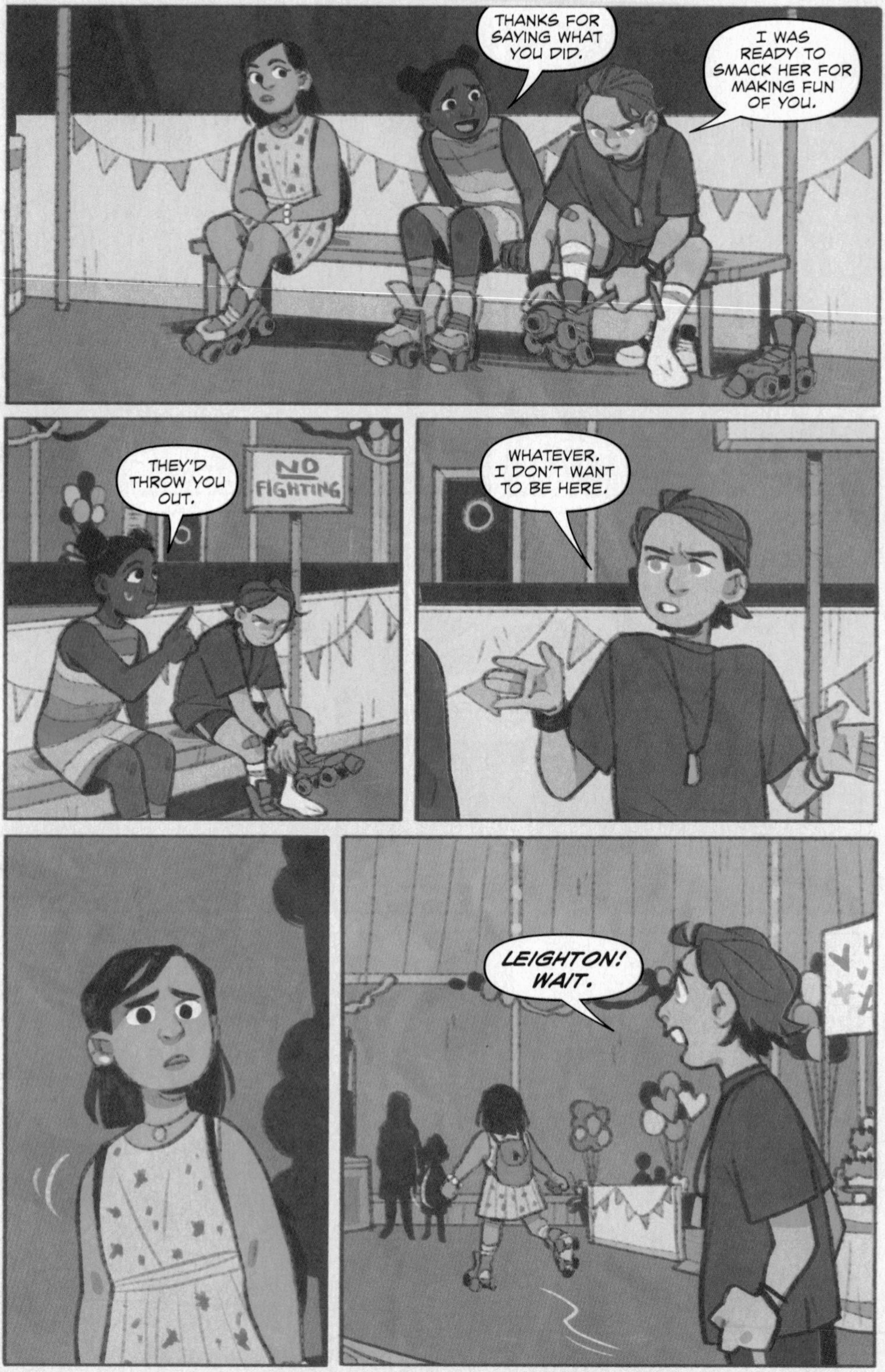
THANKS FOR SAYING WHAT YOU DID.
I WAS READY TO SMACK HER FOR MAKING FUN OF YOU.
THEY'D THROW YOU OUT.
NO FIGHTING
WHATEVER. I DON'T WANT TO BE HERE.
LEIGHTON! WAIT.

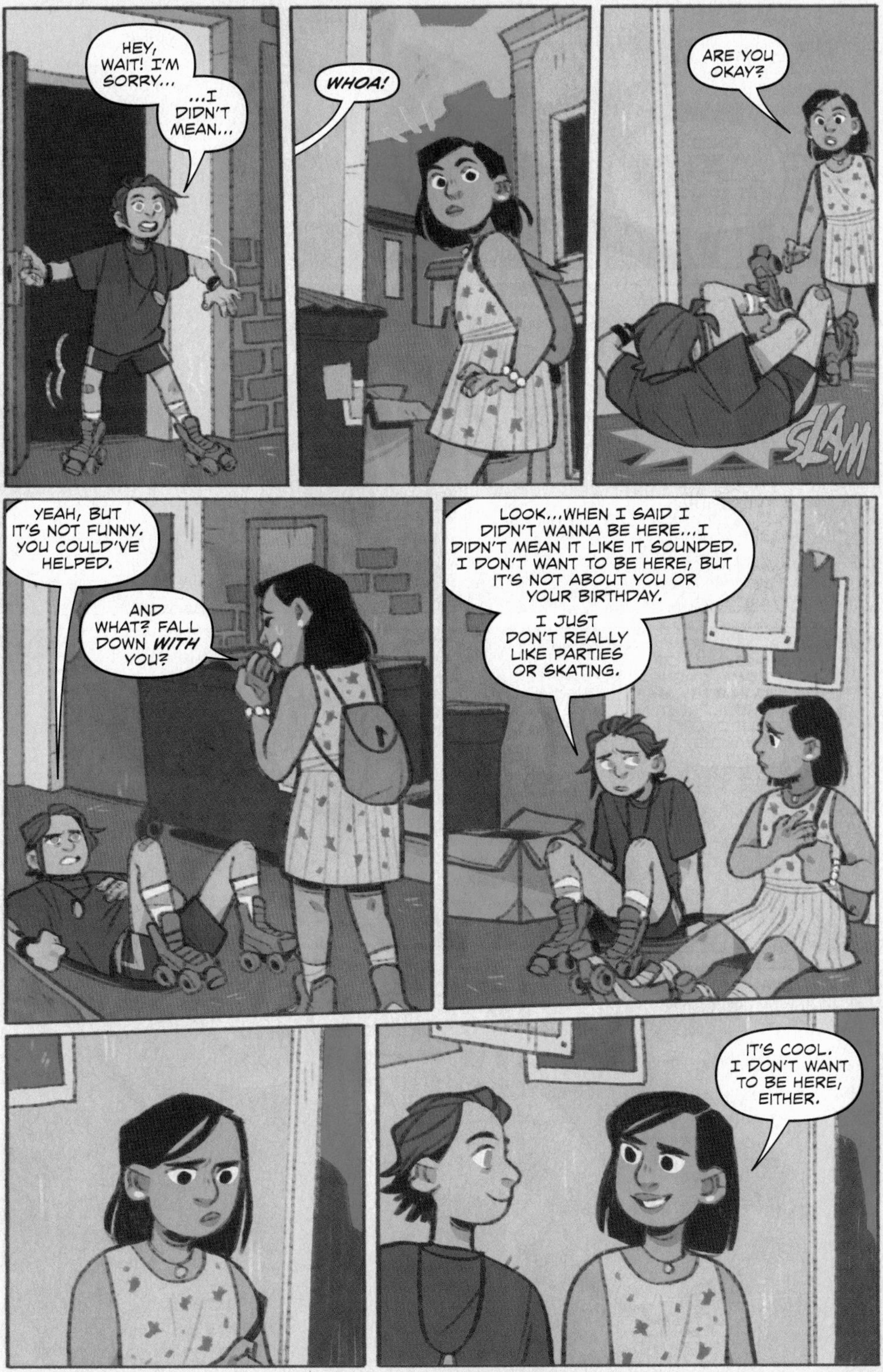
HEY, WAIT! I'M SORRY...
...I DIDN'T MEAN...
WHOA!
ARE YOU OKAY?
SLAM
YEAH, BUT IT'S NOT FUNNY. YOU COULD'VE HELPED.
AND WHAT? FALL DOWN WITH YOU?
LOOK...WHEN I SAID I DIDN'T WANNA BE HERE...I DIDN'T MEAN IT LIKE IT SOUNDED. I DON'T WANT TO BE HERE, BUT IT'S NOT ABOUT YOU OR YOUR BIRTHDAY.
I JUST DON'T REALLY LIKE PARTIES OR SKATING.
IT'S COOL. I DON'T WANT TO BE HERE, EITHER.

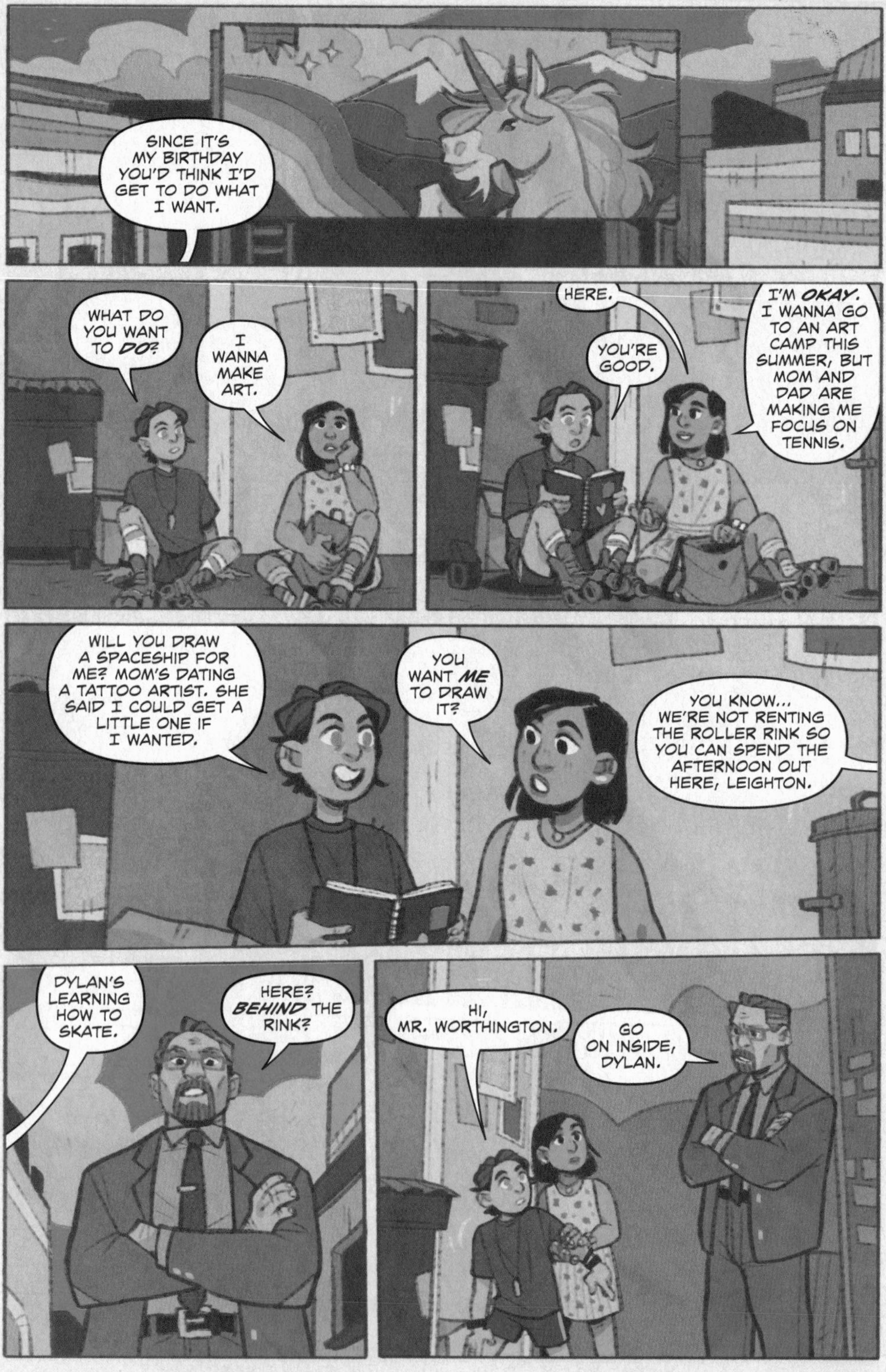
SINCE IT'S MY BIRTHDAY YOU'D THINK I'D GET TO DO WHAT I WANT.
WHAT DO YOU WANT TO *DO*?
I WANNA MAKE ART.
HERE.
YOU'RE GOOD.
I'M *OKAY*. I WANNA GO TO AN ART CAMP THIS SUMMER, BUT MOM AND DAD ARE MAKING ME FOCUS ON TENNIS.
WILL YOU DRAW A SPACESHIP FOR ME? MOM'S DATING A TATTOO ARTIST. SHE SAID I COULD GET A LITTLE ONE IF I WANTED.
YOU WANT *ME* TO DRAW IT?
YOU KNOW... WE'RE NOT RENTING THE ROLLER RINK SO YOU CAN SPEND THE AFTERNOON OUT HERE, LEIGHTON.
DYLAN'S LEARNING HOW TO SKATE.
HERE? *BEHIND* THE RINK?
HI, MR. WORTHINGTON.
GO ON INSIDE, DYLAN.

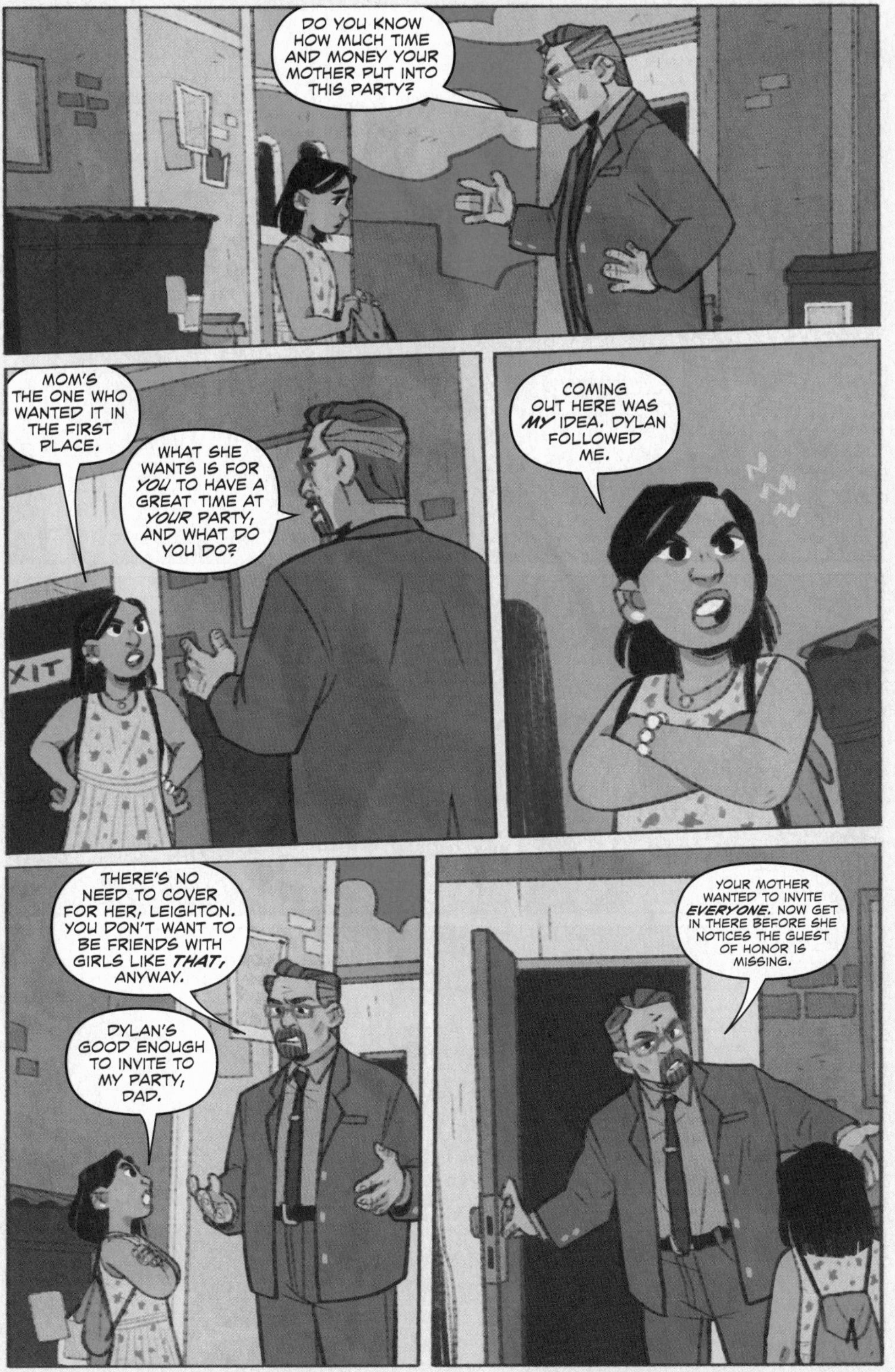
DO YOU KNOW HOW MUCH TIME AND MONEY YOUR MOTHER PUT INTO THIS PARTY?
MOM'S THE ONE WHO WANTED IT IN THE FIRST PLACE.
WHAT SHE WANTS IS FOR YOU TO HAVE A GREAT TIME AT YOUR PARTY, AND WHAT DO YOU DO?
XIT
COMING OUT HERE WAS MY IDEA. DYLAN FOLLOWED ME.
THERE'S NO NEED TO COVER FOR HER, LEIGHTON. YOU DON'T WANT TO BE FRIENDS WITH GIRLS LIKE THAT, ANYWAY.
DYLAN'S GOOD ENOUGH TO INVITE TO MY PARTY, DAD.
YOUR MOTHER WANTED TO INVITE EVERYONE. NOW GET IN THERE BEFORE SHE NOTICES THE GUEST OF HONOR IS MISSING.

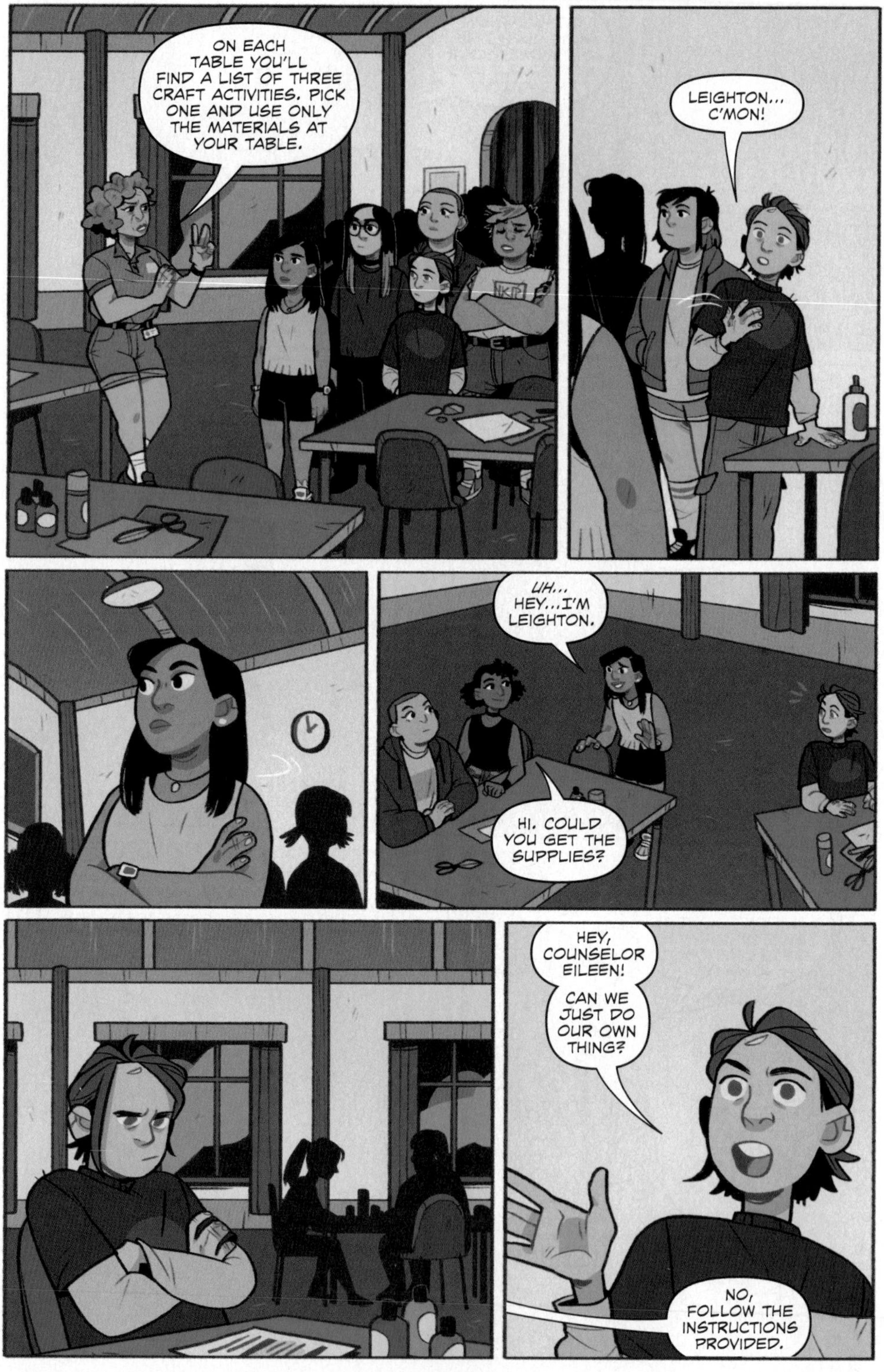
ON EACH TABLE YOU'LL FIND A LIST OF THREE CRAFT ACTIVITIES. PICK ONE AND USE ONLY THE MATERIALS AT YOUR TABLE.
LEIGHTON... C'MON!
UH... HEY...I'M LEIGHTON.
HI. COULD YOU GET THE SUPPLIES?
HEY, COUNSELOR EILEEN!
CAN WE JUST DO OUR OWN THING?
NO, FOLLOW THE INSTRUCTIONS PROVIDED.

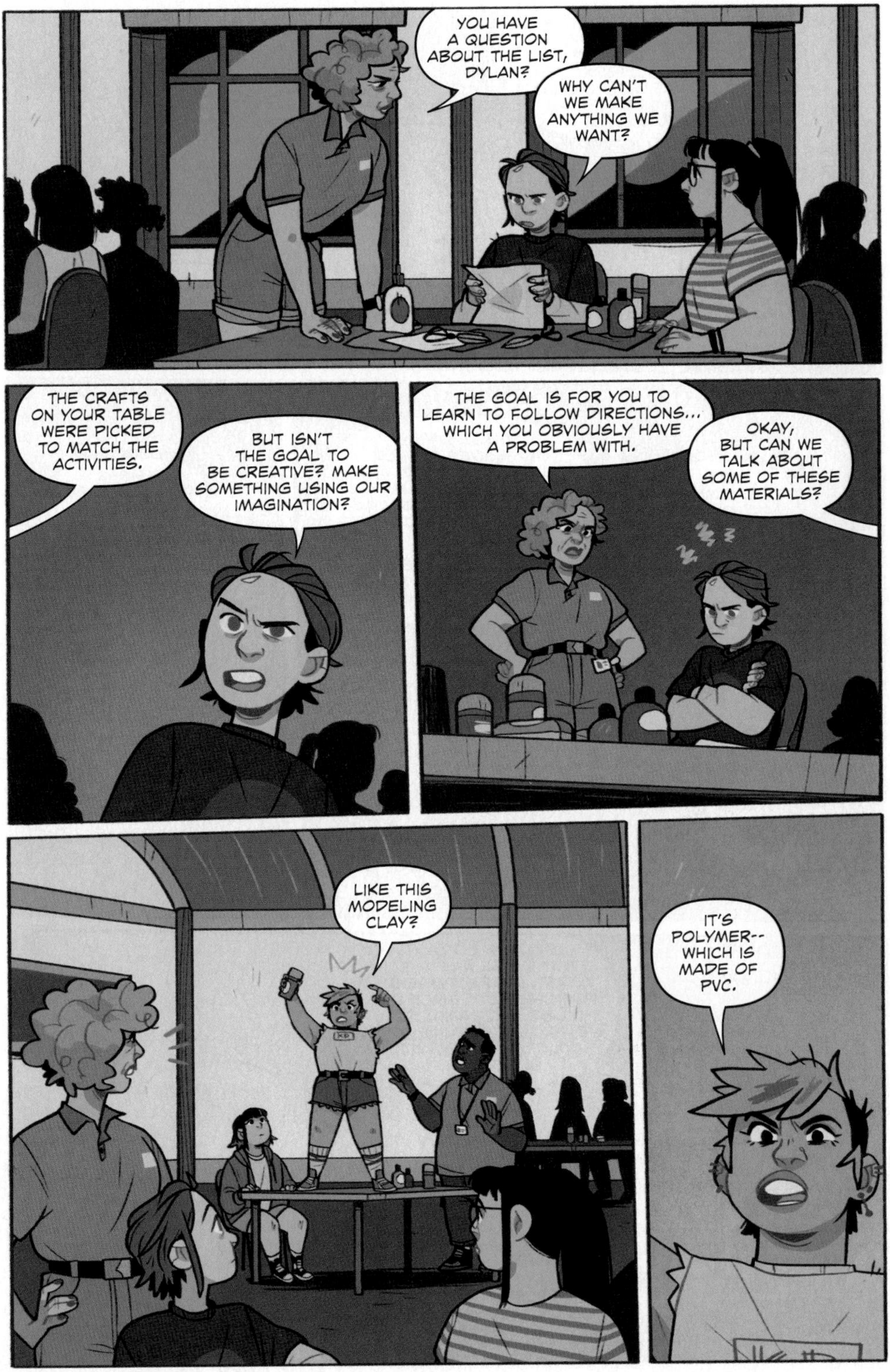
YOU HAVE A QUESTION ABOUT THE LIST, DYLAN?
WHY CAN'T WE MAKE ANYTHING WE WANT?
THE CRAFTS ON YOUR TABLE WERE PICKED TO MATCH THE ACTIVITIES.
BUT ISN'T THE GOAL TO BE CREATIVE? MAKE SOMETHING USING OUR IMAGINATION?
THE GOAL IS FOR YOU TO LEARN TO FOLLOW DIRECTIONS... WHICH YOU OBVIOUSLY HAVE A PROBLEM WITH.
OKAY, BUT CAN WE TALK ABOUT SOME OF THESE MATERIALS?
LIKE THIS MODELING CLAY?
IT'S POLYMER-- WHICH IS MADE OF PVC.

IT EMITS DANGEROUS CHEMICALS AS IT BREAKS DOWN, INCLUDING DIOXIN, A PROVEN CARCINOGEN THAT HAS BEEN LINKED TO SEVERAL HEALTH PROBLEMS.

WHAT IS *WRONG* WITH HER?

FLOUR-BASED, OR EARTH-BASED, OR EVEN OIL-BASED CLAY ARE MUCH SAFER CHOICES.

OR WE COULD MAKE OUR OWN HOMEMADE CLAY.

I THINK SHE'S DOPE.

THESE SPRAY ADHESIVES SHOULD ALSO BE AVOIDED. AND THESE OIL-BASED PAINTS CONTAIN A BUNCH OF CRAP, INCLUDING MERCURY AND LEAD.

A WATER-BASED, NON-TOXIC PAINT WOULD BE A BETTER CHOICE.

≲SIGH≳ ANYTHING ELSE, CRICKET?

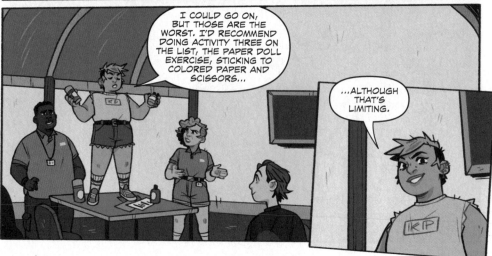

I COULD GO ON, BUT THOSE ARE THE WORST. I'D RECOMMEND DOING ACTIVITY THREE ON THE LIST, THE PAPER DOLL EXERCISE, STICKING TO COLORED PAPER AND SCISSORS...

...ALTHOUGH THAT'S LIMITING.

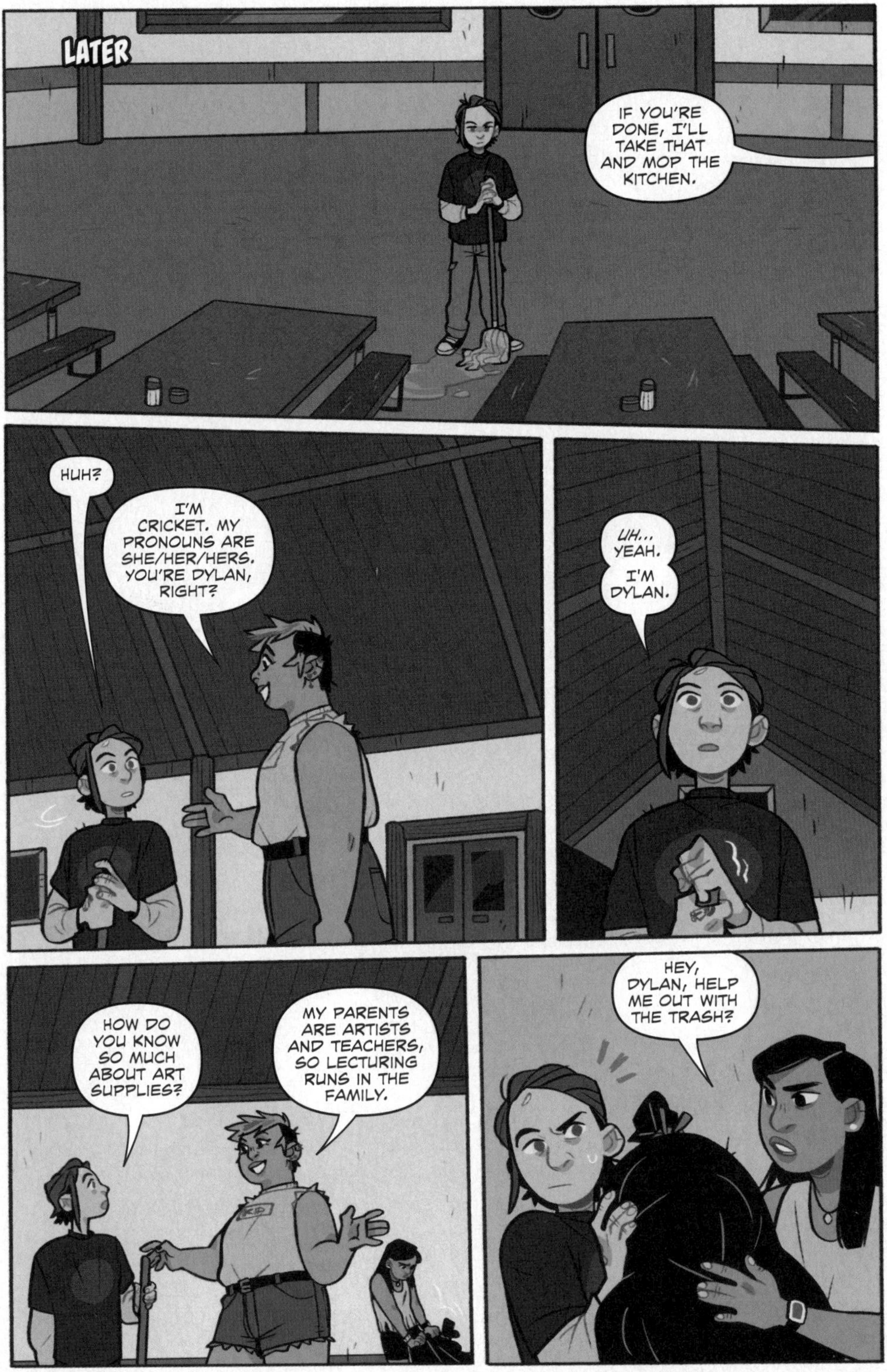
LATER
IF YOU'RE DONE, I'LL TAKE THAT AND MOP THE KITCHEN.
HUH?
I'M CRICKET. MY PRONOUNS ARE SHE/HER/HERS. YOU'RE DYLAN, RIGHT?
UH... YEAH.
I'M DYLAN.
HOW DO YOU KNOW SO MUCH ABOUT ART SUPPLIES?
MY PARENTS ARE ARTISTS AND TEACHERS, SO LECTURING RUNS IN THE FAMILY.
HEY, DYLAN, HELP ME OUT WITH THE TRASH?

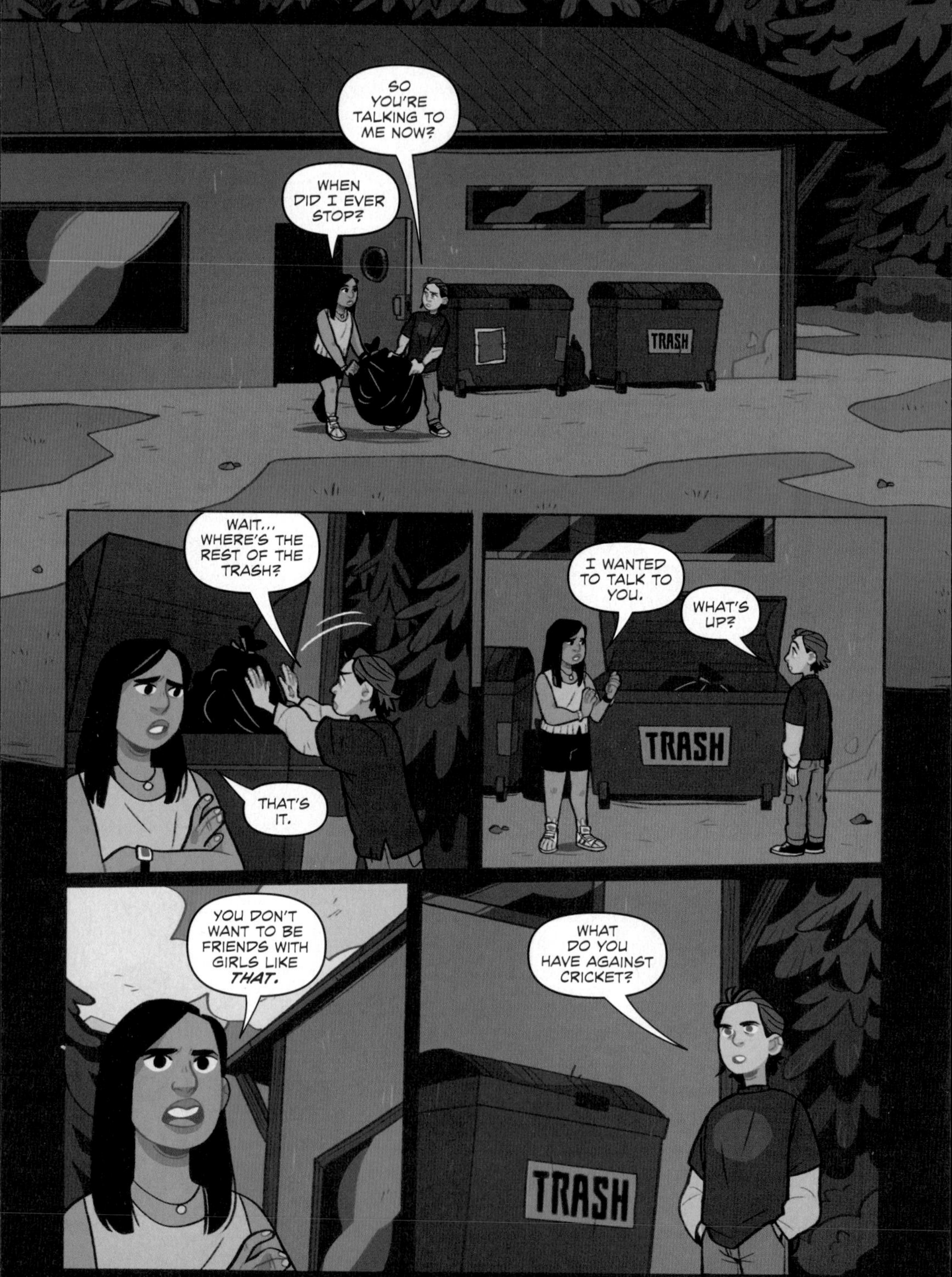
SO YOU'RE TALKING TO ME NOW?
WHEN DID I EVER STOP?
TRASH
WAIT... WHERE'S THE REST OF THE TRASH?
THAT'S IT.
I WANTED TO TALK TO YOU.
WHAT'S UP?
TRASH
YOU DON'T WANT TO BE FRIENDS WITH GIRLS LIKE *THAT.*
WHAT DO YOU HAVE AGAINST CRICKET?
TRASH

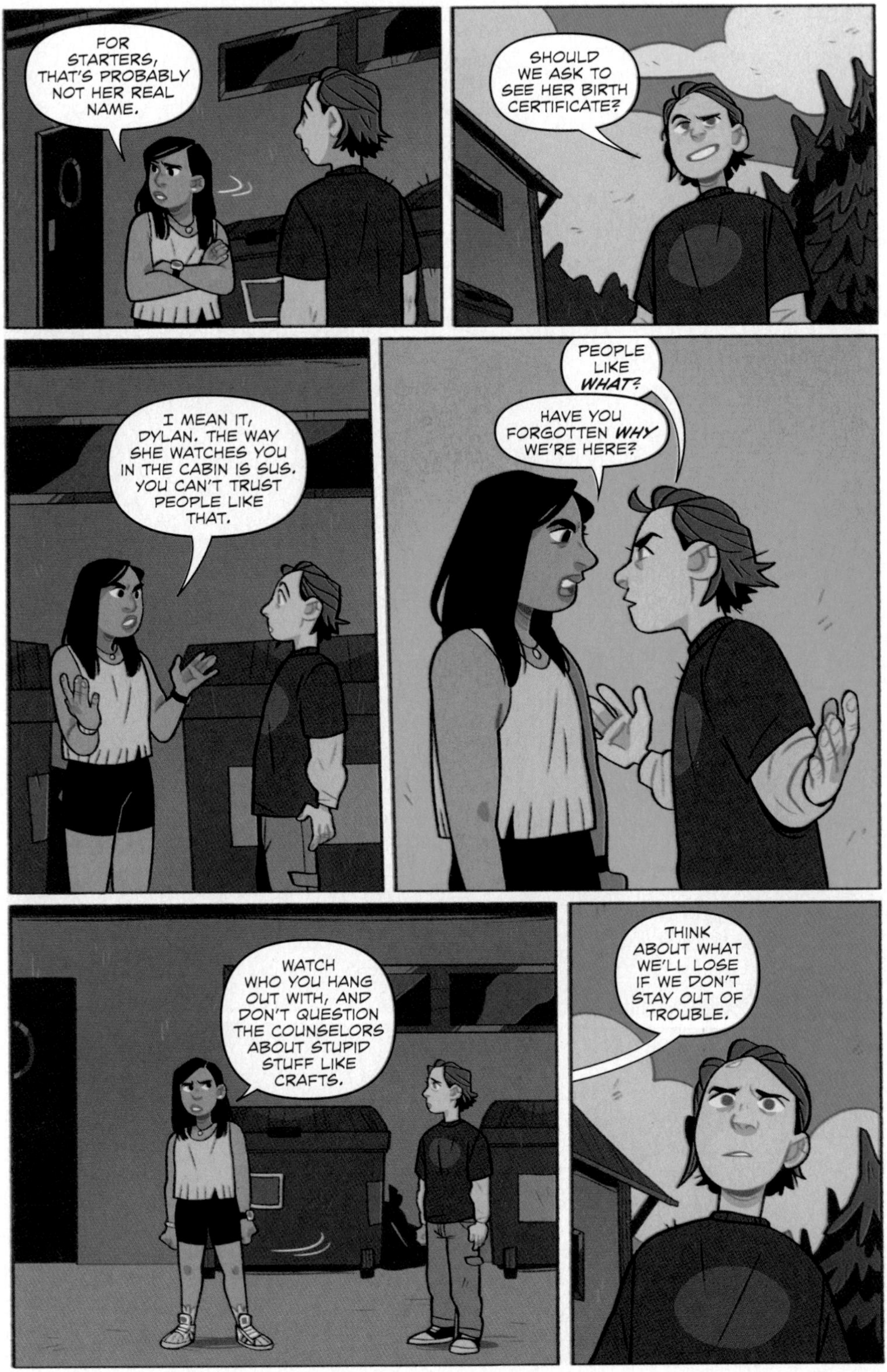
FOR STARTERS, THAT'S PROBABLY NOT HER REAL NAME.
SHOULD WE ASK TO SEE HER BIRTH CERTIFICATE?
I MEAN IT, DYLAN. THE WAY SHE WATCHES YOU IN THE CABIN IS SUS. YOU CAN'T TRUST PEOPLE LIKE THAT.
PEOPLE LIKE *WHAT*?
HAVE YOU FORGOTTEN *WHY* WE'RE HERE?
WATCH WHO YOU HANG OUT WITH, AND DON'T QUESTION THE COUNSELORS ABOUT STUPID STUFF LIKE CRAFTS.
THINK ABOUT WHAT WE'LL LOSE IF WE DON'T STAY OUT OF TROUBLE.

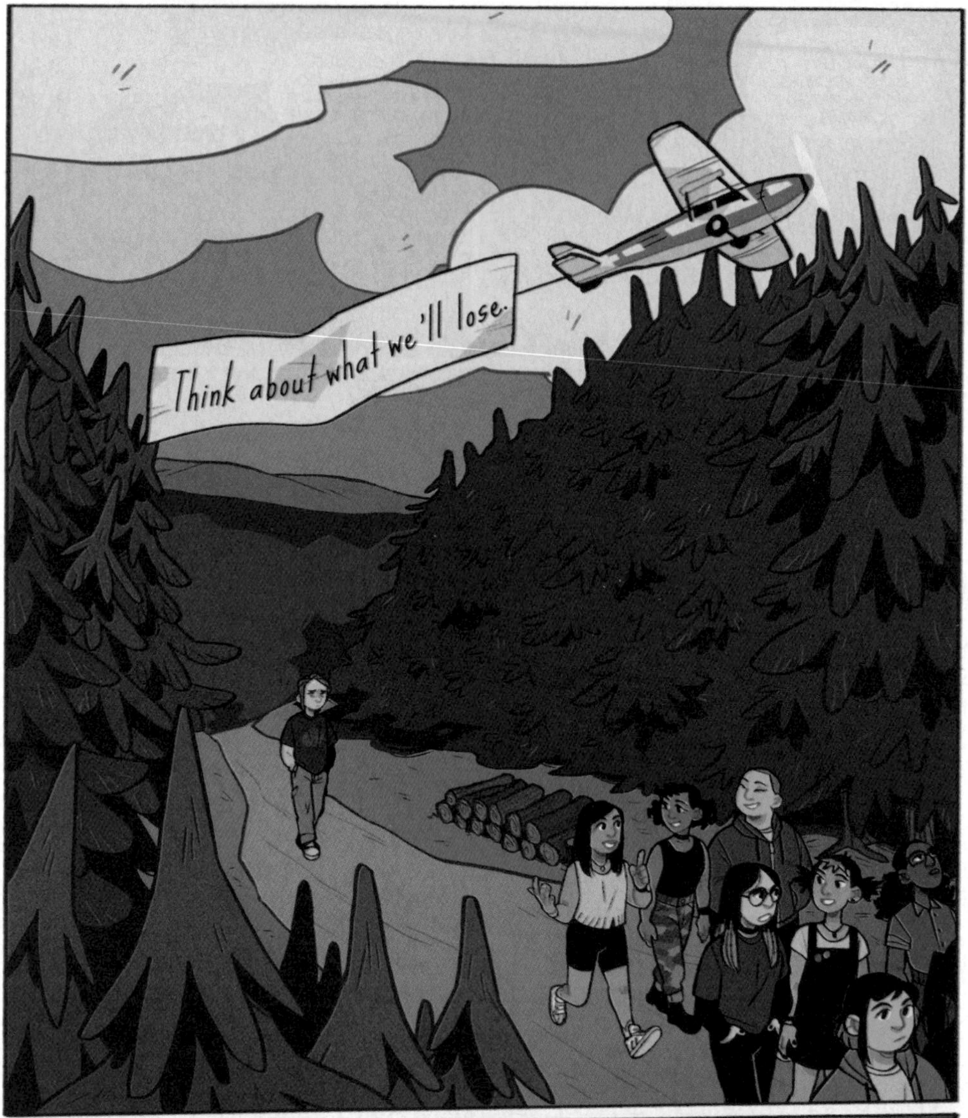
Think about what we'll lose.

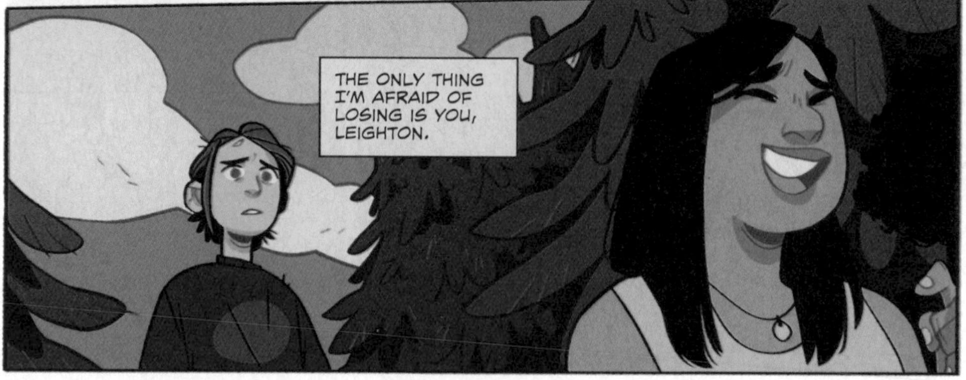
THE ONLY THING I'M AFRAID OF LOSING IS YOU, LEIGHTON.

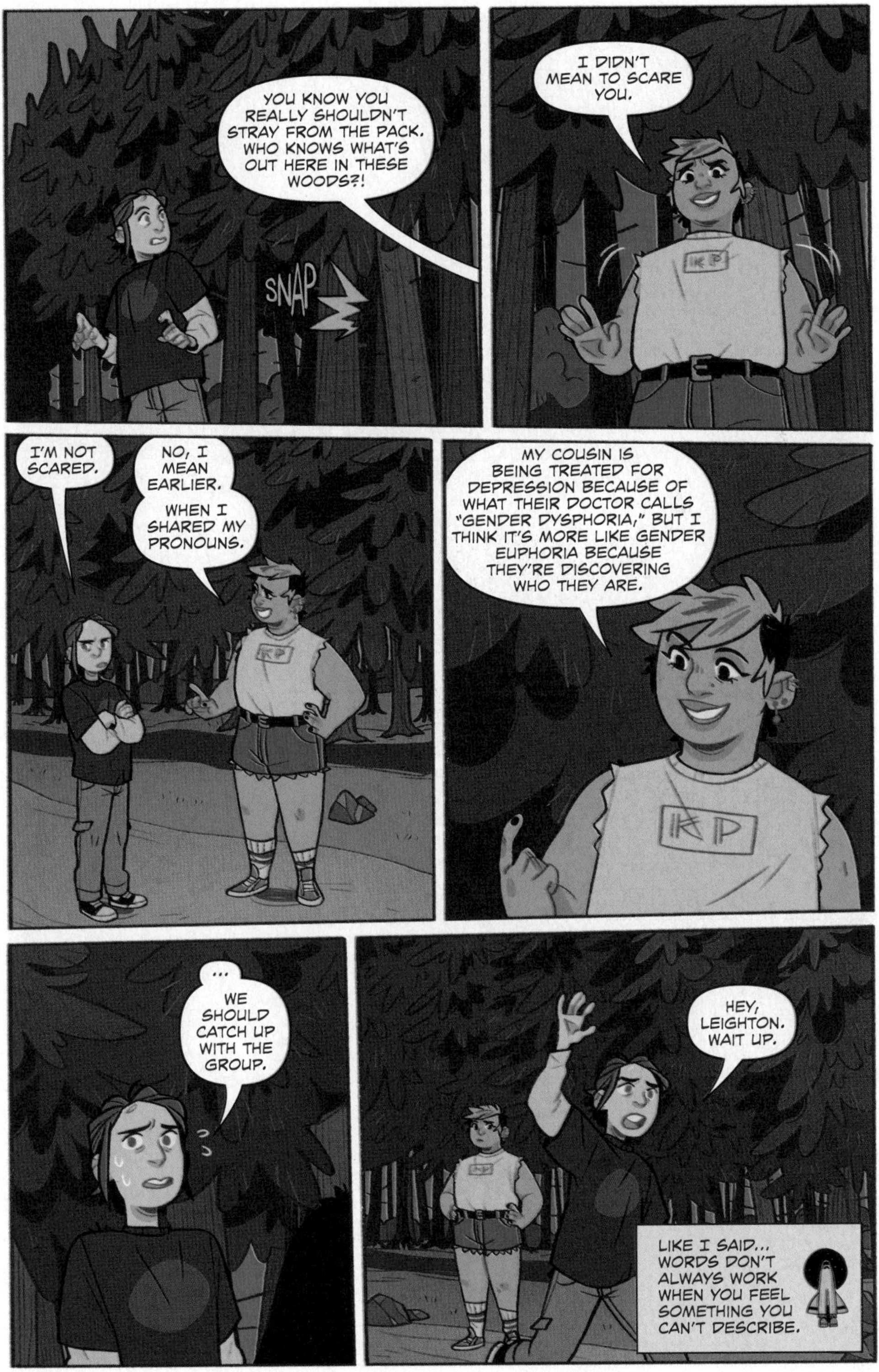
YOU KNOW YOU REALLY SHOULDN'T STRAY FROM THE PACK. WHO KNOWS WHAT'S OUT HERE IN THESE WOODS?!
SNAP
I DIDN'T MEAN TO SCARE YOU.
I'M NOT SCARED.
NO, I MEAN EARLIER.
WHEN I SHARED MY PRONOUNS.
MY COUSIN IS BEING TREATED FOR DEPRESSION BECAUSE OF WHAT THEIR DOCTOR CALLS "GENDER DYSPHORIA," BUT I THINK IT'S MORE LIKE GENDER EUPHORIA BECAUSE THEY'RE DISCOVERING WHO THEY ARE.
...
WE SHOULD CATCH UP WITH THE GROUP.
HEY, LEIGHTON. WAIT UP.
LIKE I SAID... WORDS DON'T ALWAYS WORK WHEN YOU FEEL SOMETHING YOU CAN'T DESCRIBE.

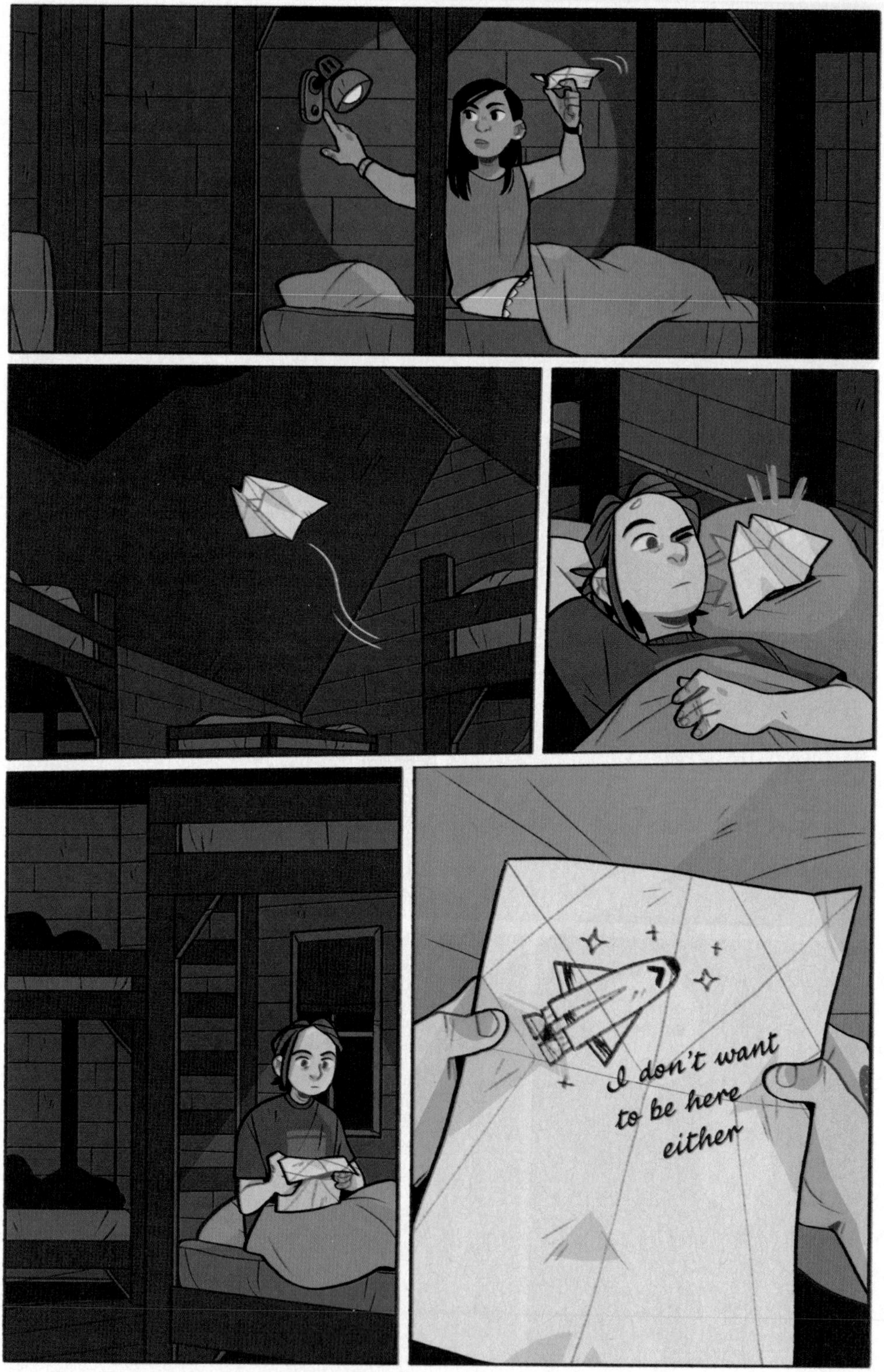
I don't want
to be here
either

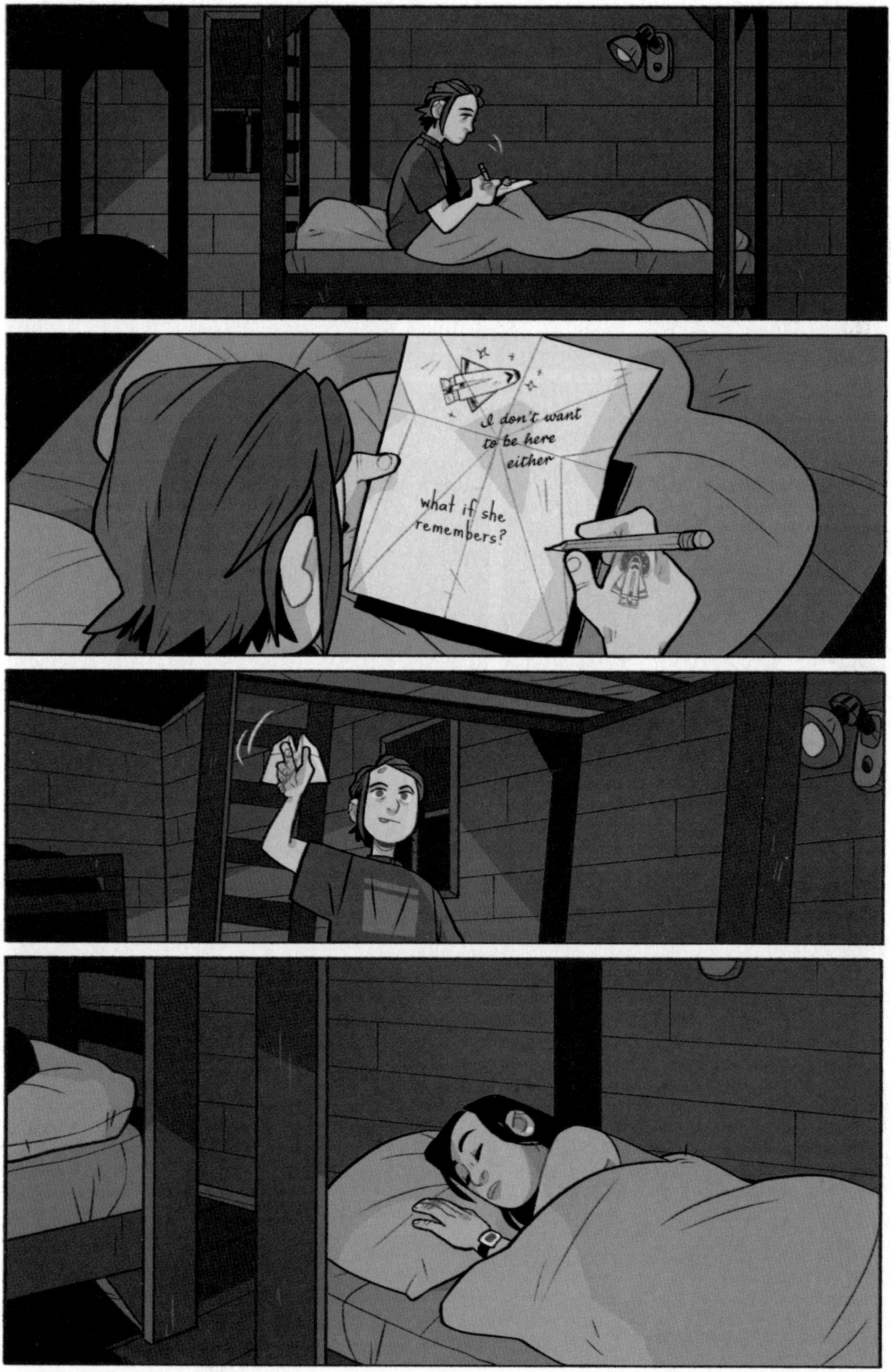
I don't want to be here either
what if she remembers?

WASTE OF TIME.

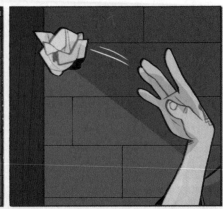

CRAP!

YOU OKAY OVER THERE?

QUIT SPYING ON ME, AND GO BACK TO SLEEP, CRICKET.

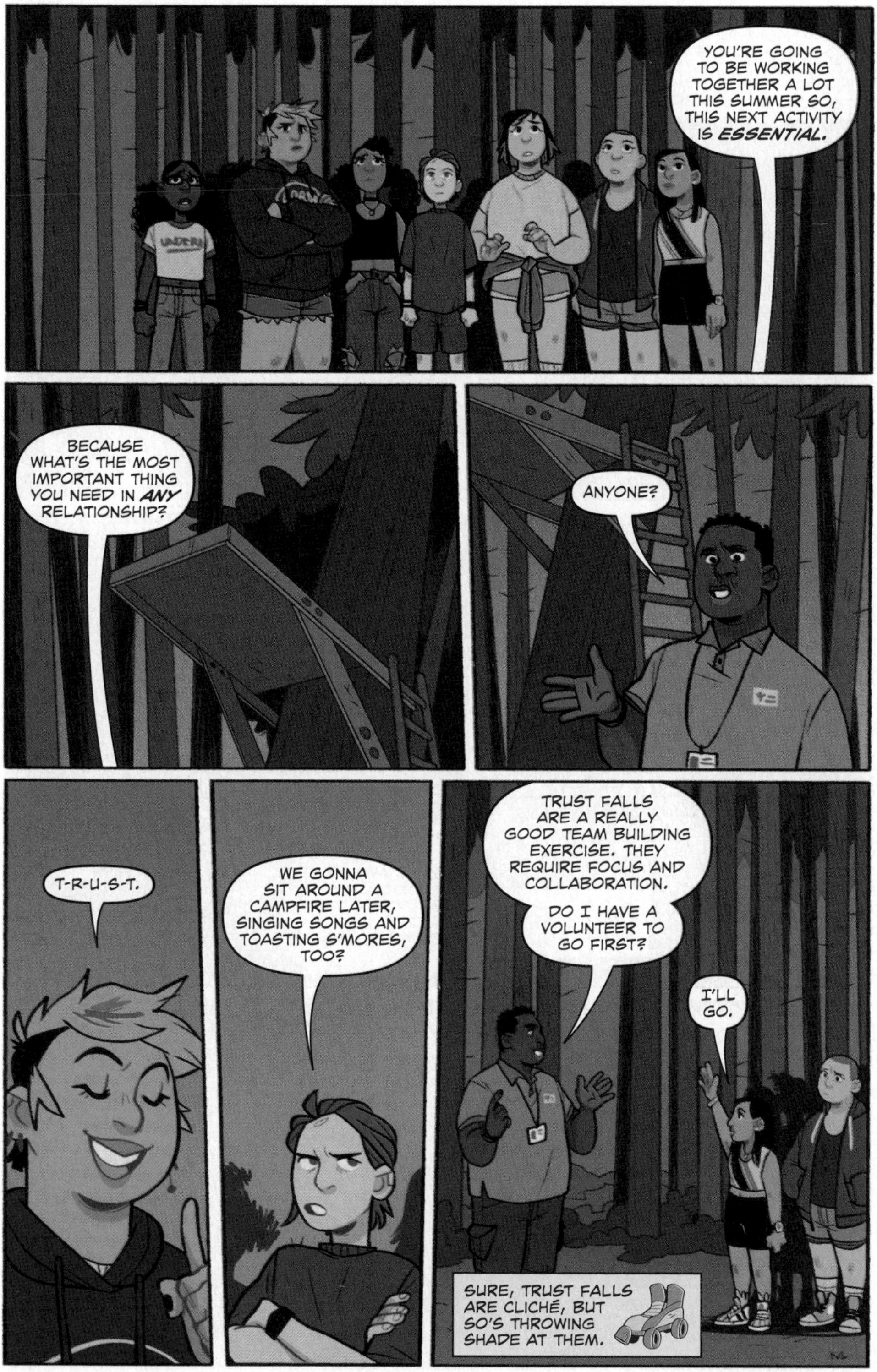
YOU'RE GOING TO BE WORKING TOGETHER A LOT THIS SUMMER SO, THIS NEXT ACTIVITY IS ESSENTIAL.
BECAUSE WHAT'S THE MOST IMPORTANT THING YOU NEED IN ANY RELATIONSHIP?
ANYONE?
T-R-U-S-T.
WE GONNA SIT AROUND A CAMPFIRE LATER, SINGING SONGS AND TOASTING S'MORES, TOO?
TRUST FALLS ARE A REALLY GOOD TEAM BUILDING EXERCISE. THEY REQUIRE FOCUS AND COLLABORATION.
DO I HAVE A VOLUNTEER TO GO FIRST?
I'LL GO.
SURE, TRUST FALLS ARE CLICHÉ, BUT SO'S THROWING SHADE AT THEM.

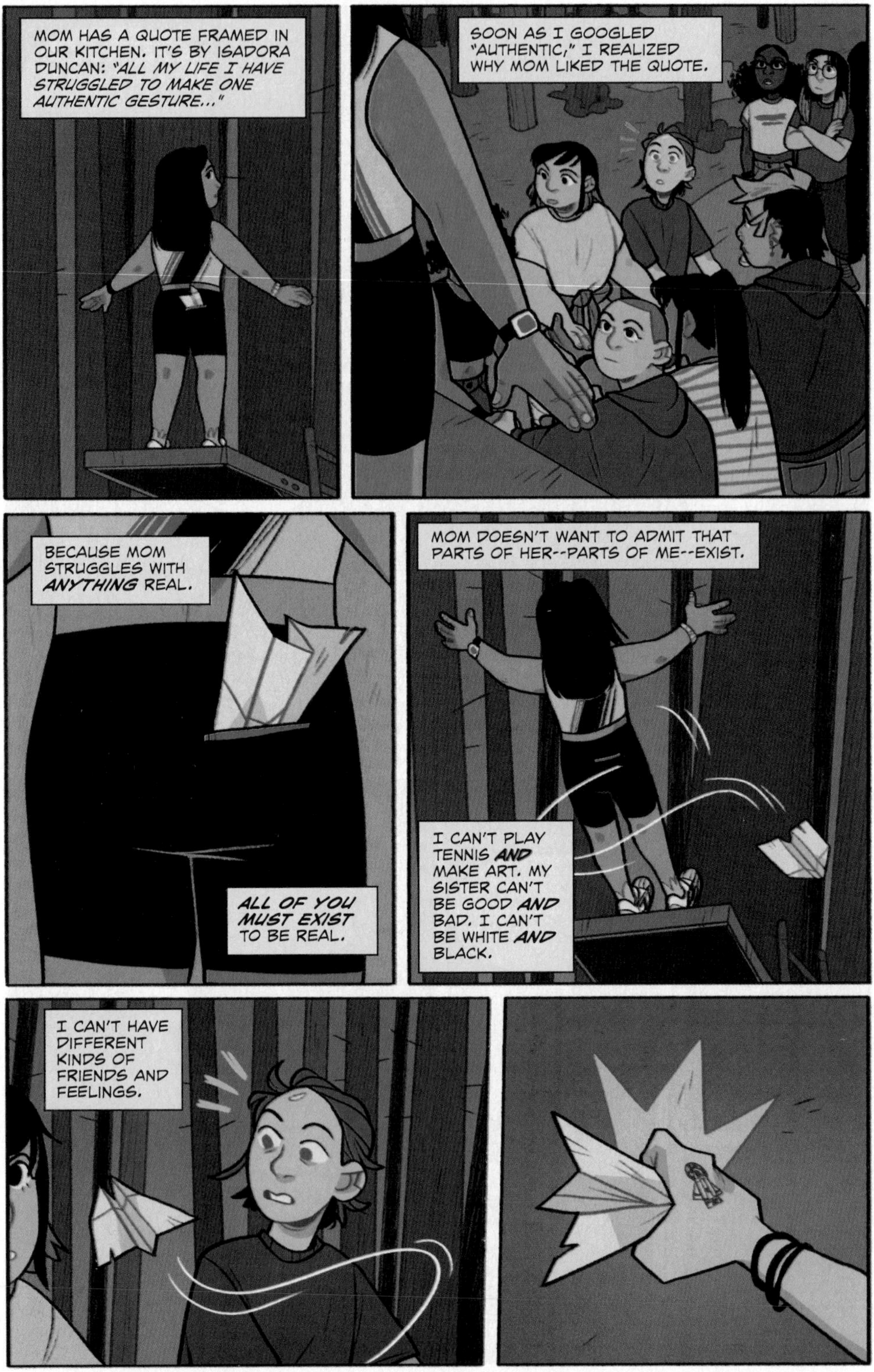
MOM HAS A QUOTE FRAMED IN OUR KITCHEN. IT'S BY ISADORA DUNCAN: "ALL MY LIFE I HAVE STRUGGLED TO MAKE ONE AUTHENTIC GESTURE..."
SOON AS I GOOGLED "AUTHENTIC," I REALIZED WHY MOM LIKED THE QUOTE.
BECAUSE MOM STRUGGLES WITH ANYTHING REAL.
ALL OF YOU MUST EXIST TO BE REAL.
MOM DOESN'T WANT TO ADMIT THAT PARTS OF HER--PARTS OF ME--EXIST.
I CAN'T PLAY TENNIS AND MAKE ART. MY SISTER CAN'T BE GOOD AND BAD. I CAN'T BE WHITE AND BLACK.
I CAN'T HAVE DIFFERENT KINDS OF FRIENDS AND FEELINGS.

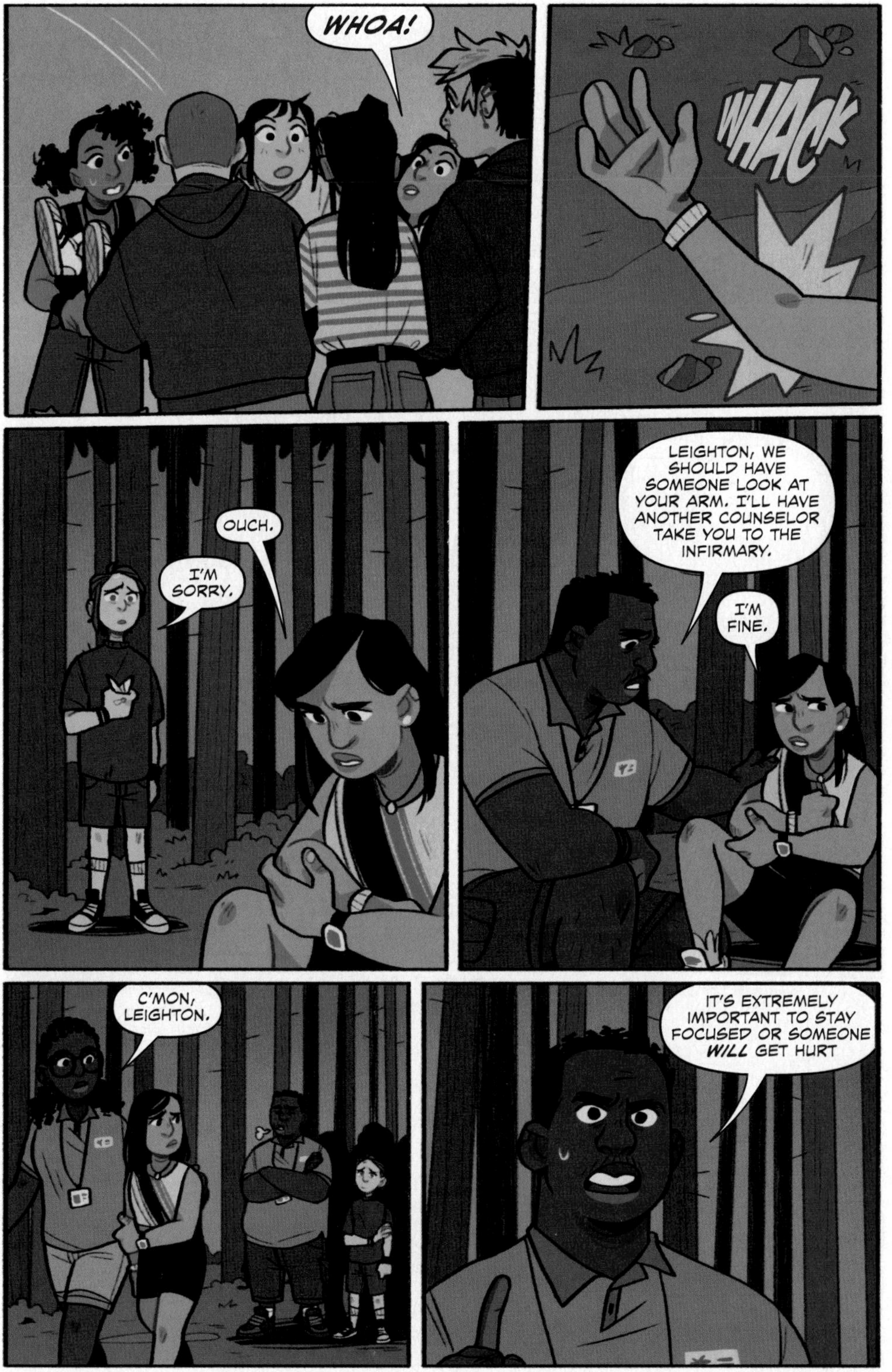
WHOA!
WHACK
OUCH.
I'M SORRY.
LEIGHTON, WE SHOULD HAVE SOMEONE LOOK AT YOUR ARM. I'LL HAVE ANOTHER COUNSELOR TAKE YOU TO THE INFIRMARY.
I'M FINE.
C'MON, LEIGHTON.
IT'S EXTREMELY IMPORTANT TO STAY FOCUSED OR SOMEONE *WILL* GET HURT

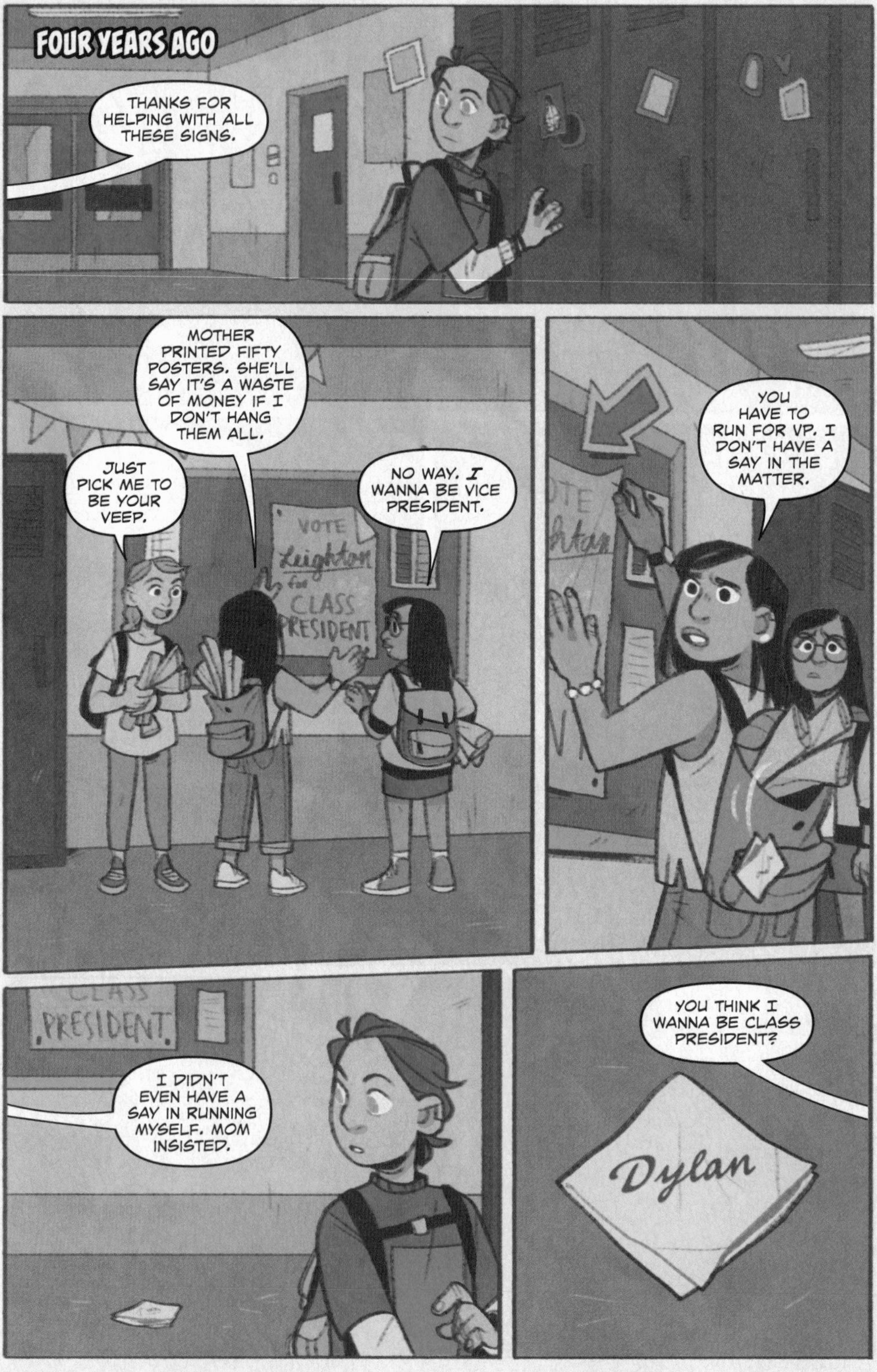
FOUR YEARS AGO
THANKS FOR HELPING WITH ALL THESE SIGNS.
MOTHER PRINTED FIFTY POSTERS. SHE'LL SAY IT'S A WASTE OF MONEY IF I DON'T HANG THEM ALL.
JUST PICK ME TO BE YOUR VEEP.
VOTE Leighton for CLASS PRESIDENT
NO WAY. *I* WANNA BE VICE PRESIDENT.
YOU HAVE TO RUN FOR VP. I DON'T HAVE A SAY IN THE MATTER.
PRESIDENT
I DIDN'T EVEN HAVE A SAY IN RUNNING MYSELF. MOM INSISTED.
YOU THINK I WANNA BE CLASS PRESIDENT?
Dylan

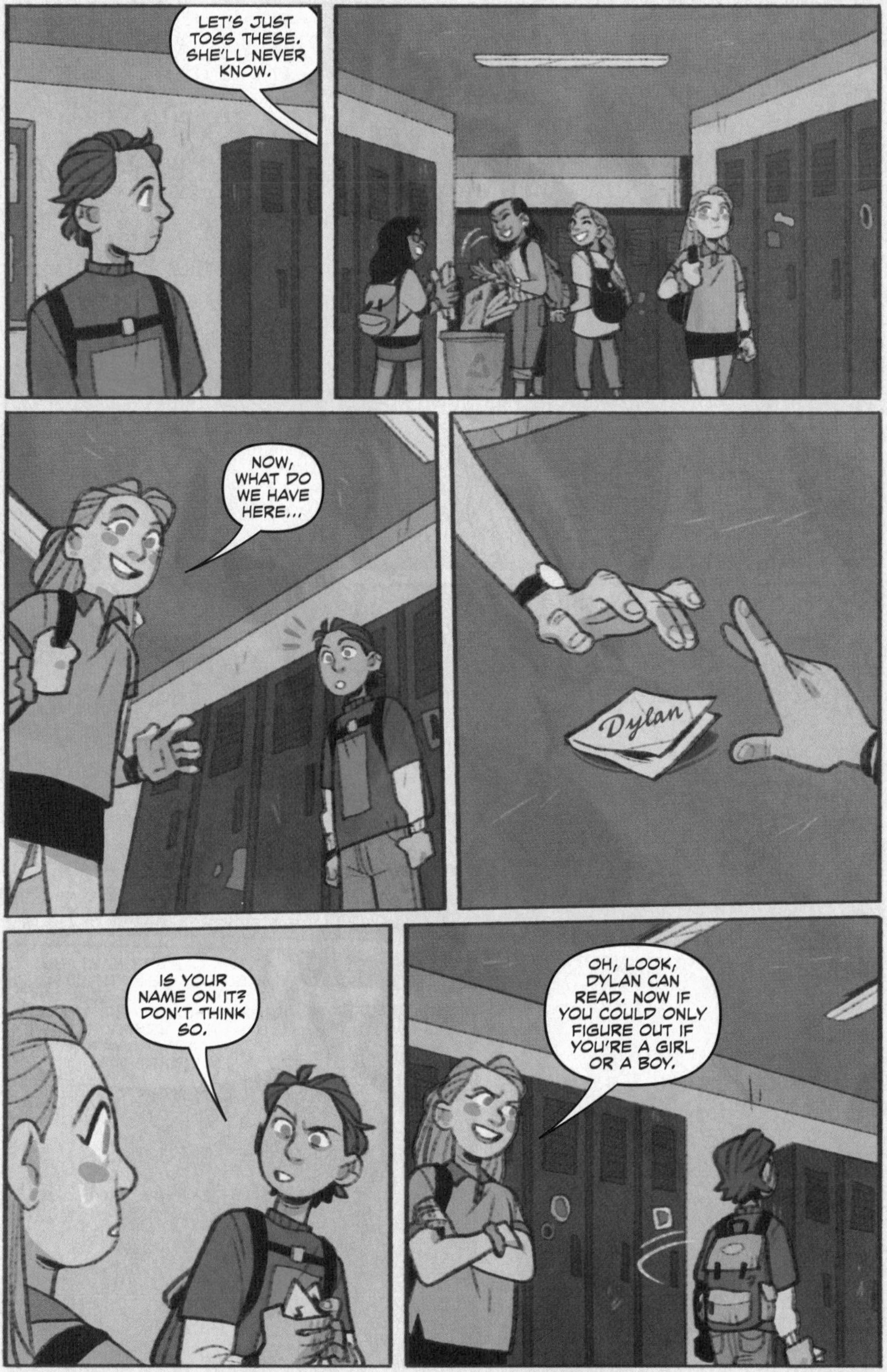
LET'S JUST TOSS THESE. SHE'LL NEVER KNOW.
NOW, WHAT DO WE HAVE HERE...
Dylan
IS YOUR NAME ON IT? DON'T THINK SO.
OH, LOOK, DYLAN CAN READ. NOW IF YOU COULD ONLY FIGURE OUT IF YOU'RE A GIRL OR A BOY.

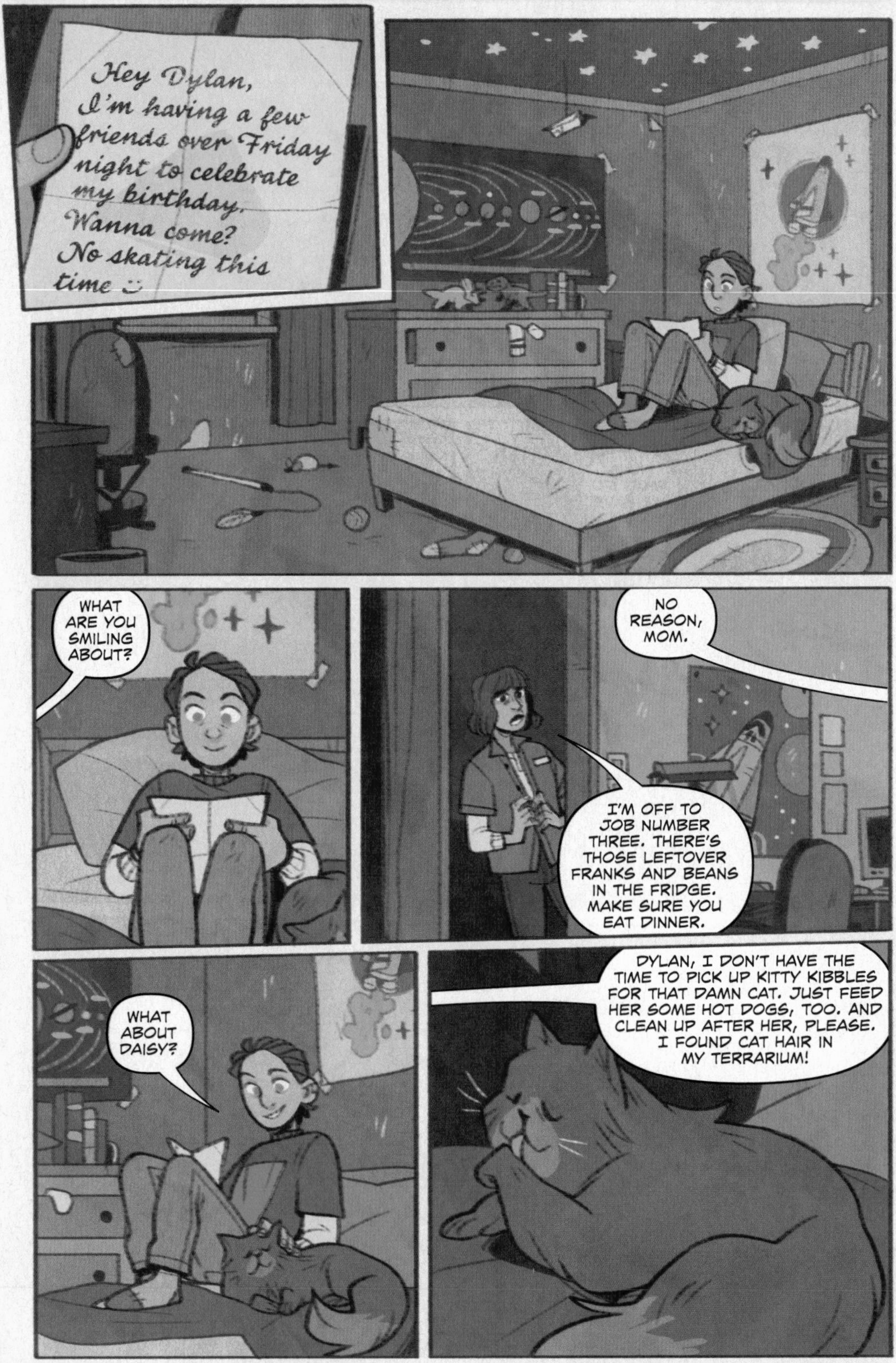

Hey Dylan,
I'm having a few friends over Friday night to celebrate my birthday.
Wanna come?
No skating this time ☺
WHAT ARE YOU SMILING ABOUT?
NO REASON, MOM.
I'M OFF TO JOB NUMBER THREE. THERE'S THOSE LEFTOVER FRANKS AND BEANS IN THE FRIDGE. MAKE SURE YOU EAT DINNER.
WHAT ABOUT DAISY?
DYLAN, I DON'T HAVE THE TIME TO PICK UP KITTY KIBBLES FOR THAT DAMN CAT. JUST FEED HER SOME HOT DOGS, TOO. AND CLEAN UP AFTER HER, PLEASE. I FOUND CAT HAIR IN MY TERRARIUM!

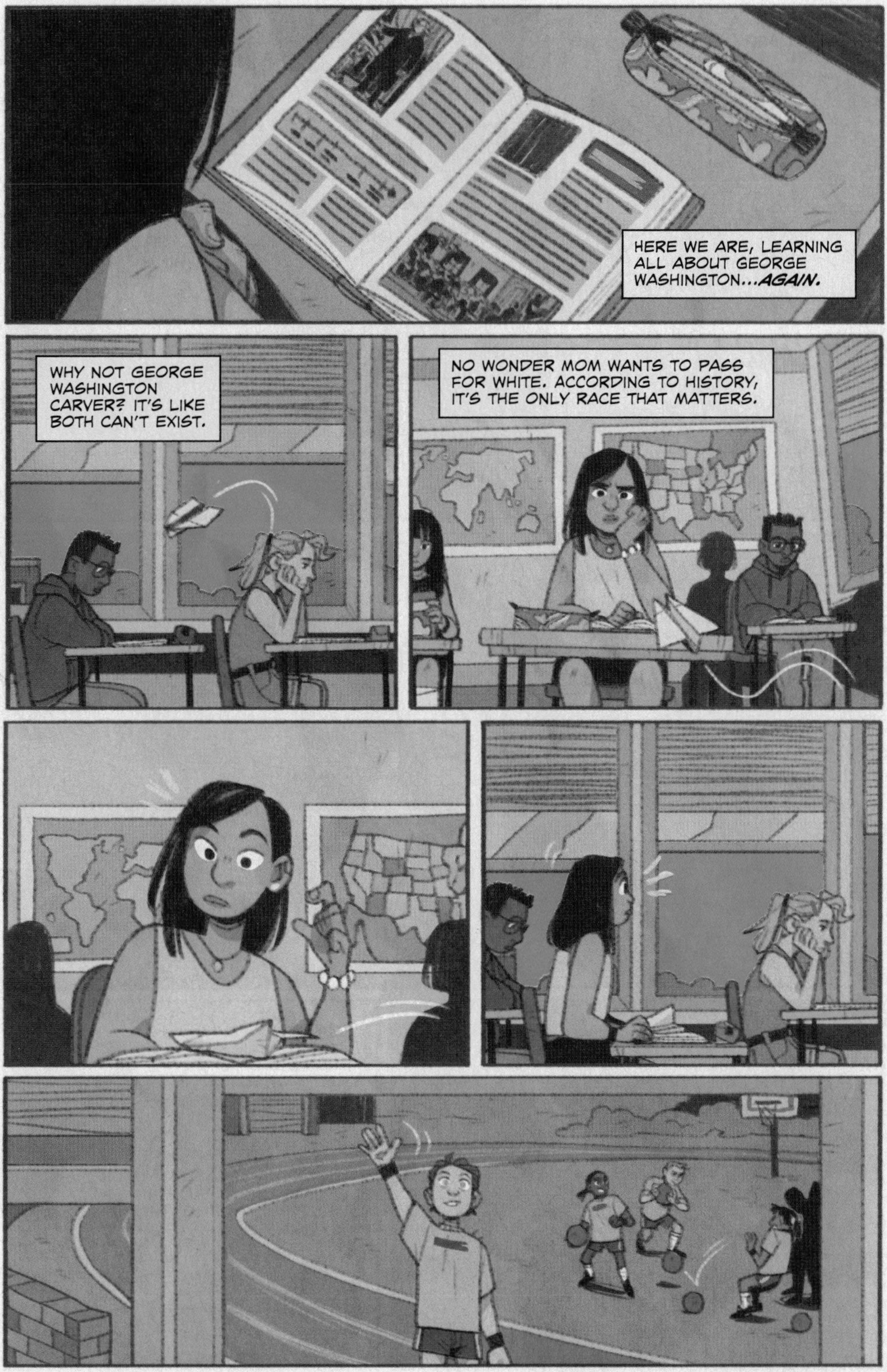
HERE WE ARE, LEARNING ALL ABOUT GEORGE WASHINGTON...*AGAIN.*
WHY NOT GEORGE WASHINGTON CARVER? IT'S LIKE BOTH CAN'T EXIST.
NO WONDER MOM WANTS TO PASS FOR WHITE. ACCORDING TO HISTORY, IT'S THE ONLY RACE THAT MATTERS.

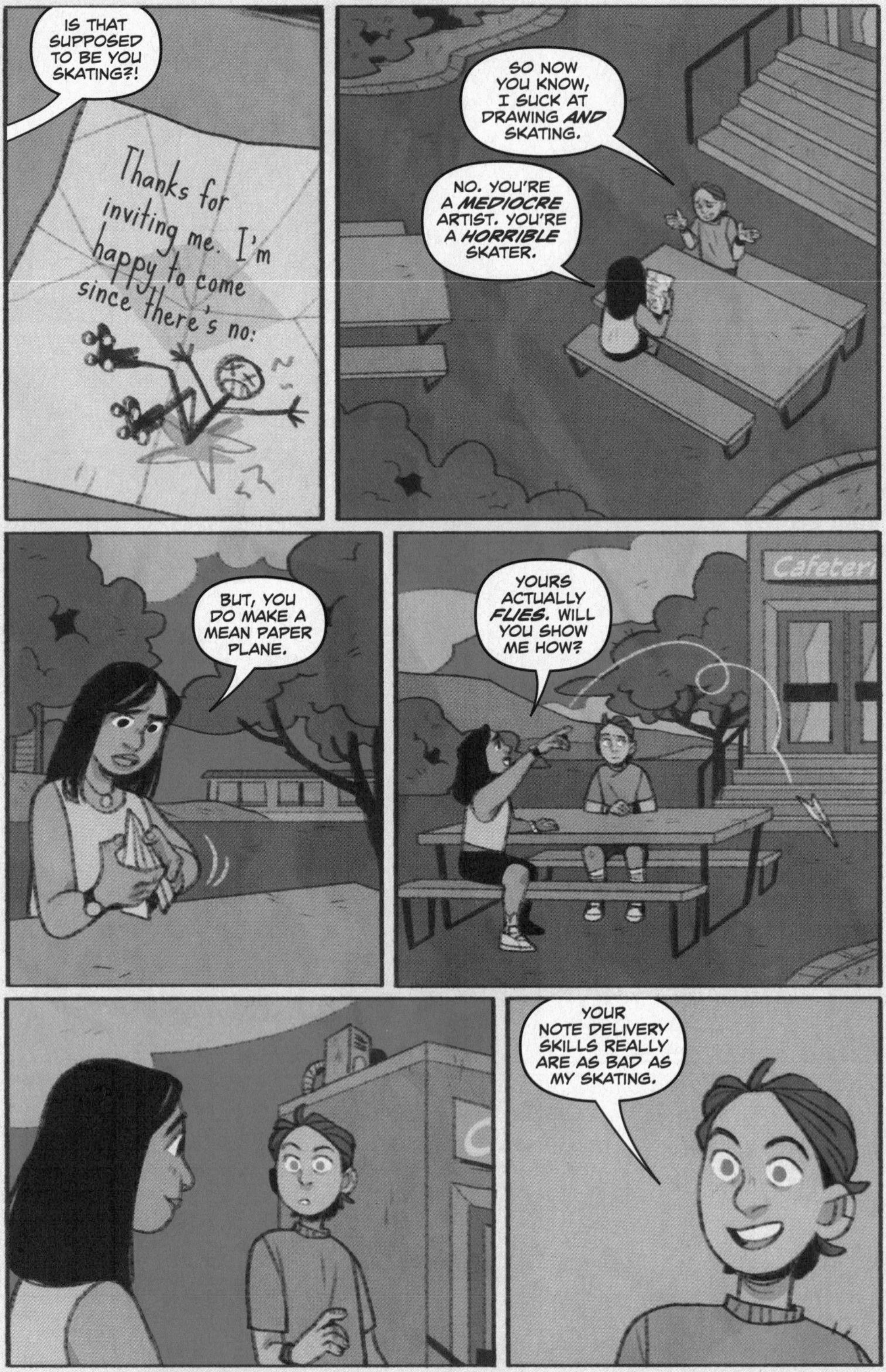
IS THAT SUPPOSED TO BE YOU SKATING?!
Thanks for inviting me. I'm happy to come since there's no:
SO NOW YOU KNOW, I SUCK AT DRAWING *AND* SKATING.
NO. YOU'RE A *MEDIOCRE* ARTIST. YOU'RE A *HORRIBLE* SKATER.
BUT, YOU DO MAKE A MEAN PAPER PLANE.
Cafeteri
YOURS ACTUALLY *FLIES*. WILL YOU SHOW ME HOW?
YOUR NOTE DELIVERY SKILLS REALLY ARE AS BAD AS MY SKATING.

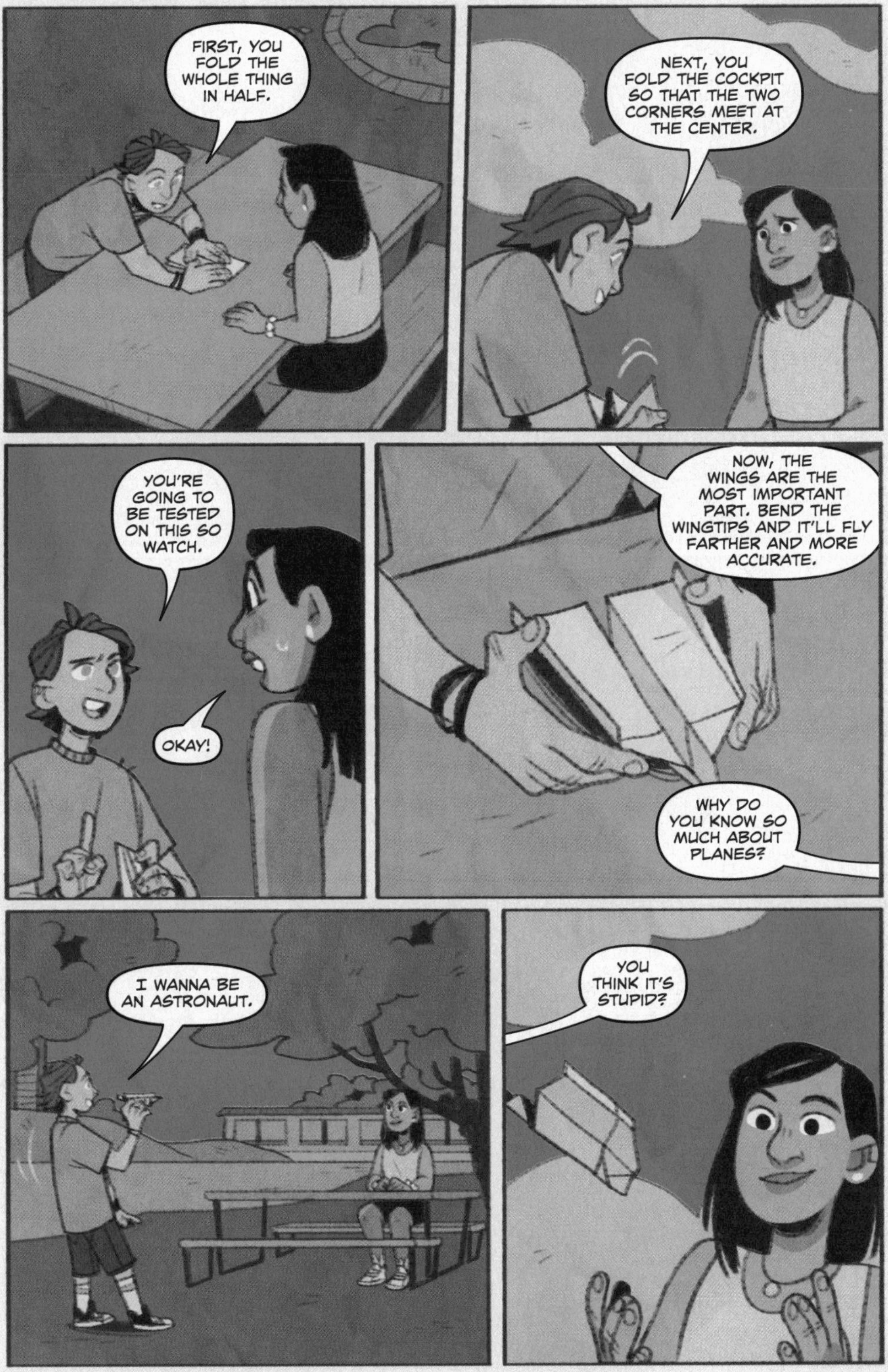
FIRST, YOU FOLD THE WHOLE THING IN HALF.
NEXT, YOU FOLD THE COCKPIT SO THAT THE TWO CORNERS MEET AT THE CENTER.
YOU'RE GOING TO BE TESTED ON THIS SO WATCH.
OKAY!
NOW, THE WINGS ARE THE MOST IMPORTANT PART. BEND THE WINGTIPS AND IT'LL FLY FARTHER AND MORE ACCURATE.
WHY DO YOU KNOW SO MUCH ABOUT PLANES?
I WANNA BE AN ASTRONAUT.
YOU THINK IT'S STUPID?

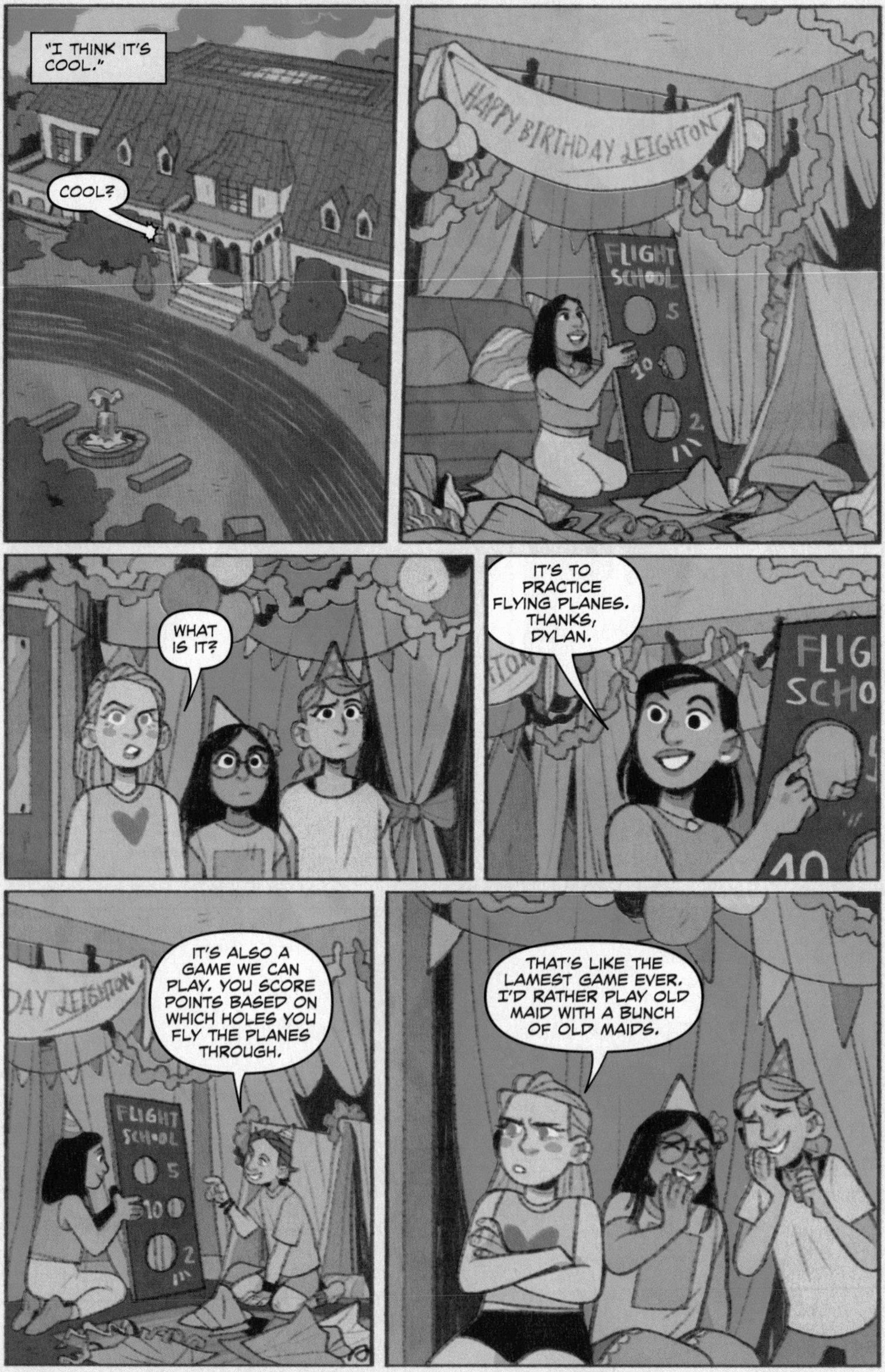
"I THINK IT'S COOL."
COOL?
HAPPY BIRTHDAY LEIGHTON
FLIGHT SCHOOL
5
10
2
WHAT IS IT?
IT'S TO PRACTICE FLYING PLANES. THANKS, DYLAN.
IT'S ALSO A GAME WE CAN PLAY. YOU SCORE POINTS BASED ON WHICH HOLES YOU FLY THE PLANES THROUGH.
THAT'S LIKE THE LAMEST GAME EVER. I'D RATHER PLAY OLD MAID WITH A BUNCH OF OLD MAIDS.

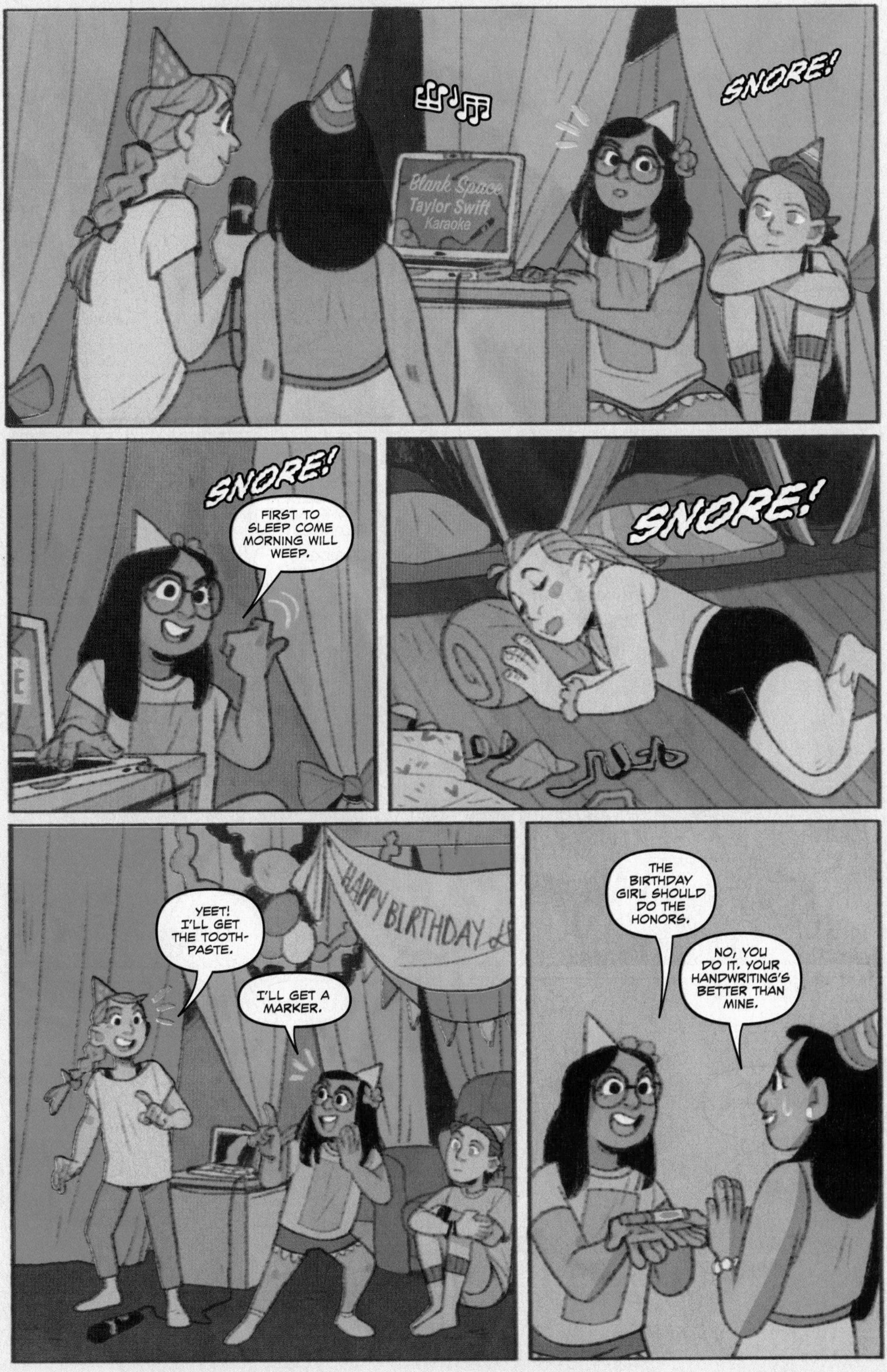
Blank Space
Taylor Swift
Karaoke
SNORE!
SNORE!
FIRST TO SLEEP COME MORNING WILL WEEP.
SNORE!
HAPPY BIRTHDAY
YEET! I'LL GET THE TOOTH-PASTE.
I'LL GET A MARKER.
THE BIRTHDAY GIRL SHOULD DO THE HONORS.
NO, YOU DO IT. YOUR HANDWRITING'S BETTER THAN MINE.

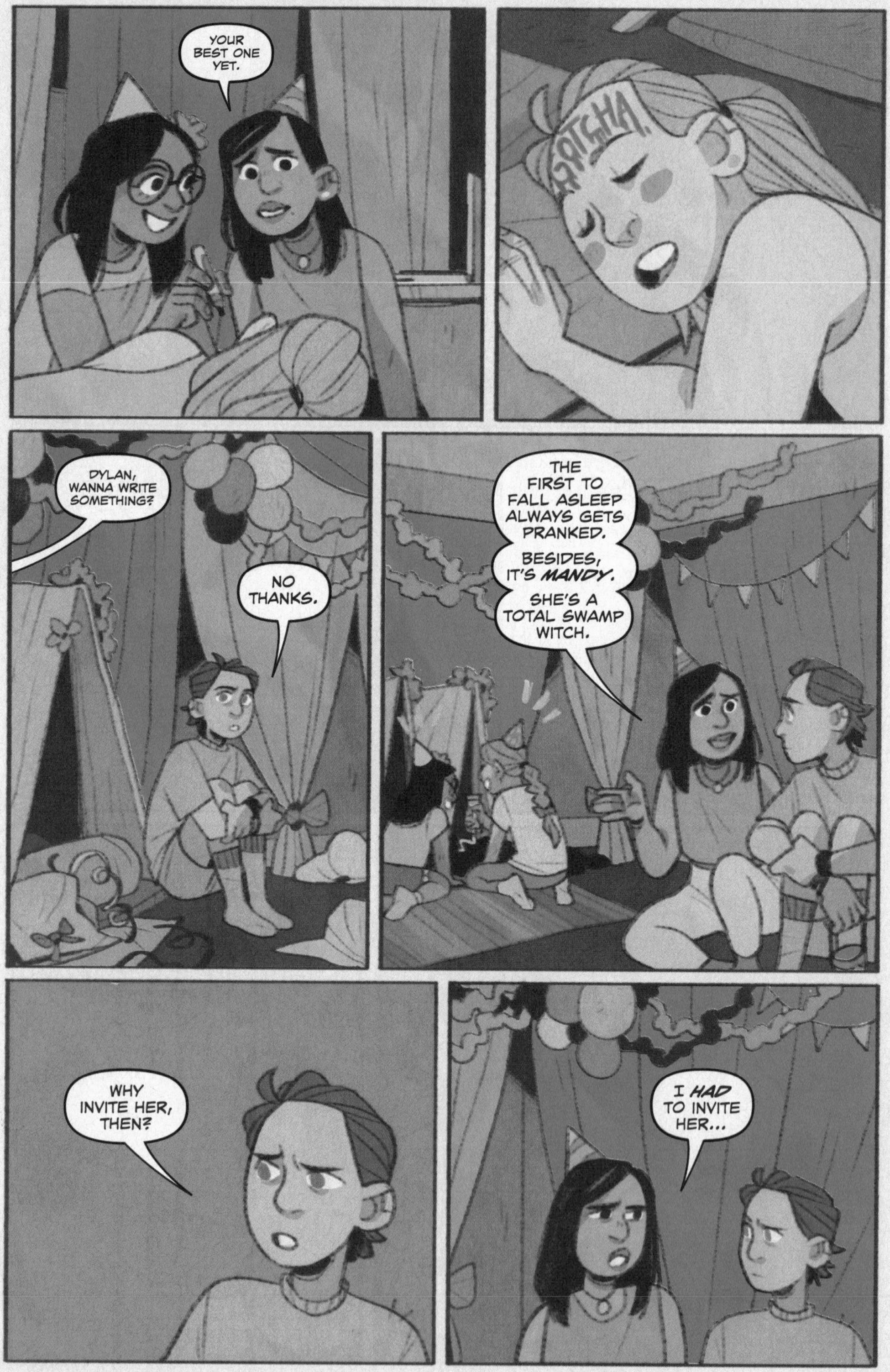
YOUR BEST ONE YET.
DYLAN, WANNA WRITE SOMETHING?
NO THANKS.
THE FIRST TO FALL ASLEEP ALWAYS GETS PRANKED.
BESIDES, IT'S *MANDY*.
SHE'S A TOTAL SWAMP WITCH.
WHY INVITE HER, THEN?
I *HAD* TO INVITE HER...

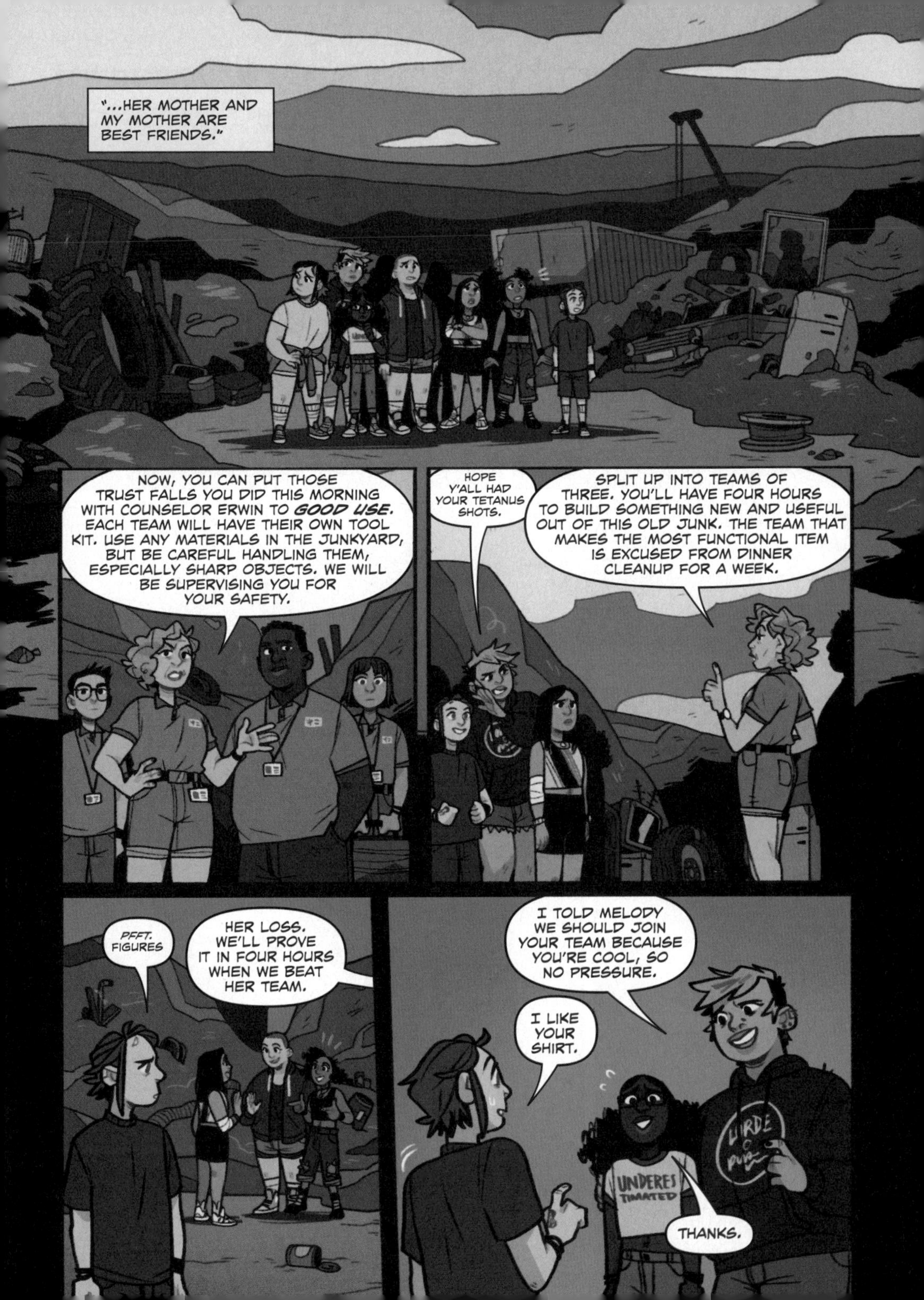
"...HER MOTHER AND MY MOTHER ARE BEST FRIENDS."
NOW, YOU CAN PUT THOSE TRUST FALLS YOU DID THIS MORNING WITH COUNSELOR ERWIN TO GOOD USE. EACH TEAM WILL HAVE THEIR OWN TOOL KIT. USE ANY MATERIALS IN THE JUNKYARD, BUT BE CAREFUL HANDLING THEM, ESPECIALLY SHARP OBJECTS. WE WILL BE SUPERVISING YOU FOR YOUR SAFETY.
HOPE Y'ALL HAD YOUR TETANUS SHOTS.
SPLIT UP INTO TEAMS OF THREE. YOU'LL HAVE FOUR HOURS TO BUILD SOMETHING NEW AND USEFUL OUT OF THIS OLD JUNK. THE TEAM THAT MAKES THE MOST FUNCTIONAL ITEM IS EXCUSED FROM DINNER CLEANUP FOR A WEEK.
PFFT. FIGURES
HER LOSS. WE'LL PROVE IT IN FOUR HOURS WHEN WE BEAT HER TEAM.
I TOLD MELODY WE SHOULD JOIN YOUR TEAM BECAUSE YOU'RE COOL, SO NO PRESSURE.
I LIKE YOUR SHIRT.
UNDERESTIMATED
THANKS.

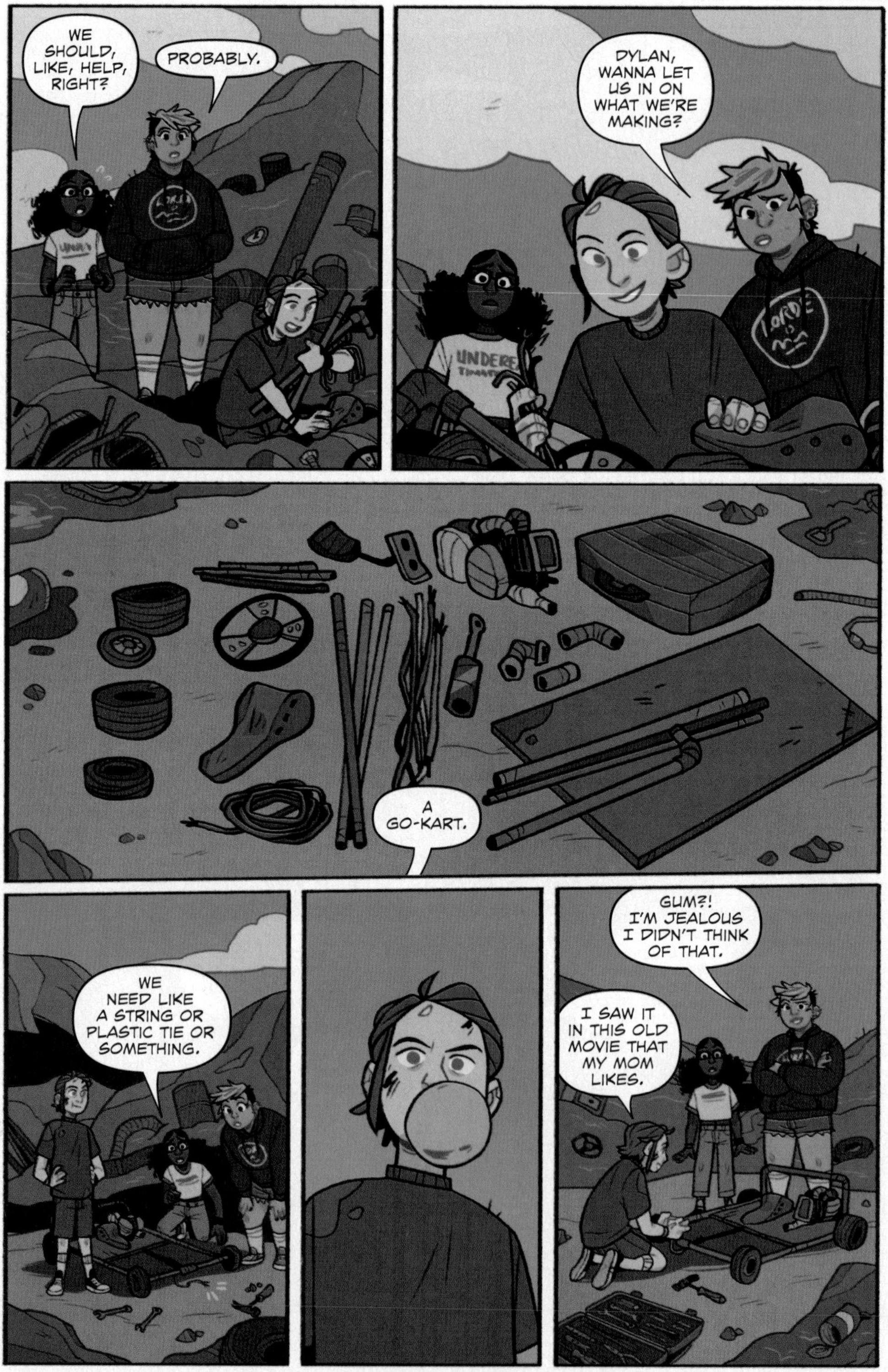
WE SHOULD, LIKE, HELP, RIGHT?
PROBABLY.
DYLAN, WANNA LET US IN ON WHAT WE'RE MAKING?
A GO-KART.
WE NEED LIKE A STRING OR PLASTIC TIE OR SOMETHING.
GUM?! I'M JEALOUS I DIDN'T THINK OF THAT.
I SAW IT IN THIS OLD MOVIE THAT MY MOM LIKES.

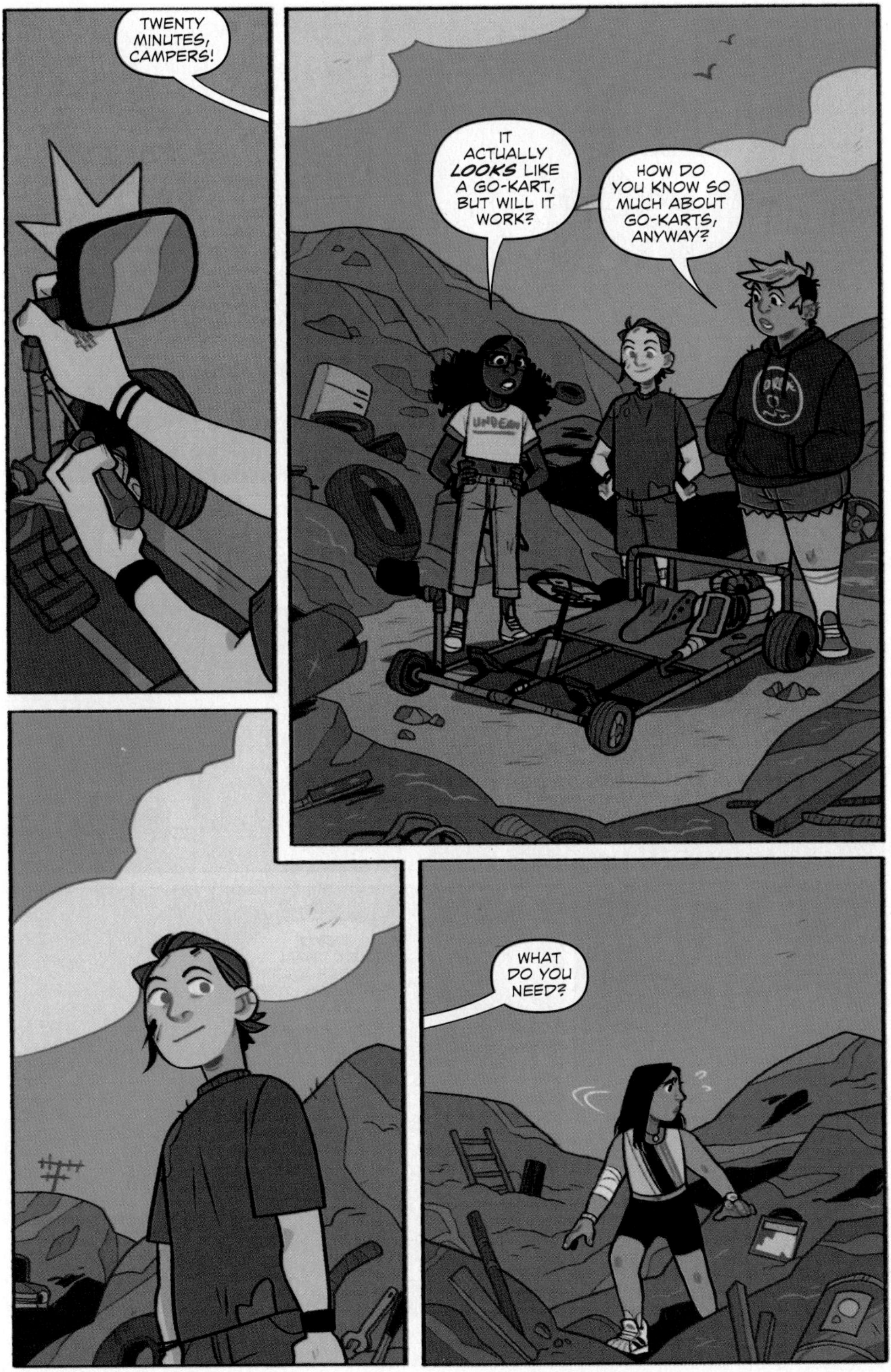
TWENTY MINUTES, CAMPERS!
IT ACTUALLY LOOKS LIKE A GO-KART, BUT WILL IT WORK?
HOW DO YOU KNOW SO MUCH ABOUT GO-KARTS, ANYWAY?
WHAT DO YOU NEED?

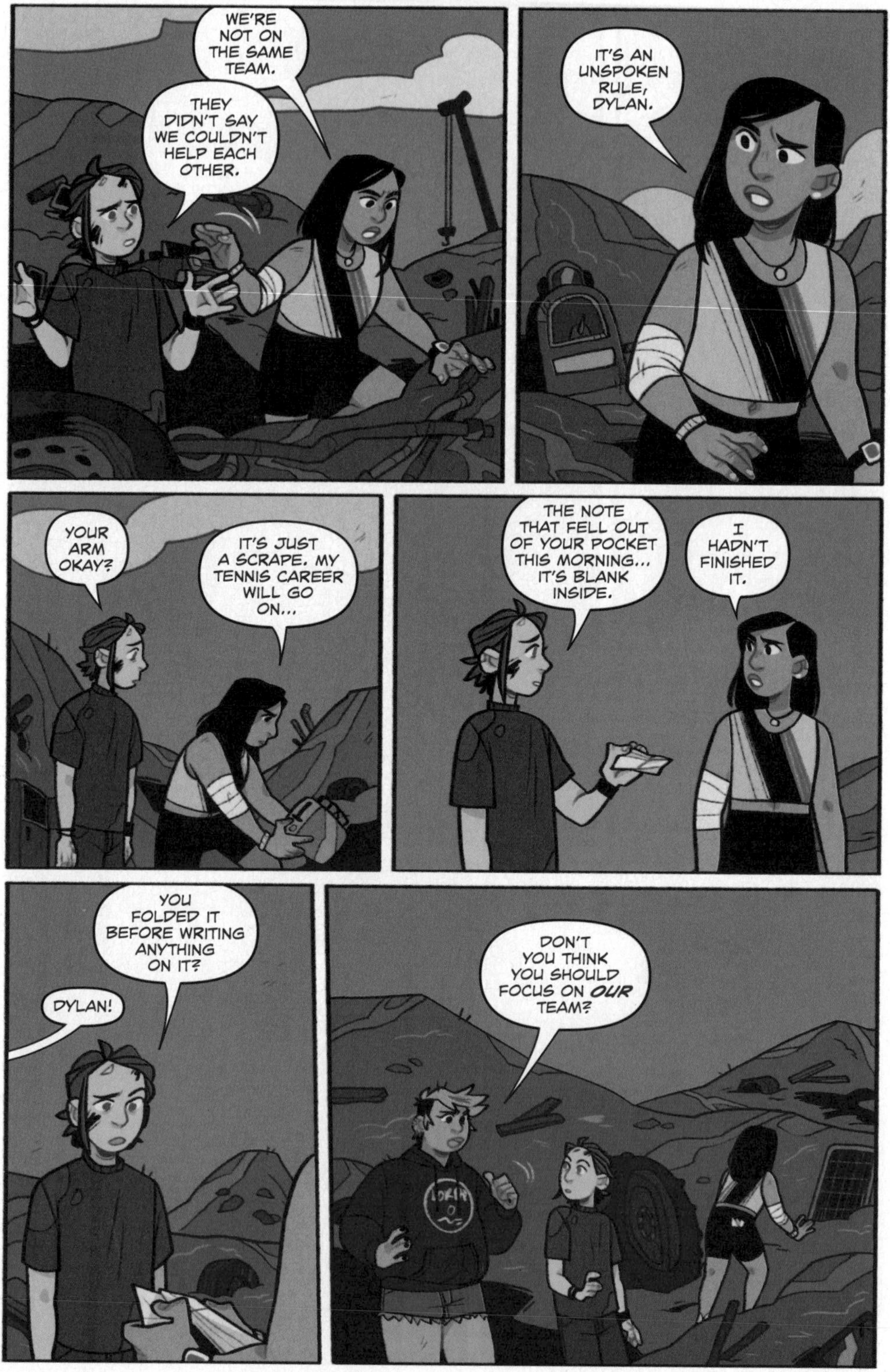
WE'RE NOT ON THE SAME TEAM.
THEY DIDN'T SAY WE COULDN'T HELP EACH OTHER.
IT'S AN UNSPOKEN RULE, DYLAN.
YOUR ARM OKAY?
IT'S JUST A SCRAPE. MY TENNIS CAREER WILL GO ON...
THE NOTE THAT FELL OUT OF YOUR POCKET THIS MORNING... IT'S BLANK INSIDE.
I HADN'T FINISHED IT.
YOU FOLDED IT BEFORE WRITING ANYTHING ON IT?
DYLAN!
DON'T YOU THINK YOU SHOULD FOCUS ON *OUR* TEAM?

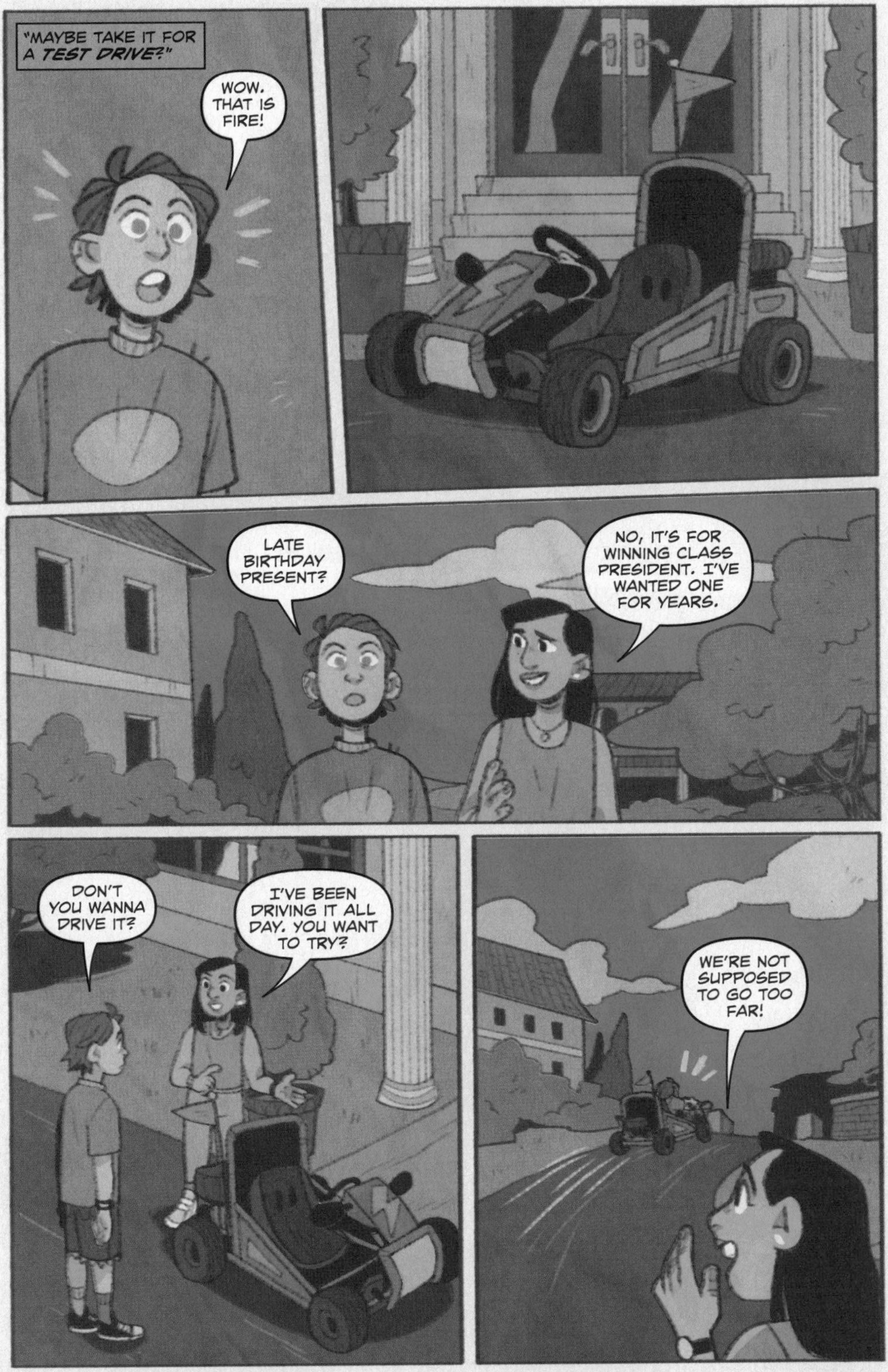
"MAYBE TAKE IT FOR A *TEST DRIVE?*"
WOW. THAT IS FIRE!
LATE BIRTHDAY PRESENT?
NO, IT'S FOR WINNING CLASS PRESIDENT. I'VE WANTED ONE FOR YEARS.
DON'T YOU WANNA DRIVE IT?
I'VE BEEN DRIVING IT ALL DAY. YOU WANT TO TRY?
WE'RE NOT SUPPOSED TO GO TOO FAR!

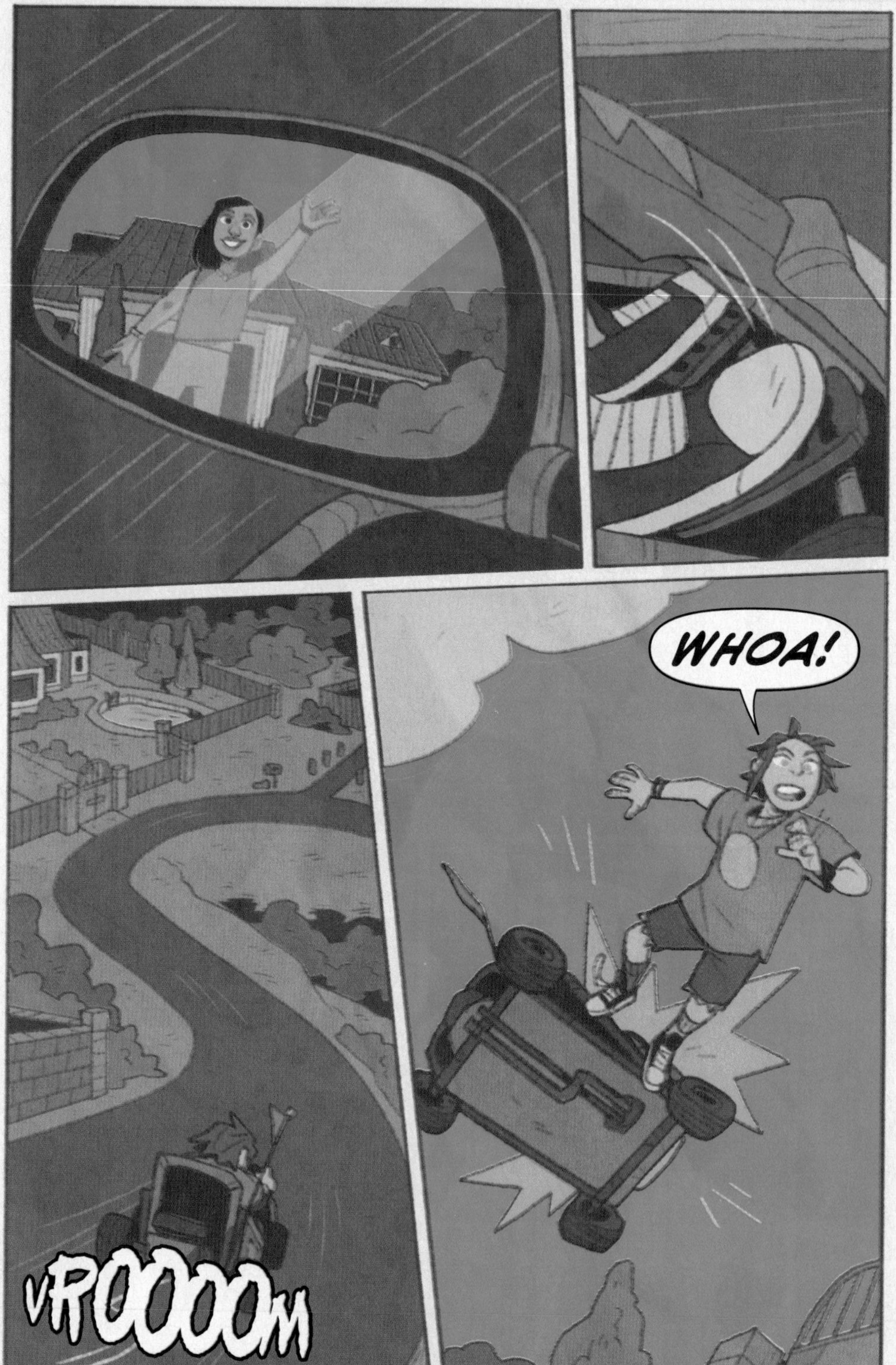
VROOOOM
WHOA!

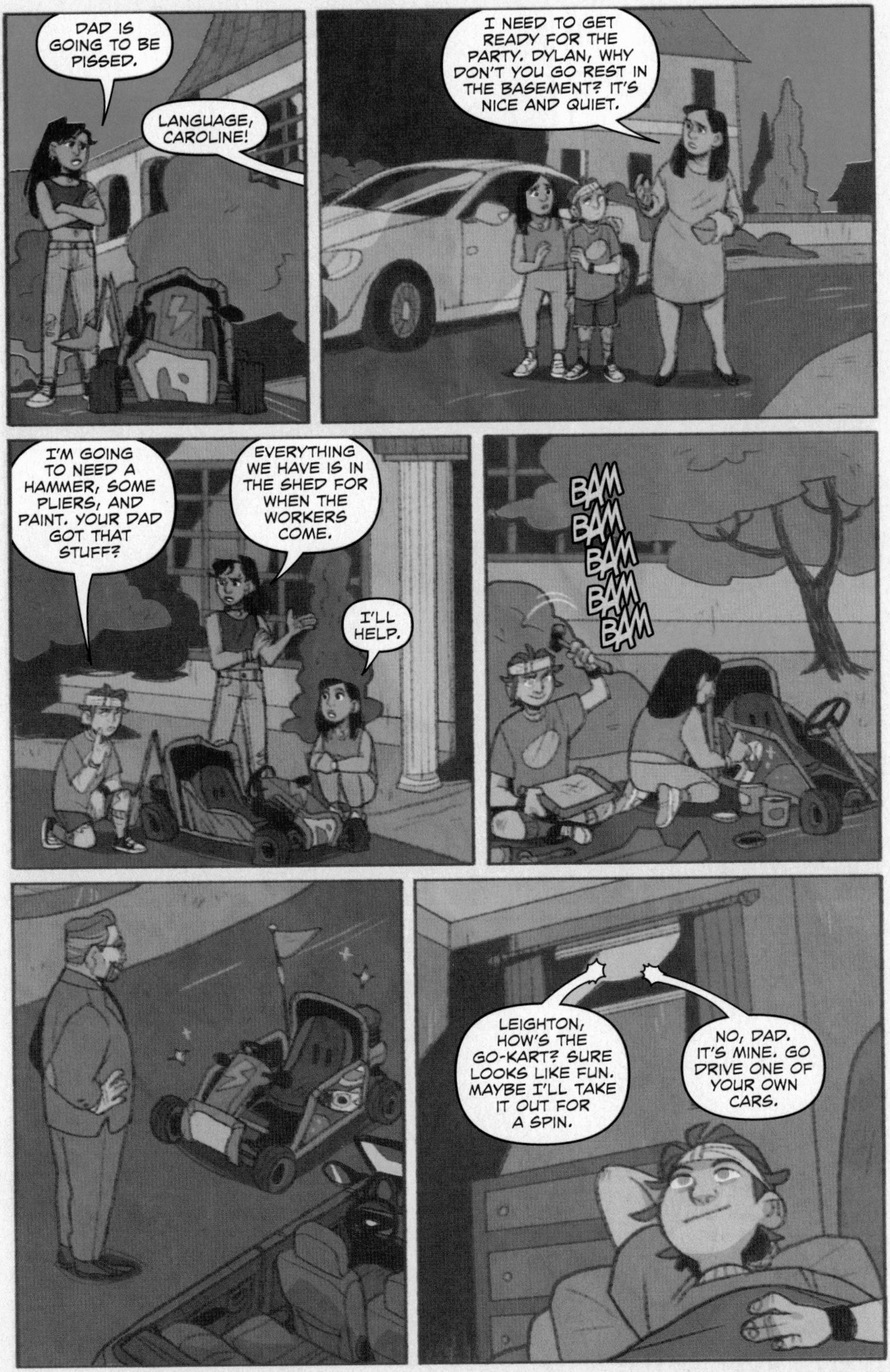
DAD IS GOING TO BE PISSED.
LANGUAGE, CAROLINE!
I NEED TO GET READY FOR THE PARTY. DYLAN, WHY DON'T YOU GO REST IN THE BASEMENT? IT'S NICE AND QUIET.
I'M GOING TO NEED A HAMMER, SOME PLIERS, AND PAINT. YOUR DAD GOT THAT STUFF?
EVERYTHING WE HAVE IS IN THE SHED FOR WHEN THE WORKERS COME.
I'LL HELP.
BAM BAM BAM BAM BAM
LEIGHTON, HOW'S THE GO-KART? SURE LOOKS LIKE FUN. MAYBE I'LL TAKE IT OUT FOR A SPIN.
NO, DAD. IT'S MINE. GO DRIVE ONE OF YOUR OWN CARS.

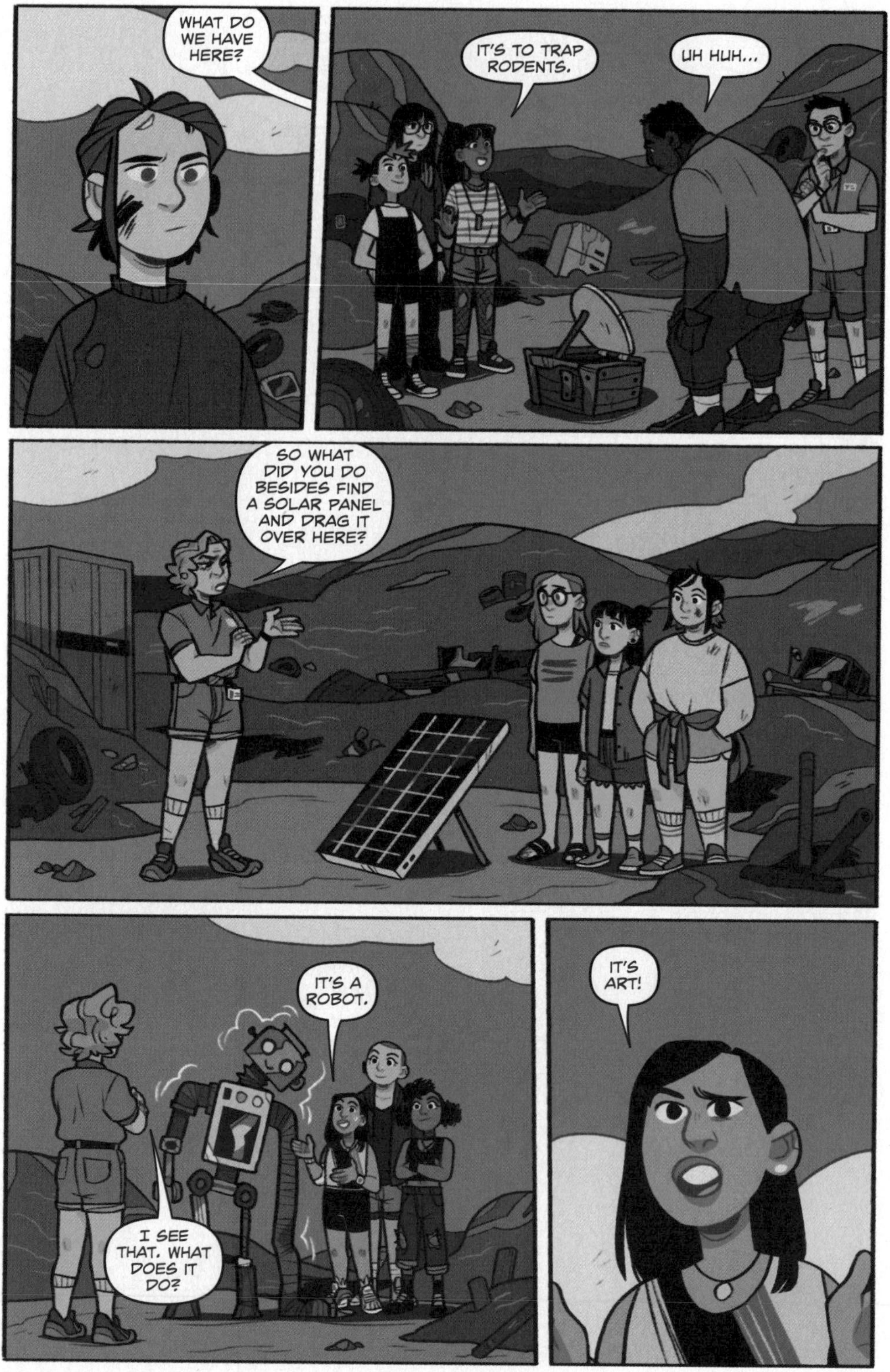
WHAT DO WE HAVE HERE?
IT'S TO TRAP RODENTS.
UH HUH...
SO WHAT DID YOU DO BESIDES FIND A SOLAR PANEL AND DRAG IT OVER HERE?
IT'S A ROBOT.
I SEE THAT. WHAT DOES IT DO?
IT'S ART!

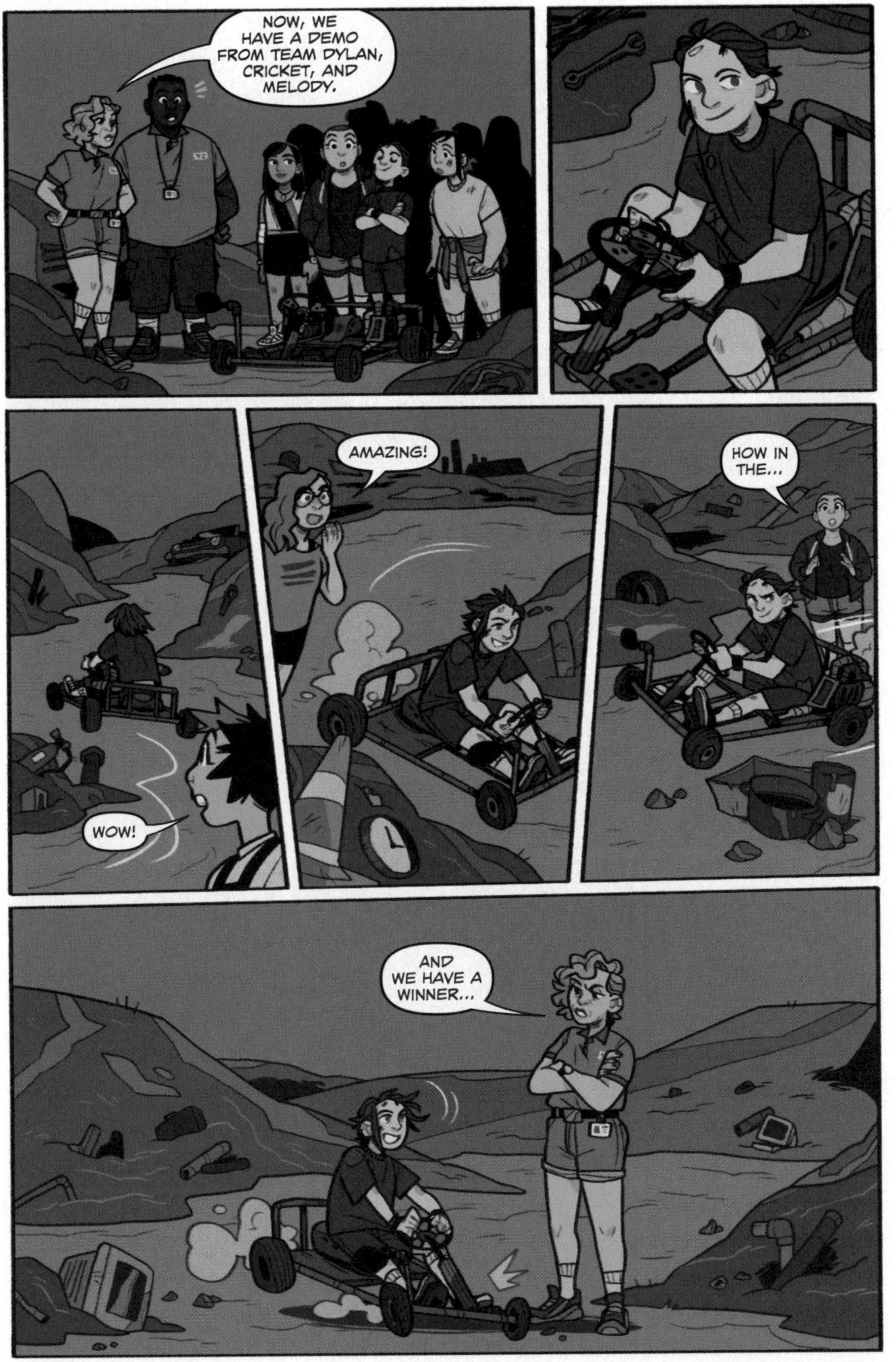
NOW, WE HAVE A DEMO FROM TEAM DYLAN, CRICKET, AND MELODY.
WOW!
AMAZING!
HOW IN THE...
AND WE HAVE A WINNER...

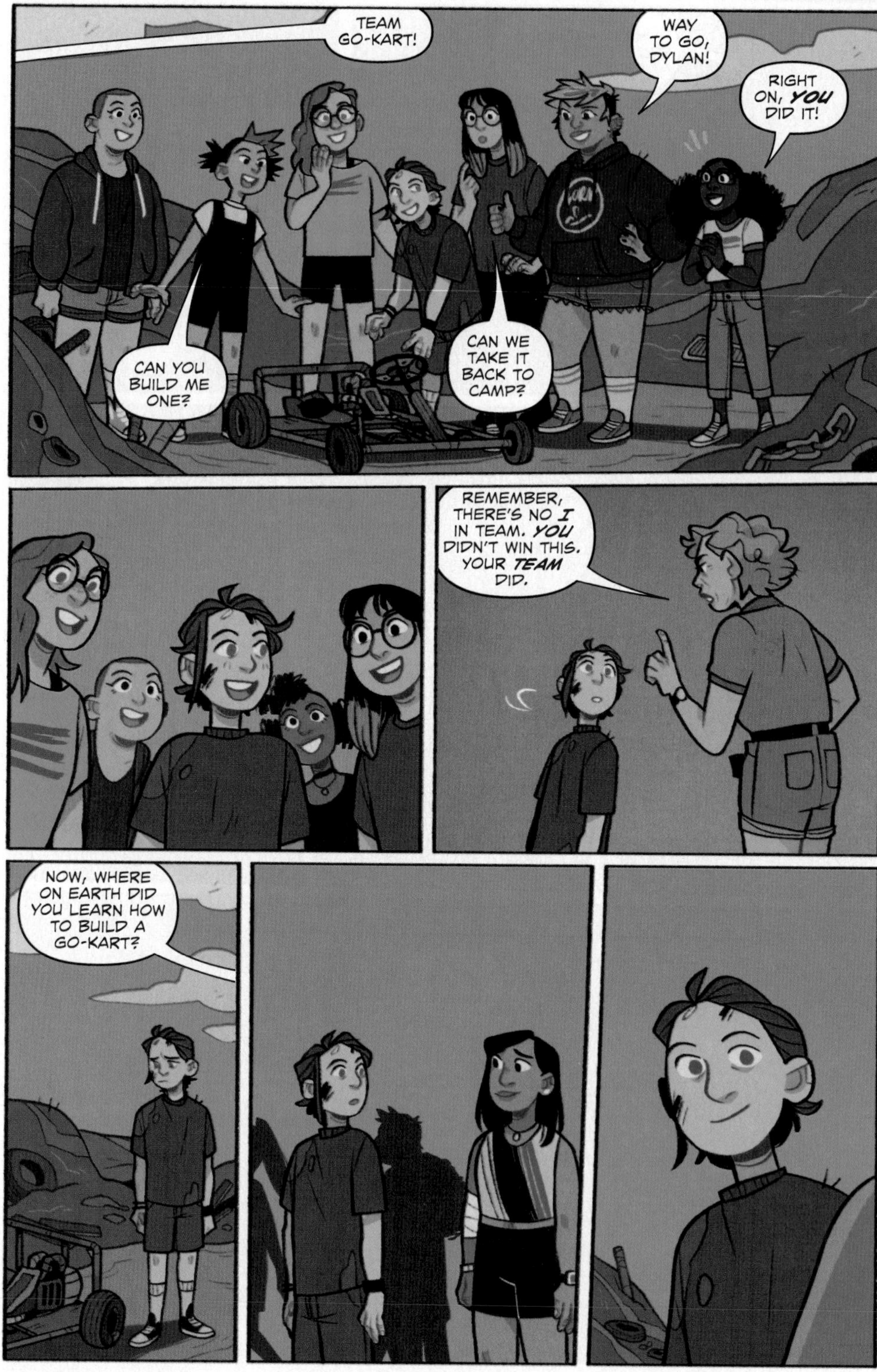
TEAM GO-KART!
WAY TO GO, DYLAN!
RIGHT ON, YOU DID IT!
CAN YOU BUILD ME ONE?
CAN WE TAKE IT BACK TO CAMP?
REMEMBER, THERE'S NO I IN TEAM. YOU DIDN'T WIN THIS. YOUR TEAM DID.
NOW, WHERE ON EARTH DID YOU LEARN HOW TO BUILD A GO-KART?

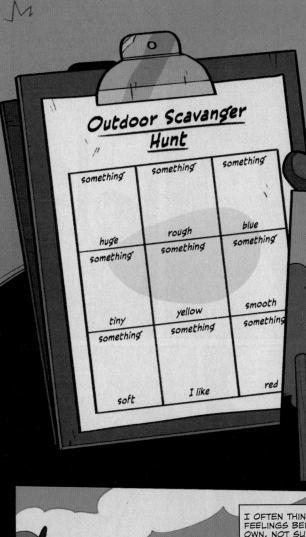

Outdoor Scavanger Hunt

something	something	something
huge	rough	blue
something	something	something
tiny	yellow	smooth
something	something	something
soft	I like	red

OKAY CAMPERS, HERE'S THE DEAL. GO OFF ON YOUR OWN IN THIS WOODED AREA, FIND ITEMS THAT CORRESPOND TO THE PROMPTS ON THE SHEET, AND DRAW THEM. DON'T GO TOO FAR OFF THE MAIN PATH, AND MEET BACK HERE IN TWO HOURS.

COUNSELORS WILL BE HANGING OUT ALL ALONG THE PATH SHOULD YOU NEED US. THE PURPOSE OF THIS ACTIVITY IS TO BE SELF-RELIANT AND *CREATIVE.* IN TWO HOURS.

SO, FOR THOSE OF YOU YEARNING TO USE YOUR IMAGINATION AND WORK WITH MORE ORGANIC MATERIALS, HERE YOU GO.

I OFTEN THINK ABOUT LEIGHTON'S FEELINGS BEFORE I THINK ABOUT MY OWN. NOT SURE IF THAT'S HEALTHY OR NOT, BUT IT IS WHAT IT IS. LIKE THIS ACTIVITY...I KNEW SHE'D BE ALL INTO IT AS SOON AS COUNSELOR ERWIN TOLD US ABOUT IT.

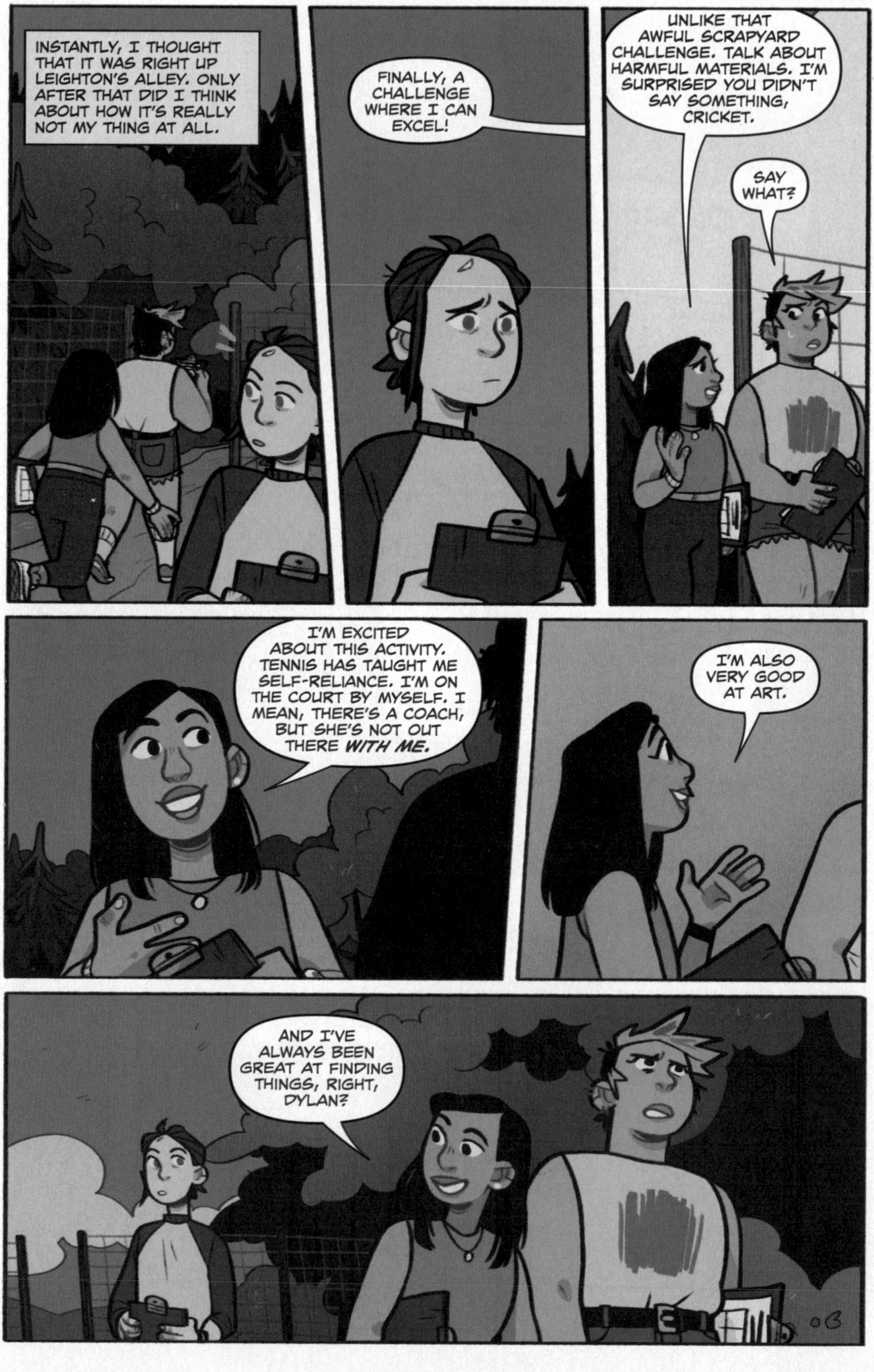
INSTANTLY, I THOUGHT THAT IT WAS RIGHT UP LEIGHTON'S ALLEY. ONLY AFTER THAT DID I THINK ABOUT HOW IT'S REALLY NOT MY THING AT ALL.
FINALLY, A CHALLENGE WHERE I CAN EXCEL!
UNLIKE THAT AWFUL SCRAPYARD CHALLENGE. TALK ABOUT HARMFUL MATERIALS. I'M SURPRISED YOU DIDN'T SAY SOMETHING, CRICKET.
SAY WHAT?
I'M EXCITED ABOUT THIS ACTIVITY. TENNIS HAS TAUGHT ME SELF-RELIANCE. I'M ON THE COURT BY MYSELF. I MEAN, THERE'S A COACH, BUT SHE'S NOT OUT THERE *WITH ME.*
I'M ALSO VERY GOOD AT ART.
AND I'VE ALWAYS BEEN GREAT AT FINDING THINGS, RIGHT, DYLAN?

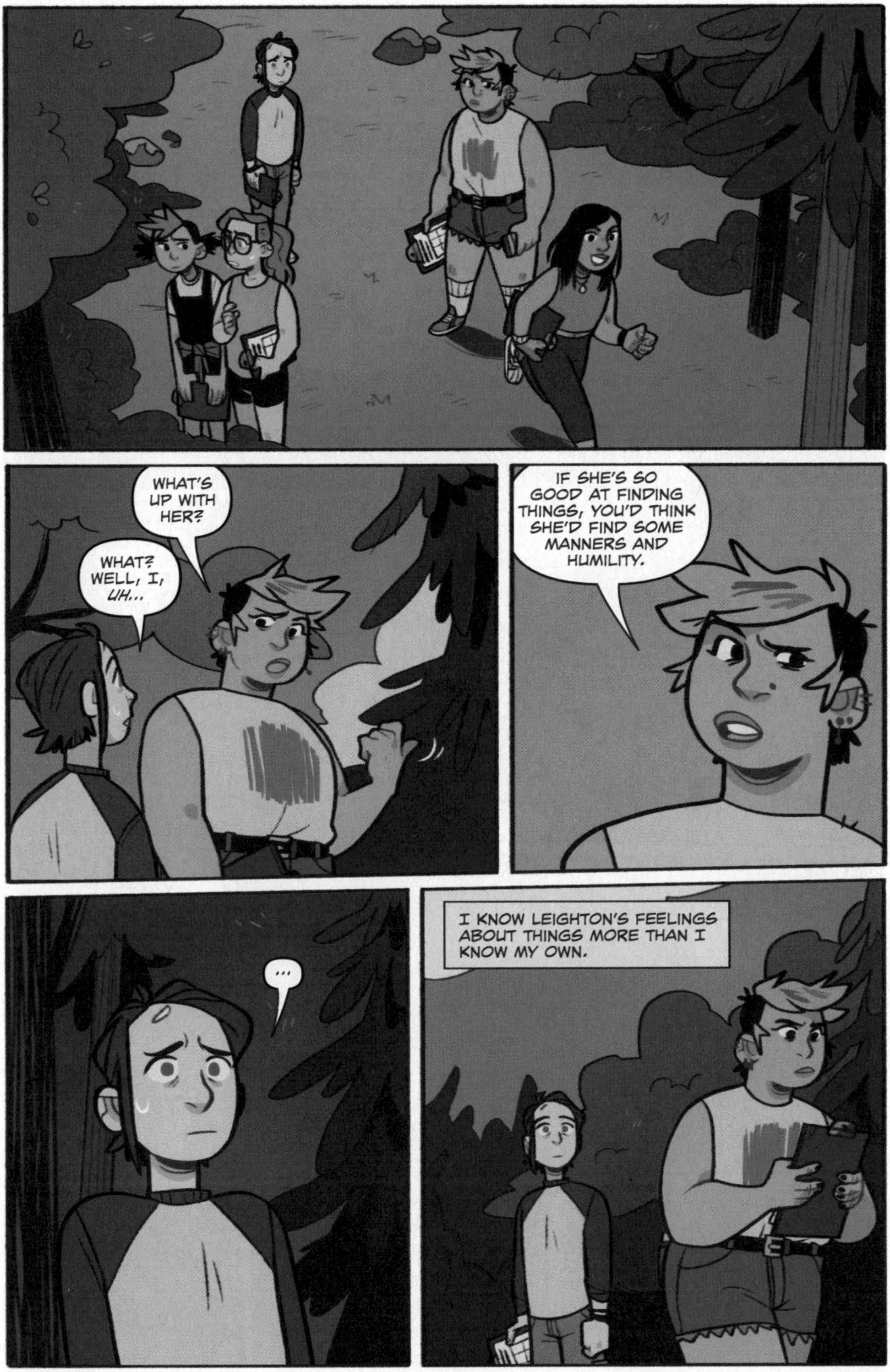
WHAT'S UP WITH HER?
WHAT? WELL, I, UH...
IF SHE'S SO GOOD AT FINDING THINGS, YOU'D THINK SHE'D FIND SOME MANNERS AND HUMILITY.
...
I KNOW LEIGHTON'S FEELINGS ABOUT THINGS MORE THAN I KNOW MY OWN.

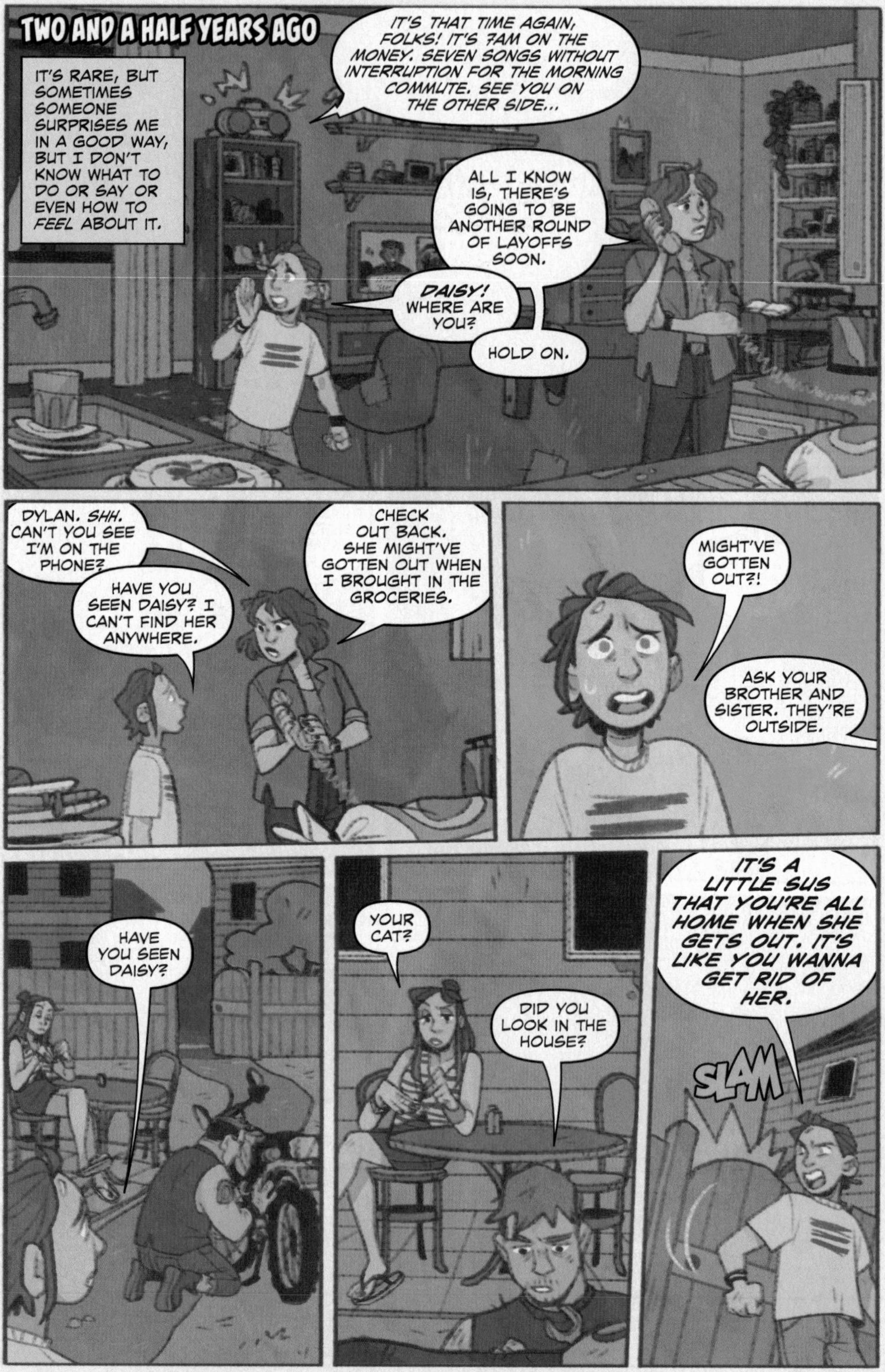
TWO AND A HALF YEARS AGO
IT'S RARE, BUT SOMETIMES SOMEONE SURPRISES ME IN A GOOD WAY, BUT I DON'T KNOW WHAT TO DO OR SAY OR EVEN HOW TO *FEEL* ABOUT IT.
IT'S THAT TIME AGAIN, FOLKS! IT'S 7AM ON THE MONEY. SEVEN SONGS WITHOUT INTERRUPTION FOR THE MORNING COMMUTE. SEE YOU ON THE OTHER SIDE...
ALL I KNOW IS, THERE'S GOING TO BE ANOTHER ROUND OF LAYOFFS SOON.
DAISY! WHERE ARE YOU?
HOLD ON.
DYLAN. *SHH.* CAN'T YOU SEE I'M ON THE PHONE?
HAVE YOU SEEN DAISY? I CAN'T FIND HER ANYWHERE.
CHECK OUT BACK. SHE MIGHT'VE GOTTEN OUT WHEN I BROUGHT IN THE GROCERIES.
MIGHT'VE GOTTEN OUT?!
ASK YOUR BROTHER AND SISTER. THEY'RE OUTSIDE.
HAVE YOU SEEN DAISY?
YOUR CAT?
DID YOU LOOK IN THE HOUSE?
IT'S A LITTLE SUS THAT YOU'RE ALL HOME WHEN SHE GETS OUT. IT'S LIKE YOU WANNA GET RID OF HER.
SLAM

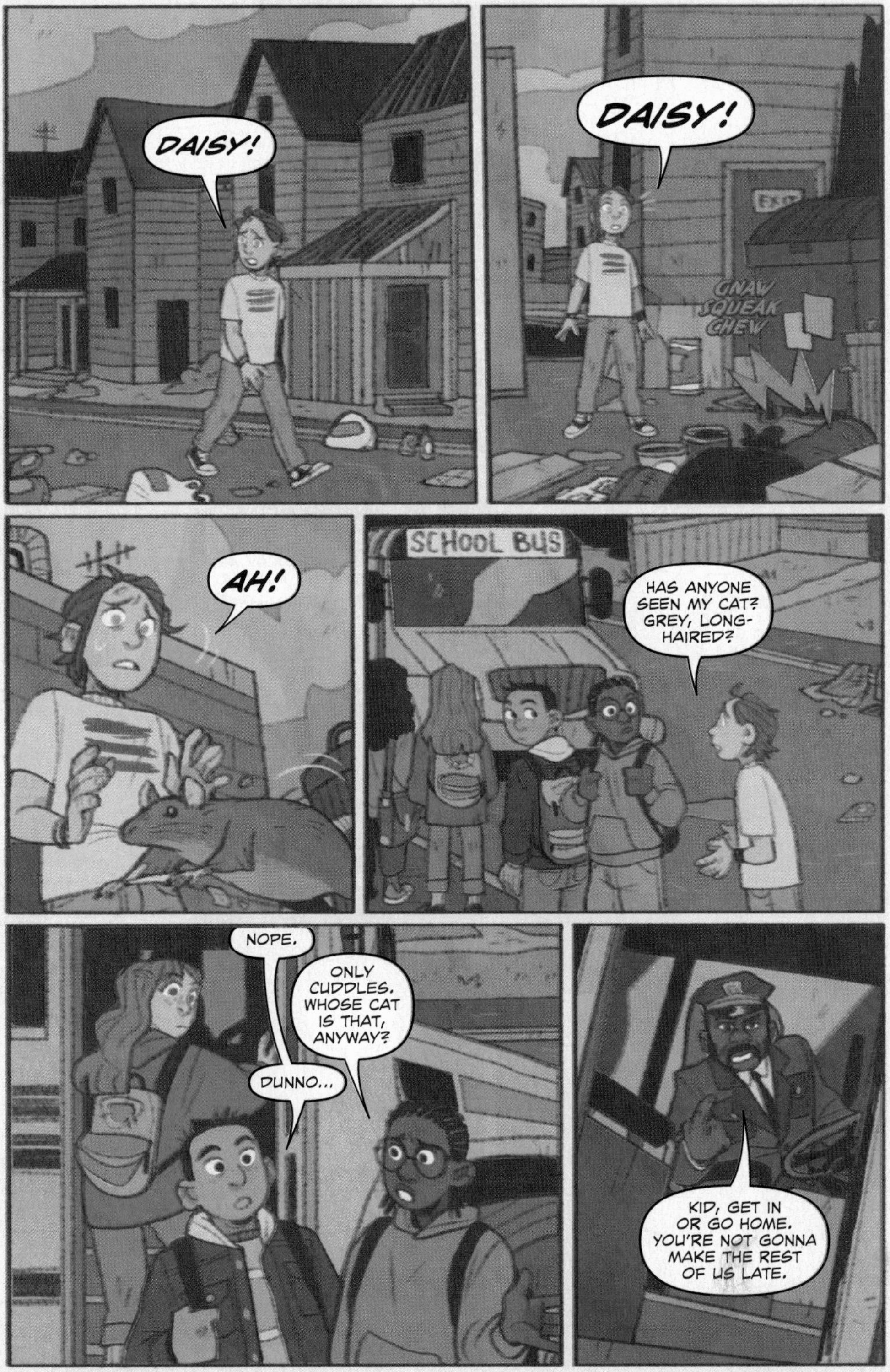
DAISY!
DAISY!
GNAW SQUEAK CHEW
AH!
SCHOOL BUS
HAS ANYONE SEEN MY CAT? GREY, LONG-HAIRED?
NOPE.
ONLY CUDDLES. WHOSE CAT IS THAT, ANYWAY?
DUNNO...
KID, GET IN OR GO HOME. YOU'RE NOT GONNA MAKE THE REST OF US LATE.

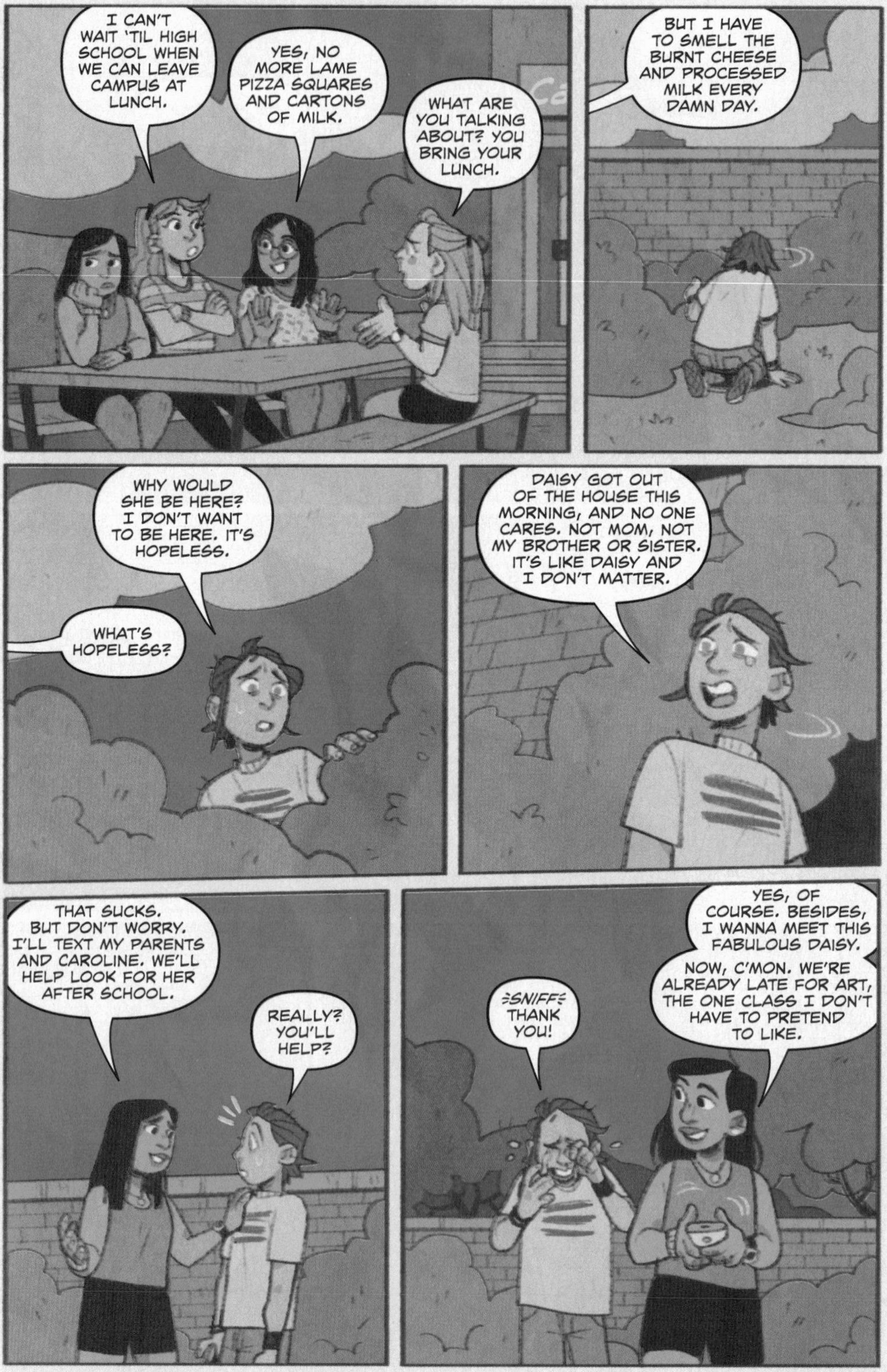
I CAN'T WAIT 'TIL HIGH SCHOOL WHEN WE CAN LEAVE CAMPUS AT LUNCH.
YES, NO MORE LAME PIZZA SQUARES AND CARTONS OF MILK.
WHAT ARE YOU TALKING ABOUT? YOU BRING YOUR LUNCH.
BUT I HAVE TO SMELL THE BURNT CHEESE AND PROCESSED MILK EVERY DAMN DAY.
WHY WOULD SHE BE HERE? I DON'T WANT TO BE HERE. IT'S HOPELESS.
WHAT'S HOPELESS?
DAISY GOT OUT OF THE HOUSE THIS MORNING, AND NO ONE CARES. NOT MOM, NOT MY BROTHER OR SISTER. IT'S LIKE DAISY AND I DON'T MATTER.
THAT SUCKS. BUT DON'T WORRY. I'LL TEXT MY PARENTS AND CAROLINE. WE'LL HELP LOOK FOR HER AFTER SCHOOL.
REALLY? YOU'LL HELP?
SNIFF THANK YOU!
YES, OF COURSE. BESIDES, I WANNA MEET THIS FABULOUS DAISY.
NOW, C'MON. WE'RE ALREADY LATE FOR ART, THE ONE CLASS I DON'T HAVE TO PRETEND TO LIKE.

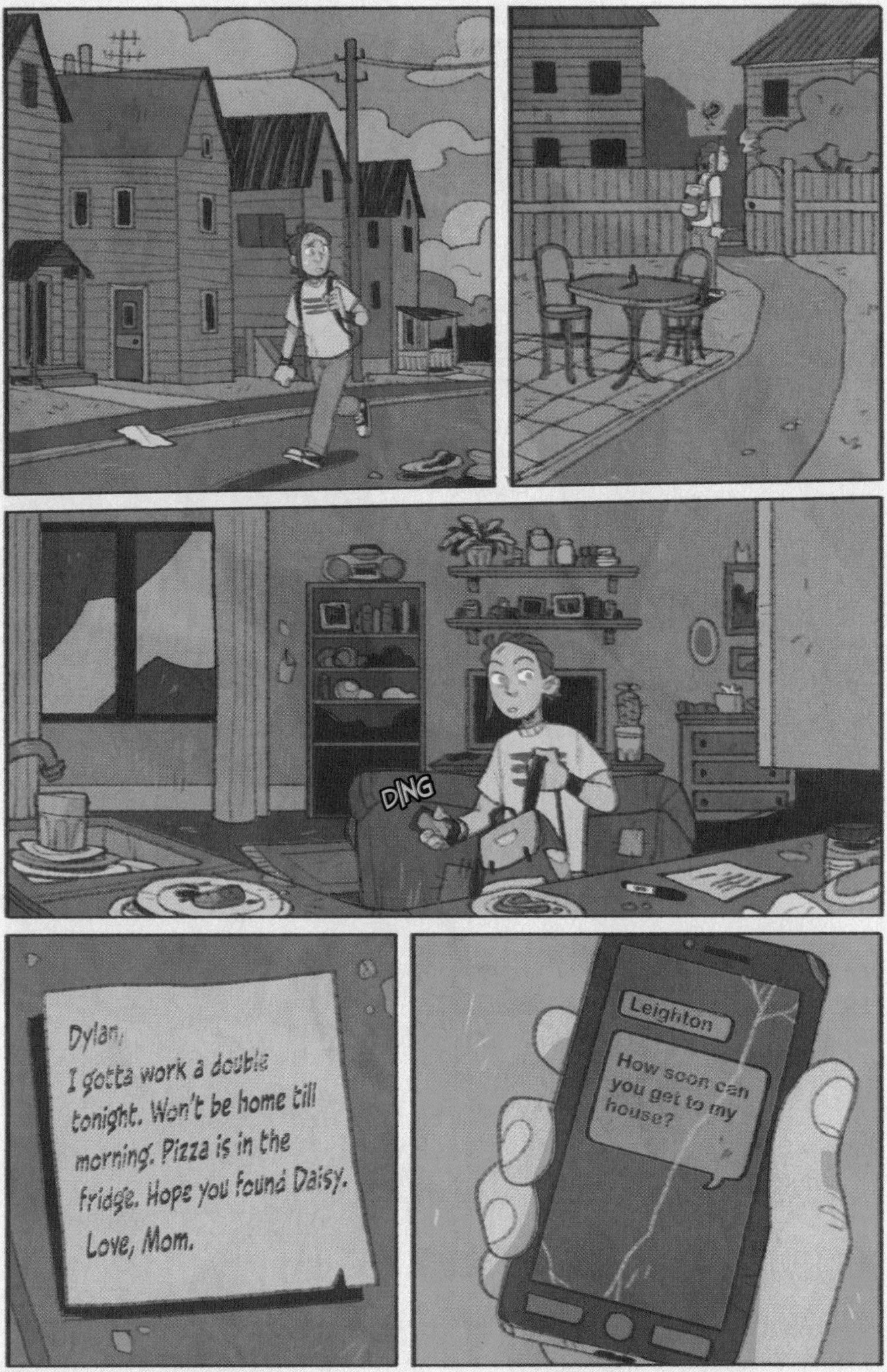
DING
Dylan,
I gotta work a double tonight. Won't be home till morning. Pizza is in the fridge. Hope you found Daisy.
Love, Mom.
Leighton
How soon can you get to my house?

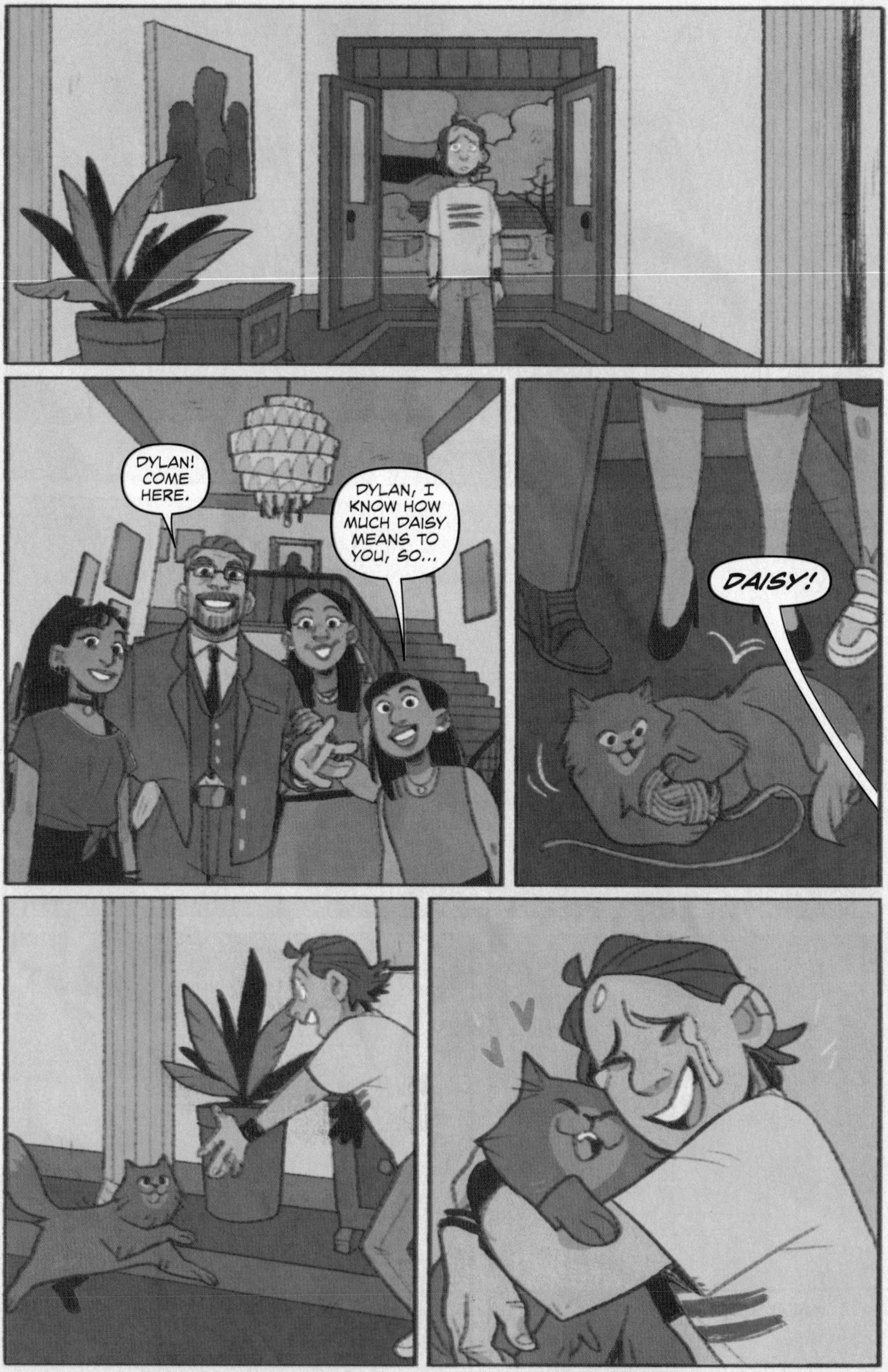
DYLAN! COME HERE.
DYLAN, I KNOW HOW MUCH DAISY MEANS TO YOU, SO...
DAISY!

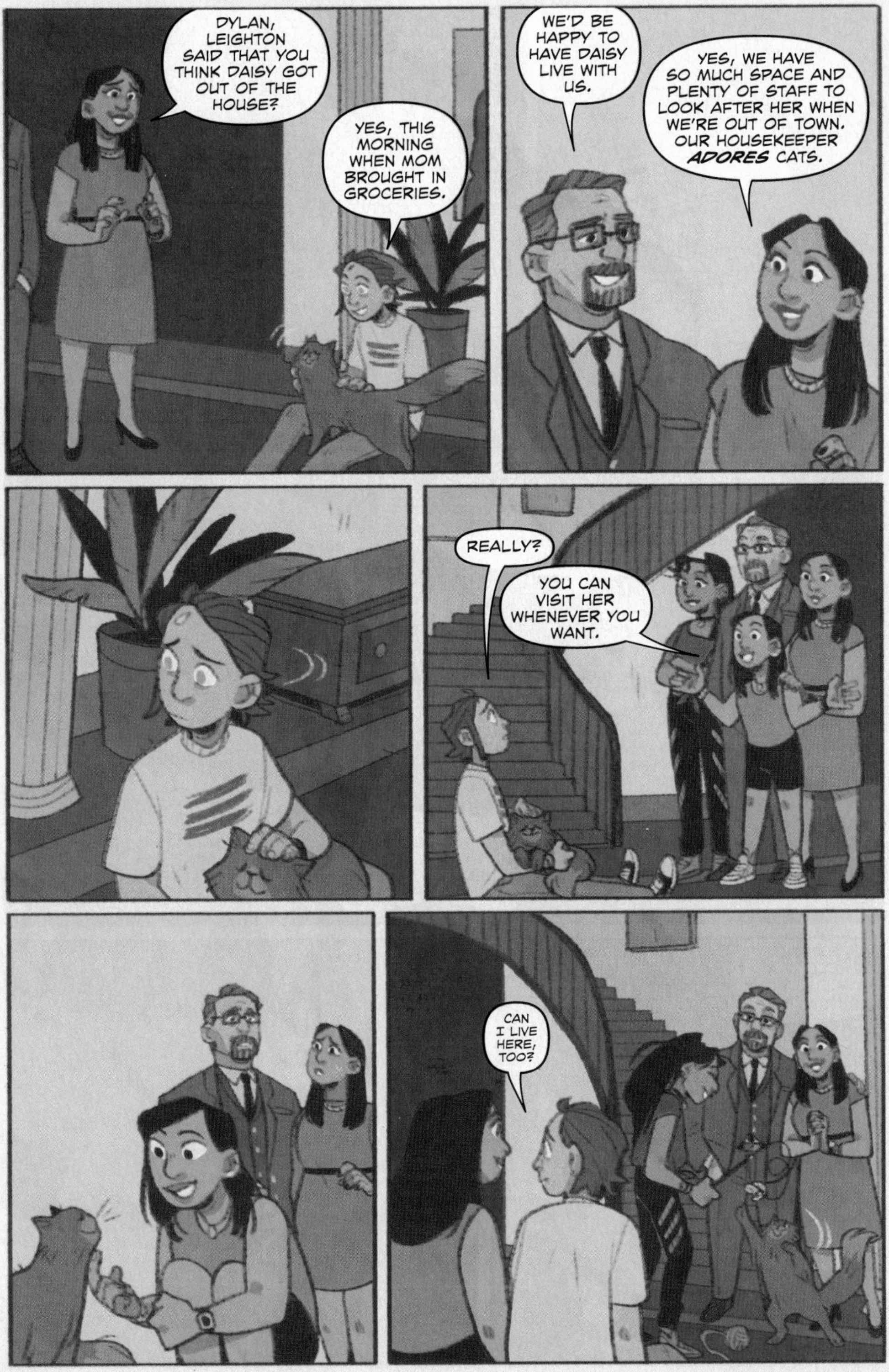
DYLAN, LEIGHTON SAID THAT YOU THINK DAISY GOT OUT OF THE HOUSE?
YES, THIS MORNING WHEN MOM BROUGHT IN GROCERIES.
WE'D BE HAPPY TO HAVE DAISY LIVE WITH US.
YES, WE HAVE SO MUCH SPACE AND PLENTY OF STAFF TO LOOK AFTER HER WHEN WE'RE OUT OF TOWN. OUR HOUSEKEEPER **ADORES** CATS.
REALLY?
YOU CAN VISIT HER WHENEVER YOU WANT.
CAN I LIVE HERE, TOO?

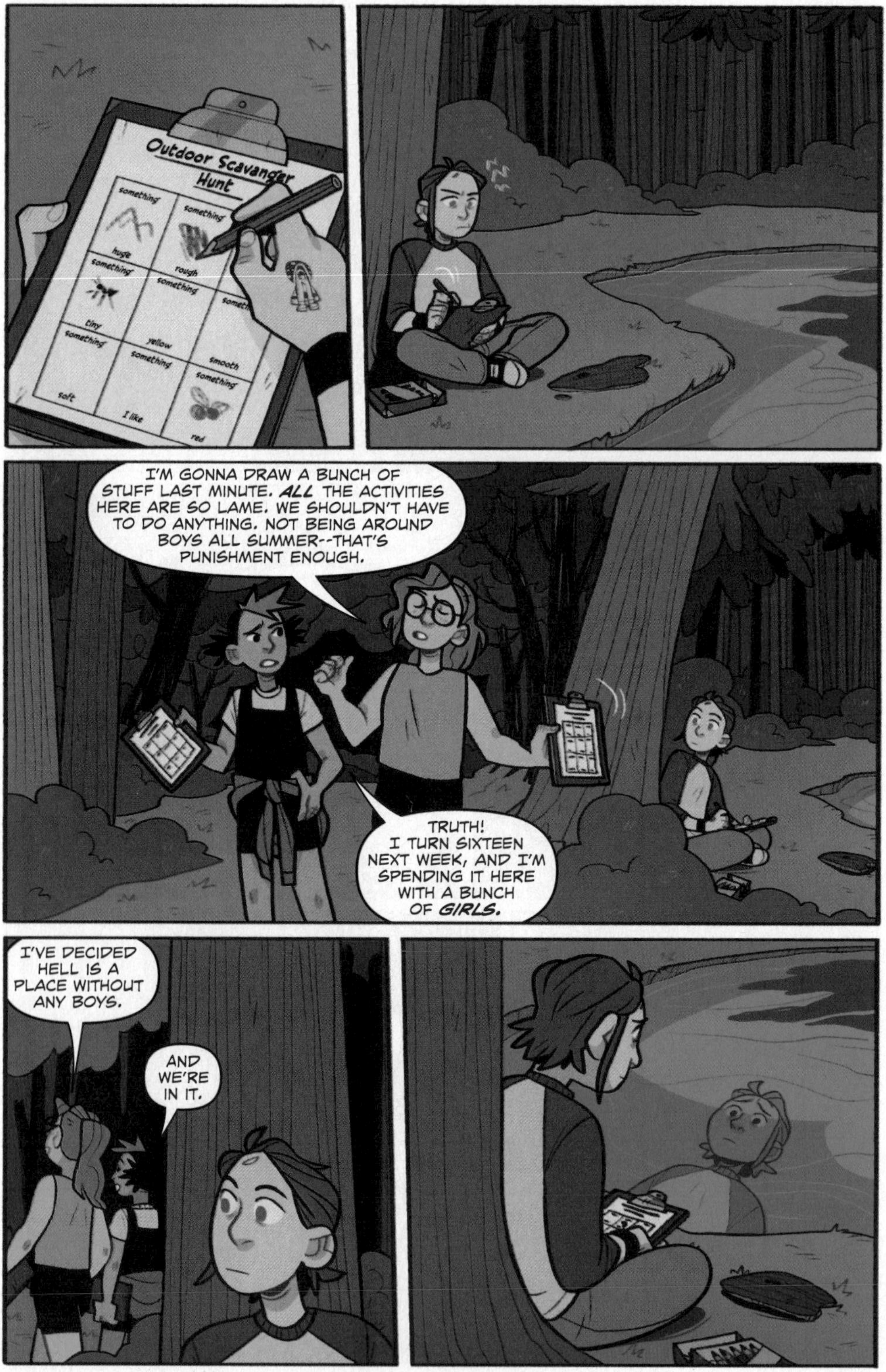

Outdoor Scavanger Hunt
something huge
something rough
something tiny
something yellow
something soft
something I like
something smooth
something red
I'M GONNA DRAW A BUNCH OF STUFF LAST MINUTE. ***ALL*** THE ACTIVITIES HERE ARE SO LAME. WE SHOULDN'T HAVE TO DO ANYTHING. NOT BEING AROUND BOYS ALL SUMMER--THAT'S PUNISHMENT ENOUGH.
TRUTH! I TURN SIXTEEN NEXT WEEK, AND I'M SPENDING IT HERE WITH A BUNCH OF ***GIRLS.***
I'VE DECIDED HELL IS A PLACE WITHOUT ANY BOYS.
AND WE'RE IN IT.

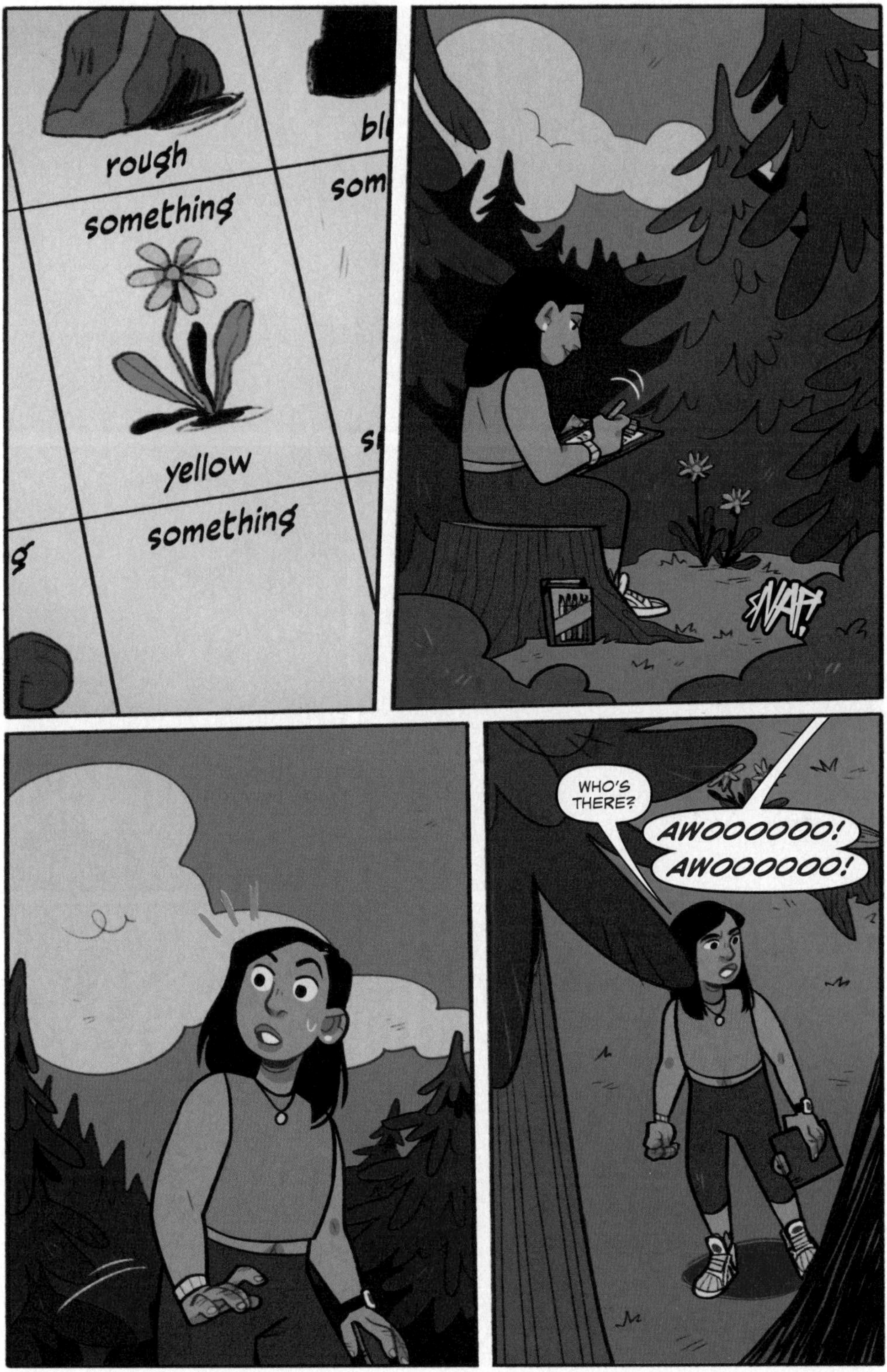

rough
something
yellow
something
SNAP!
WHO'S THERE?
AWOOOOOOO! AWOOOOOOO!

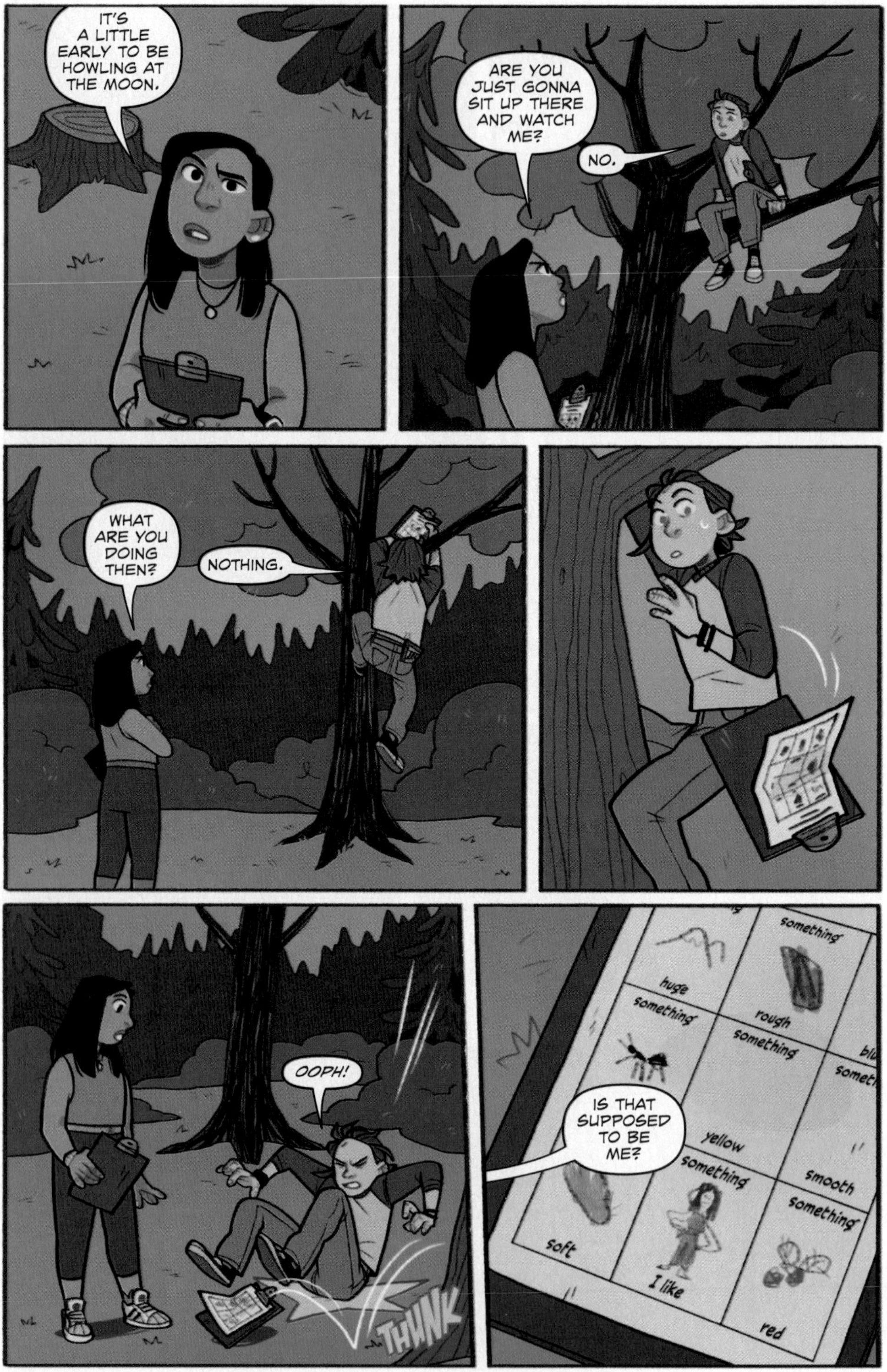
IT'S A LITTLE EARLY TO BE HOWLING AT THE MOON.
ARE YOU JUST GONNA SIT UP THERE AND WATCH ME?
NO.
WHAT ARE YOU DOING THEN?
NOTHING.
OOPH!
THUNK
something
huge
something
rough
something
yellow
something
smooth
something
soft
I like
red
IS THAT SUPPOSED TO BE ME?

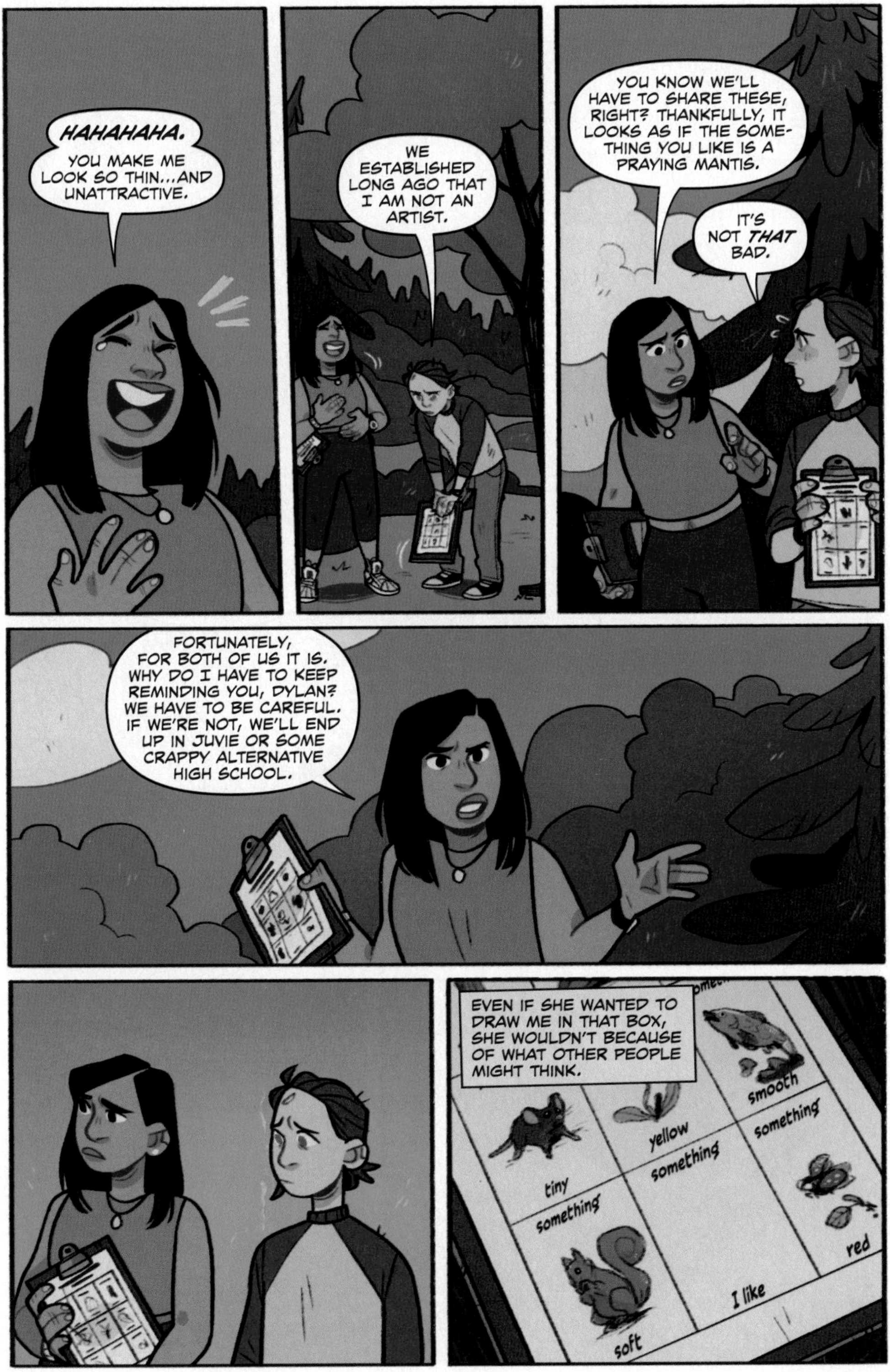
HAHAHAHA.
YOU MAKE ME LOOK SO THIN...AND UNATTRACTIVE.
WE ESTABLISHED LONG AGO THAT I AM NOT AN ARTIST.
YOU KNOW WE'LL HAVE TO SHARE THESE, RIGHT? THANKFULLY, IT LOOKS AS IF THE SOME-THING YOU LIKE IS A PRAYING MANTIS.
IT'S NOT THAT BAD.
FORTUNATELY, FOR BOTH OF US IT IS. WHY DO I HAVE TO KEEP REMINDING YOU, DYLAN? WE HAVE TO BE CAREFUL. IF WE'RE NOT, WE'LL END UP IN JUVIE OR SOME CRAPPY ALTERNATIVE HIGH SCHOOL.
EVEN IF SHE WANTED TO DRAW ME IN THAT BOX, SHE WOULDN'T BECAUSE OF WHAT OTHER PEOPLE MIGHT THINK.
smooth
yellow
something
tiny
something
something
red
I like
soft

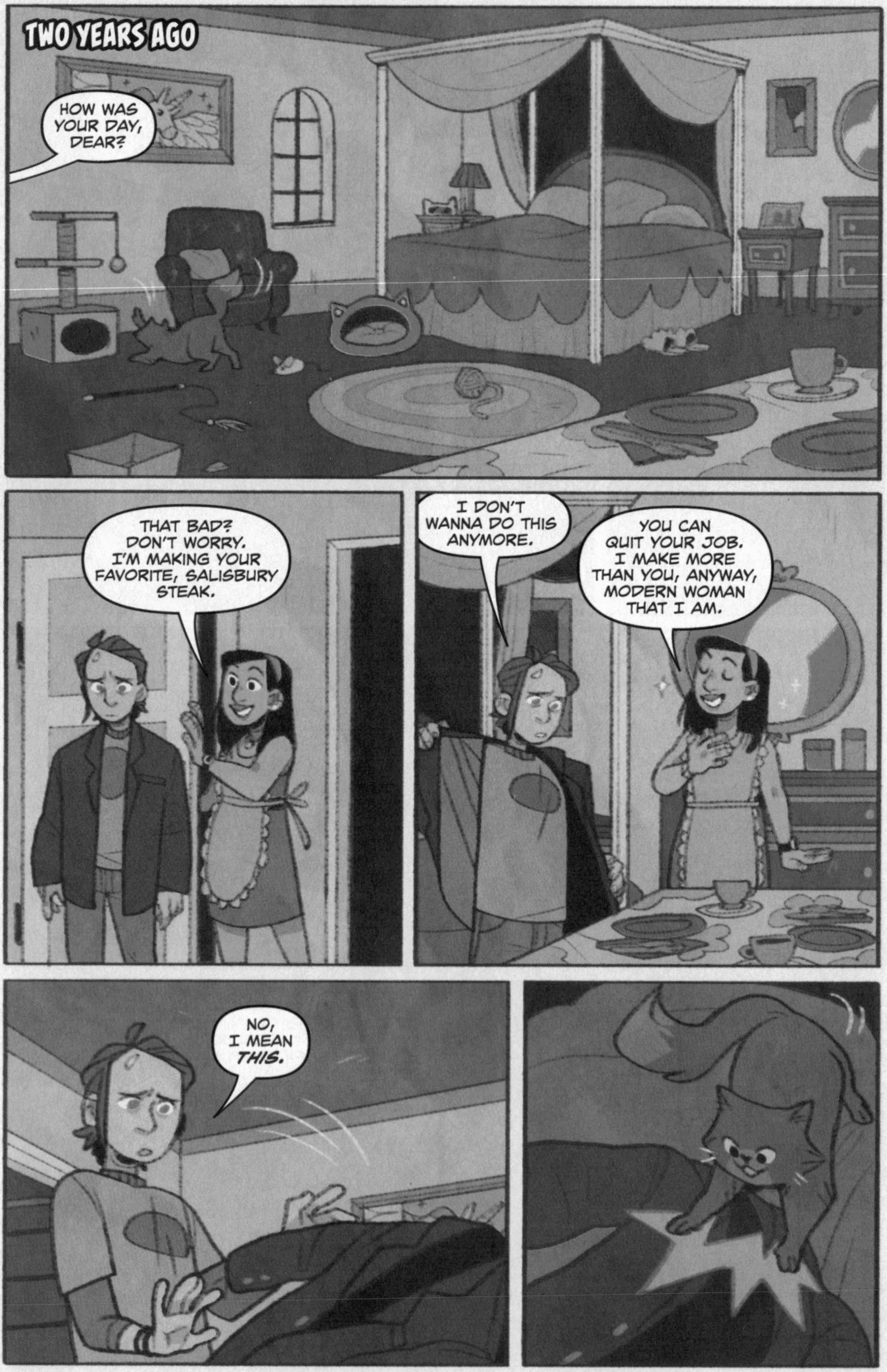
TWO YEARS AGO
HOW WAS YOUR DAY, DEAR?
THAT BAD? DON'T WORRY. I'M MAKING YOUR FAVORITE, SALISBURY STEAK.
I DON'T WANNA DO THIS ANYMORE.
YOU CAN QUIT YOUR JOB. I MAKE MORE THAN YOU, ANYWAY, MODERN WOMAN THAT I AM.
NO, I MEAN *THIS*.

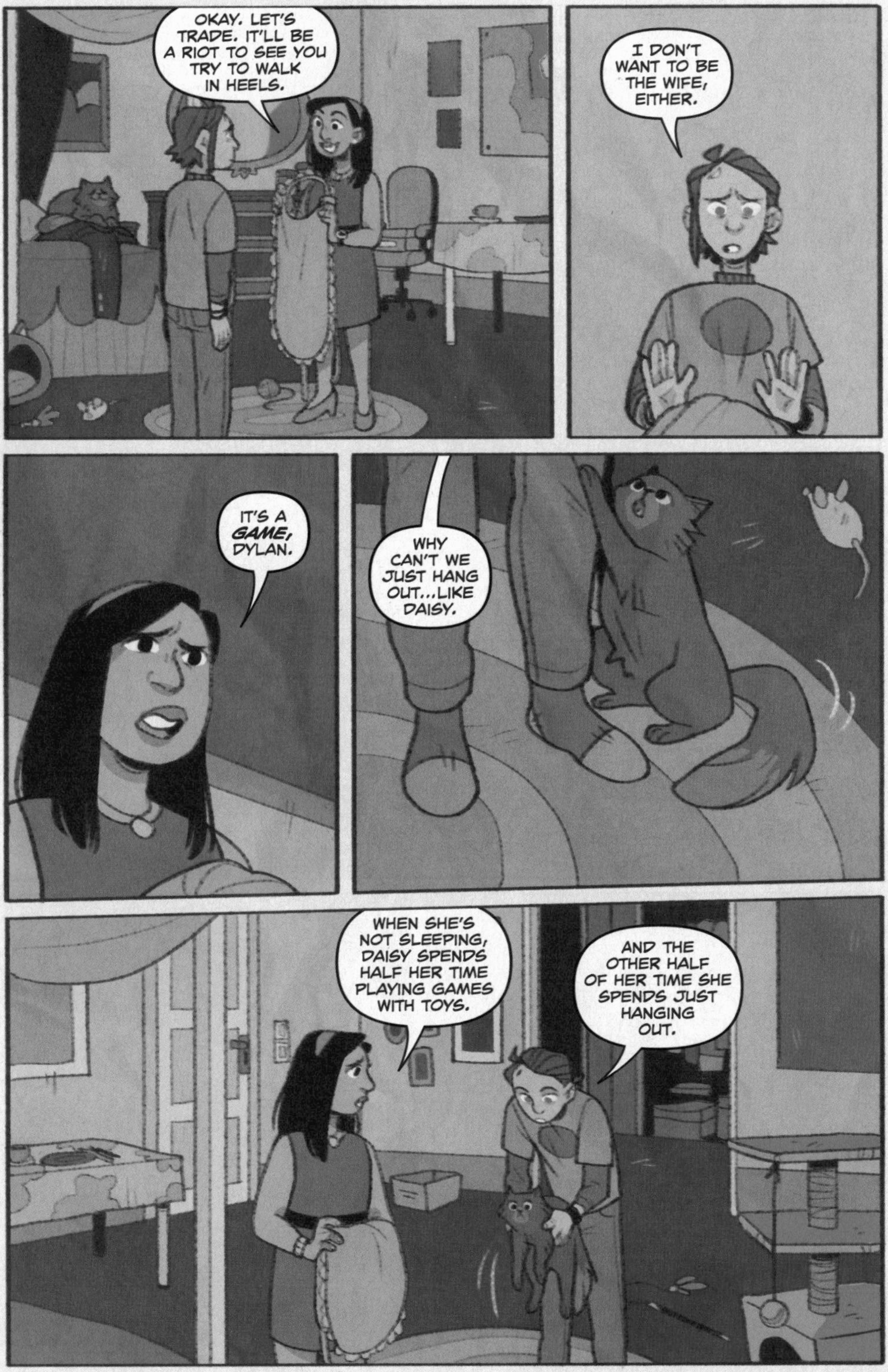
OKAY. LET'S TRADE. IT'LL BE A RIOT TO SEE YOU TRY TO WALK IN HEELS.
I DON'T WANT TO BE THE WIFE, EITHER.
IT'S A *GAME,* DYLAN.
WHY CAN'T WE JUST HANG OUT...LIKE DAISY.
WHEN SHE'S NOT SLEEPING, DAISY SPENDS HALF HER TIME PLAYING GAMES WITH TOYS.
AND THE OTHER HALF OF HER TIME SHE SPENDS JUST HANGING OUT.

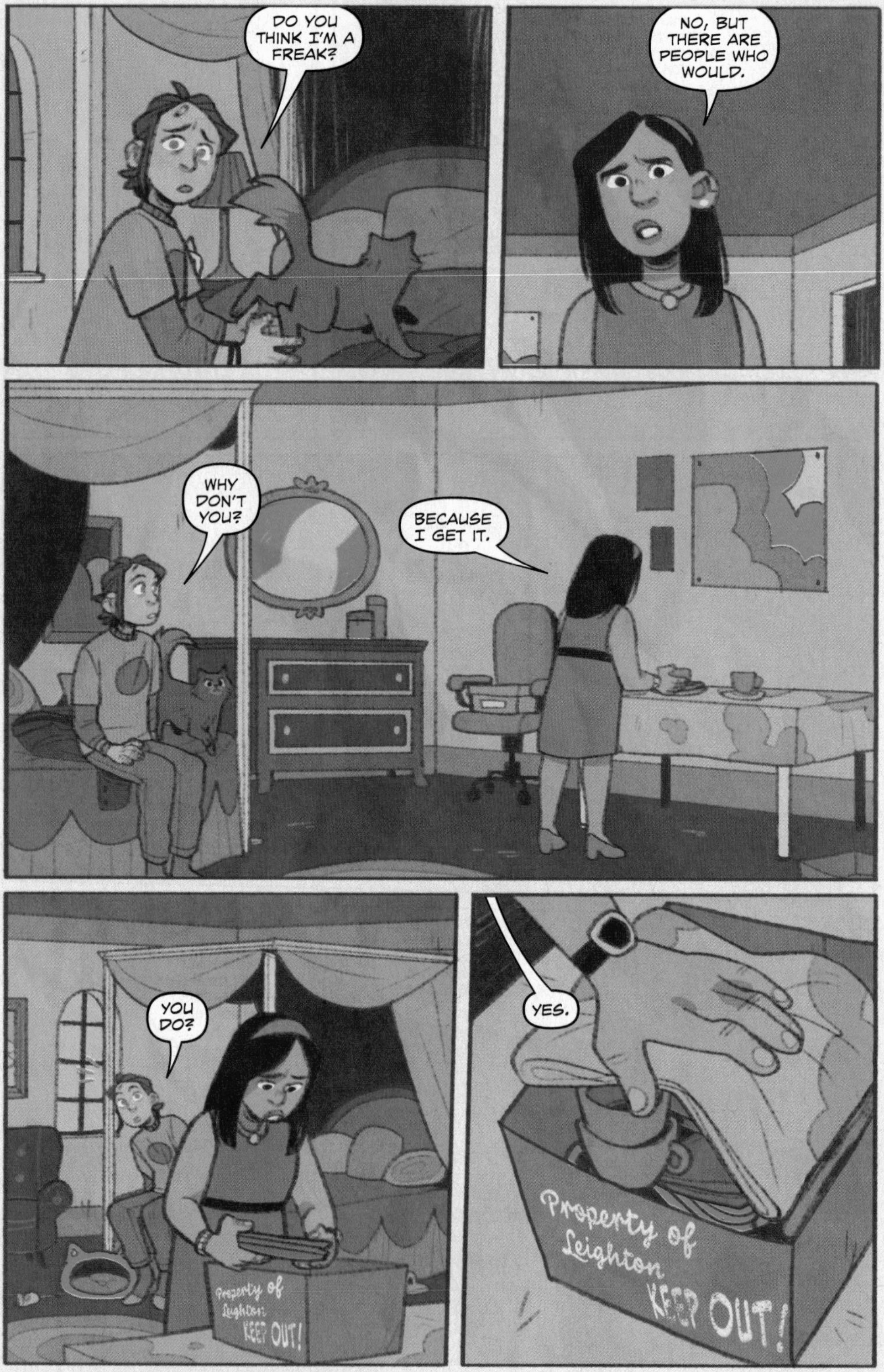
DO YOU THINK I'M A FREAK?
NO, BUT THERE ARE PEOPLE WHO WOULD.
WHY DON'T YOU?
BECAUSE I GET IT.
YOU DO?
YES.
Property of Leighton KEEP OUT!
Property of Leighton KEEP OUT!

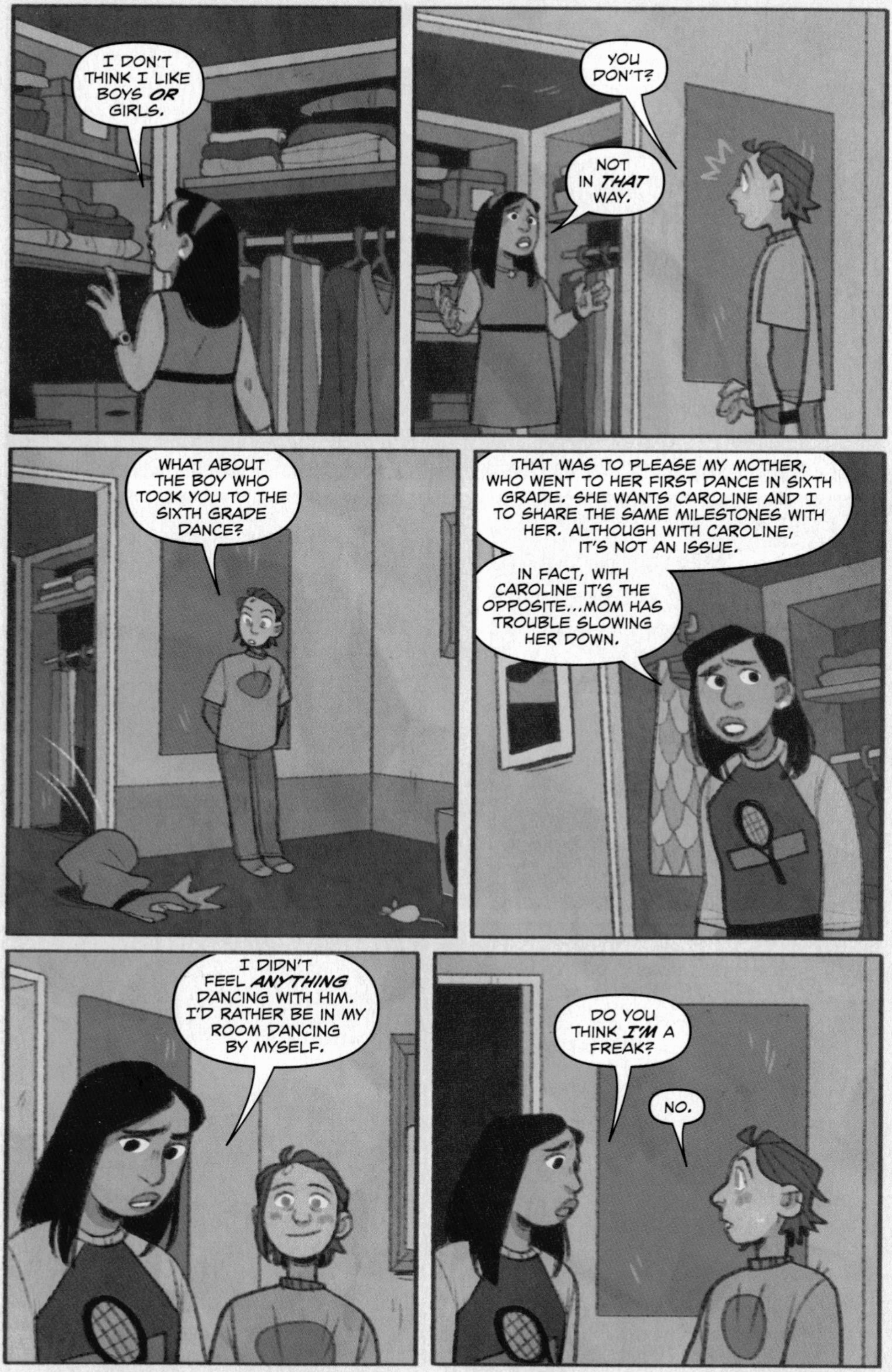
I DON'T THINK I LIKE BOYS *OR* GIRLS.
YOU DON'T?
NOT IN *THAT* WAY.
WHAT ABOUT THE BOY WHO TOOK YOU TO THE SIXTH GRADE DANCE?
THAT WAS TO PLEASE MY MOTHER, WHO WENT TO HER FIRST DANCE IN SIXTH GRADE. SHE WANTS CAROLINE AND I TO SHARE THE SAME MILESTONES WITH HER. ALTHOUGH WITH CAROLINE, IT'S NOT AN ISSUE.
IN FACT, WITH CAROLINE IT'S THE OPPOSITE...MOM HAS TROUBLE SLOWING HER DOWN.
I DIDN'T FEEL *ANYTHING* DANCING WITH HIM. I'D RATHER BE IN MY ROOM DANCING BY MYSELF.
DO YOU THINK *I'M* A FREAK?
NO.

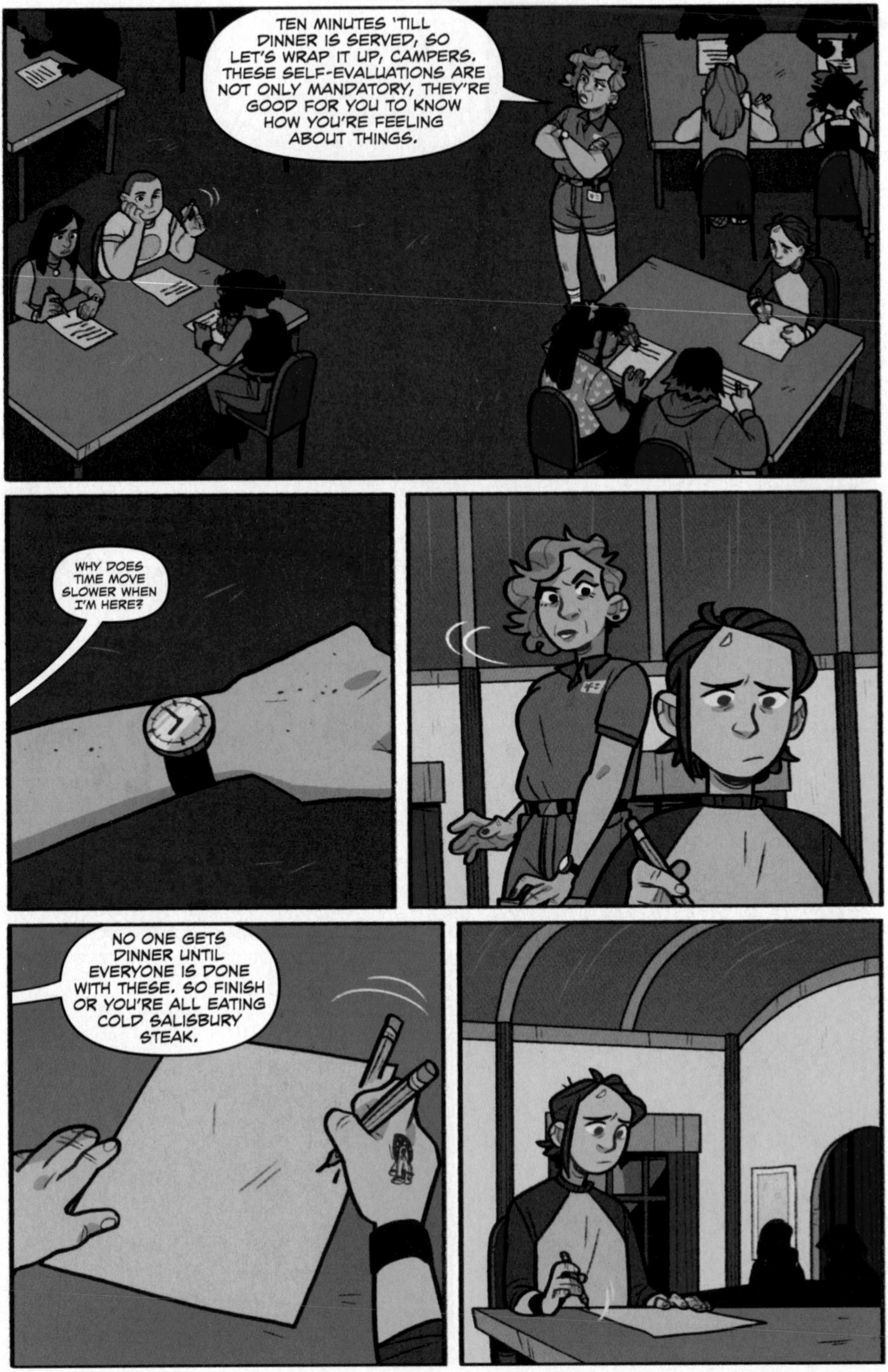
TEN MINUTES 'TILL DINNER IS SERVED, SO LET'S WRAP IT UP, CAMPERS. THESE SELF-EVALUATIONS ARE NOT ONLY MANDATORY, THEY'RE GOOD FOR YOU TO KNOW HOW YOU'RE FEELING ABOUT THINGS.
WHY DOES TIME MOVE SLOWER WHEN I'M HERE?
NO ONE GETS DINNER UNTIL EVERYONE IS DONE WITH THESE. SO FINISH OR YOU'RE ALL EATING COLD SALISBURY STEAK.

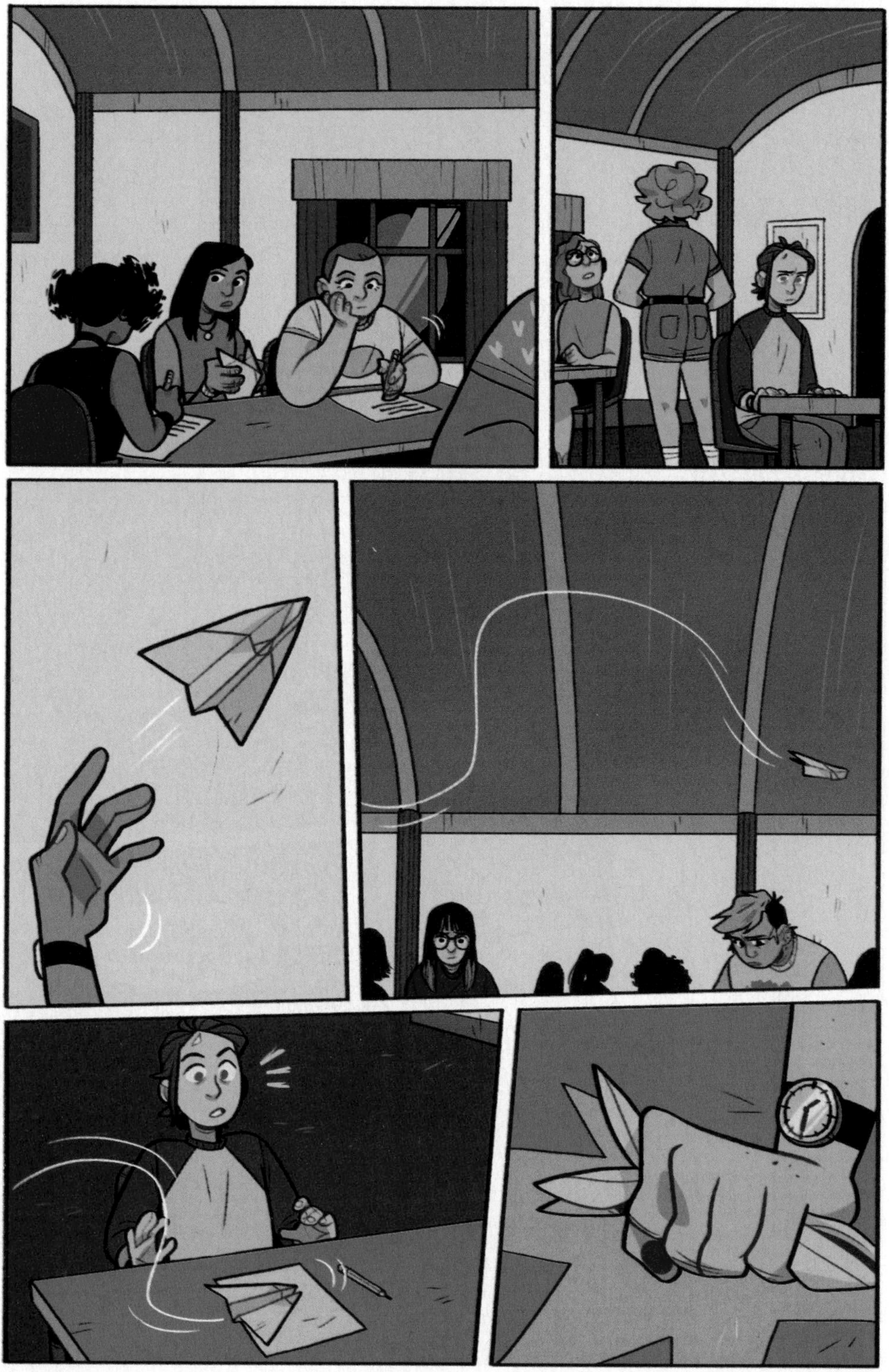

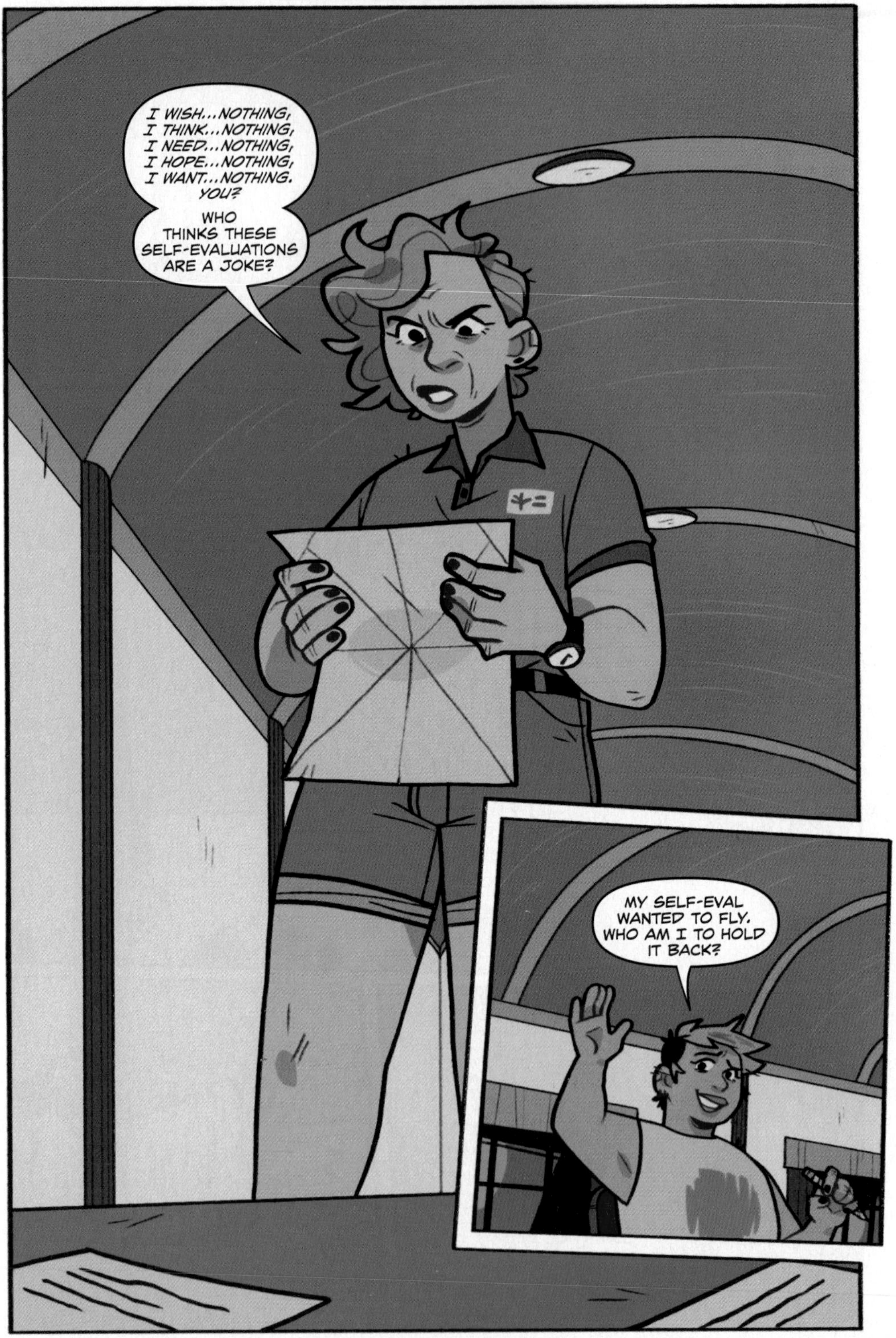
I WISH...NOTHING, I THINK...NOTHING, I NEED...NOTHING, I HOPE...NOTHING, I WANT...NOTHING. YOU?
WHO THINKS THESE SELF-EVALUATIONS ARE A JOKE?
MY SELF-EVAL WANTED TO FLY. WHO AM I TO HOLD IT BACK?

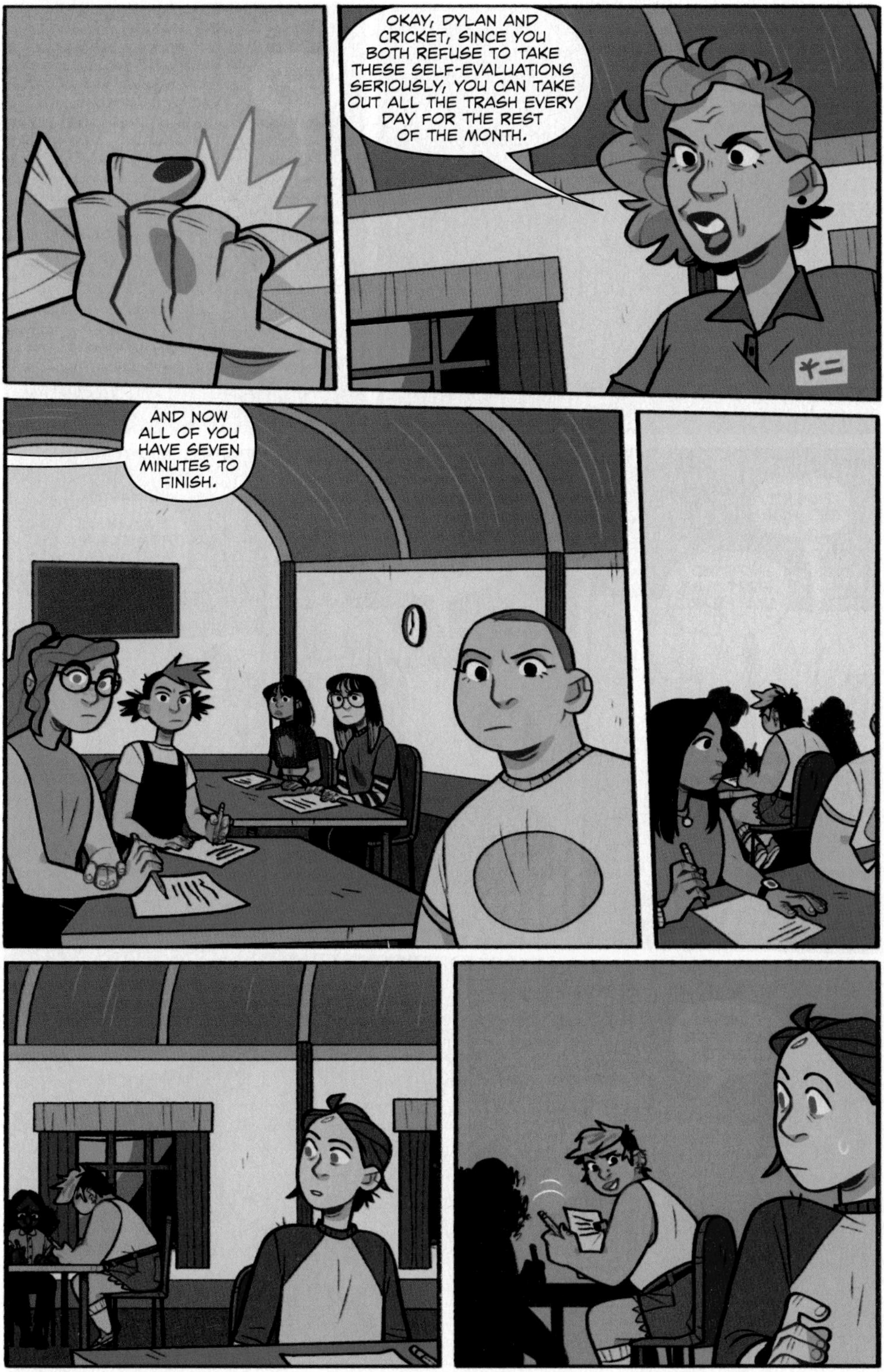

OKAY, DYLAN AND CRICKET, SINCE YOU BOTH REFUSE TO TAKE THESE SELF-EVALUATIONS SERIOUSLY, YOU CAN TAKE OUT ALL THE TRASH EVERY DAY FOR THE REST OF THE MONTH.
AND NOW ALL OF YOU HAVE SEVEN MINUTES TO FINISH.

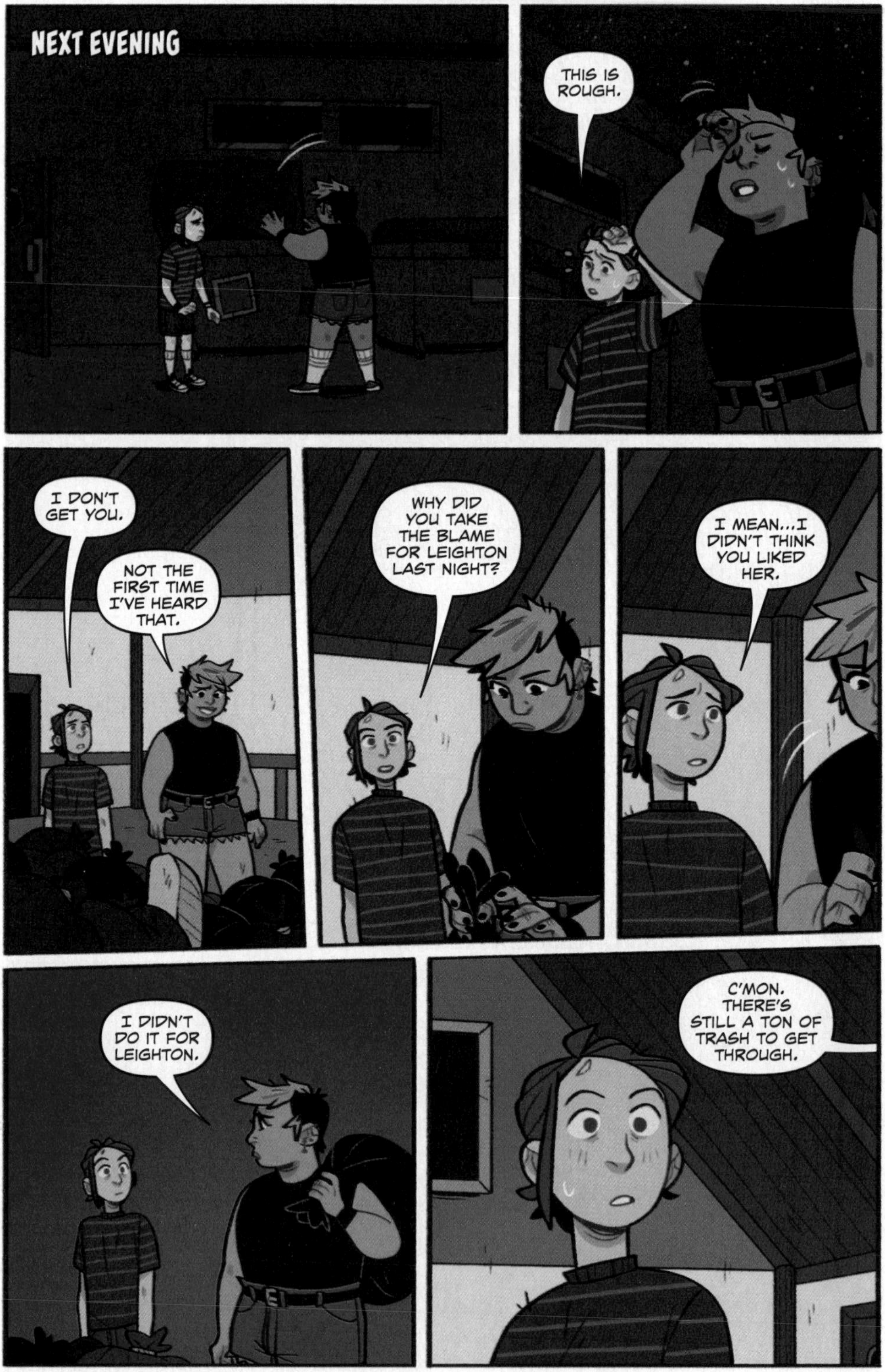

NEXT EVENING
THIS IS ROUGH.
I DON'T GET YOU.
NOT THE FIRST TIME I'VE HEARD THAT.
WHY DID YOU TAKE THE BLAME FOR LEIGHTON LAST NIGHT?
I MEAN...I DIDN'T THINK YOU LIKED HER.
I DIDN'T DO IT FOR LEIGHTON.
C'MON. THERE'S STILL A TON OF TRASH TO GET THROUGH.

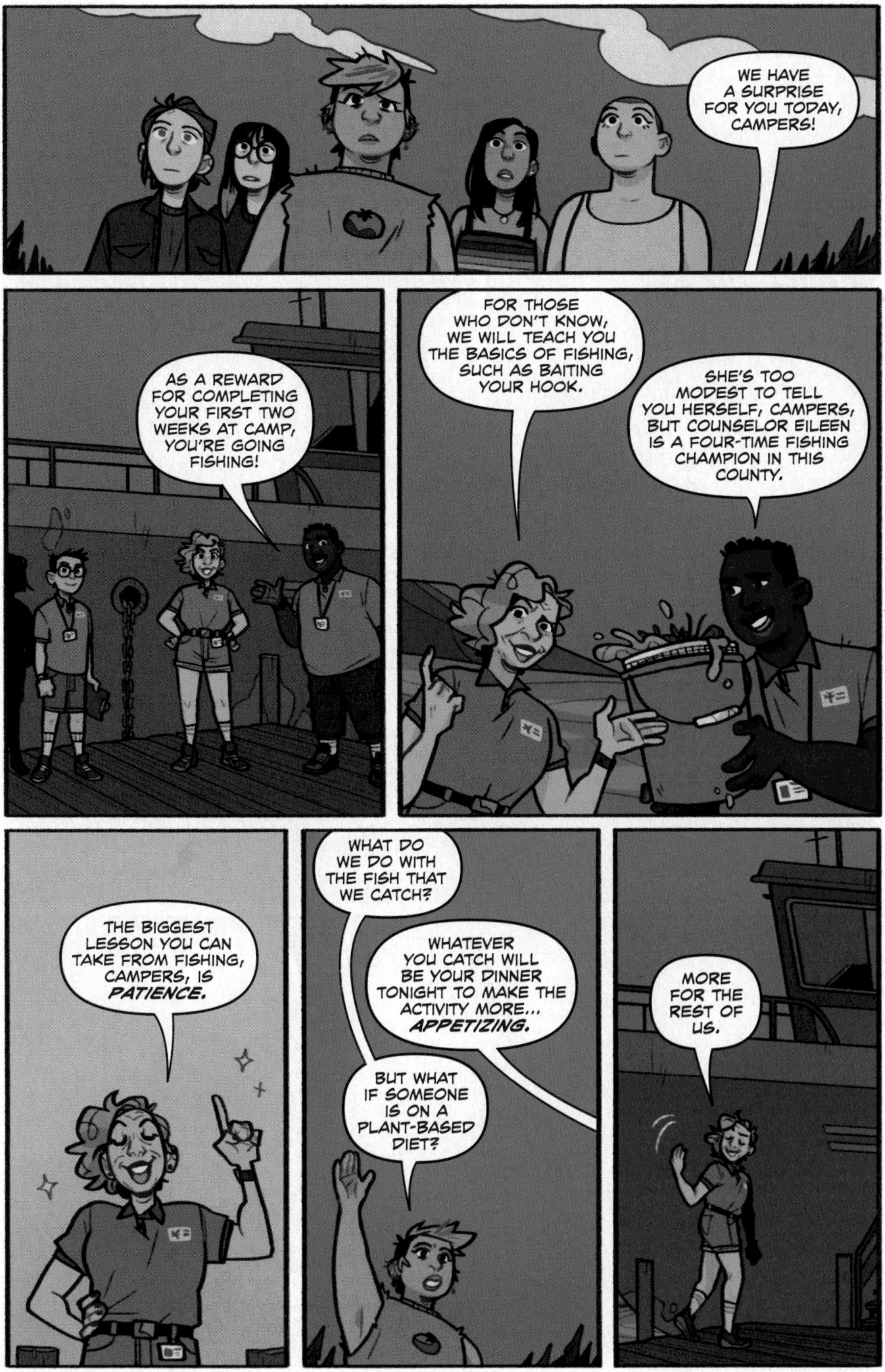

WE HAVE A SURPRISE FOR YOU TODAY, CAMPERS!
AS A REWARD FOR COMPLETING YOUR FIRST TWO WEEKS AT CAMP, YOU'RE GOING FISHING!
FOR THOSE WHO DON'T KNOW, WE WILL TEACH YOU THE BASICS OF FISHING, SUCH AS BAITING YOUR HOOK.
SHE'S TOO MODEST TO TELL YOU HERSELF, CAMPERS, BUT COUNSELOR EILEEN IS A FOUR-TIME FISHING CHAMPION IN THIS COUNTY.
THE BIGGEST LESSON YOU CAN TAKE FROM FISHING, CAMPERS, IS ***PATIENCE.***
WHAT DO WE DO WITH THE FISH THAT WE CATCH?
WHATEVER YOU CATCH WILL BE YOUR DINNER TONIGHT TO MAKE THE ACTIVITY MORE... ***APPETIZING.***
BUT WHAT IF SOMEONE IS ON A PLANT-BASED DIET?
MORE FOR THE REST OF US.

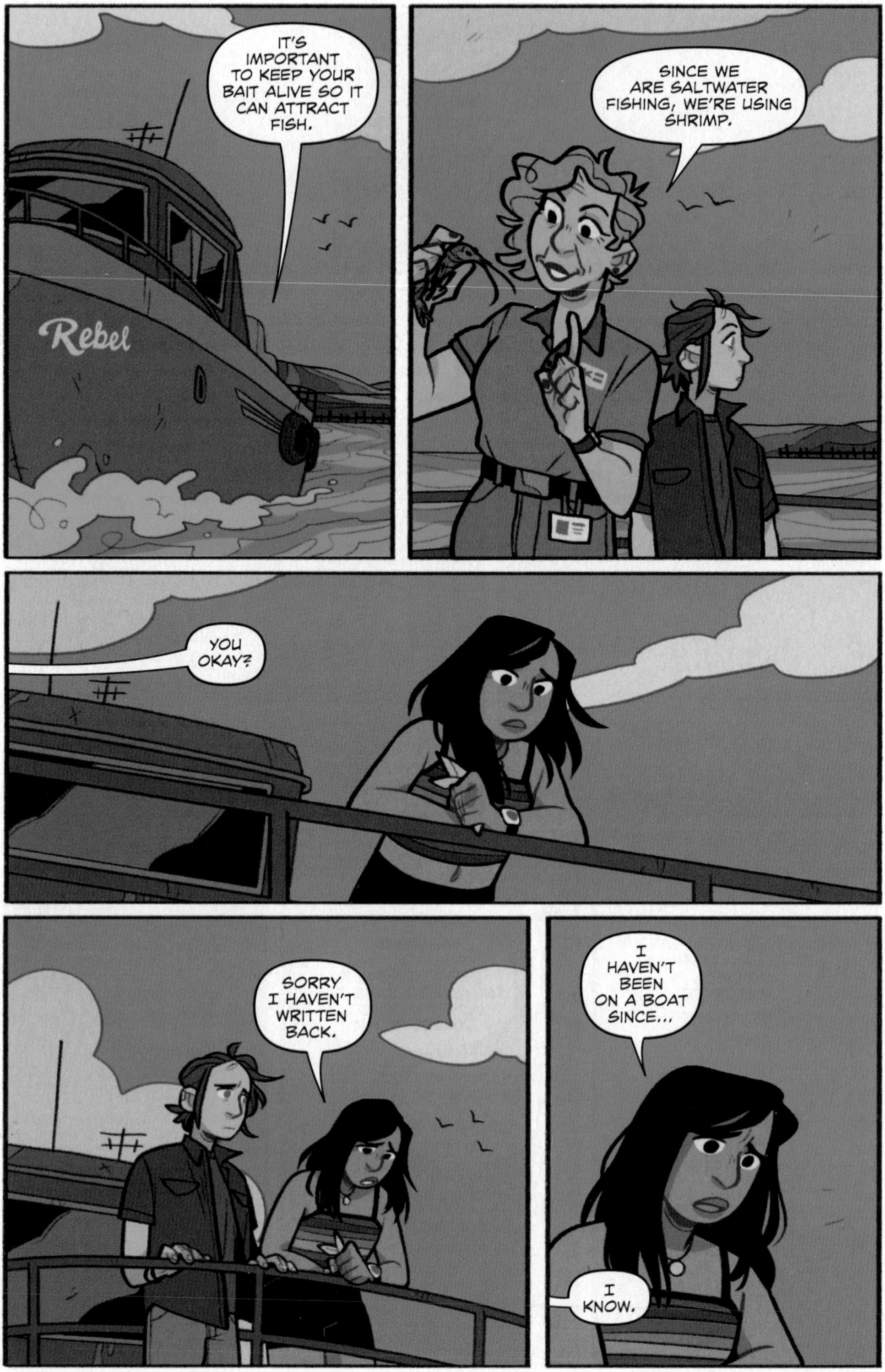
IT'S IMPORTANT TO KEEP YOUR BAIT ALIVE SO IT CAN ATTRACT FISH.
Rebel
SINCE WE ARE SALTWATER FISHING, WE'RE USING SHRIMP.
YOU OKAY?
SORRY I HAVEN'T WRITTEN BACK.
I HAVEN'T BEEN ON A BOAT SINCE...
I KNOW.

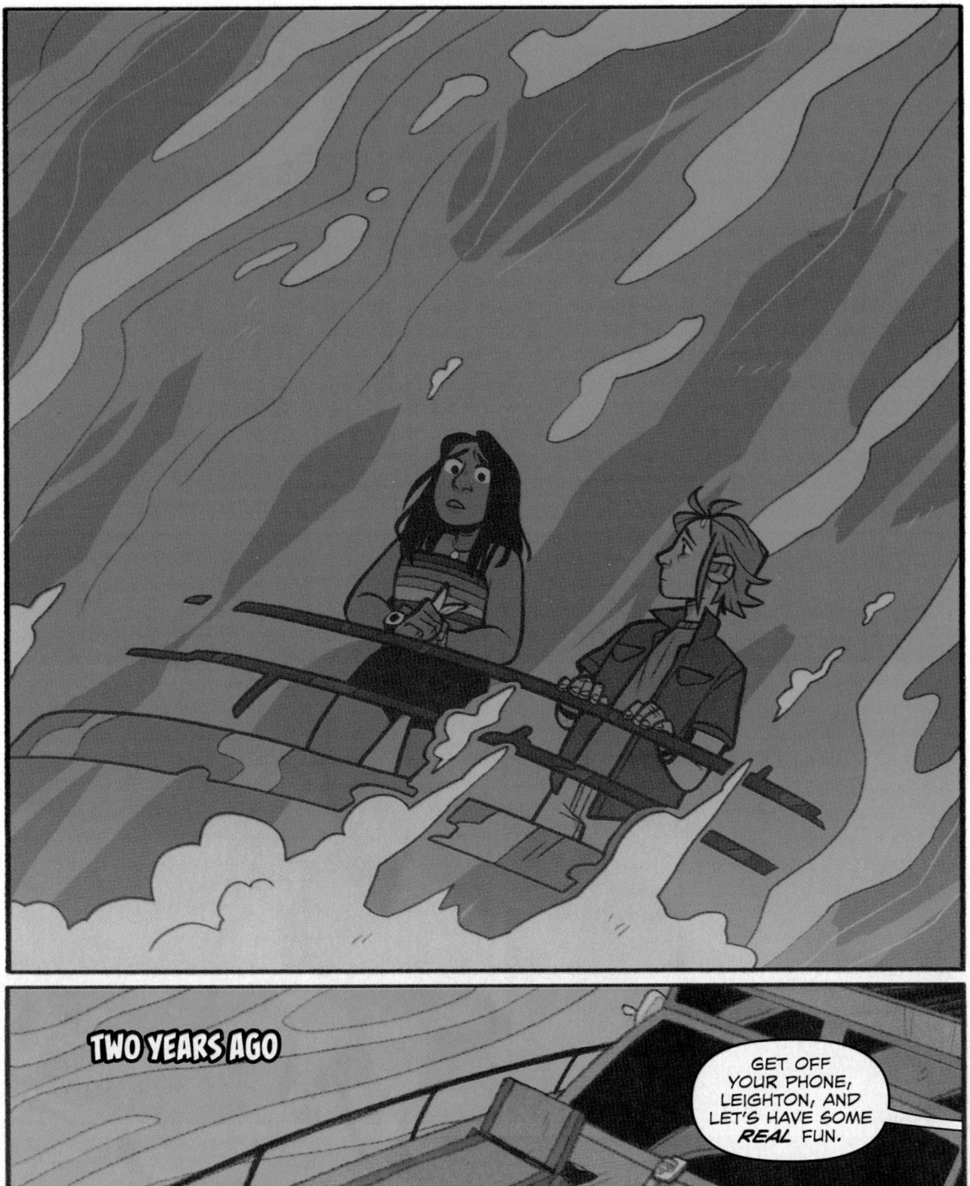

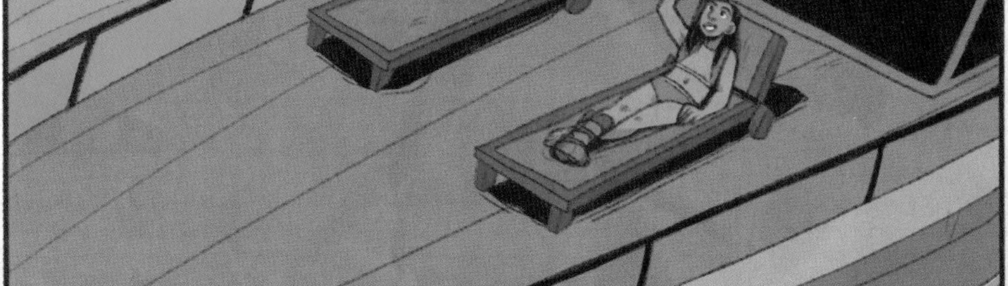
TWO YEARS AGO
GET OFF YOUR PHONE, LEIGHTON, AND LET'S HAVE SOME *REAL* FUN.

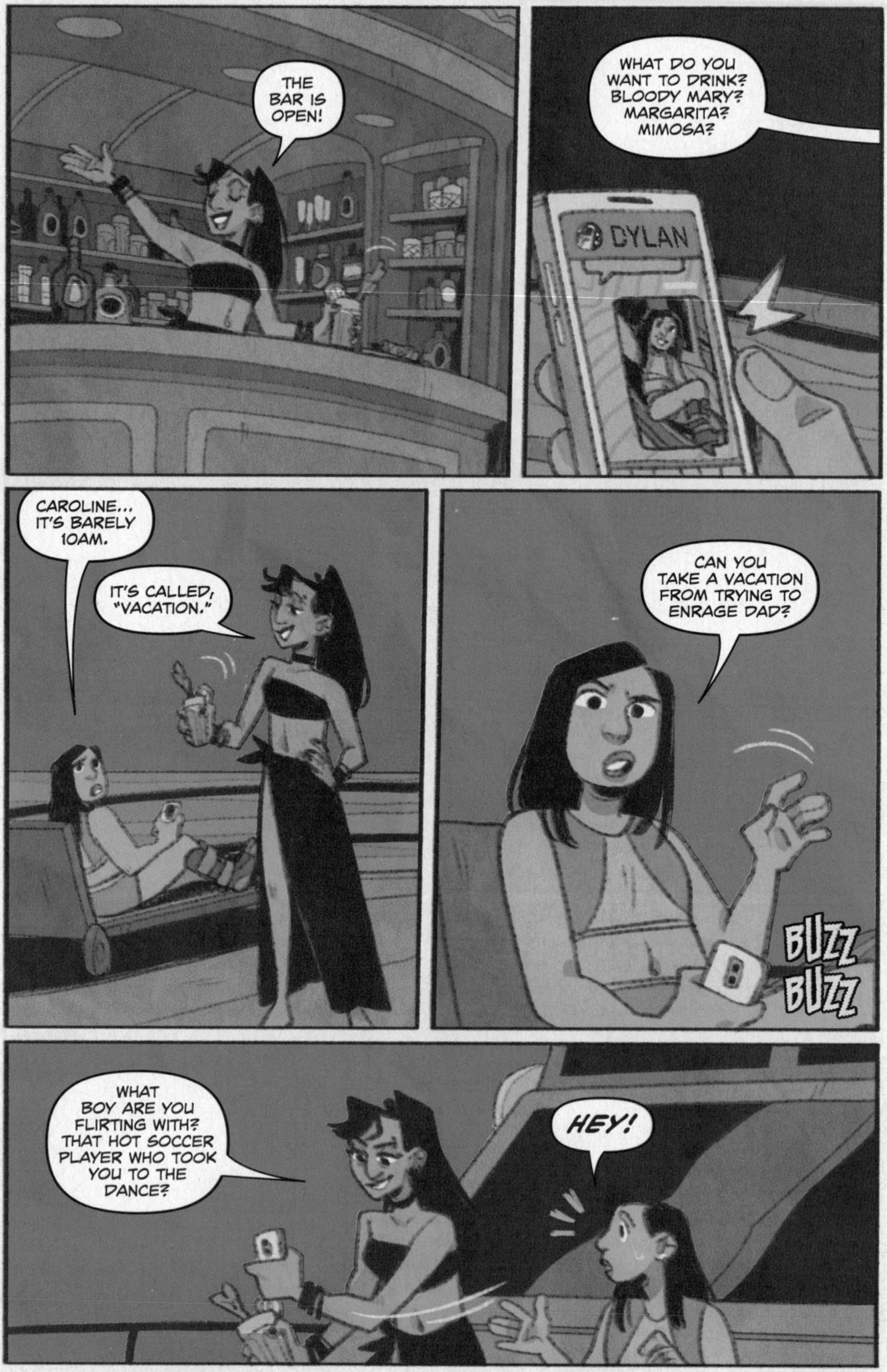

THE BAR IS OPEN!
WHAT DO YOU WANT TO DRINK? BLOODY MARY? MARGARITA? MIMOSA?
DYLAN
CAROLINE... IT'S BARELY 10AM.
IT'S CALLED, "VACATION."
CAN YOU TAKE A VACATION FROM TRYING TO ENRAGE DAD?
BUZZ BUZZ
WHAT BOY ARE YOU FLIRTING WITH? THAT HOT SOCCER PLAYER WHO TOOK YOU TO THE DANCE?
HEY!

GIVE IT BACK!

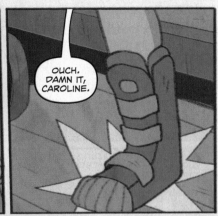

OUCH. DAMN IT, CAROLINE.

I NEED TO STAY OFF MY ANKLE.

THAT'S WHY I OFFERED TO *BRING* YOU A DRINK.

DYLAN

That cast is fire. ♥♥ ♥♡♥♥ ♢♥♡♥

How's it going?

ALCOHOL IS NOT *YOUR* VICE. GOT IT. BUT MAYBE DYL--

THERE'S NOTHING GOING ON WITH DYLAN, BUT IF THERE WAS, IT'S *NOT* A VICE.

I WANNA HEAR YOU TELL MOM AND DAD THAT.

Fine, except I wish my sister would jump into the ocean & get eaten by a Humpback whale.

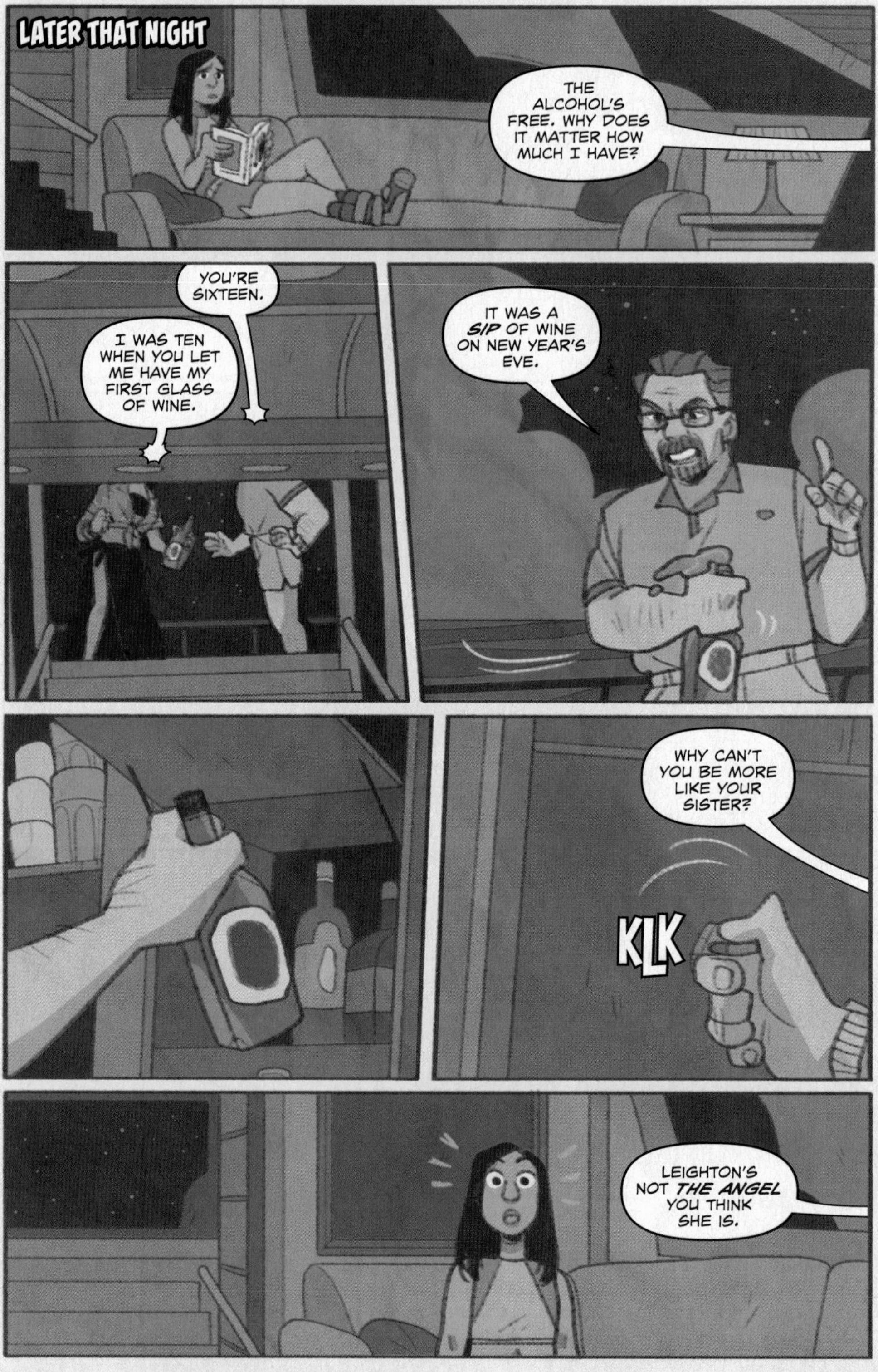
LATER THAT NIGHT
THE ALCOHOL'S FREE. WHY DOES IT MATTER HOW MUCH I HAVE?
YOU'RE SIXTEEN.
I WAS TEN WHEN YOU LET ME HAVE MY FIRST GLASS OF WINE.
IT WAS A *SIP* OF WINE ON NEW YEAR'S EVE.
WHY CAN'T YOU BE MORE LIKE YOUR SISTER?
KLK
LEIGHTON'S NOT *THE ANGEL* YOU THINK SHE IS.

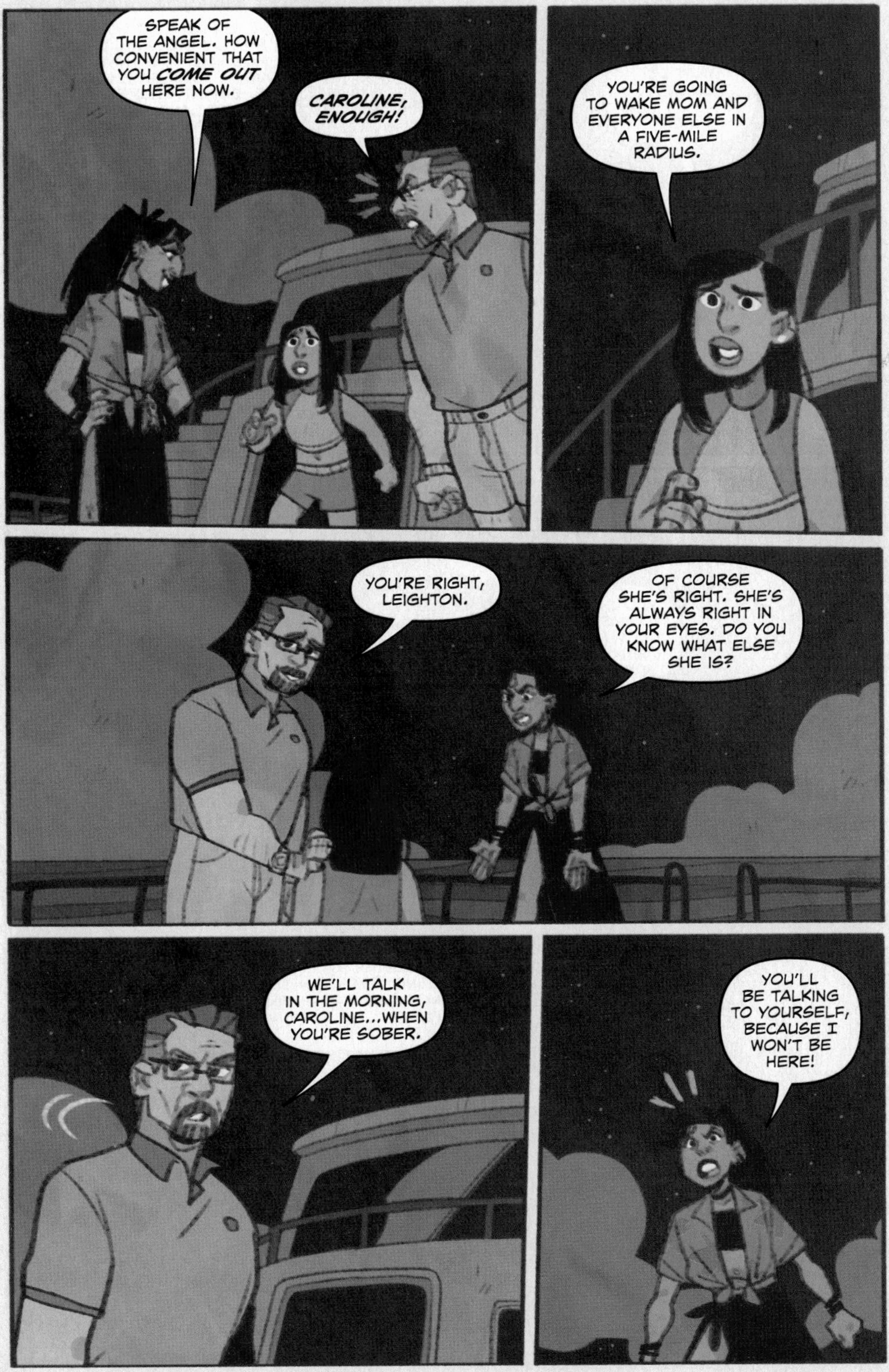
SPEAK OF THE ANGEL. HOW CONVENIENT THAT YOU *COME OUT* HERE NOW.
CAROLINE, ENOUGH!
YOU'RE GOING TO WAKE MOM AND EVERYONE ELSE IN A FIVE-MILE RADIUS.
YOU'RE RIGHT, LEIGHTON.
OF COURSE SHE'S RIGHT. SHE'S ALWAYS RIGHT IN YOUR EYES. DO YOU KNOW WHAT ELSE SHE IS?
WE'LL TALK IN THE MORNING, CAROLINE...WHEN YOU'RE SOBER.
YOU'LL BE TALKING TO YOURSELF, BECAUSE I WON'T BE HERE!

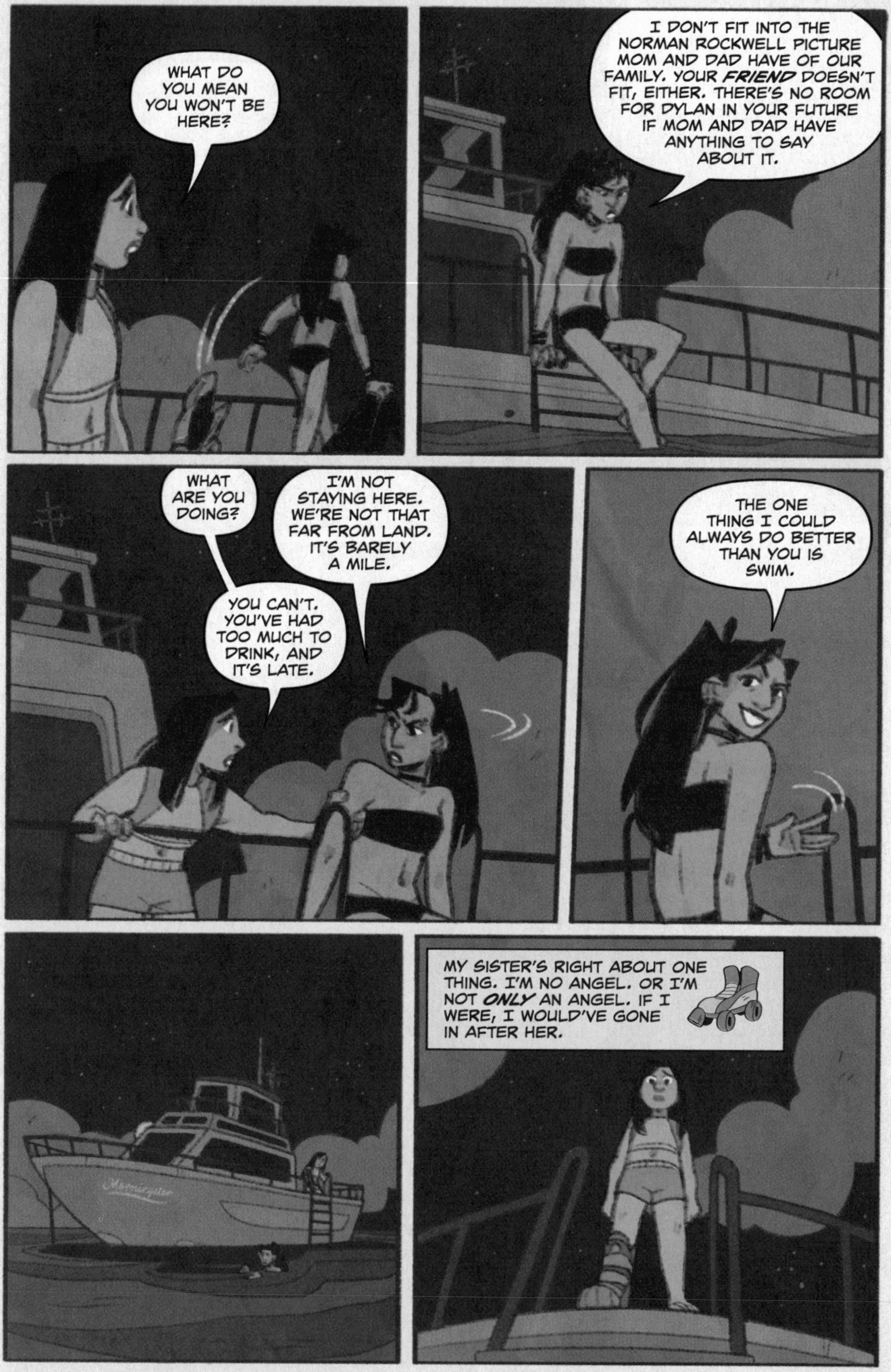
WHAT DO YOU MEAN YOU WON'T BE HERE?
I DON'T FIT INTO THE NORMAN ROCKWELL PICTURE MOM AND DAD HAVE OF OUR FAMILY. YOUR *FRIEND* DOESN'T FIT, EITHER. THERE'S NO ROOM FOR DYLAN IN YOUR FUTURE IF MOM AND DAD HAVE ANYTHING TO SAY ABOUT IT.
WHAT ARE YOU DOING?
I'M NOT STAYING HERE. WE'RE NOT THAT FAR FROM LAND. IT'S BARELY A MILE.
YOU CAN'T. YOU'VE HAD TOO MUCH TO DRINK, AND IT'S LATE.
THE ONE THING I COULD ALWAYS DO BETTER THAN YOU IS SWIM.
MY SISTER'S RIGHT ABOUT ONE THING. I'M NO ANGEL. OR I'M NOT *ONLY* AN ANGEL. IF I WERE, I WOULD'VE GONE IN AFTER HER.

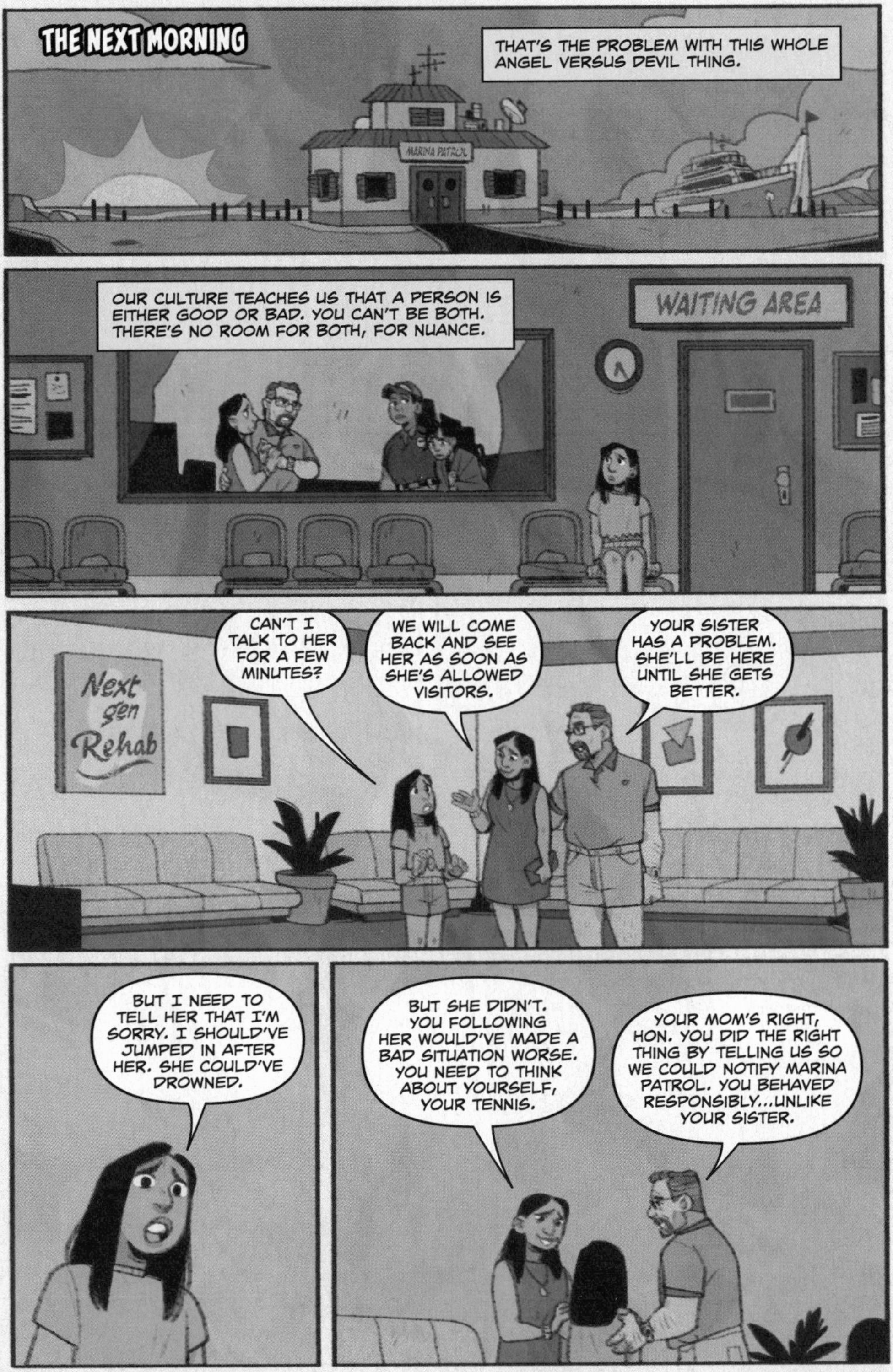
THE NEXT MORNING
THAT'S THE PROBLEM WITH THIS WHOLE ANGEL VERSUS DEVIL THING.
MARINA PATROL
OUR CULTURE TEACHES US THAT A PERSON IS EITHER GOOD OR BAD. YOU CAN'T BE BOTH. THERE'S NO ROOM FOR BOTH, FOR NUANCE.
WAITING AREA
Next gen Rehab
CAN'T I TALK TO HER FOR A FEW MINUTES?
WE WILL COME BACK AND SEE HER AS SOON AS SHE'S ALLOWED VISITORS.
YOUR SISTER HAS A PROBLEM. SHE'LL BE HERE UNTIL SHE GETS BETTER.
BUT I NEED TO TELL HER THAT I'M SORRY. I SHOULD'VE JUMPED IN AFTER HER. SHE COULD'VE DROWNED.
BUT SHE DIDN'T. YOU FOLLOWING HER WOULD'VE MADE A BAD SITUATION WORSE. YOU NEED TO THINK ABOUT YOURSELF, YOUR TENNIS.
YOUR MOM'S RIGHT, HON. YOU DID THE RIGHT THING BY TELLING US SO WE COULD NOTIFY MARINA PATROL. YOU BEHAVED RESPONSIBLY...UNLIKE YOUR SISTER.

I DON'T KNOW ONE PERSON WHO IS ALL GOOD OR ALL BAD. THAT'S BECAUSE WE'RE ALL BOTH, OFTEN AT THE SAME TIME.

Rebel

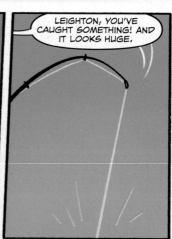

LEIGHTON, YOU'VE CAUGHT SOMETHING! AND IT LOOKS HUGE.

NEED HELP?

NO, I'VE GOT IT.

REEL IT IN SLOW AND STEADY.

GREAT JOB, LEIGHTON. I THINK WE HAVE THE CATCH OF THE DAY. THIS WILL BE HARD TO BEAT!

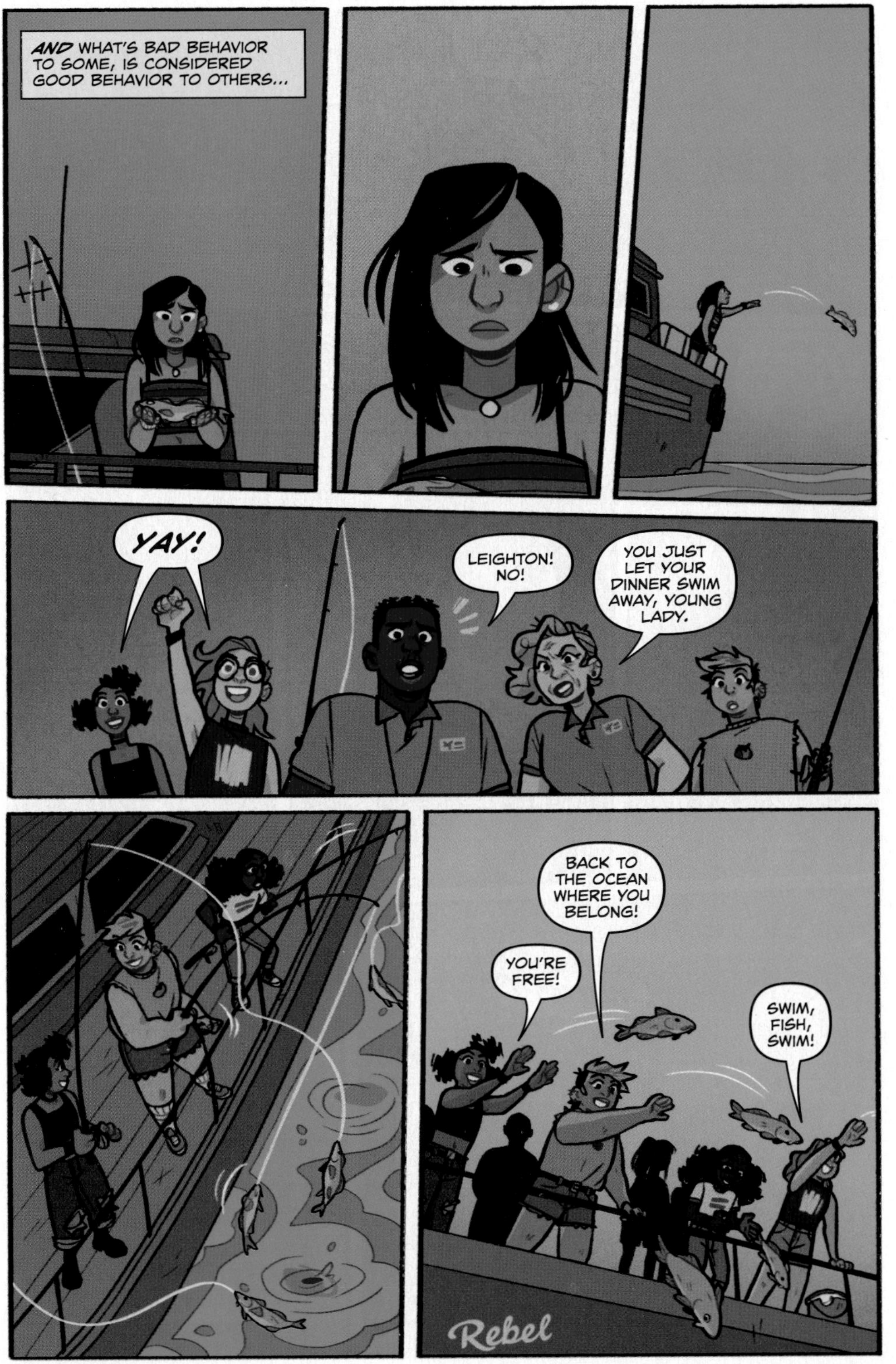
AND WHAT'S BAD BEHAVIOR TO SOME, IS CONSIDERED GOOD BEHAVIOR TO OTHERS...
YAY!
LEIGHTON! NO!
YOU JUST LET YOUR DINNER SWIM AWAY, YOUNG LADY.
BACK TO THE OCEAN WHERE YOU BELONG!
YOU'RE FREE!
SWIM, FISH, SWIM!
Rebel

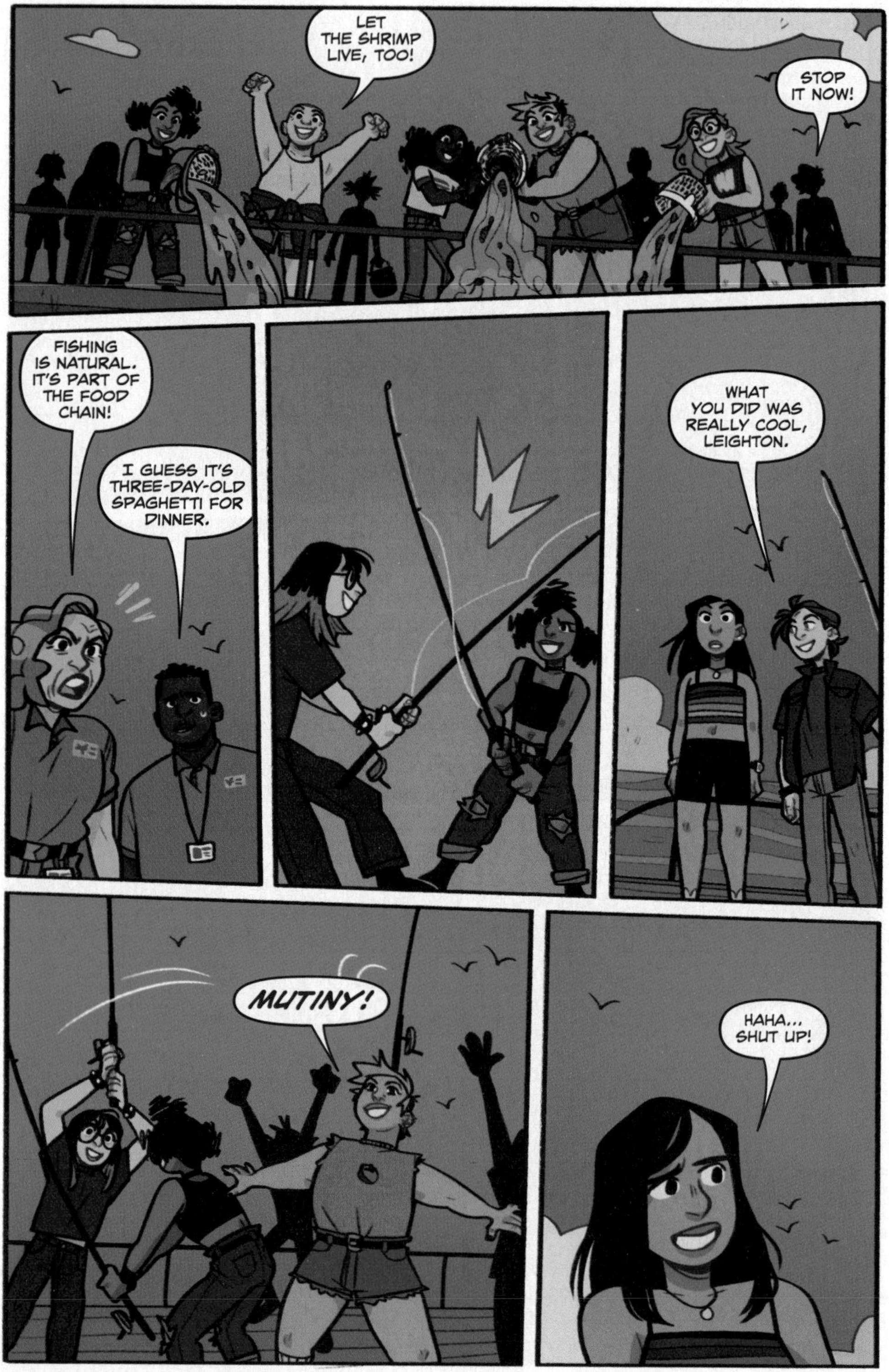
LET THE SHRIMP LIVE, TOO!
STOP IT NOW!
FISHING IS NATURAL. IT'S PART OF THE FOOD CHAIN!
I GUESS IT'S THREE-DAY-OLD SPAGHETTI FOR DINNER.
WHAT YOU DID WAS REALLY COOL, LEIGHTON.
MUTINY!
HAHA... SHUT UP!

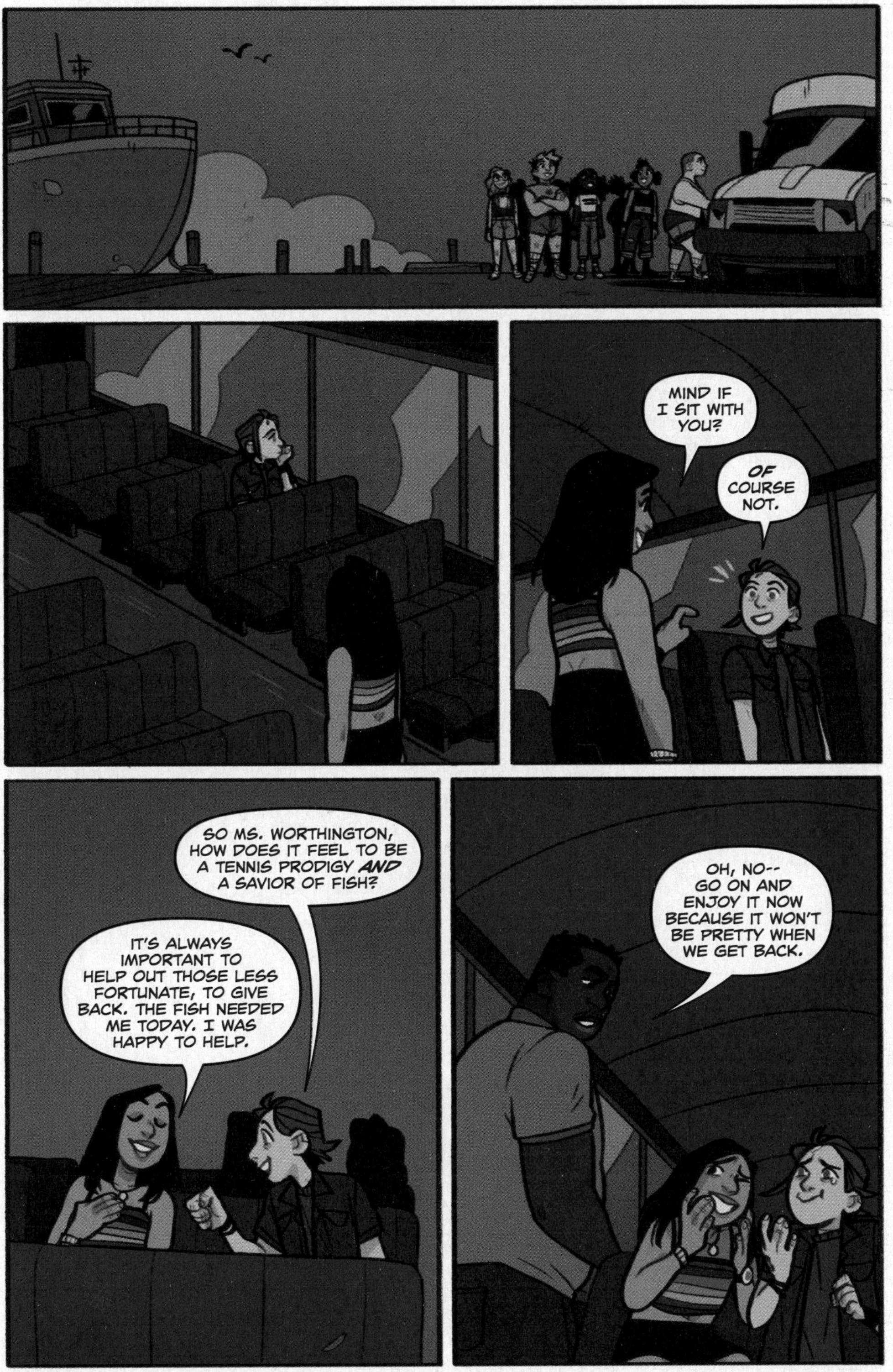
MIND IF I SIT WITH YOU?
OF COURSE NOT.
SO MS. WORTHINGTON, HOW DOES IT FEEL TO BE A TENNIS PRODIGY AND A SAVIOR OF FISH?
IT'S ALWAYS IMPORTANT TO HELP OUT THOSE LESS FORTUNATE, TO GIVE BACK. THE FISH NEEDED ME TODAY. I WAS HAPPY TO HELP.
OH, NO-- GO ON AND ENJOY IT NOW BECAUSE IT WON'T BE PRETTY WHEN WE GET BACK.

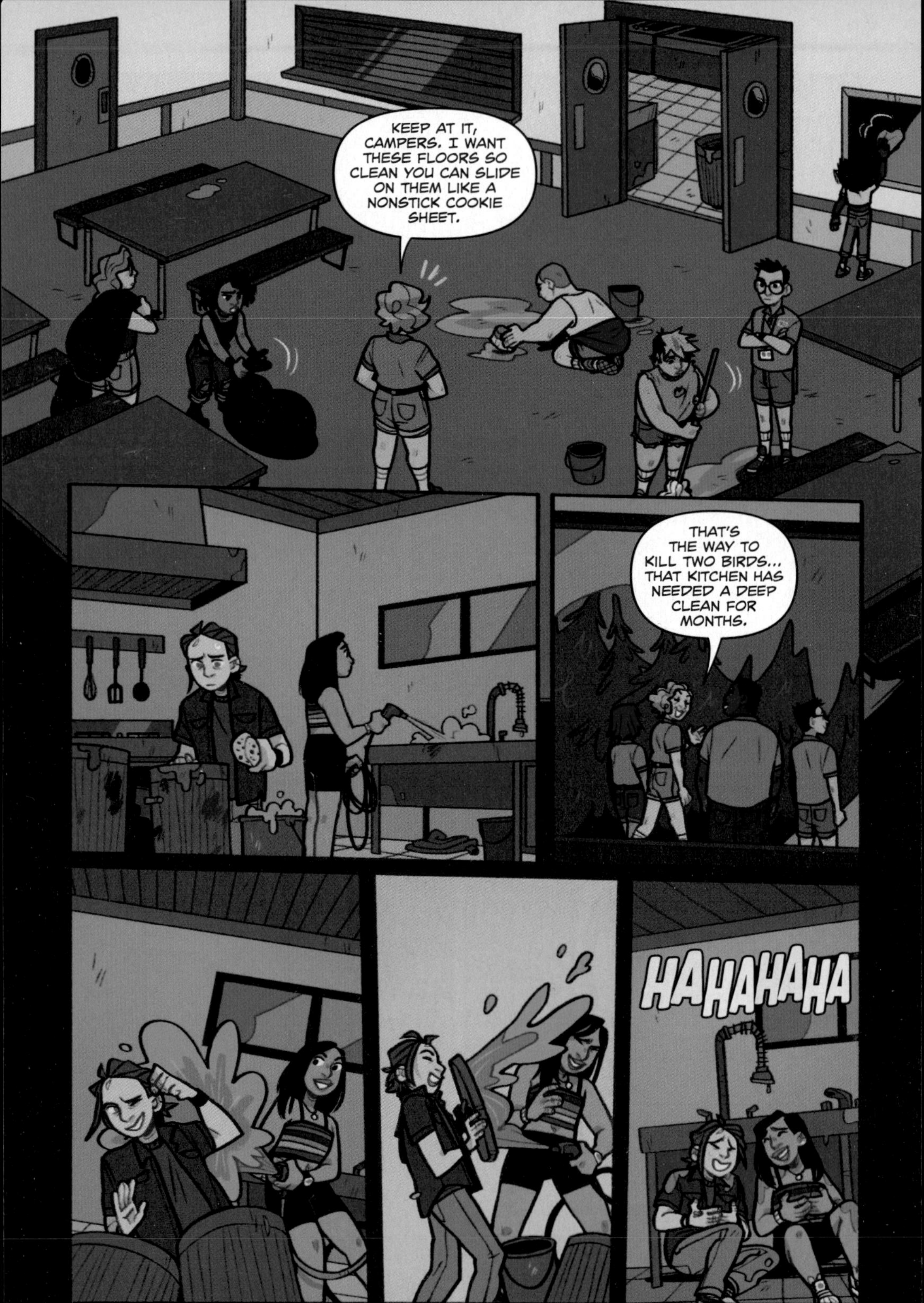
KEEP AT IT, CAMPERS. I WANT THESE FLOORS SO CLEAN YOU CAN SLIDE ON THEM LIKE A NONSTICK COOKIE SHEET.
THAT'S THE WAY TO KILL TWO BIRDS... THAT KITCHEN HAS NEEDED A DEEP CLEAN FOR MONTHS.
HAHAHAHA

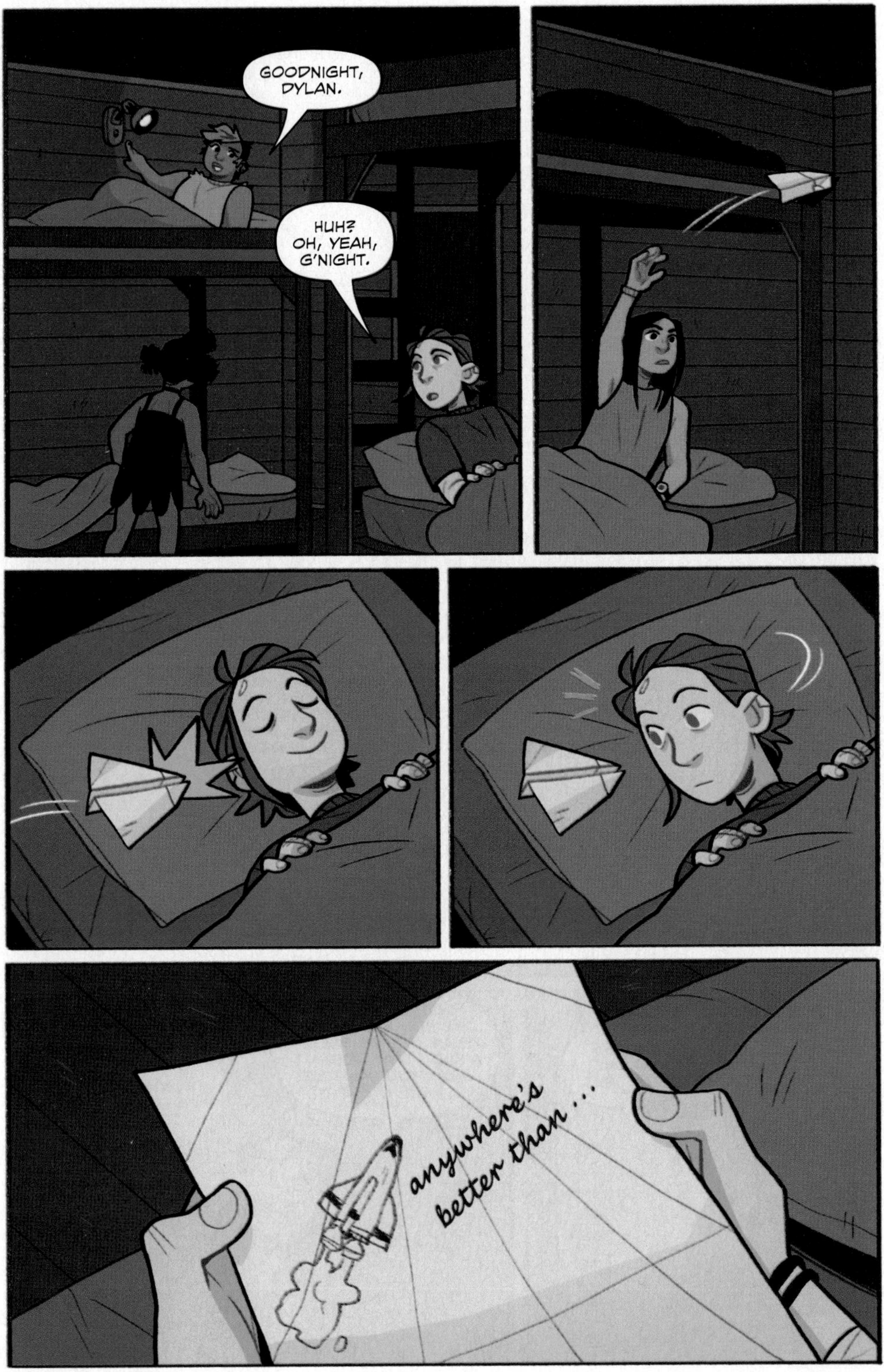
GOODNIGHT, DYLAN.
HUH? OH, YEAH, G'NIGHT.
anywhere's better than ...

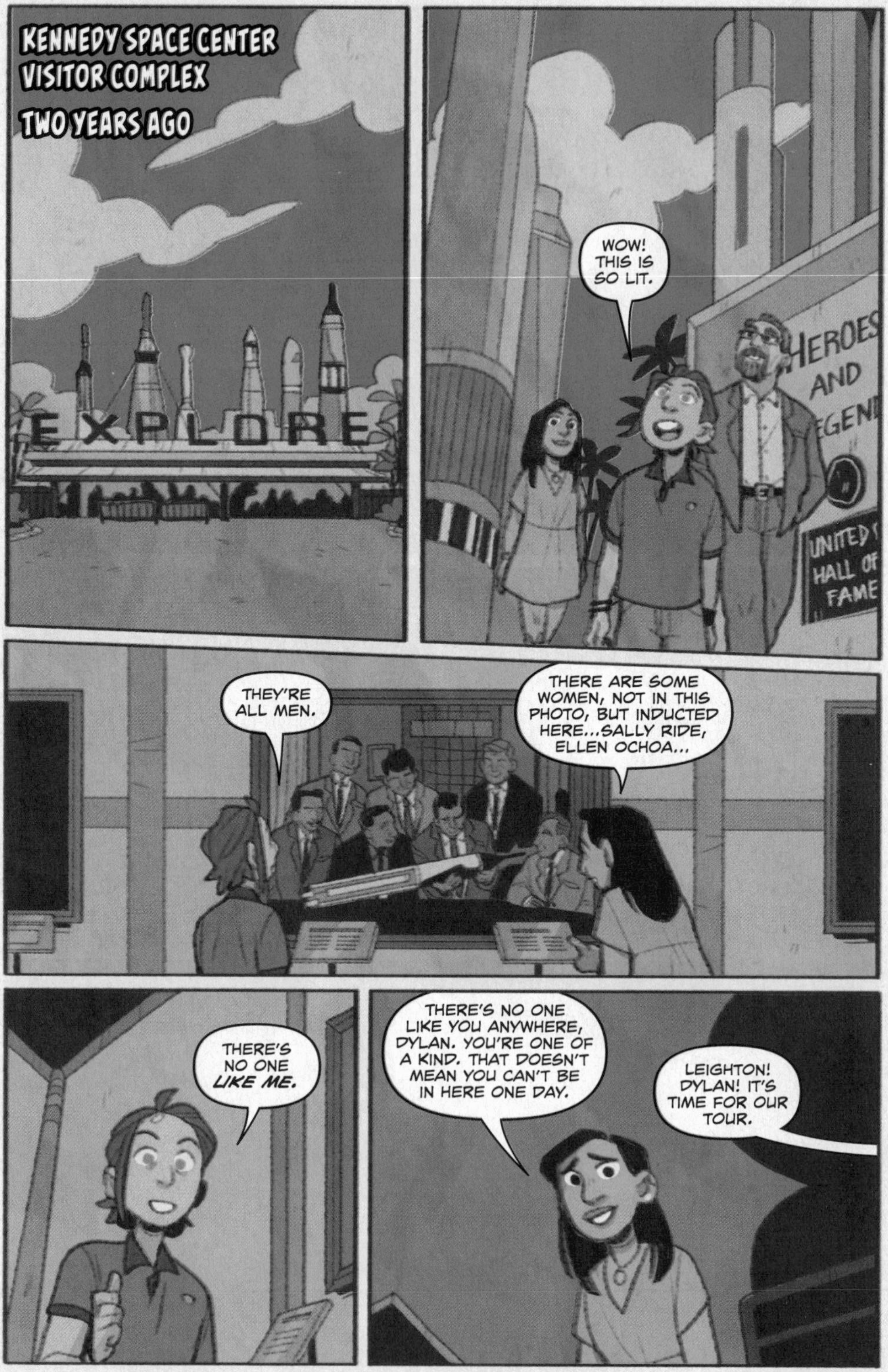
KENNEDY SPACE CENTER
VISITOR COMPLEX
TWO YEARS AGO
EXPLORE
WOW! THIS IS SO LIT.
HEROES AND LEGEND
UNITED HALL OF FAME
THEY'RE ALL MEN.
THERE ARE SOME WOMEN, NOT IN THIS PHOTO, BUT INDUCTED HERE...SALLY RIDE, ELLEN OCHOA...
THERE'S NO ONE *LIKE ME.*
THERE'S NO ONE LIKE YOU ANYWHERE, DYLAN. YOU'RE ONE OF A KIND. THAT DOESN'T MEAN YOU CAN'T BE IN HERE ONE DAY.
LEIGHTON! DYLAN! IT'S TIME FOR OUR TOUR.

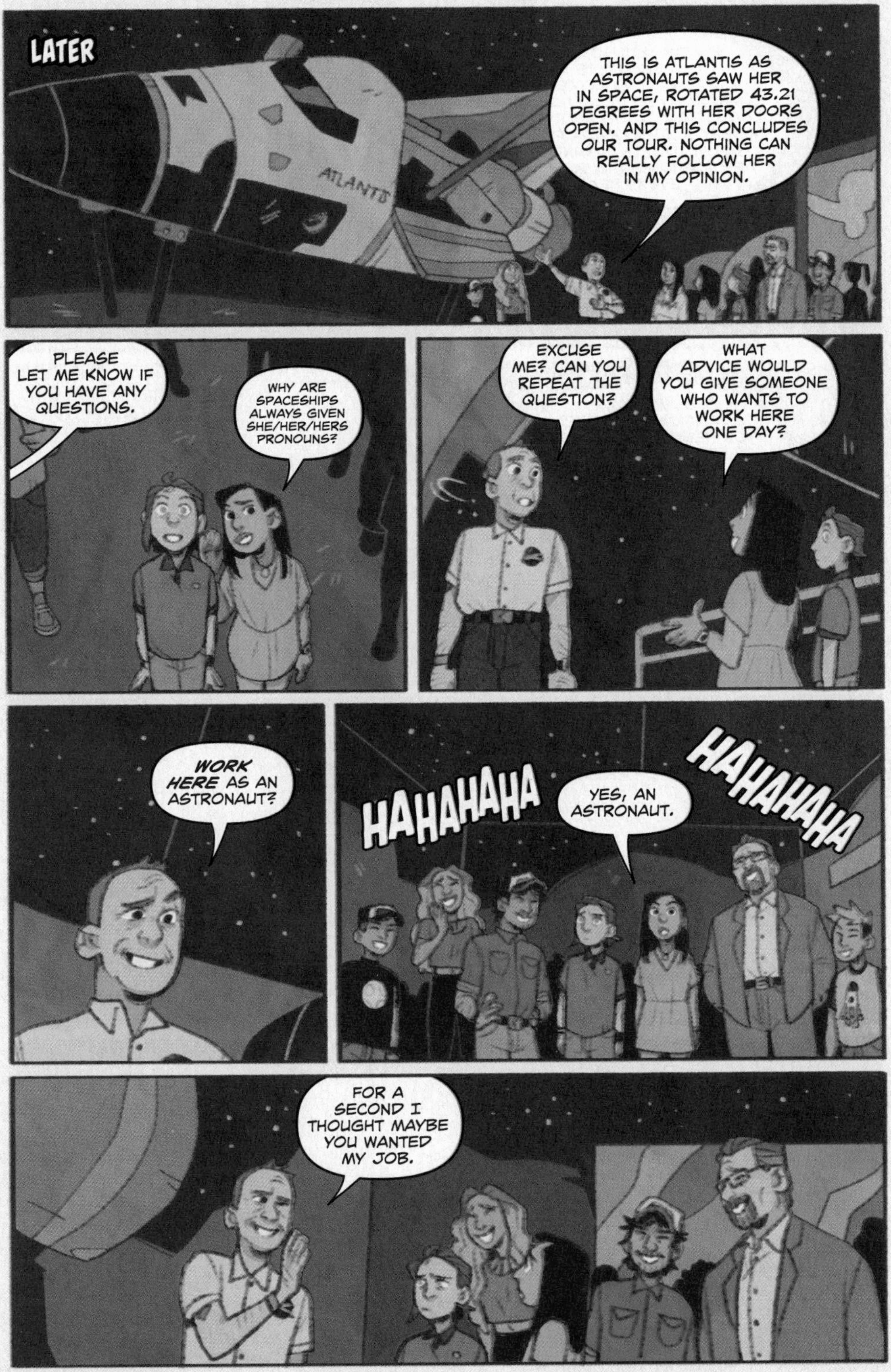
LATER
THIS IS ATLANTIS AS ASTRONAUTS SAW HER IN SPACE, ROTATED 43.21 DEGREES WITH HER DOORS OPEN. AND THIS CONCLUDES OUR TOUR. NOTHING CAN REALLY FOLLOW HER IN MY OPINION.
ATLANTIS
PLEASE LET ME KNOW IF YOU HAVE ANY QUESTIONS.
WHY ARE SPACESHIPS ALWAYS GIVEN SHE/HER/HERS PRONOUNS?
EXCUSE ME? CAN YOU REPEAT THE QUESTION?
WHAT ADVICE WOULD YOU GIVE SOMEONE WHO WANTS TO WORK HERE ONE DAY?
WORK HERE AS AN ASTRONAUT?
HAHAHAHA
YES, AN ASTRONAUT.
HAHAHAHA
FOR A SECOND I THOUGHT MAYBE YOU WANTED MY JOB.

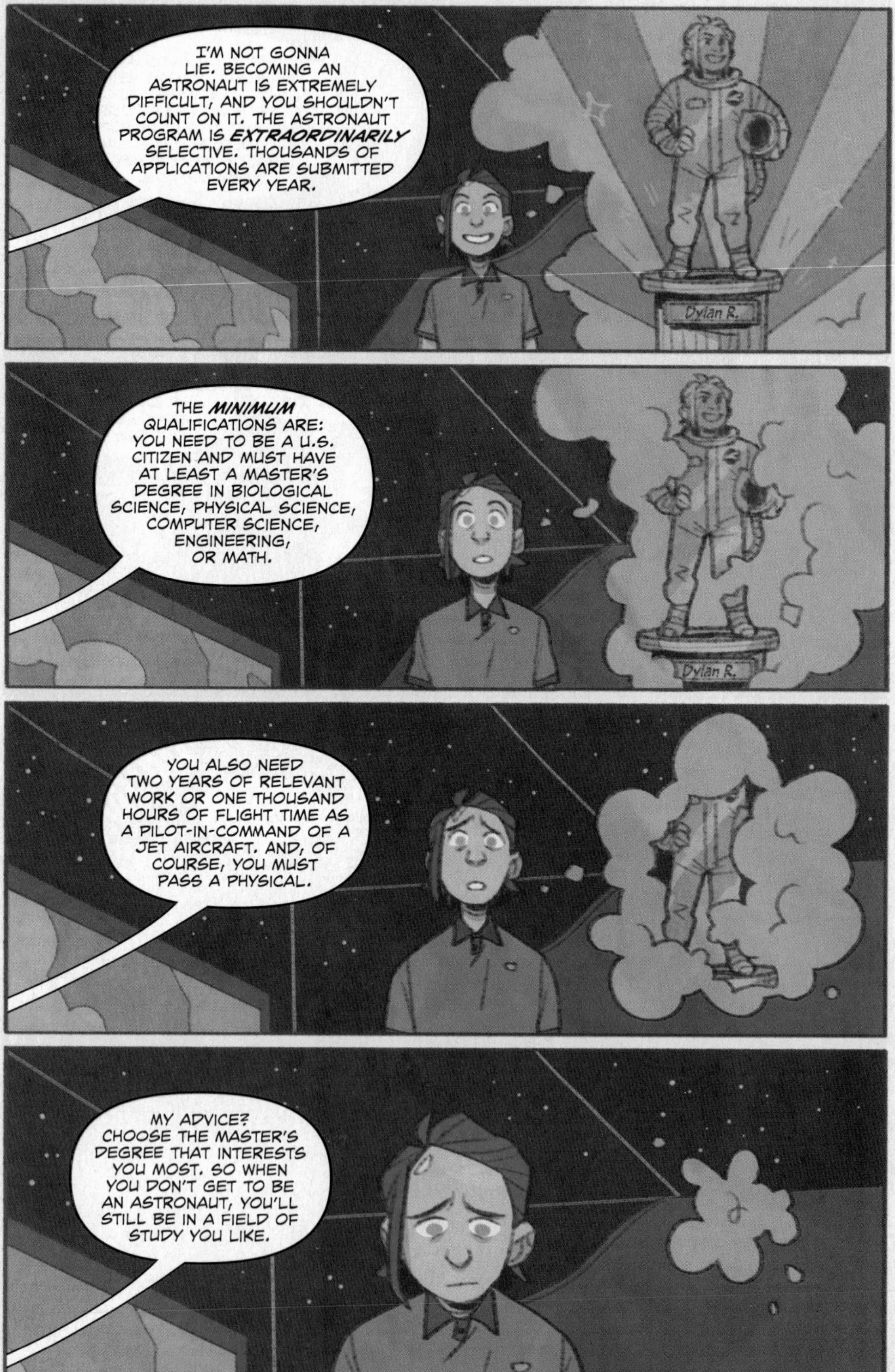
I'M NOT GONNA LIE. BECOMING AN ASTRONAUT IS EXTREMELY DIFFICULT, AND YOU SHOULDN'T COUNT ON IT. THE ASTRONAUT PROGRAM IS EXTRAORDINARILY SELECTIVE. THOUSANDS OF APPLICATIONS ARE SUBMITTED EVERY YEAR.
Dylan R.
THE MINIMUM QUALIFICATIONS ARE: YOU NEED TO BE A U.S. CITIZEN AND MUST HAVE AT LEAST A MASTER'S DEGREE IN BIOLOGICAL SCIENCE, PHYSICAL SCIENCE, COMPUTER SCIENCE, ENGINEERING, OR MATH.
Dylan R.
YOU ALSO NEED TWO YEARS OF RELEVANT WORK OR ONE THOUSAND HOURS OF FLIGHT TIME AS A PILOT-IN-COMMAND OF A JET AIRCRAFT. AND, OF COURSE, YOU MUST PASS A PHYSICAL.
MY ADVICE? CHOOSE THE MASTER'S DEGREE THAT INTERESTS YOU MOST. SO WHEN YOU DON'T GET TO BE AN ASTRONAUT, YOU'LL STILL BE IN A FIELD OF STUDY YOU LIKE.

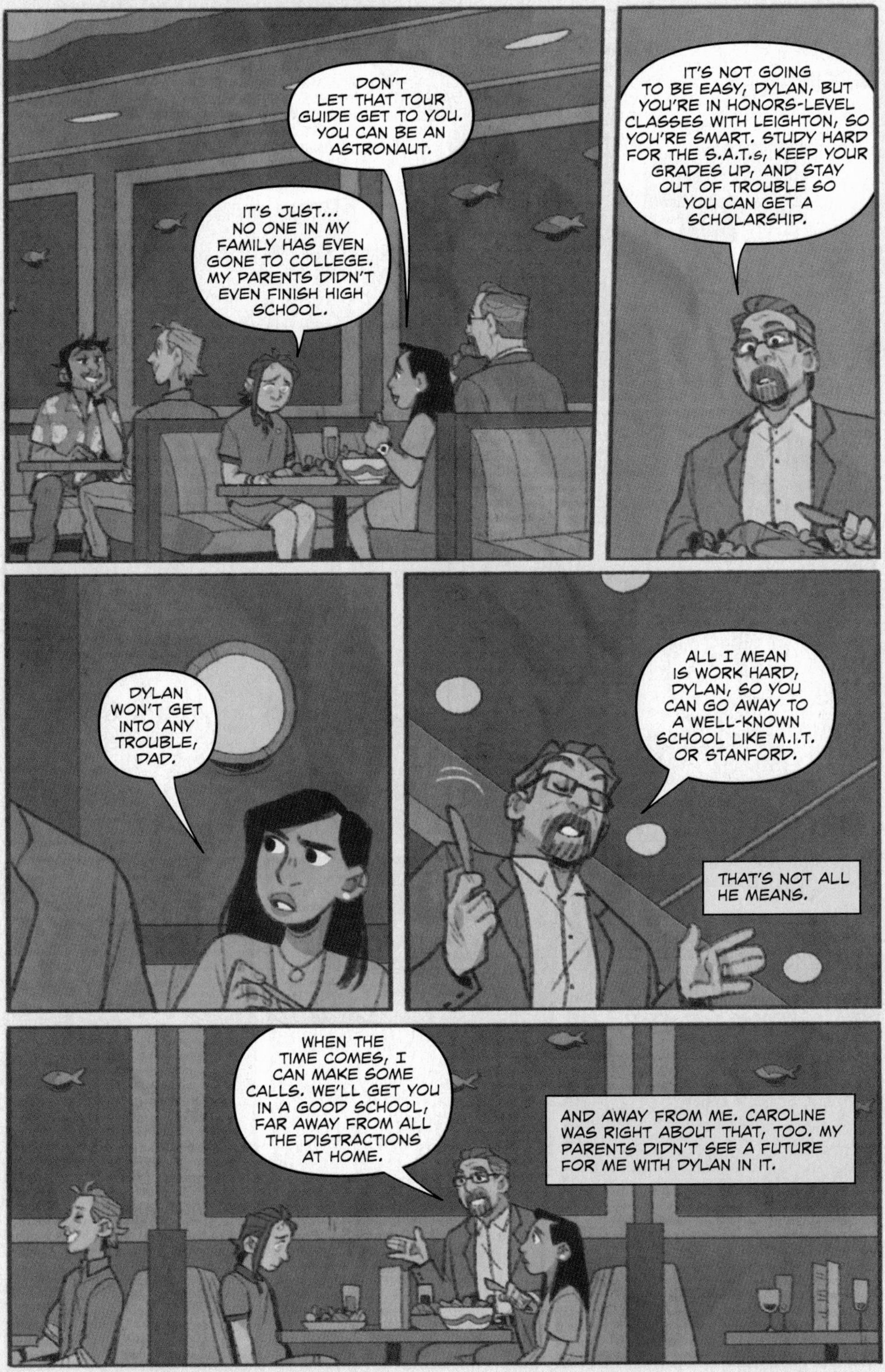
DON'T LET THAT TOUR GUIDE GET TO YOU. YOU CAN BE AN ASTRONAUT.
IT'S JUST... NO ONE IN MY FAMILY HAS EVEN GONE TO COLLEGE. MY PARENTS DIDN'T EVEN FINISH HIGH SCHOOL.
IT'S NOT GOING TO BE EASY, DYLAN, BUT YOU'RE IN HONORS-LEVEL CLASSES WITH LEIGHTON, SO YOU'RE SMART. STUDY HARD FOR THE S.A.T.s, KEEP YOUR GRADES UP, AND STAY OUT OF TROUBLE SO YOU CAN GET A SCHOLARSHIP.
DYLAN WON'T GET INTO ANY TROUBLE, DAD.
ALL I MEAN IS WORK HARD, DYLAN, SO YOU CAN GO AWAY TO A WELL-KNOWN SCHOOL LIKE M.I.T. OR STANFORD.
THAT'S NOT ALL HE MEANS.
WHEN THE TIME COMES, I CAN MAKE SOME CALLS. WE'LL GET YOU IN A GOOD SCHOOL, FAR AWAY FROM ALL THE DISTRACTIONS AT HOME.
AND AWAY FROM ME. CAROLINE WAS RIGHT ABOUT THAT, TOO. MY PARENTS DIDN'T SEE A FUTURE FOR ME WITH DYLAN IN IT.

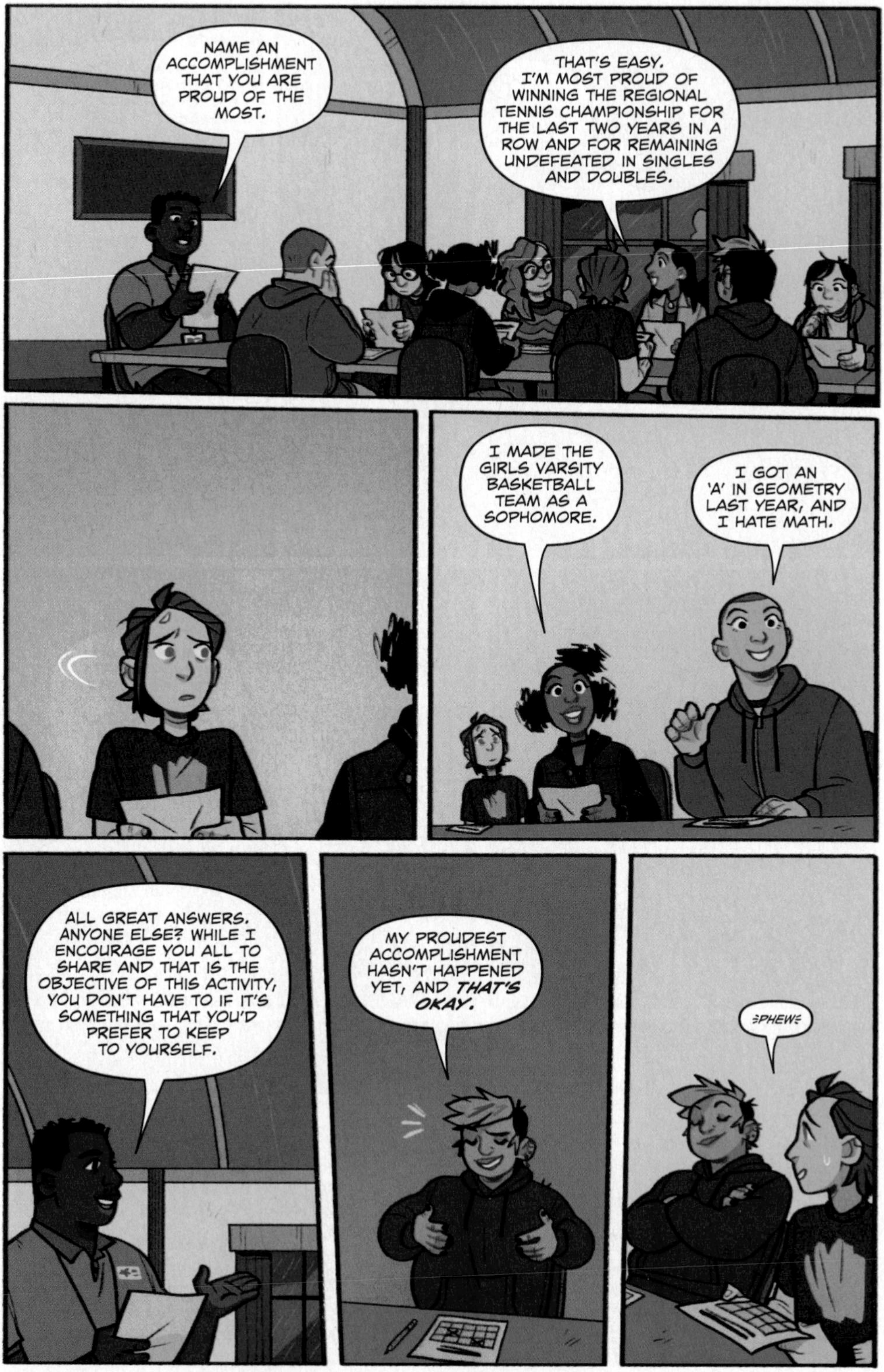
NAME AN ACCOMPLISHMENT THAT YOU ARE PROUD OF THE MOST.
THAT'S EASY. I'M MOST PROUD OF WINNING THE REGIONAL TENNIS CHAMPIONSHIP FOR THE LAST TWO YEARS IN A ROW AND FOR REMAINING UNDEFEATED IN SINGLES AND DOUBLES.
I MADE THE GIRLS VARSITY BASKETBALL TEAM AS A SOPHOMORE.
I GOT AN 'A' IN GEOMETRY LAST YEAR, AND I HATE MATH.
ALL GREAT ANSWERS. ANYONE ELSE? WHILE I ENCOURAGE YOU ALL TO SHARE AND THAT IS THE OBJECTIVE OF THIS ACTIVITY, YOU DON'T HAVE TO IF IT'S SOMETHING THAT YOU'D PREFER TO KEEP TO YOURSELF.
MY PROUDEST ACCOMPLISHMENT HASN'T HAPPENED YET, AND *THAT'S OKAY.*
PHEW

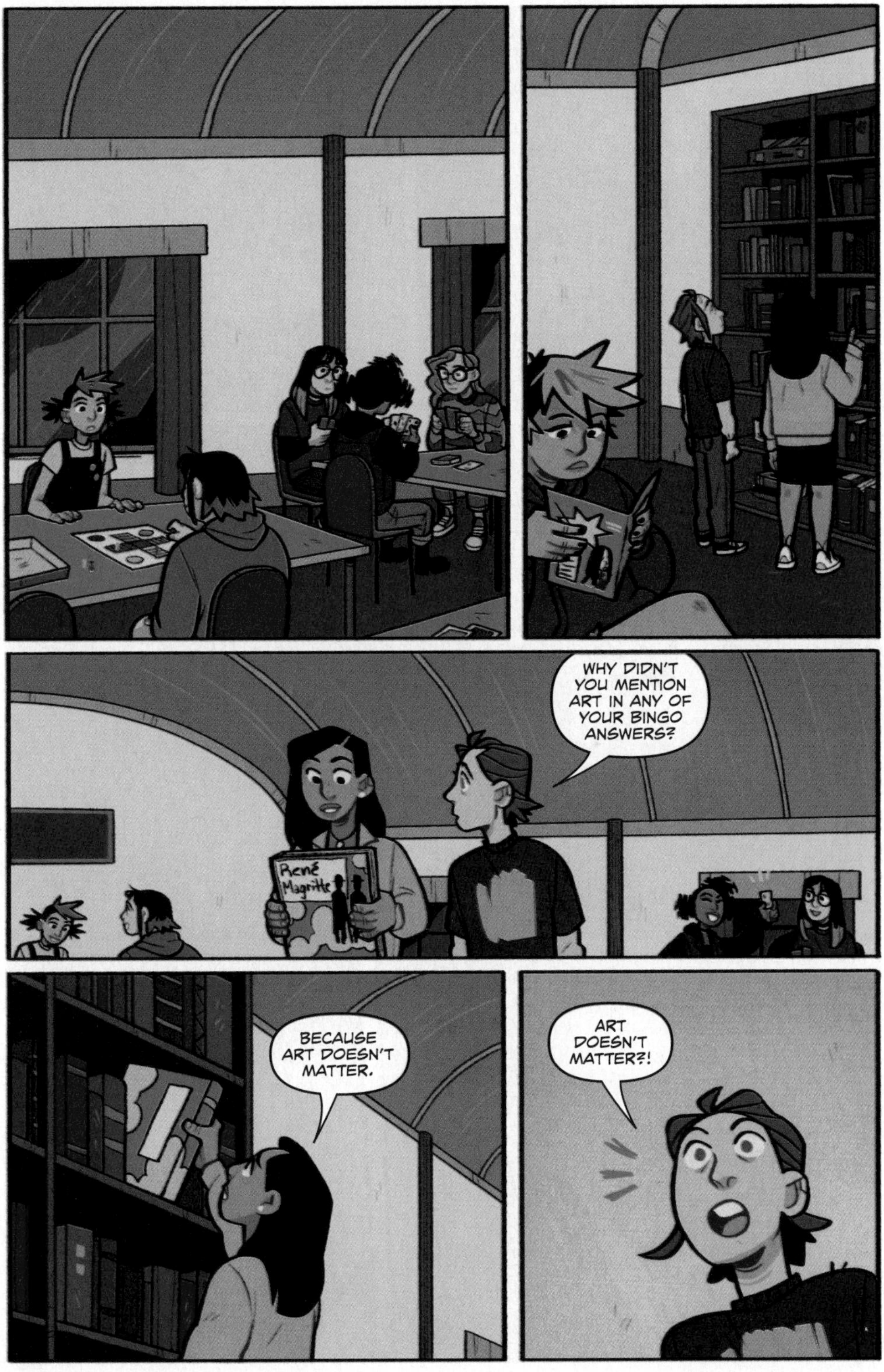
René Magritte
WHY DIDN'T YOU MENTION ART IN ANY OF YOUR BINGO ANSWERS?
BECAUSE ART DOESN'T MATTER.
ART DOESN'T MATTER?!

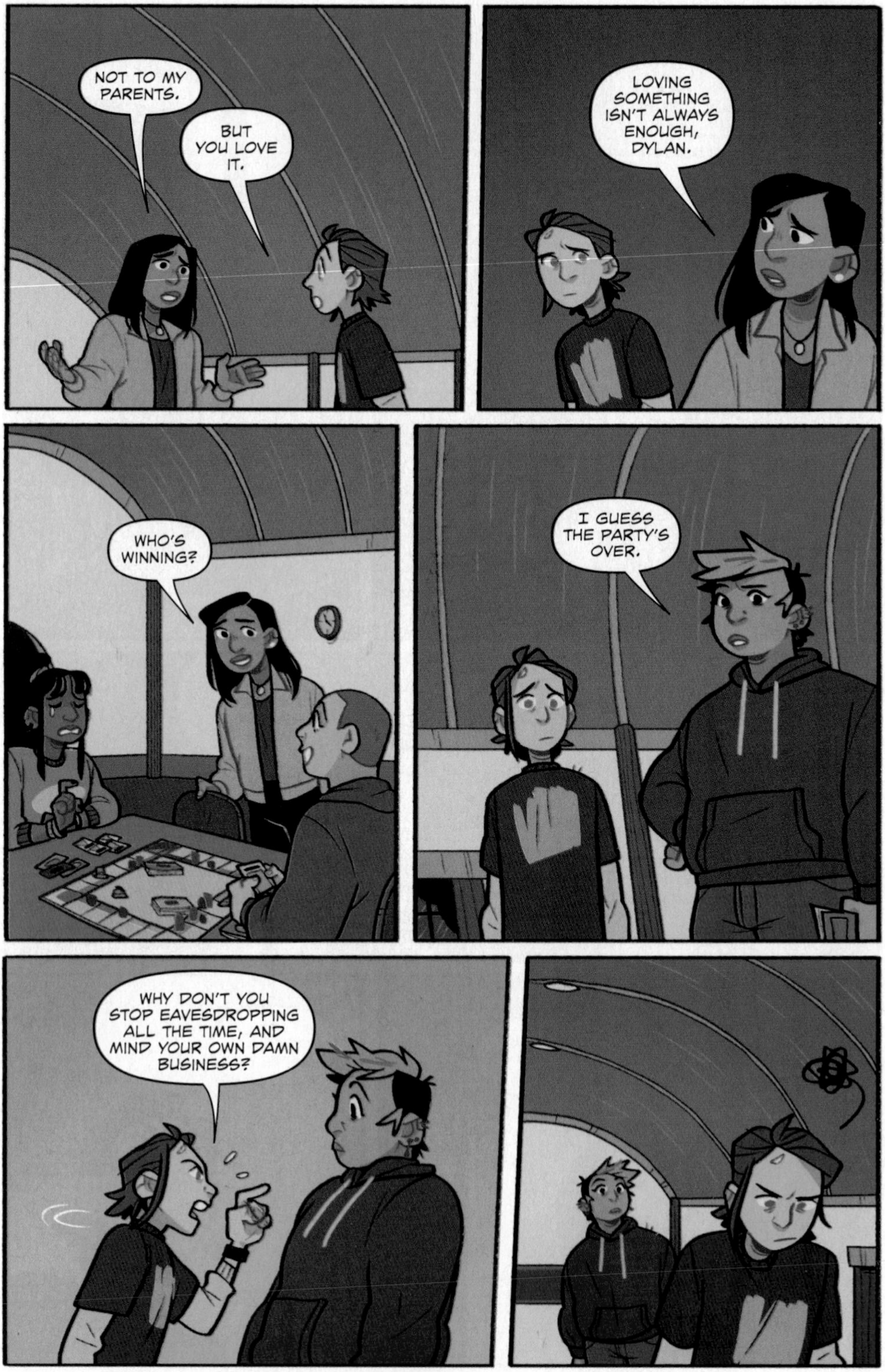
NOT TO MY PARENTS.
BUT YOU LOVE IT.
LOVING SOMETHING ISN'T ALWAYS ENOUGH, DYLAN.
WHO'S WINNING?
I GUESS THE PARTY'S OVER.
WHY DON'T YOU STOP EAVESDROPPING ALL THE TIME, AND MIND YOUR OWN DAMN BUSINESS?

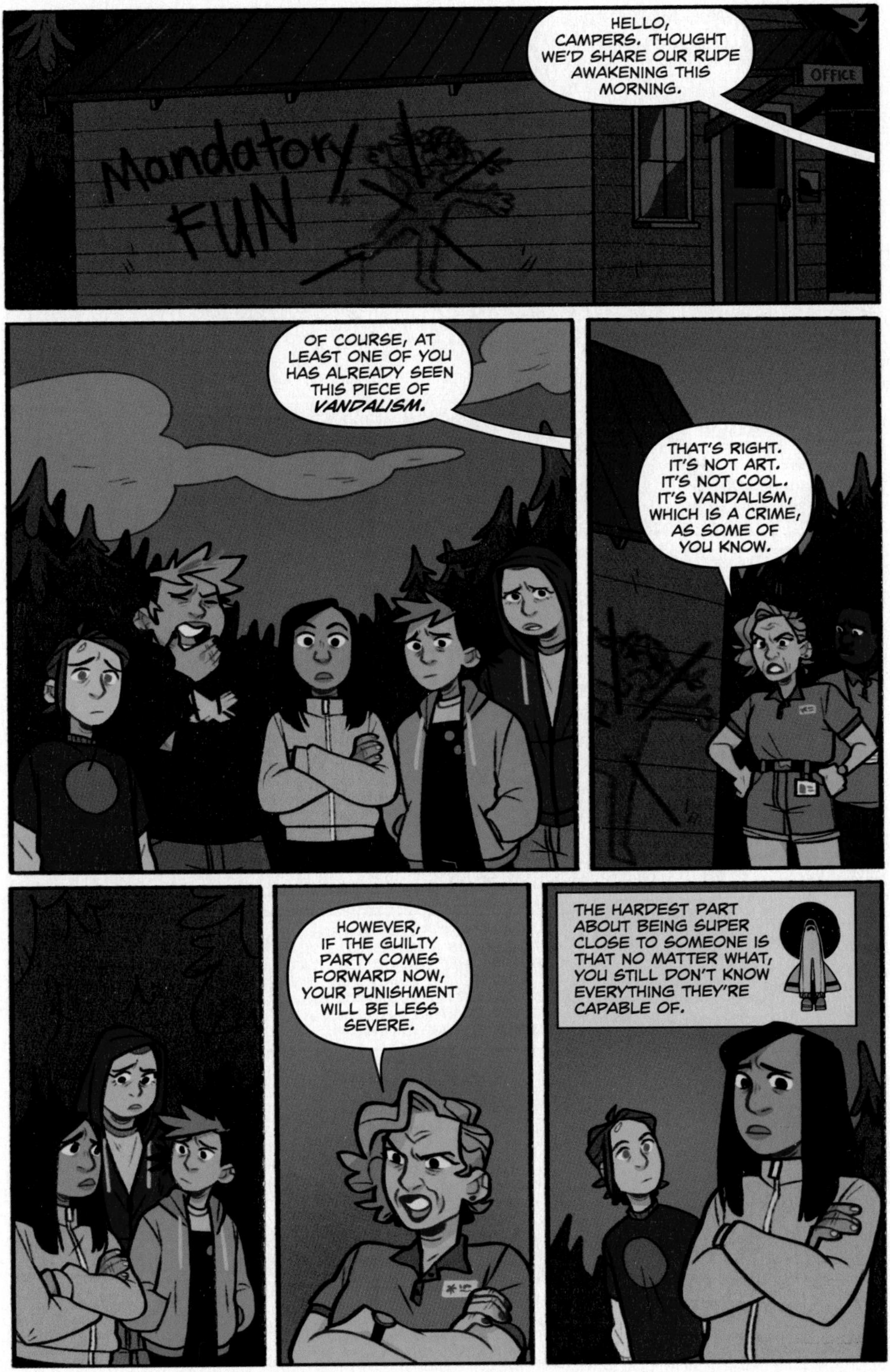

OFFICE
Mandatory FUN
HELLO, CAMPERS. THOUGHT WE'D SHARE OUR RUDE AWAKENING THIS MORNING.
OF COURSE, AT LEAST ONE OF YOU HAS ALREADY SEEN THIS PIECE OF VANDALISM.
THAT'S RIGHT. IT'S NOT ART. IT'S NOT COOL. IT'S VANDALISM, WHICH IS A CRIME, AS SOME OF YOU KNOW.
HOWEVER, IF THE GUILTY PARTY COMES FORWARD NOW, YOUR PUNISHMENT WILL BE LESS SEVERE.
THE HARDEST PART ABOUT BEING SUPER CLOSE TO SOMEONE IS THAT NO MATTER WHAT, YOU STILL DON'T KNOW EVERYTHING THEY'RE CAPABLE OF.

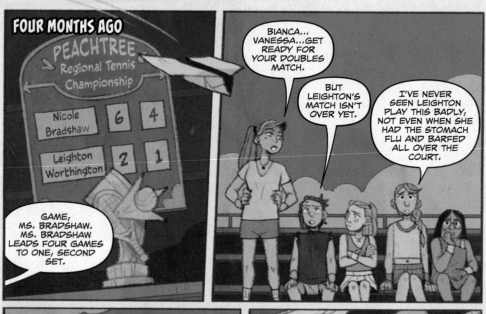

FOUR MONTHS AGO

PEACHTREE
Regional Tennis
Championship

| Nicole Bradshaw | 6 | 4 |
| Leighton Worthington | 2 | 1 |

GAME, MS. BRADSHAW. MS. BRADSHAW LEADS FOUR GAMES TO ONE, SECOND SET.

BIANCA... VANESSA...GET READY FOR YOUR DOUBLES MATCH.

BUT LEIGHTON'S MATCH ISN'T OVER YET.

I'VE NEVER SEEN LEIGHTON PLAY THIS BADLY, NOT EVEN WHEN SHE HAD THE STOMACH FLU AND BARFED ALL OVER THE COURT.

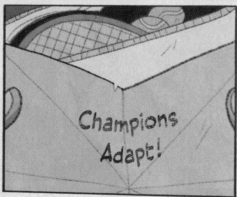

Champions Adapt!

Leighton

I'VE WATCHED EVERY SINGLE ONE OF LEIGHTON'S MATCHES. I'VE SEEN ALL HER PRACTICES, TOO, SOMETIMES FROM ACROSS THE NET AS HER HITTING PARTNER. SHE'S A CLASSIC BASELINER, RARELY COMING TO THE NET.

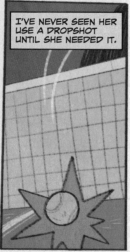

I'VE NEVER SEEN HER USE A DROPSHOT UNTIL SHE NEEDED IT.

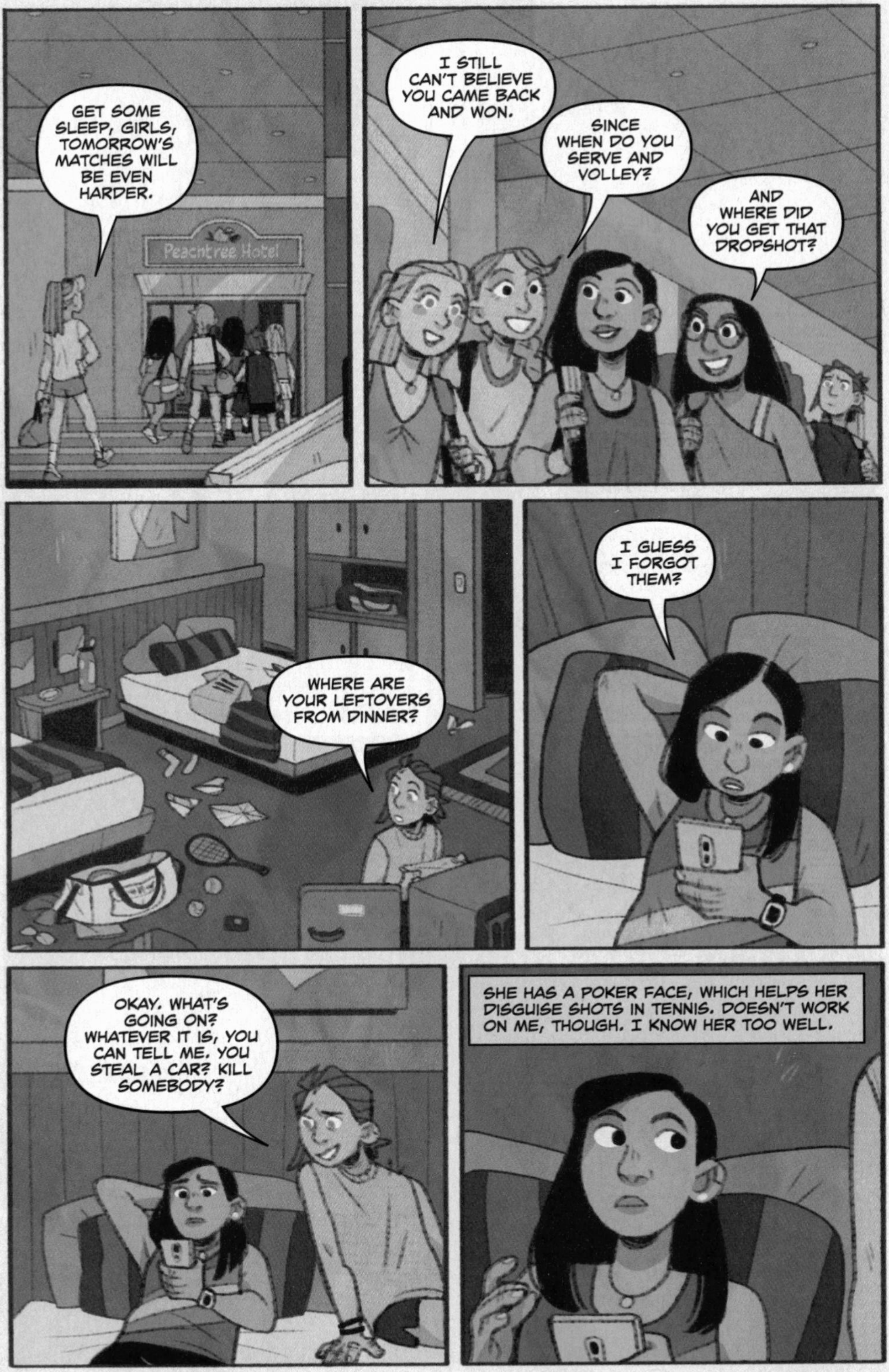
GET SOME SLEEP, GIRLS, TOMORROW'S MATCHES WILL BE EVEN HARDER.
Peachtree Hotel
I STILL CAN'T BELIEVE YOU CAME BACK AND WON.
SINCE WHEN DO YOU SERVE AND VOLLEY?
AND WHERE DID YOU GET THAT DROPSHOT?
WHERE ARE YOUR LEFTOVERS FROM DINNER?
I GUESS I FORGOT THEM?
OKAY. WHAT'S GOING ON? WHATEVER IT IS, YOU CAN TELL ME. YOU STEAL A CAR? KILL SOMEBODY?
SHE HAS A POKER FACE, WHICH HELPS HER DISGUISE SHOTS IN TENNIS. DOESN'T WORK ON ME, THOUGH. I KNOW HER TOO WELL.

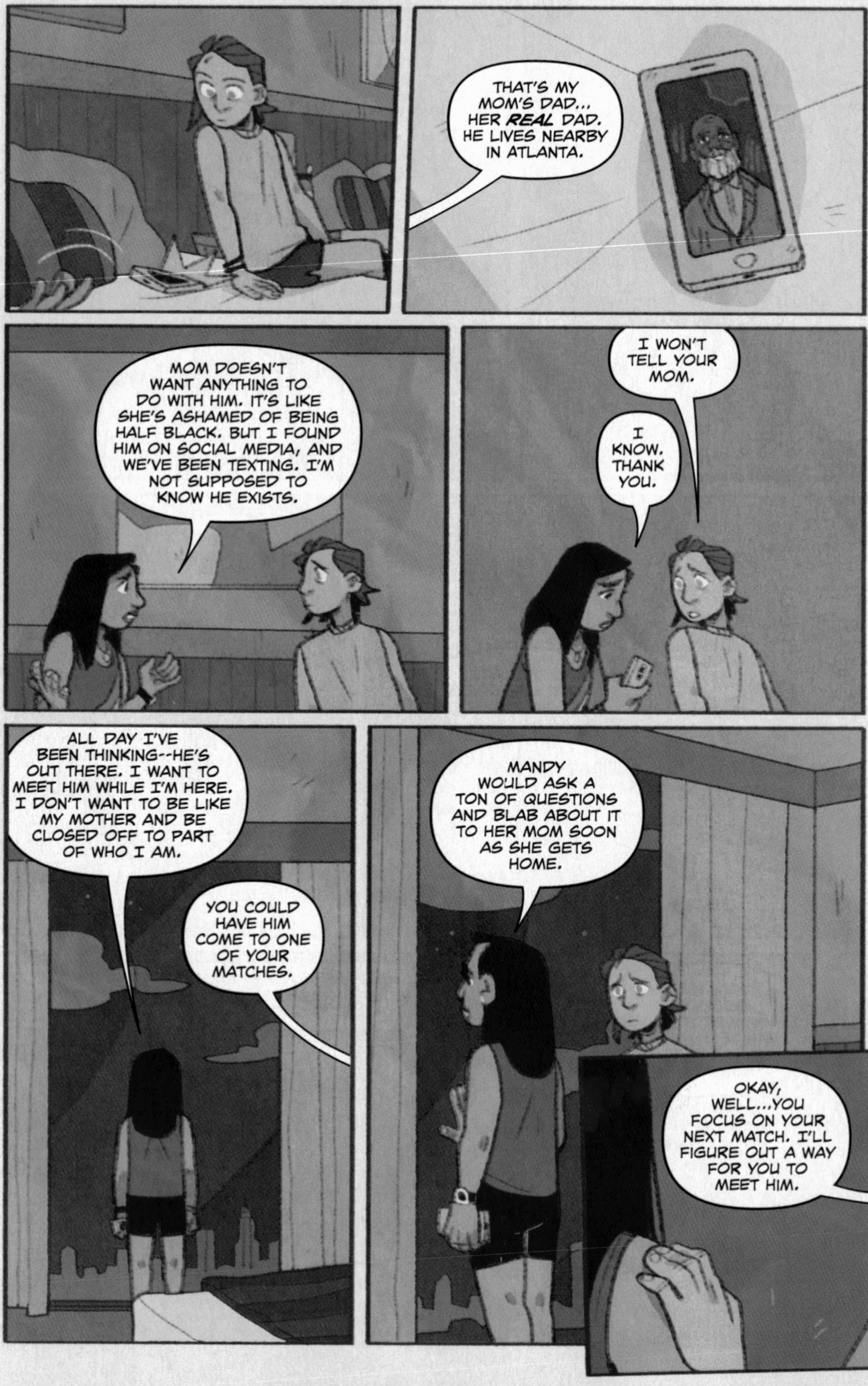
THAT'S MY MOM'S DAD... HER **REAL** DAD. HE LIVES NEARBY IN ATLANTA.
MOM DOESN'T WANT ANYTHING TO DO WITH HIM. IT'S LIKE SHE'S ASHAMED OF BEING HALF BLACK. BUT I FOUND HIM ON SOCIAL MEDIA, AND WE'VE BEEN TEXTING. I'M NOT SUPPOSED TO KNOW HE EXISTS.
I WON'T TELL YOUR MOM.
I KNOW. THANK YOU.
ALL DAY I'VE BEEN THINKING--HE'S OUT THERE. I WANT TO MEET HIM WHILE I'M HERE. I DON'T WANT TO BE LIKE MY MOTHER AND BE CLOSED OFF TO PART OF WHO I AM.
YOU COULD HAVE HIM COME TO ONE OF YOUR MATCHES.
MANDY WOULD ASK A TON OF QUESTIONS AND BLAB ABOUT IT TO HER MOM SOON AS SHE GETS HOME.
OKAY, WELL...YOU FOCUS ON YOUR NEXT MATCH. I'LL FIGURE OUT A WAY FOR YOU TO MEET HIM.

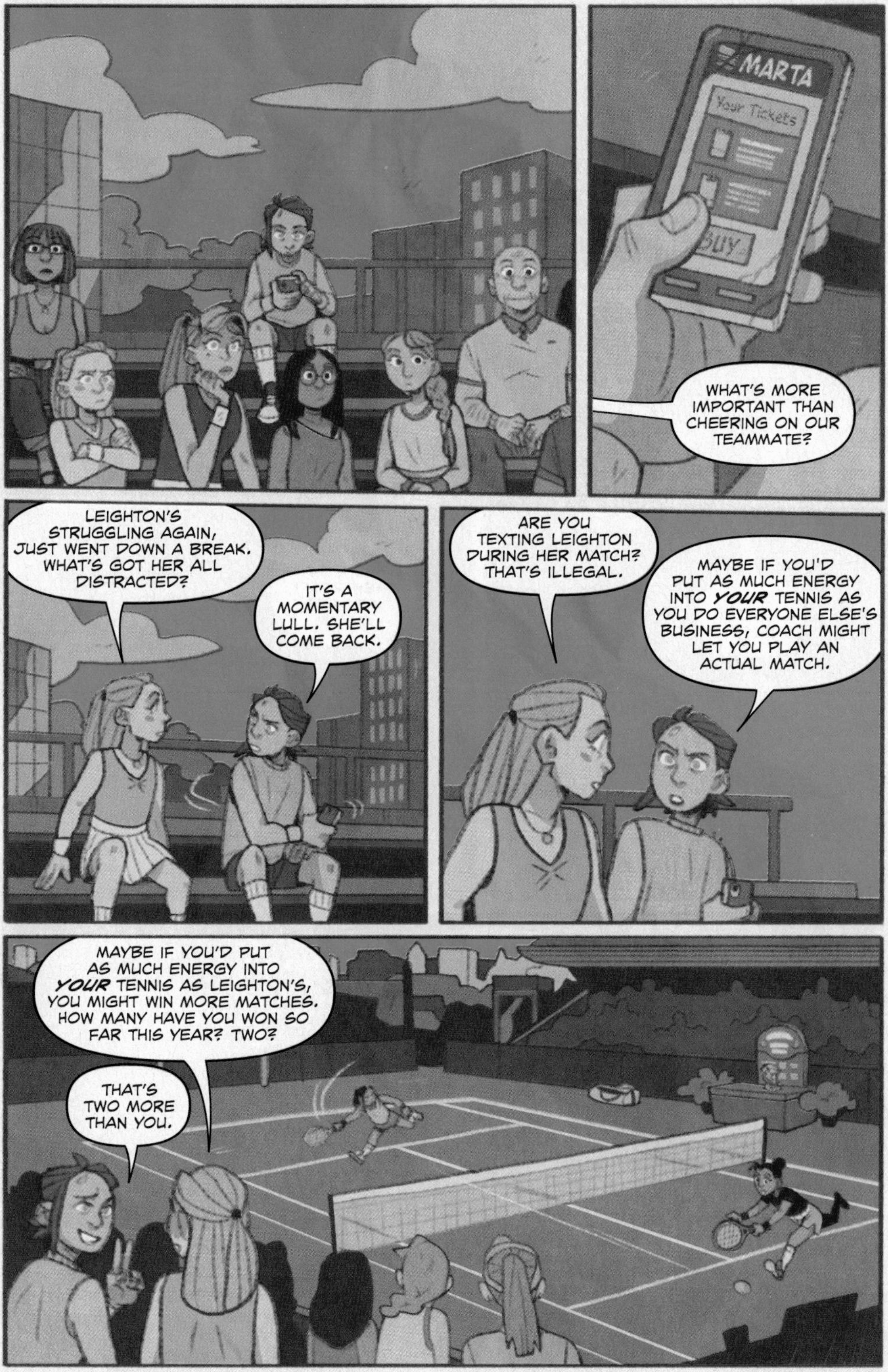
MARTA
Your Tickets
Buy
WHAT'S MORE IMPORTANT THAN CHEERING ON OUR TEAMMATE?
LEIGHTON'S STRUGGLING AGAIN, JUST WENT DOWN A BREAK. WHAT'S GOT HER ALL DISTRACTED?
IT'S A MOMENTARY LULL. SHE'LL COME BACK.
ARE YOU TEXTING LEIGHTON DURING HER MATCH? THAT'S ILLEGAL.
MAYBE IF YOU'D PUT AS MUCH ENERGY INTO ***YOUR*** TENNIS AS YOU DO EVERYONE ELSE'S BUSINESS, COACH MIGHT LET YOU PLAY AN ACTUAL MATCH.
MAYBE IF YOU'D PUT AS MUCH ENERGY INTO ***YOUR*** TENNIS AS LEIGHTON'S, YOU MIGHT WIN MORE MATCHES. HOW MANY HAVE YOU WON SO FAR THIS YEAR? TWO?
THAT'S TWO MORE THAN YOU.

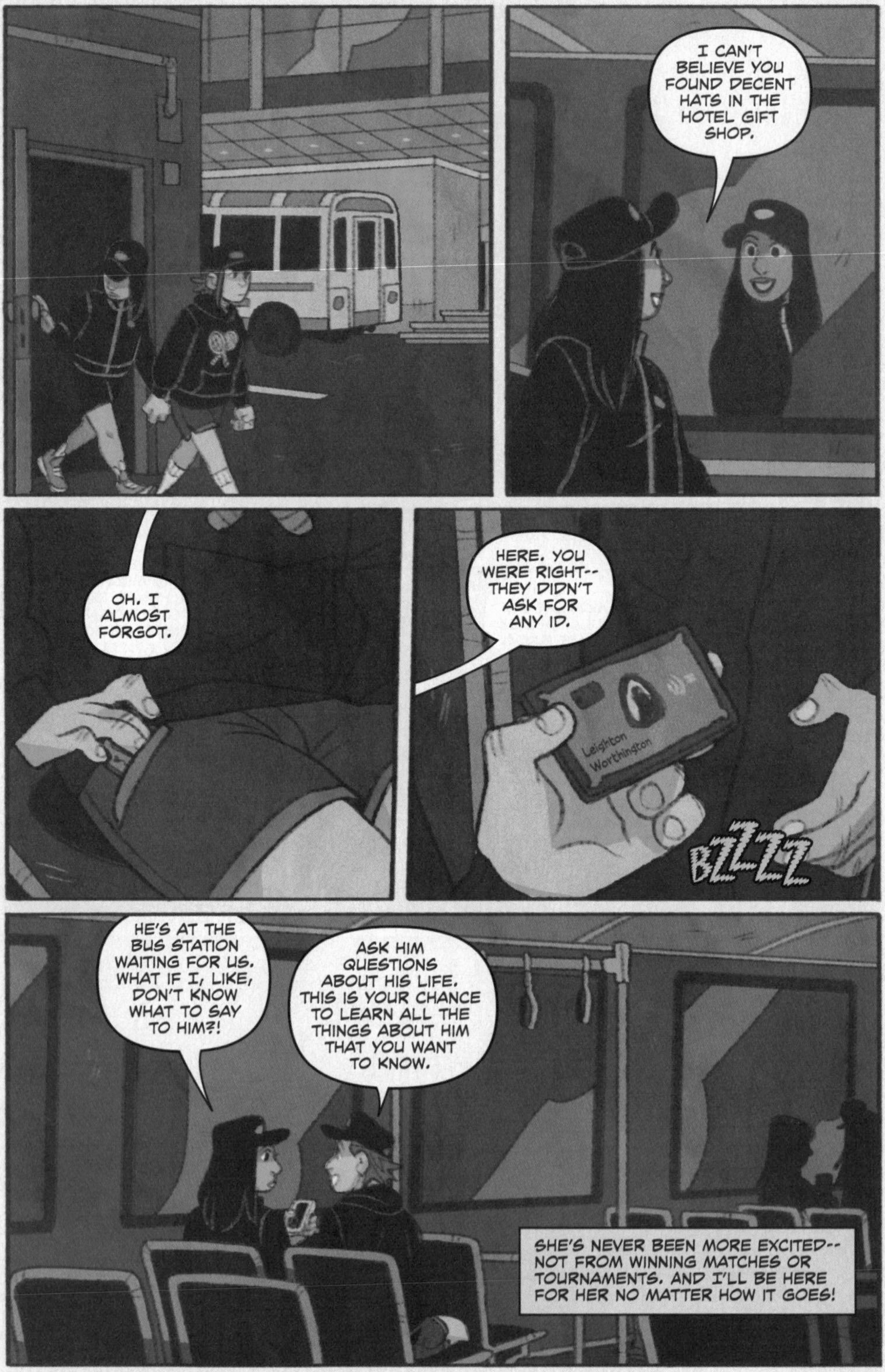
I CAN'T BELIEVE YOU FOUND DECENT HATS IN THE HOTEL GIFT SHOP.
OH. I ALMOST FORGOT.
HERE. YOU WERE RIGHT-- THEY DIDN'T ASK FOR ANY ID.
Leighton Worthington
BZZZZ
HE'S AT THE BUS STATION WAITING FOR US. WHAT IF I, LIKE, DON'T KNOW WHAT TO SAY TO HIM?!
ASK HIM QUESTIONS ABOUT HIS LIFE. THIS IS YOUR CHANCE TO LEARN ALL THE THINGS ABOUT HIM THAT YOU WANT TO KNOW.
SHE'S NEVER BEEN MORE EXCITED-- NOT FROM WINNING MATCHES OR TOURNAMENTS. AND I'LL BE HERE FOR HER NO MATTER HOW IT GOES!

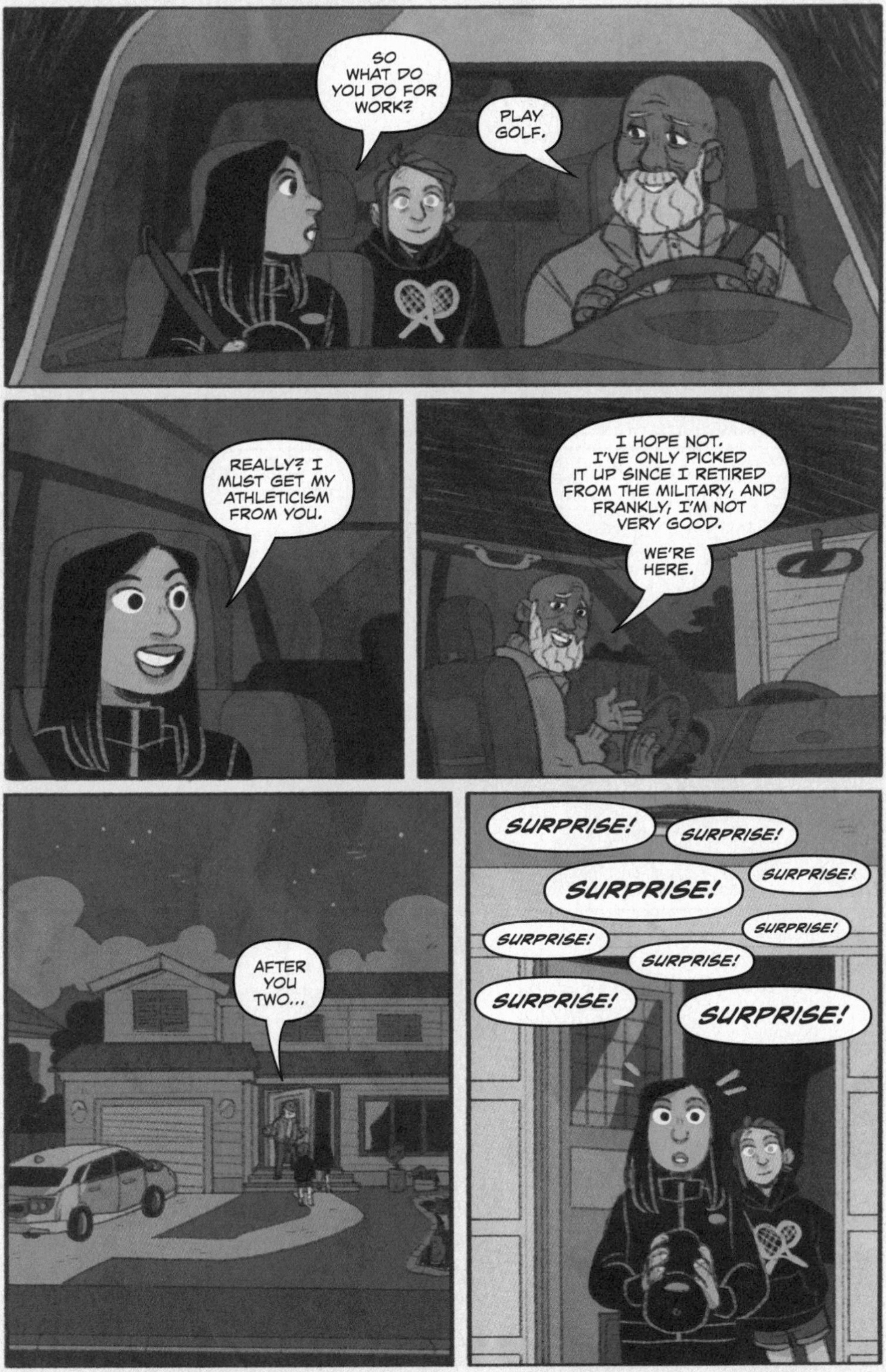
SO WHAT DO YOU DO FOR WORK?
PLAY GOLF.
REALLY? I MUST GET MY ATHLETICISM FROM YOU.
I HOPE NOT. I'VE ONLY PICKED IT UP SINCE I RETIRED FROM THE MILITARY, AND FRANKLY, I'M NOT VERY GOOD.
WE'RE HERE.
AFTER YOU TWO...
SURPRISE!
SURPRISE!
SURPRISE!
SURPRISE!
SURPRISE!
SURPRISE!
SURPRISE!
SURPRISE!
SURPRISE!

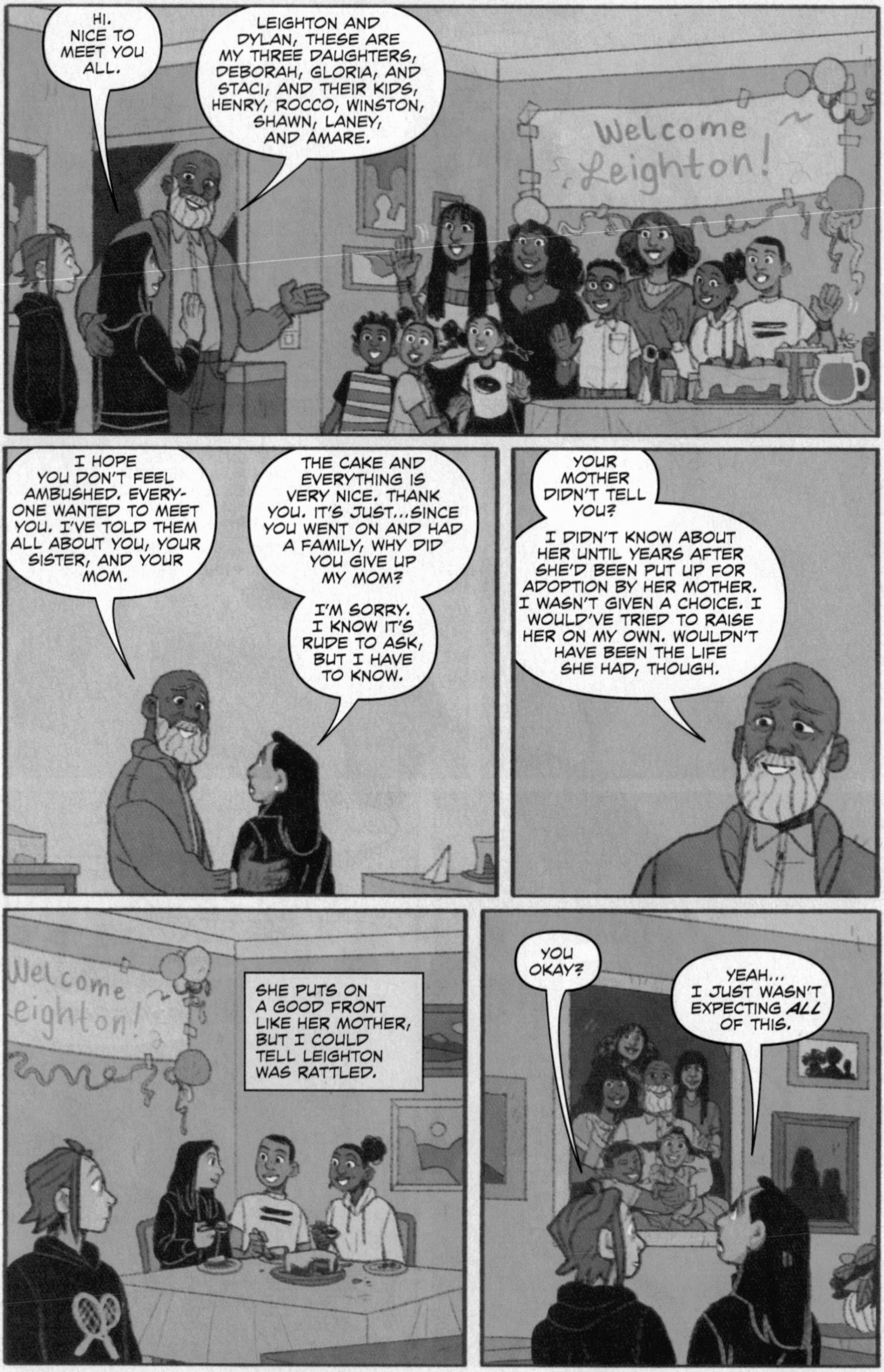

HI. NICE TO MEET YOU ALL.
LEIGHTON AND DYLAN, THESE ARE MY THREE DAUGHTERS, DEBORAH, GLORIA, AND STACI, AND THEIR KIDS, HENRY, ROCCO, WINSTON, SHAWN, LANEY, AND AMARE.
Welcome Leighton!
I HOPE YOU DON'T FEEL AMBUSHED. EVERY-ONE WANTED TO MEET YOU. I'VE TOLD THEM ALL ABOUT YOU, YOUR SISTER, AND YOUR MOM.
THE CAKE AND EVERYTHING IS VERY NICE. THANK YOU. IT'S JUST...SINCE YOU WENT ON AND HAD A FAMILY, WHY DID YOU GIVE UP MY MOM?
I'M SORRY. I KNOW IT'S RUDE TO ASK, BUT I HAVE TO KNOW.
YOUR MOTHER DIDN'T TELL YOU?
I DIDN'T KNOW ABOUT HER UNTIL YEARS AFTER SHE'D BEEN PUT UP FOR ADOPTION BY HER MOTHER. I WASN'T GIVEN A CHOICE. I WOULD'VE TRIED TO RAISE HER ON MY OWN. WOULDN'T HAVE BEEN THE LIFE SHE HAD, THOUGH.
Welcome Leighton!
SHE PUTS ON A GOOD FRONT LIKE HER MOTHER, BUT I COULD TELL LEIGHTON WAS RATTLED.
YOU OKAY?
YEAH... I JUST WASN'T EXPECTING ***ALL*** OF THIS.

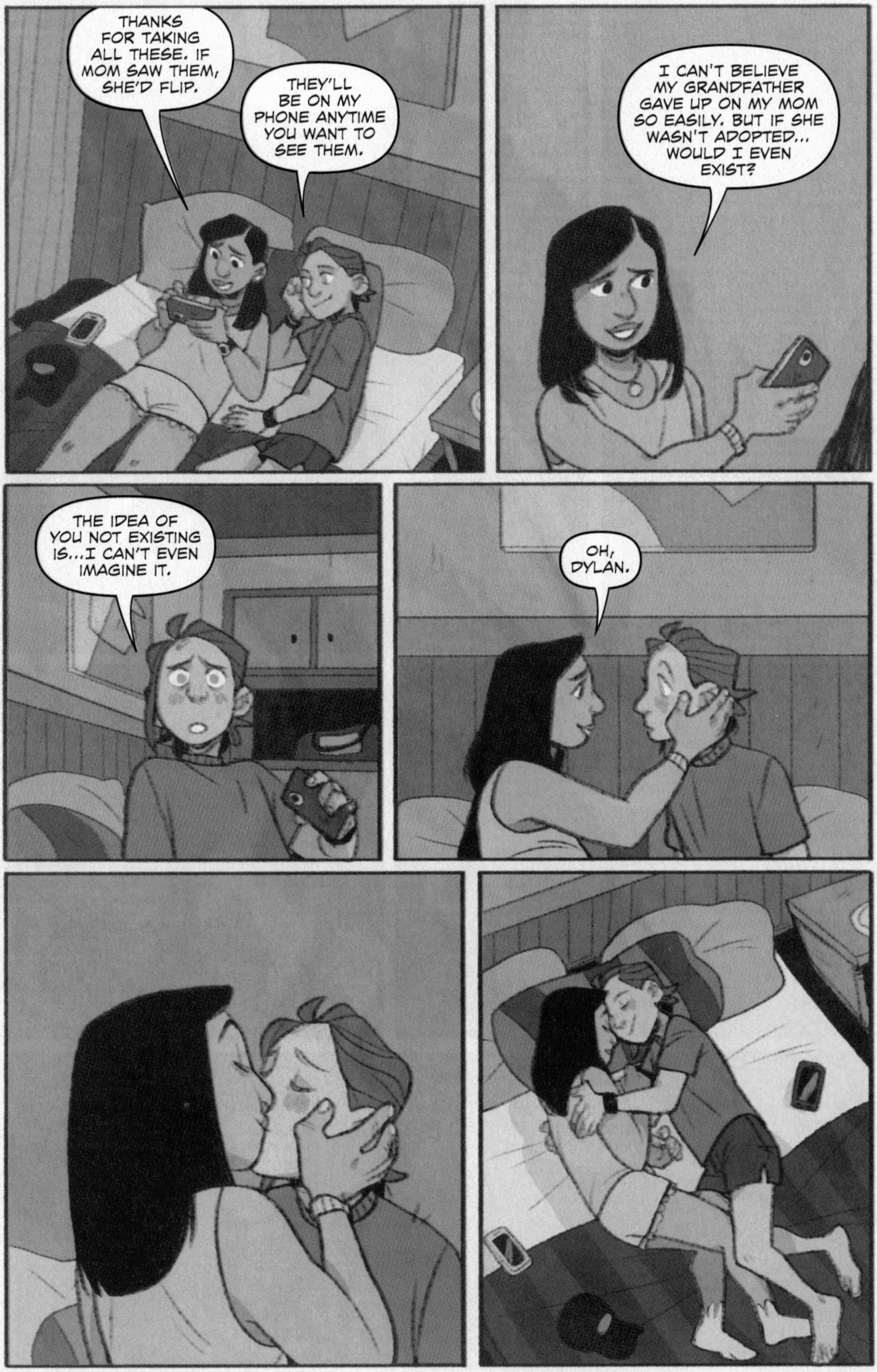
THANKS FOR TAKING ALL THESE. IF MOM SAW THEM, SHE'D FLIP.
THEY'LL BE ON MY PHONE ANYTIME YOU WANT TO SEE THEM.
I CAN'T BELIEVE MY GRANDFATHER GAVE UP ON MY MOM SO EASILY. BUT IF SHE WASN'T ADOPTED... WOULD I EVEN EXIST?
THE IDEA OF YOU NOT EXISTING IS...I CAN'T EVEN IMAGINE IT.
OH, DYLAN.

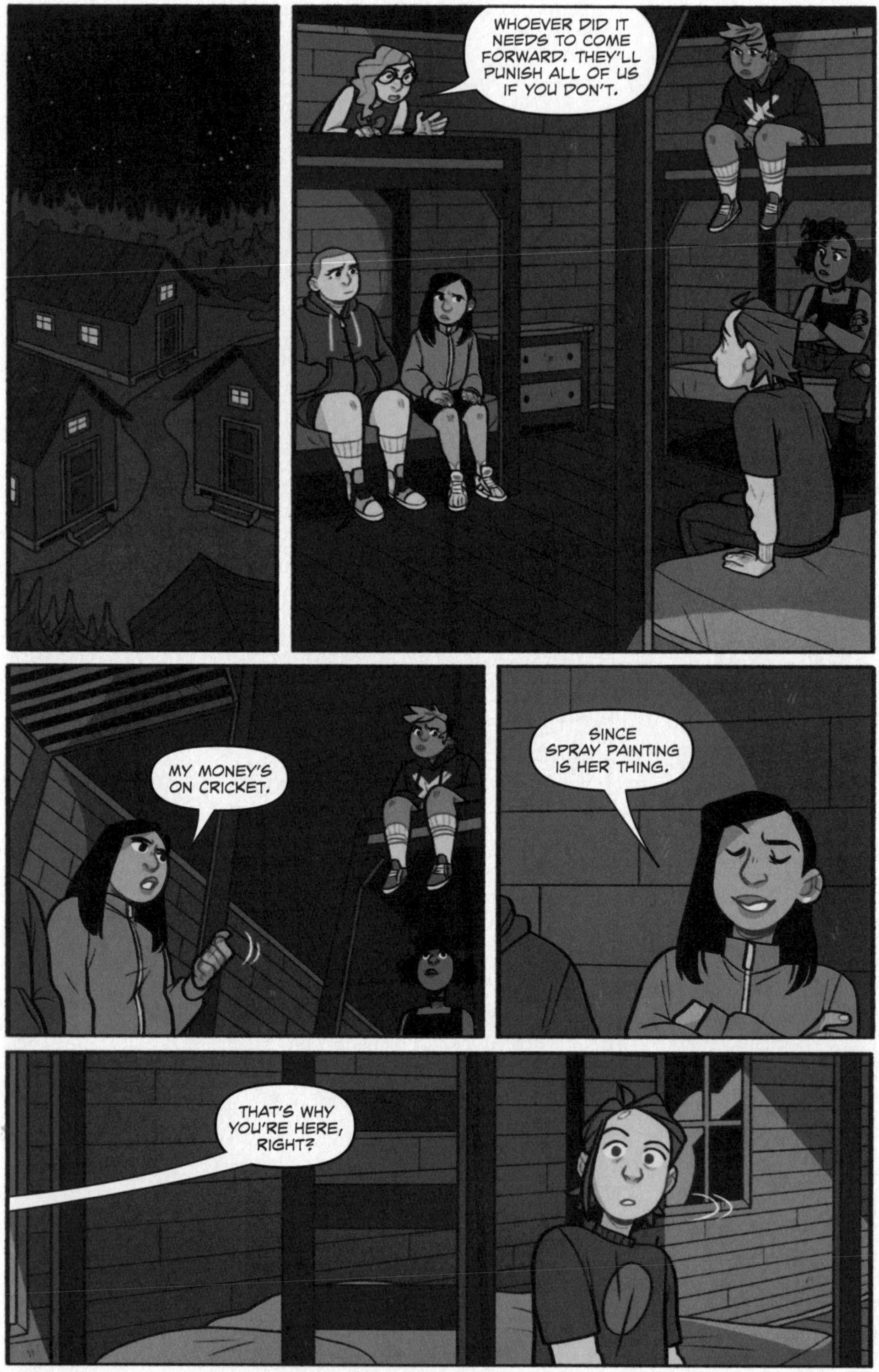
WHOEVER DID IT NEEDS TO COME FORWARD. THEY'LL PUNISH ALL OF US IF YOU DON'T.
MY MONEY'S ON CRICKET.
SINCE SPRAY PAINTING IS HER THING.
THAT'S WHY YOU'RE HERE, RIGHT?

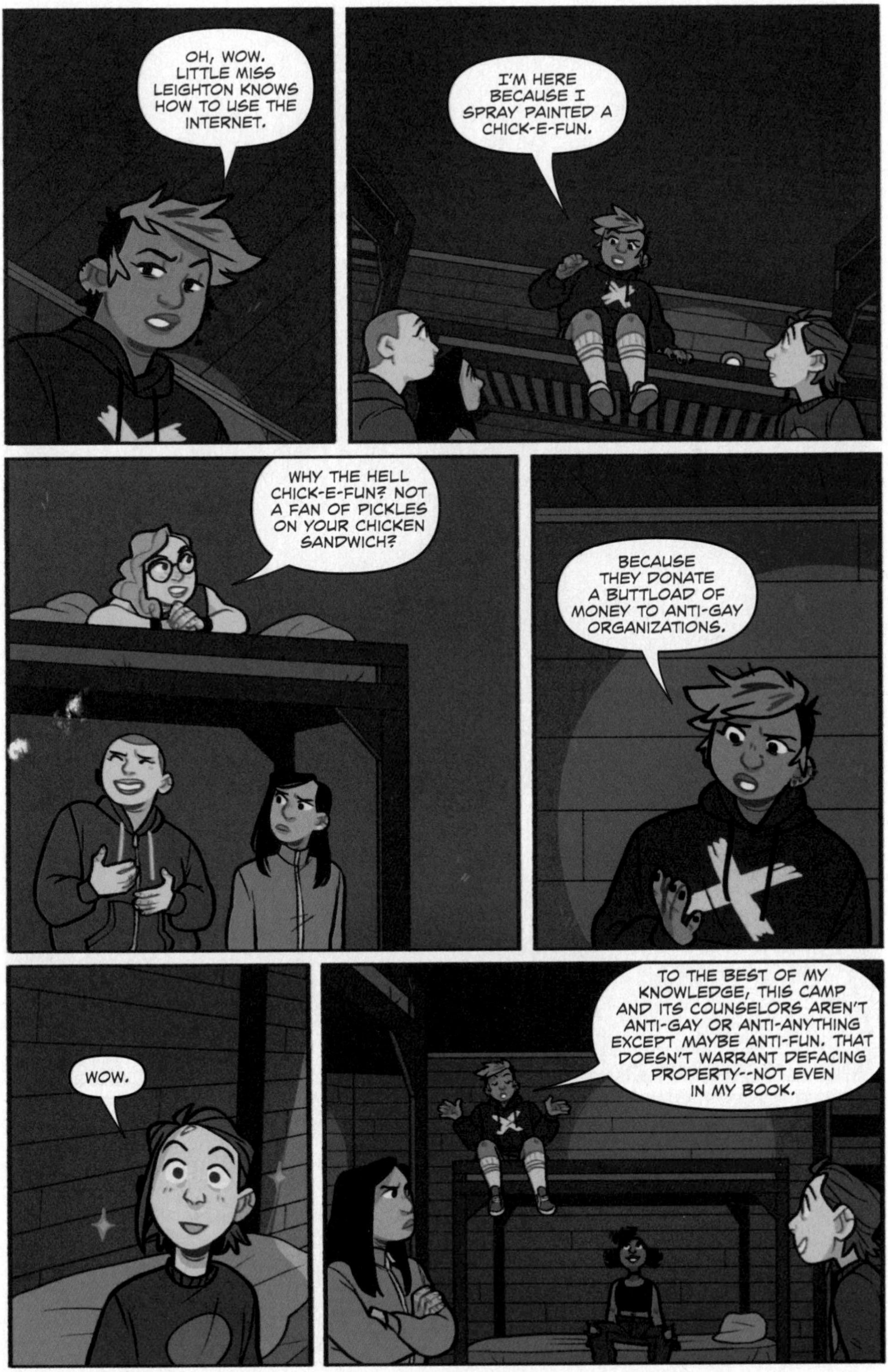
OH, WOW. LITTLE MISS LEIGHTON KNOWS HOW TO USE THE INTERNET.
I'M HERE BECAUSE I SPRAY PAINTED A CHICK-E-FUN.
WHY THE HELL CHICK-E-FUN? NOT A FAN OF PICKLES ON YOUR CHICKEN SANDWICH?
BECAUSE THEY DONATE A BUTTLOAD OF MONEY TO ANTI-GAY ORGANIZATIONS.
WOW.
TO THE BEST OF MY KNOWLEDGE, THIS CAMP AND ITS COUNSELORS AREN'T ANTI-GAY OR ANTI-ANYTHING EXCEPT MAYBE ANTI-FUN. THAT DOESN'T WARRANT DEFACING PROPERTY--NOT EVEN IN MY BOOK.

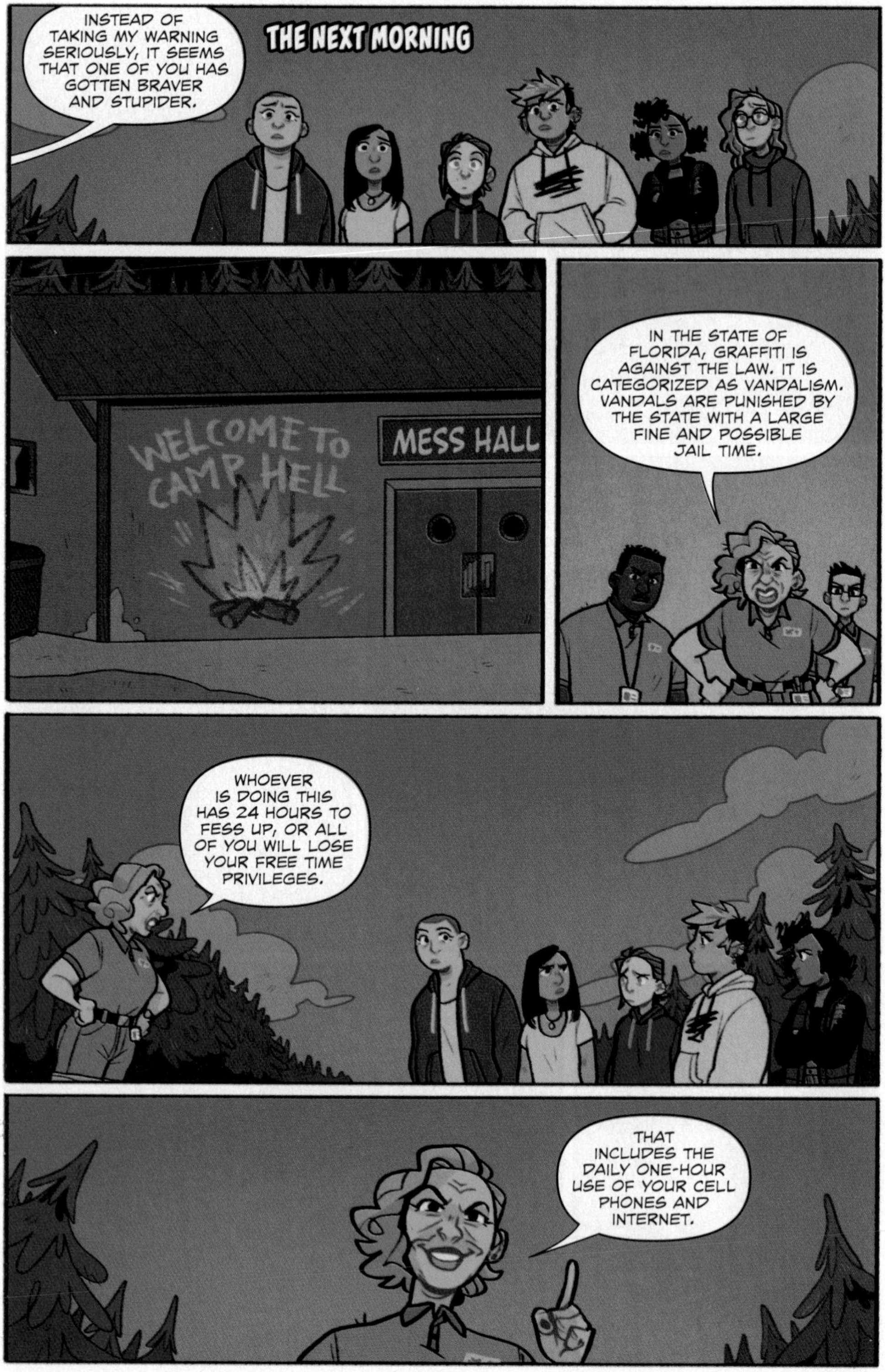
THE NEXT MORNING
INSTEAD OF TAKING MY WARNING SERIOUSLY, IT SEEMS THAT ONE OF YOU HAS GOTTEN BRAVER AND STUPIDER.
WELCOME TO CAMP HELL
MESS HALL
IN THE STATE OF FLORIDA, GRAFFITI IS AGAINST THE LAW. IT IS CATEGORIZED AS VANDALISM. VANDALS ARE PUNISHED BY THE STATE WITH A LARGE FINE AND POSSIBLE JAIL TIME.
WHOEVER IS DOING THIS HAS 24 HOURS TO FESS UP, OR ALL OF YOU WILL LOSE YOUR FREE TIME PRIVILEGES.
THAT INCLUDES THE DAILY ONE-HOUR USE OF YOUR CELL PHONES AND INTERNET.

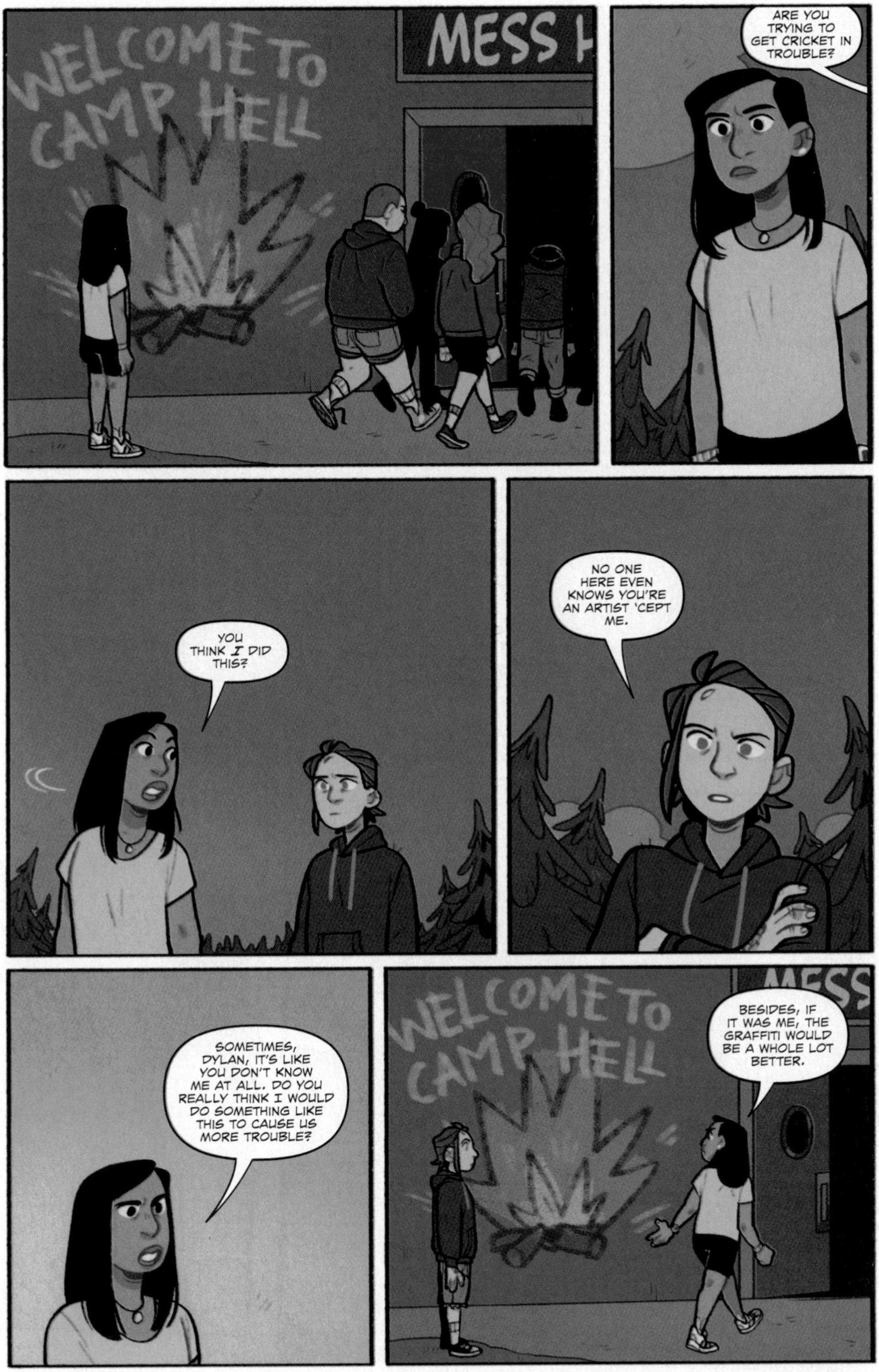

MESS H
WELCOME TO CAMP HELL
ARE YOU TRYING TO GET CRICKET IN TROUBLE?
YOU THINK *I* DID THIS?
NO ONE HERE EVEN KNOWS YOU'RE AN ARTIST 'CEPT ME.
SOMETIMES, DYLAN, IT'S LIKE YOU DON'T KNOW ME AT ALL. DO YOU REALLY THINK I WOULD DO SOMETHING LIKE THIS TO CAUSE US MORE TROUBLE?
WELCOME TO CAMP HELL
MESS
BESIDES, IF IT WAS ME, THE GRAFFITI WOULD BE A WHOLE LOT BETTER.

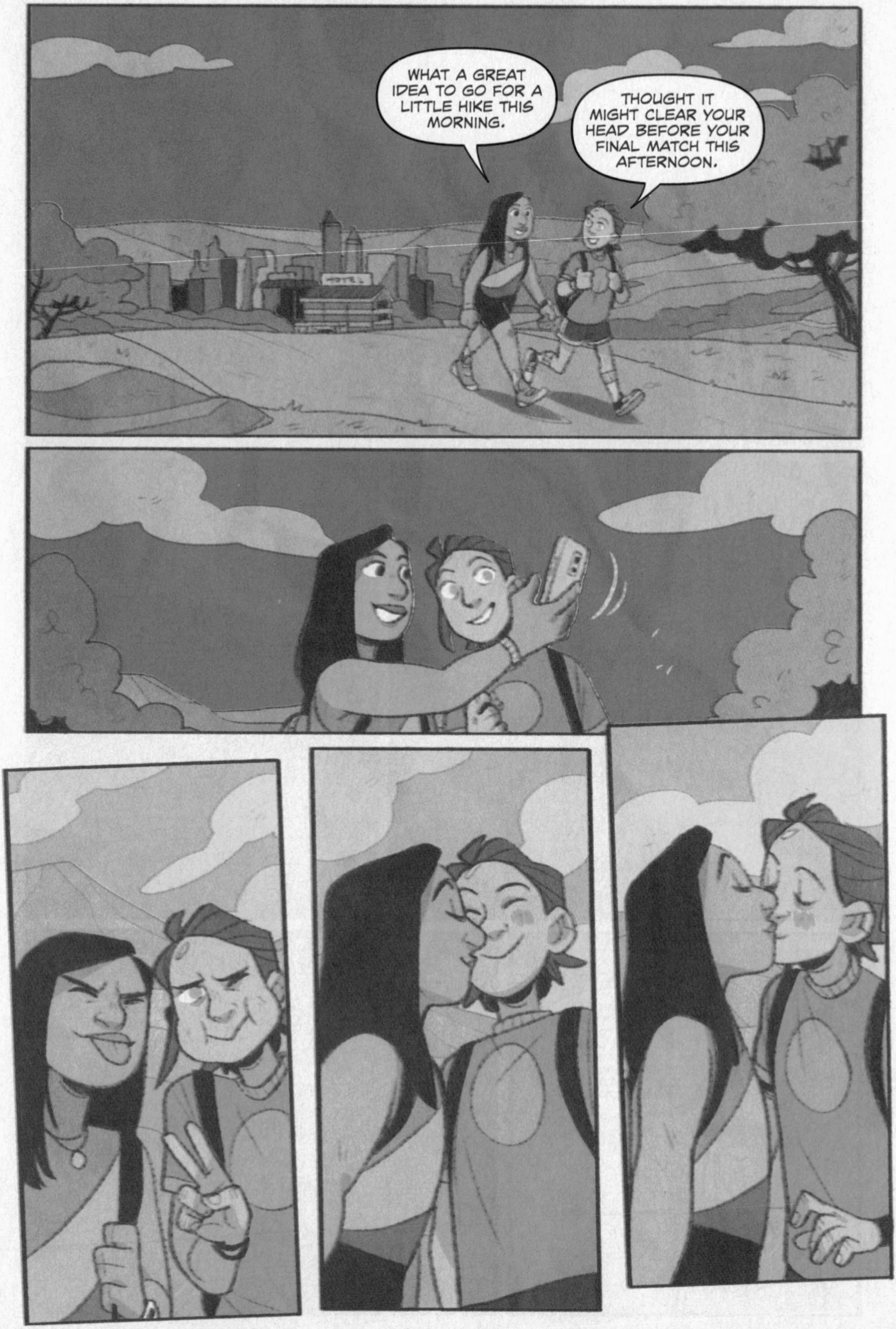
WHAT A GREAT IDEA TO GO FOR A LITTLE HIKE THIS MORNING.
THOUGHT IT MIGHT CLEAR YOUR HEAD BEFORE YOUR FINAL MATCH THIS AFTERNOON.

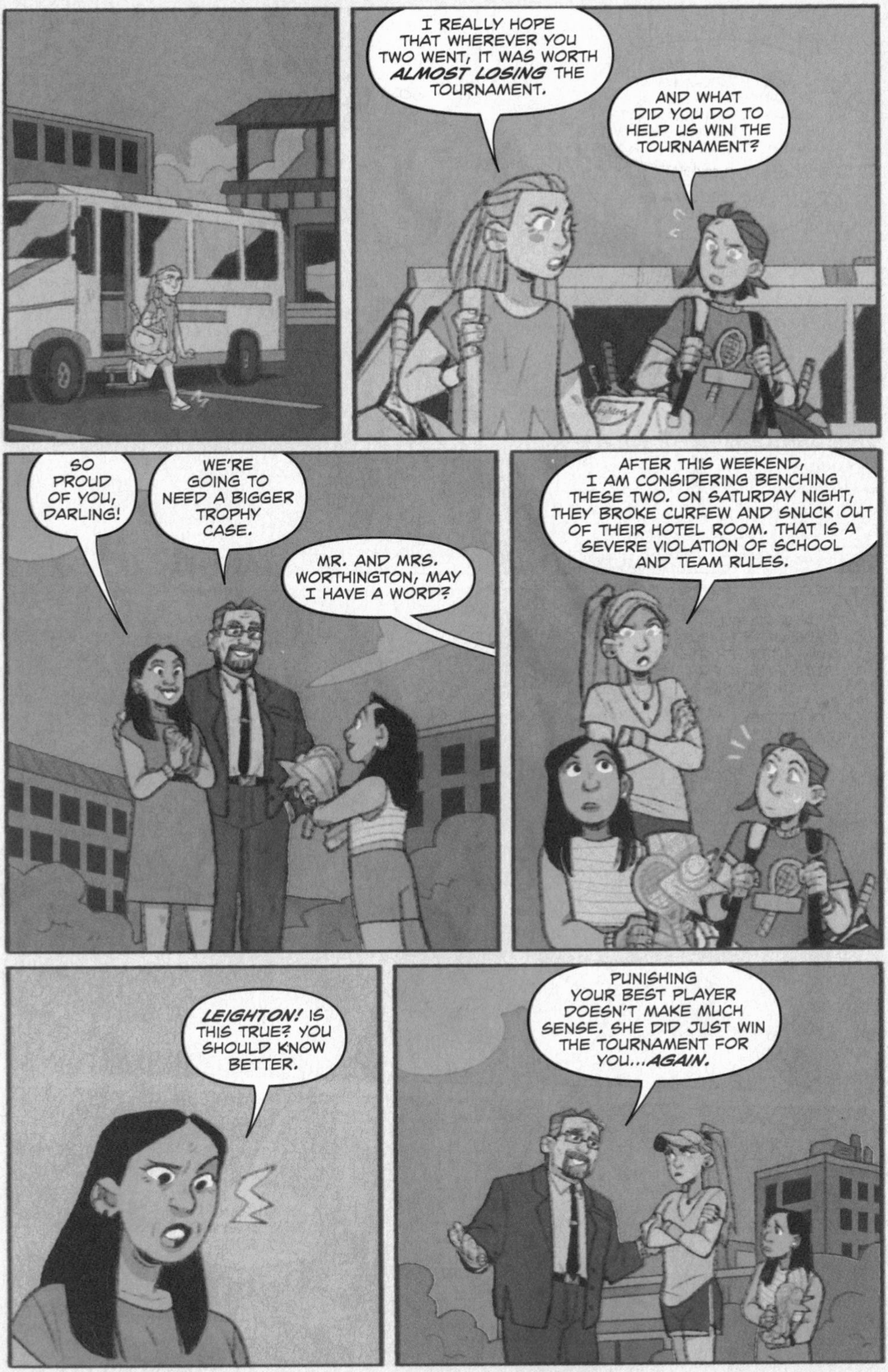
I REALLY HOPE THAT WHEREVER YOU TWO WENT, IT WAS WORTH *ALMOST LOSING* THE TOURNAMENT.
AND WHAT DID YOU DO TO HELP US WIN THE TOURNAMENT?
SO PROUD OF YOU, DARLING!
WE'RE GOING TO NEED A BIGGER TROPHY CASE.
MR. AND MRS. WORTHINGTON, MAY I HAVE A WORD?
AFTER THIS WEEKEND, I AM CONSIDERING BENCHING THESE TWO. ON SATURDAY NIGHT, THEY BROKE CURFEW AND SNUCK OUT OF THEIR HOTEL ROOM. THAT IS A SEVERE VIOLATION OF SCHOOL AND TEAM RULES.
LEIGHTON! IS THIS TRUE? YOU SHOULD KNOW BETTER.
PUNISHING YOUR BEST PLAYER DOESN'T MAKE MUCH SENSE. SHE DID JUST WIN THE TOURNAMENT FOR YOU...*AGAIN*.

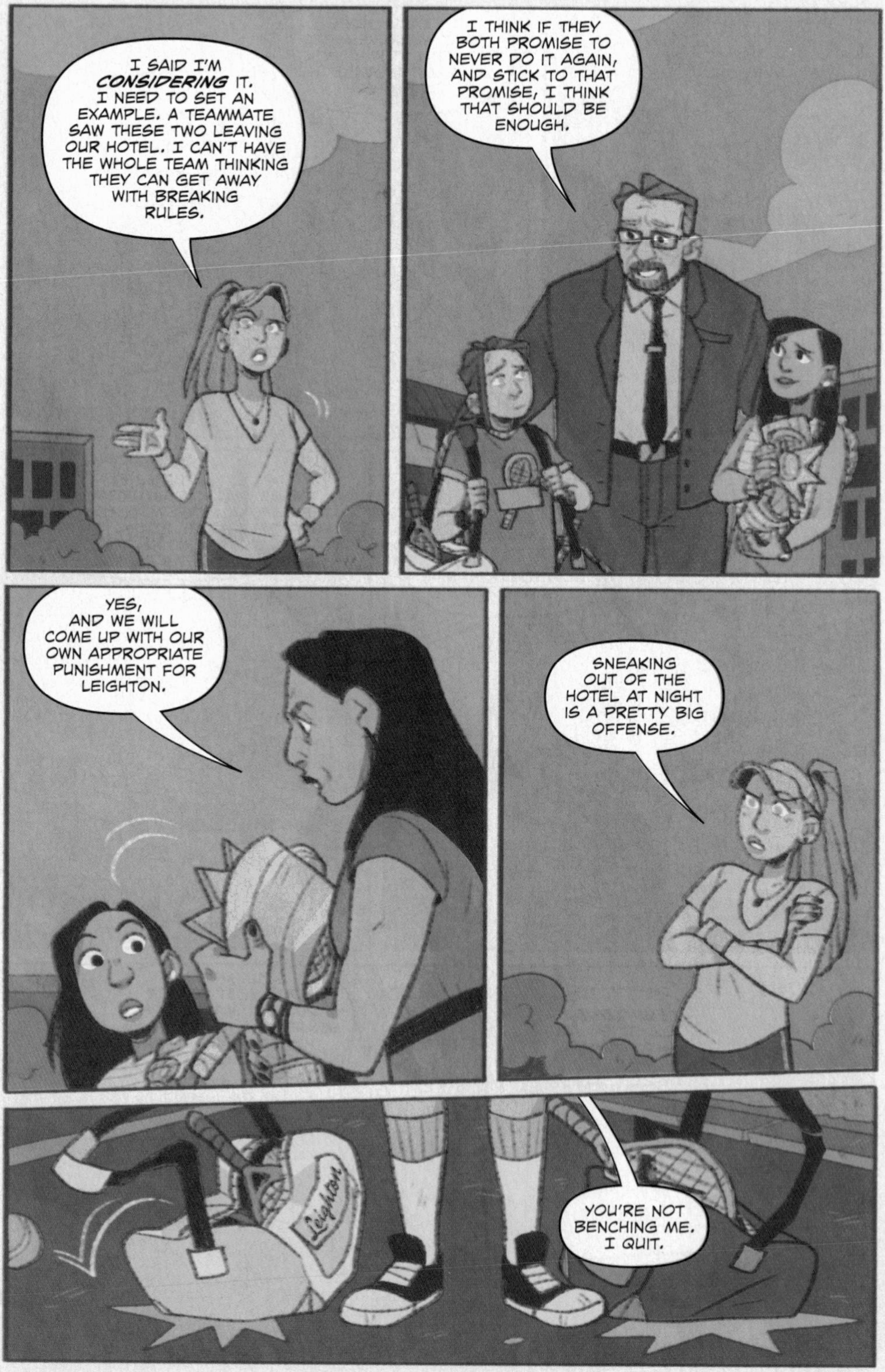
I SAID I'M *CONSIDERING* IT. I NEED TO SET AN EXAMPLE. A TEAMMATE SAW THESE TWO LEAVING OUR HOTEL. I CAN'T HAVE THE WHOLE TEAM THINKING THEY CAN GET AWAY WITH BREAKING RULES.
I THINK IF THEY BOTH PROMISE TO NEVER DO IT AGAIN, AND STICK TO THAT PROMISE, I THINK THAT SHOULD BE ENOUGH.
YES, AND WE WILL COME UP WITH OUR OWN APPROPRIATE PUNISHMENT FOR LEIGHTON.
SNEAKING OUT OF THE HOTEL AT NIGHT IS A PRETTY BIG OFFENSE.
Leighton
YOU'RE NOT BENCHING ME. I QUIT.

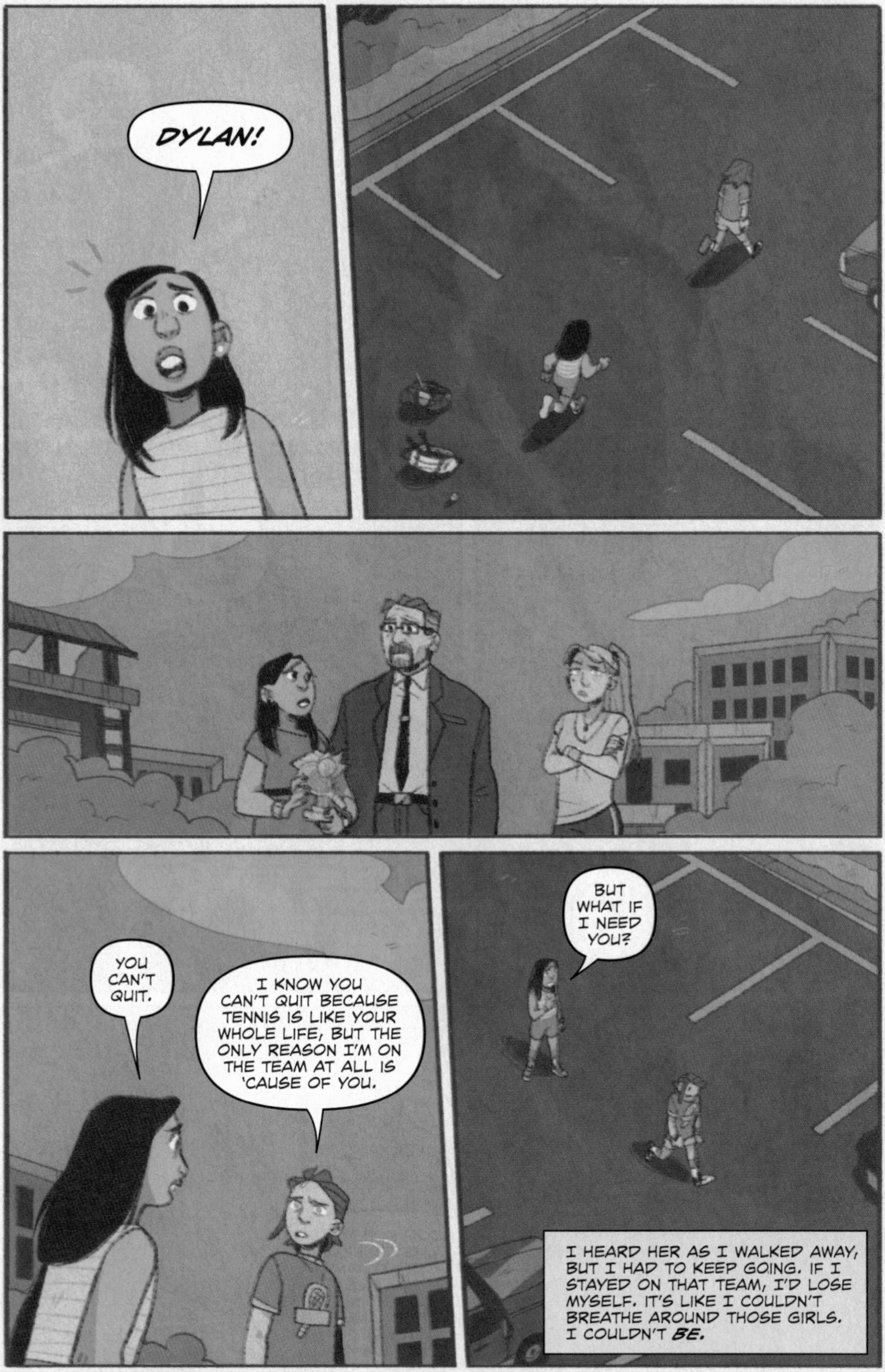
DYLAN!
YOU CAN'T QUIT.
I KNOW YOU CAN'T QUIT BECAUSE TENNIS IS LIKE YOUR WHOLE LIFE, BUT THE ONLY REASON I'M ON THE TEAM AT ALL IS 'CAUSE OF YOU.
BUT WHAT IF I NEED YOU?
I HEARD HER AS I WALKED AWAY, BUT I HAD TO KEEP GOING. IF I STAYED ON THAT TEAM, I'D LOSE MYSELF. IT'S LIKE I COULDN'T BREATHE AROUND THOSE GIRLS. I COULDN'T *BE.*

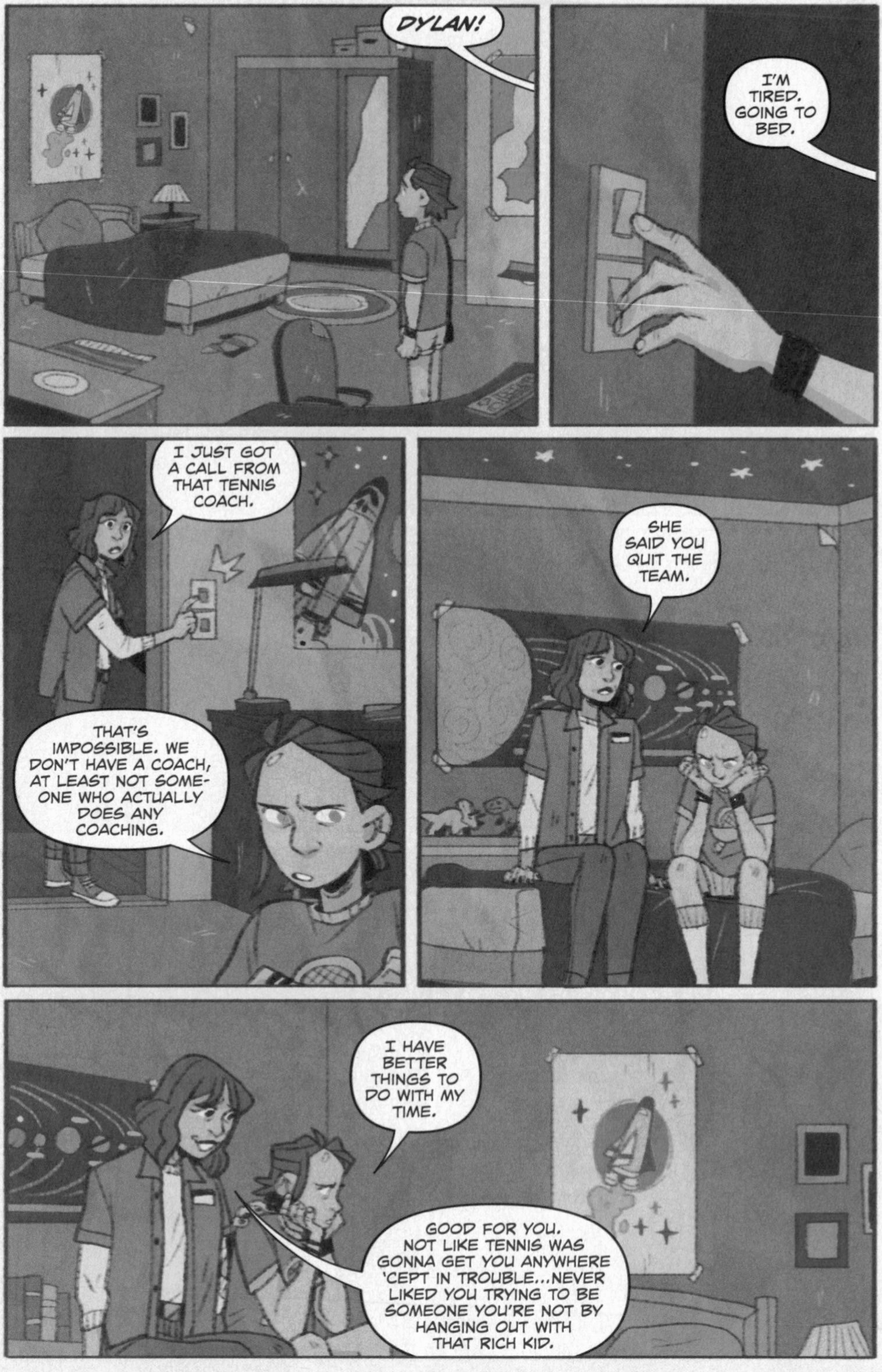
DYLAN!
I'M TIRED. GOING TO BED.
I JUST GOT A CALL FROM THAT TENNIS COACH.
THAT'S IMPOSSIBLE. WE DON'T HAVE A COACH, AT LEAST NOT SOME-ONE WHO ACTUALLY DOES ANY COACHING.
SHE SAID YOU QUIT THE TEAM.
I HAVE BETTER THINGS TO DO WITH MY TIME.
GOOD FOR YOU. NOT LIKE TENNIS WAS GONNA GET YOU ANYWHERE 'CEPT IN TROUBLE...NEVER LIKED YOU TRYING TO BE SOMEONE YOU'RE NOT BY HANGING OUT WITH THAT RICH KID.

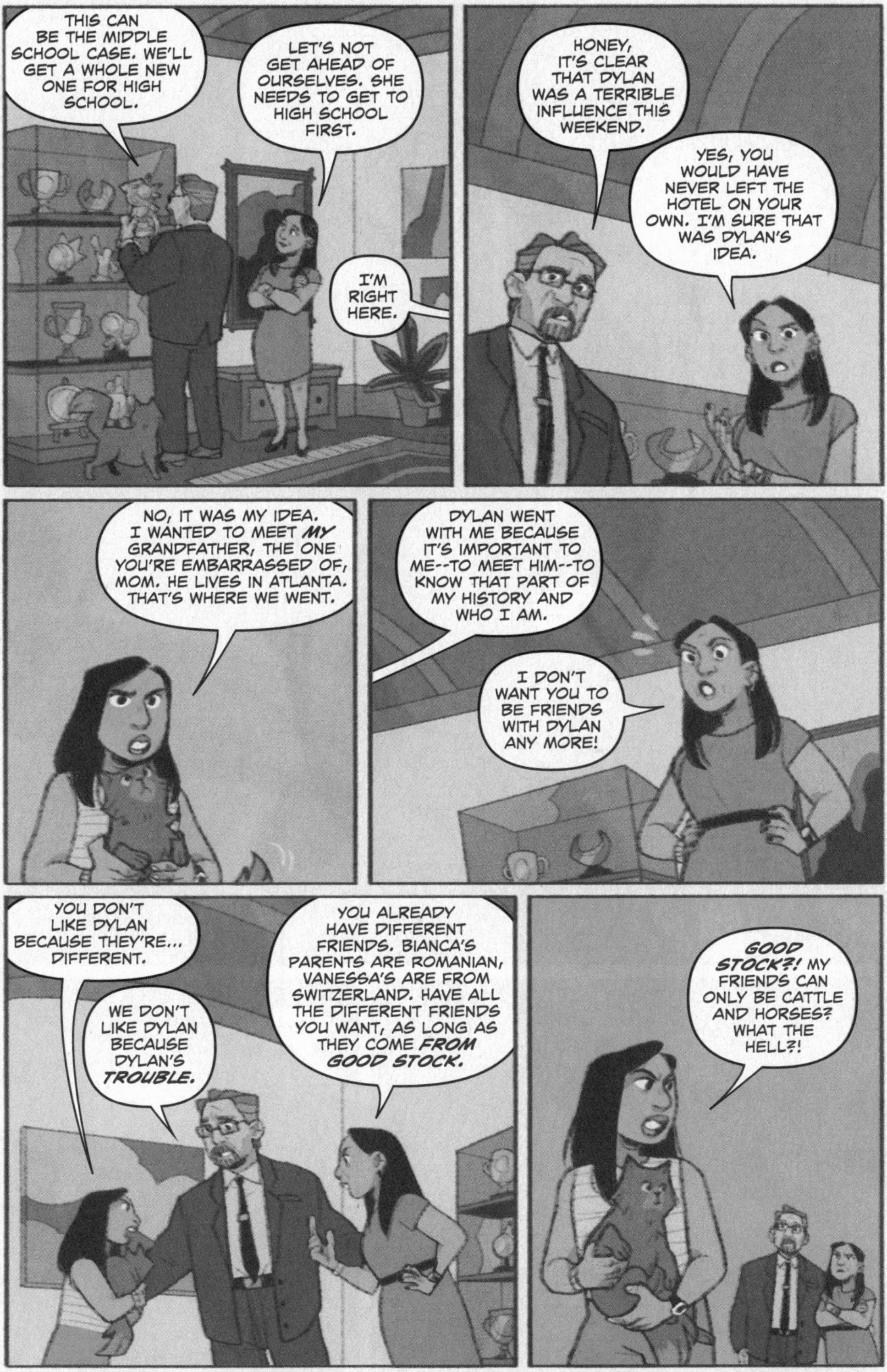

THIS CAN BE THE MIDDLE SCHOOL CASE. WE'LL GET A WHOLE NEW ONE FOR HIGH SCHOOL.
LET'S NOT GET AHEAD OF OURSELVES. SHE NEEDS TO GET TO HIGH SCHOOL FIRST.
I'M RIGHT HERE.
HONEY, IT'S CLEAR THAT DYLAN WAS A TERRIBLE INFLUENCE THIS WEEKEND.
YES, YOU WOULD HAVE NEVER LEFT THE HOTEL ON YOUR OWN. I'M SURE THAT WAS DYLAN'S IDEA.
NO, IT WAS MY IDEA. I WANTED TO MEET *MY* GRANDFATHER, THE ONE YOU'RE EMBARRASSED OF, MOM. HE LIVES IN ATLANTA. THAT'S WHERE WE WENT.
DYLAN WENT WITH ME BECAUSE IT'S IMPORTANT TO ME--TO MEET HIM--TO KNOW THAT PART OF MY HISTORY AND WHO I AM.
I DON'T WANT YOU TO BE FRIENDS WITH DYLAN ANY MORE!
YOU DON'T LIKE DYLAN BECAUSE THEY'RE... DIFFERENT.
WE DON'T LIKE DYLAN BECAUSE DYLAN'S *TROUBLE.*
YOU ALREADY HAVE DIFFERENT FRIENDS. BIANCA'S PARENTS ARE ROMANIAN, VANESSA'S ARE FROM SWITZERLAND. HAVE ALL THE DIFFERENT FRIENDS YOU WANT, AS LONG AS THEY COME *FROM GOOD STOCK.*
GOOD STOCK?! MY FRIENDS CAN ONLY BE CATTLE AND HORSES? WHAT THE HELL?!

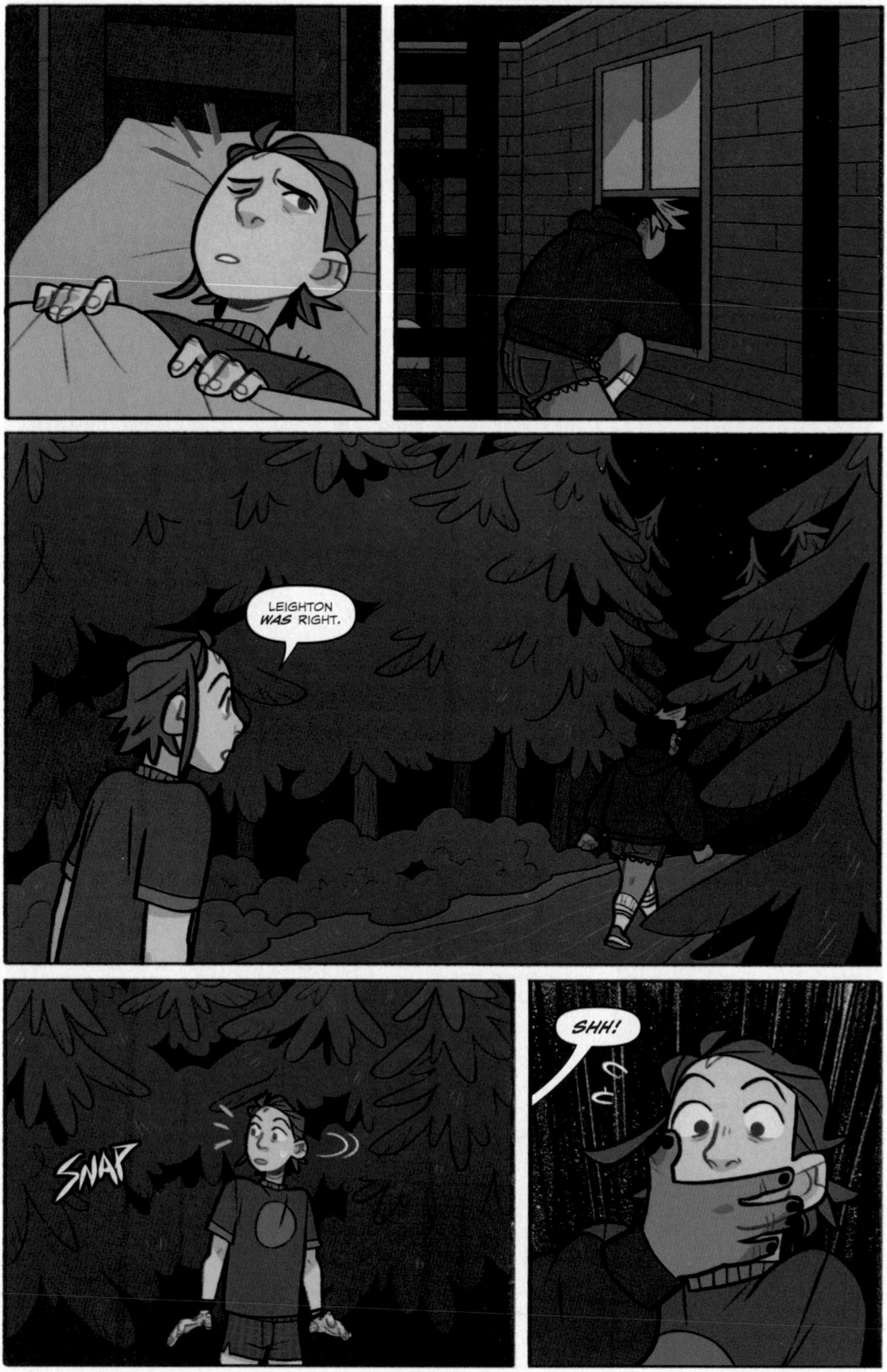
LEIGHTON WAS RIGHT.
SNAP
SHH!

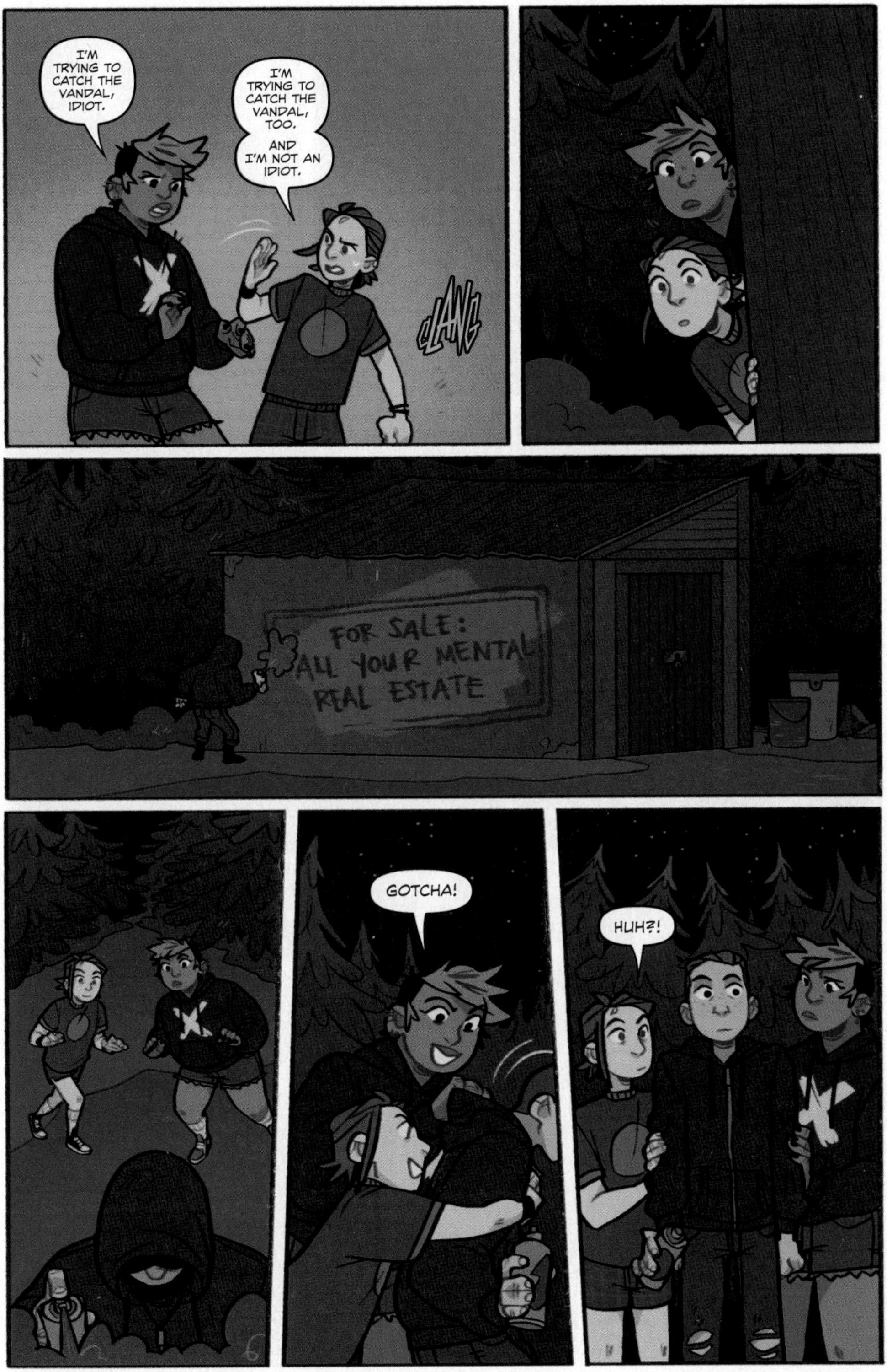
I'M TRYING TO CATCH THE VANDAL, IDIOT.
I'M TRYING TO CATCH THE VANDAL, TOO.
AND I'M NOT AN IDIOT.
CLANG
FOR SALE: ALL YOUR MENTAL REAL ESTATE
GOTCHA!
HUH?!

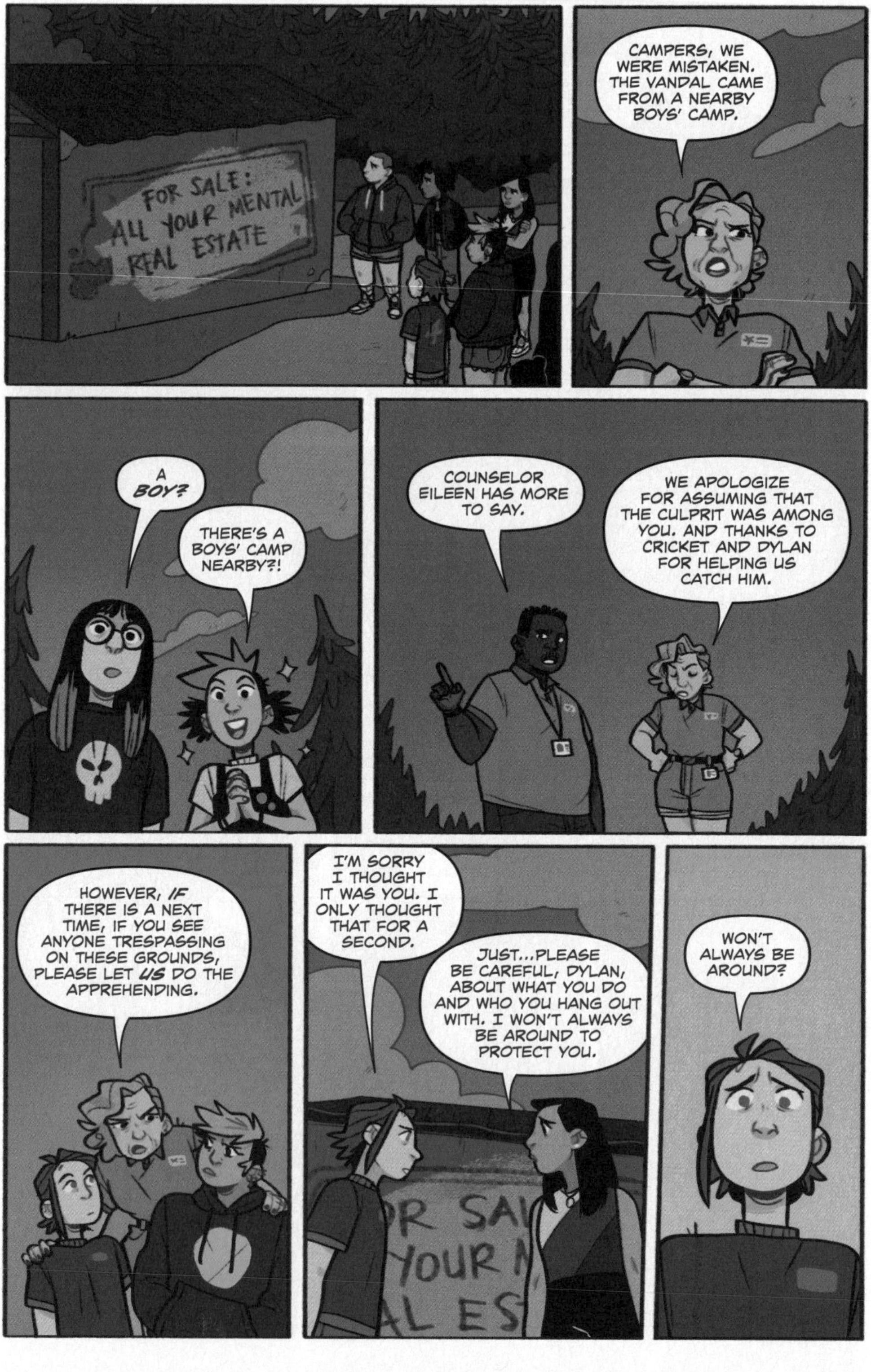
FOR SALE: ALL YOUR MENTAL REAL ESTATE
CAMPERS, WE WERE MISTAKEN. THE VANDAL CAME FROM A NEARBY BOYS' CAMP.
A *BOY*?
THERE'S A BOYS' CAMP NEARBY?!
COUNSELOR EILEEN HAS MORE TO SAY.
WE APOLOGIZE FOR ASSUMING THAT THE CULPRIT WAS AMONG YOU. AND THANKS TO CRICKET AND DYLAN FOR HELPING US CATCH HIM.
HOWEVER, *IF* THERE IS A NEXT TIME, IF YOU SEE ANYONE TRESPASSING ON THESE GROUNDS, PLEASE LET *US* DO THE APPREHENDING.
I'M SORRY I THOUGHT IT WAS YOU. I ONLY THOUGHT THAT FOR A SECOND.
JUST...PLEASE BE CAREFUL, DYLAN, ABOUT WHAT YOU DO AND WHO YOU HANG OUT WITH. I WON'T ALWAYS BE AROUND TO PROTECT YOU.
WON'T ALWAYS BE AROUND?

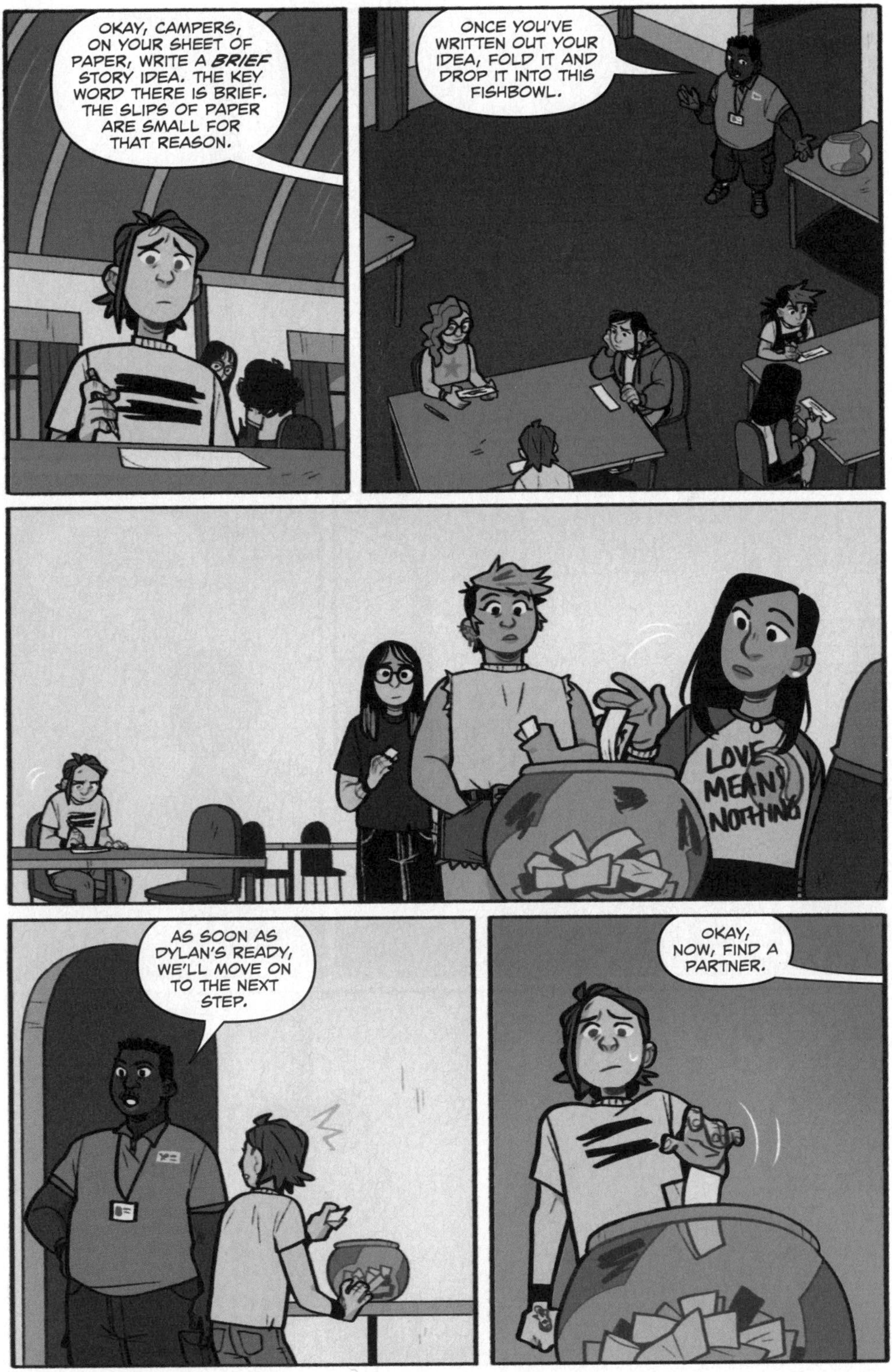
OKAY, CAMPERS, ON YOUR SHEET OF PAPER, WRITE A *BRIEF* STORY IDEA. THE KEY WORD THERE IS BRIEF. THE SLIPS OF PAPER ARE SMALL FOR THAT REASON.
ONCE YOU'VE WRITTEN OUT YOUR IDEA, FOLD IT AND DROP IT INTO THIS FISHBOWL.
LOVE MEANS NOTHING
AS SOON AS DYLAN'S READY, WE'LL MOVE ON TO THE NEXT STEP.
OKAY, NOW, FIND A PARTNER.

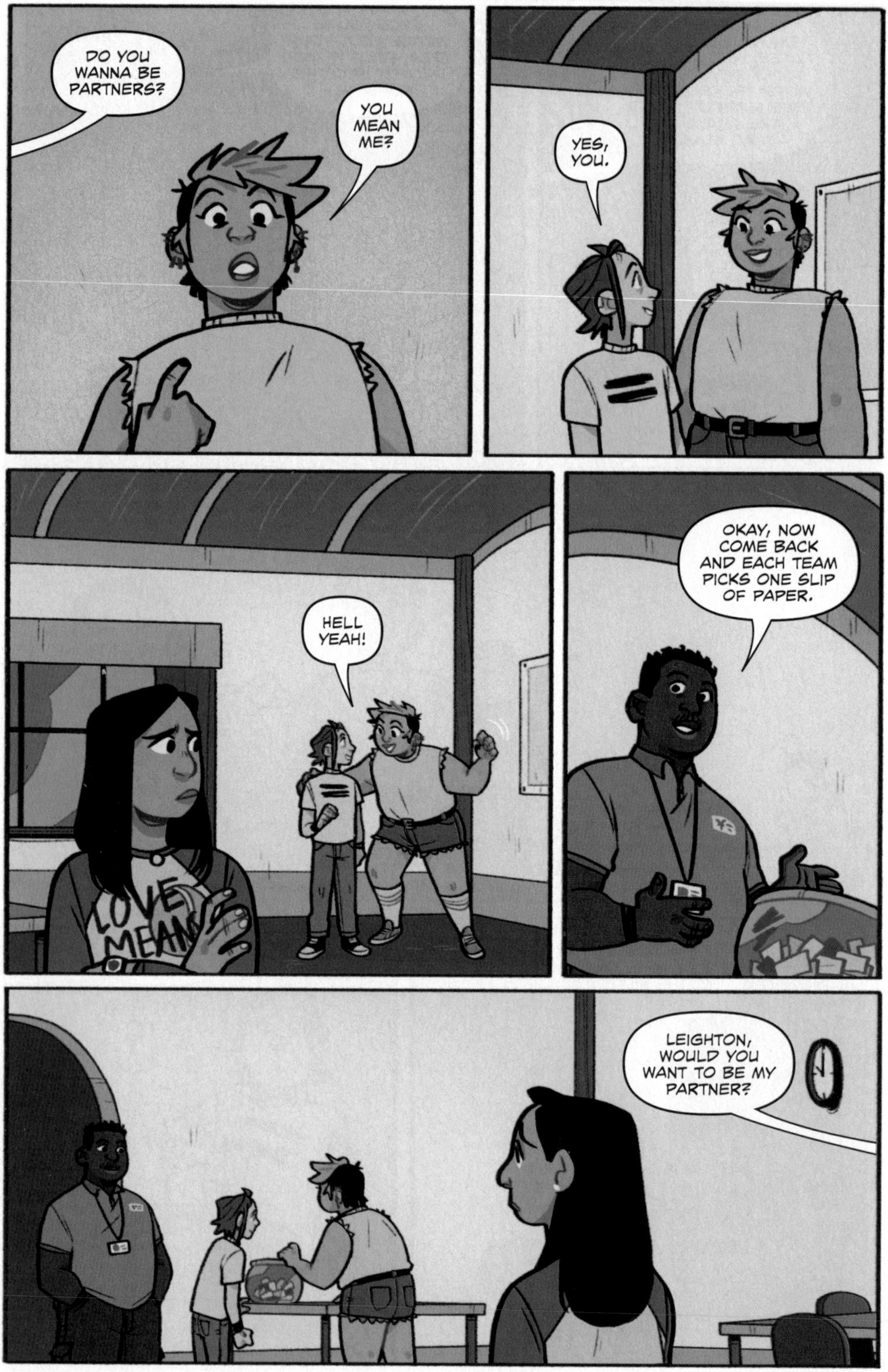
DO YOU WANNA BE PARTNERS?
YOU MEAN ME?
YES, YOU.
HELL YEAH!
LOVE MEANS
OKAY, NOW COME BACK AND EACH TEAM PICKS ONE SLIP OF PAPER.
LEIGHTON, WOULD YOU WANT TO BE MY PARTNER?

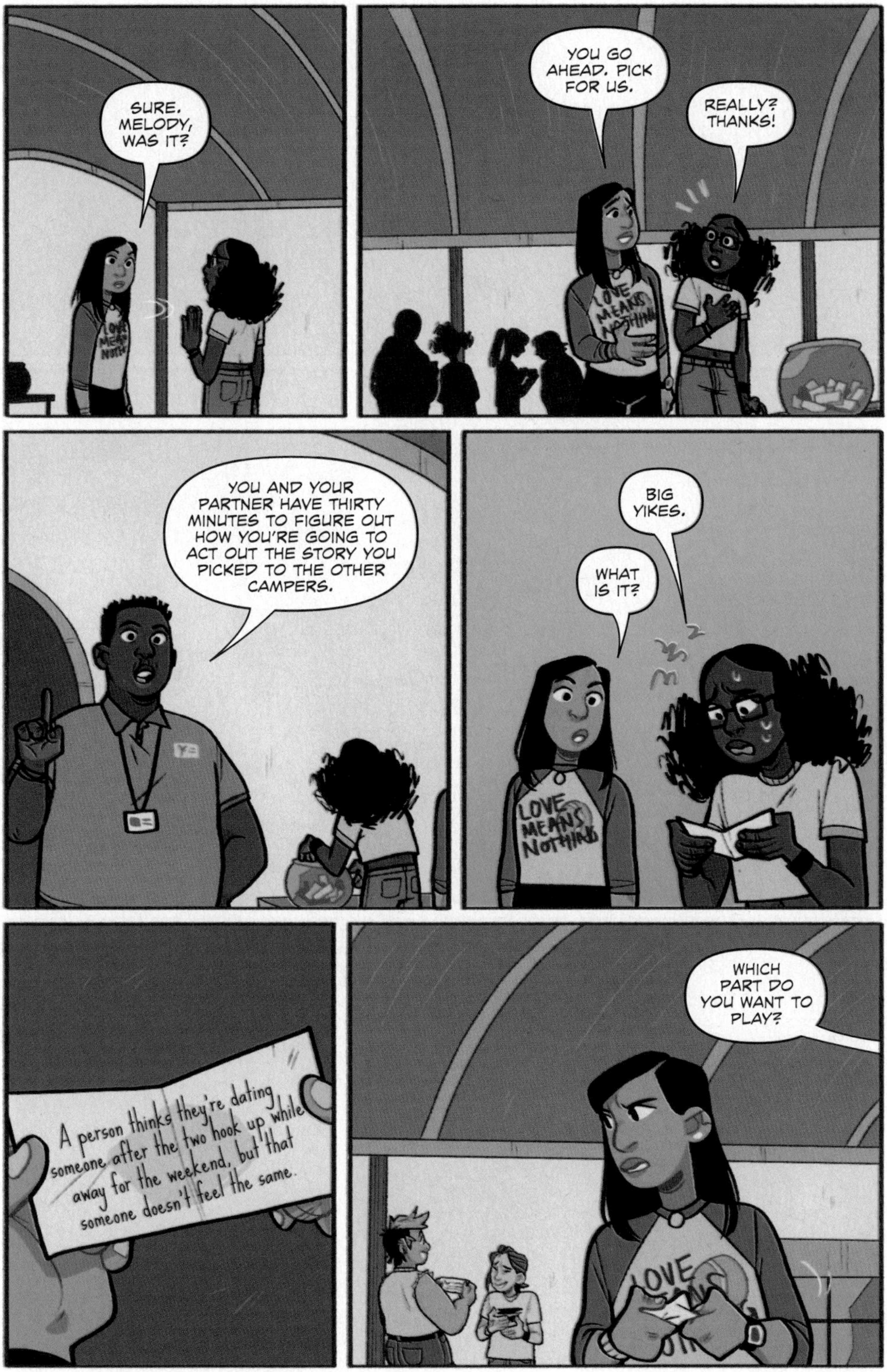
SURE. MELODY, WAS IT?
YOU GO AHEAD. PICK FOR US.
REALLY? THANKS!
YOU AND YOUR PARTNER HAVE THIRTY MINUTES TO FIGURE OUT HOW YOU'RE GOING TO ACT OUT THE STORY YOU PICKED TO THE OTHER CAMPERS.
BIG YIKES.
WHAT IS IT?
A person thinks they're dating someone after the two hook up while away for the weekend, but that someone doesn't feel the same.
WHICH PART DO YOU WANT TO PLAY?

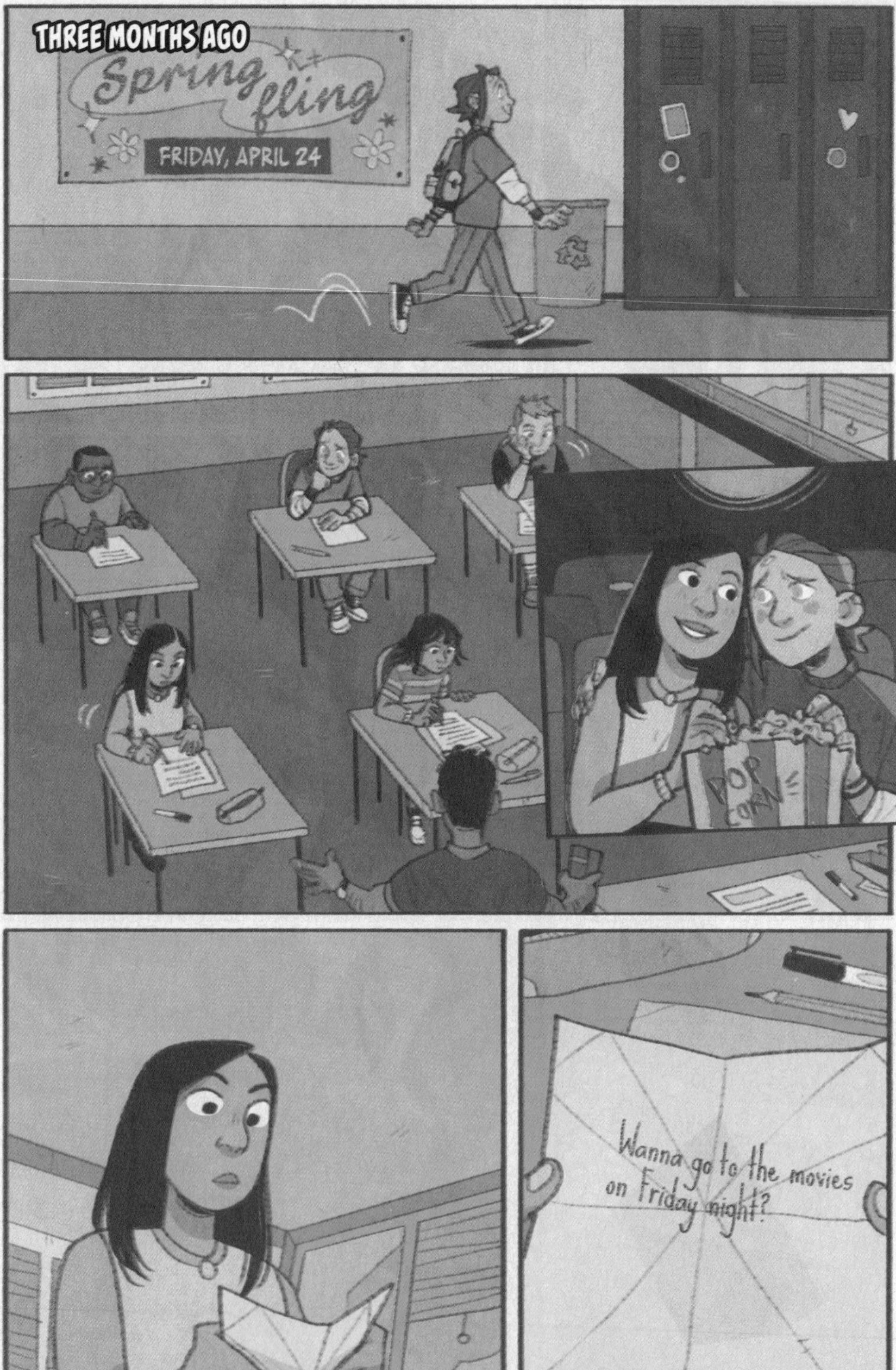
THREE MONTHS AGO
Spring fling
FRIDAY, APRIL 24
POP CORN
Wanna go to the movies on Friday night?

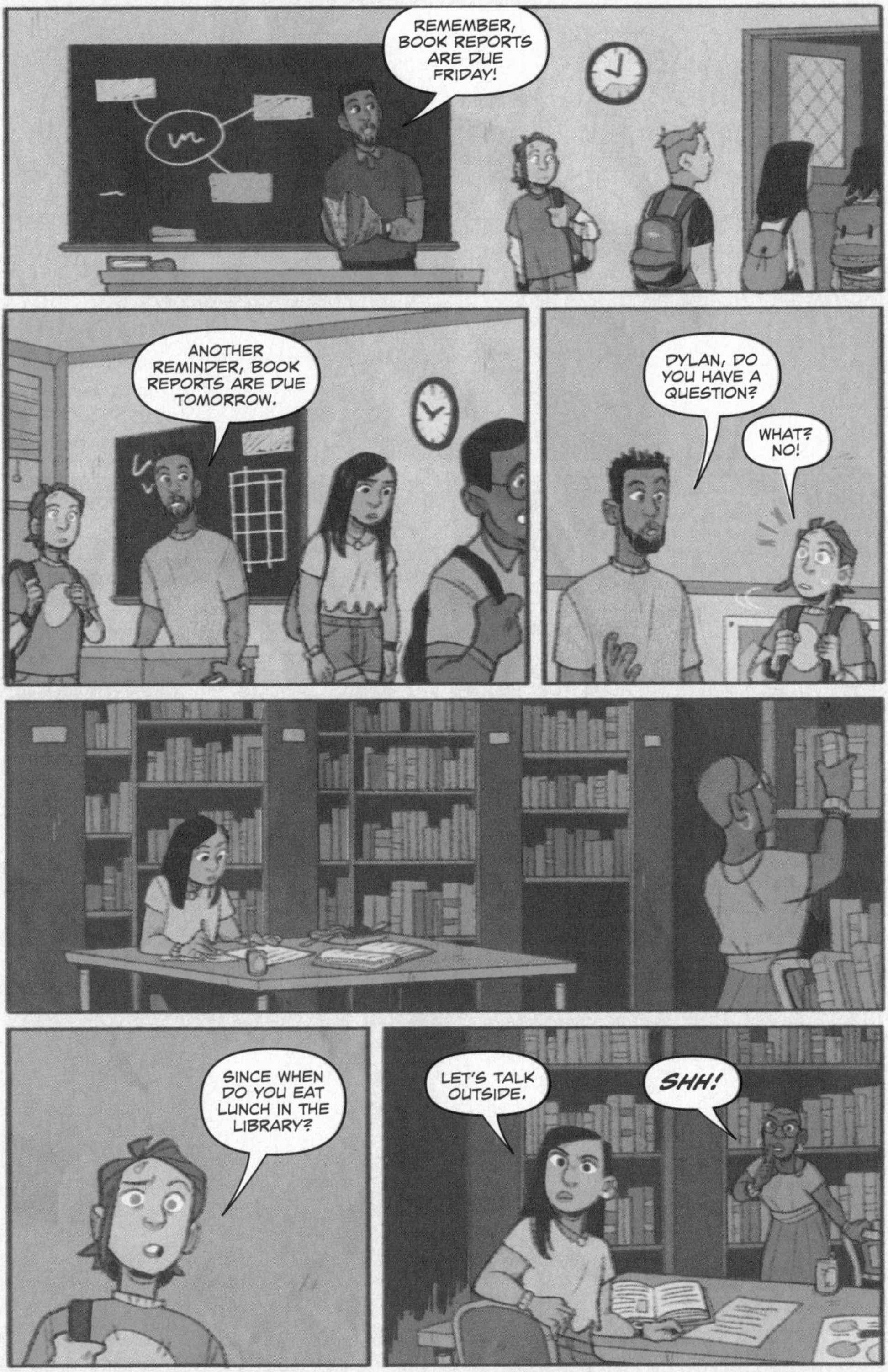
REMEMBER, BOOK REPORTS ARE DUE FRIDAY!
ANOTHER REMINDER, BOOK REPORTS ARE DUE TOMORROW.
DYLAN, DO YOU HAVE A QUESTION?
WHAT? NO!
SINCE WHEN DO YOU EAT LUNCH IN THE LIBRARY?
LET'S TALK OUTSIDE.
SHH!

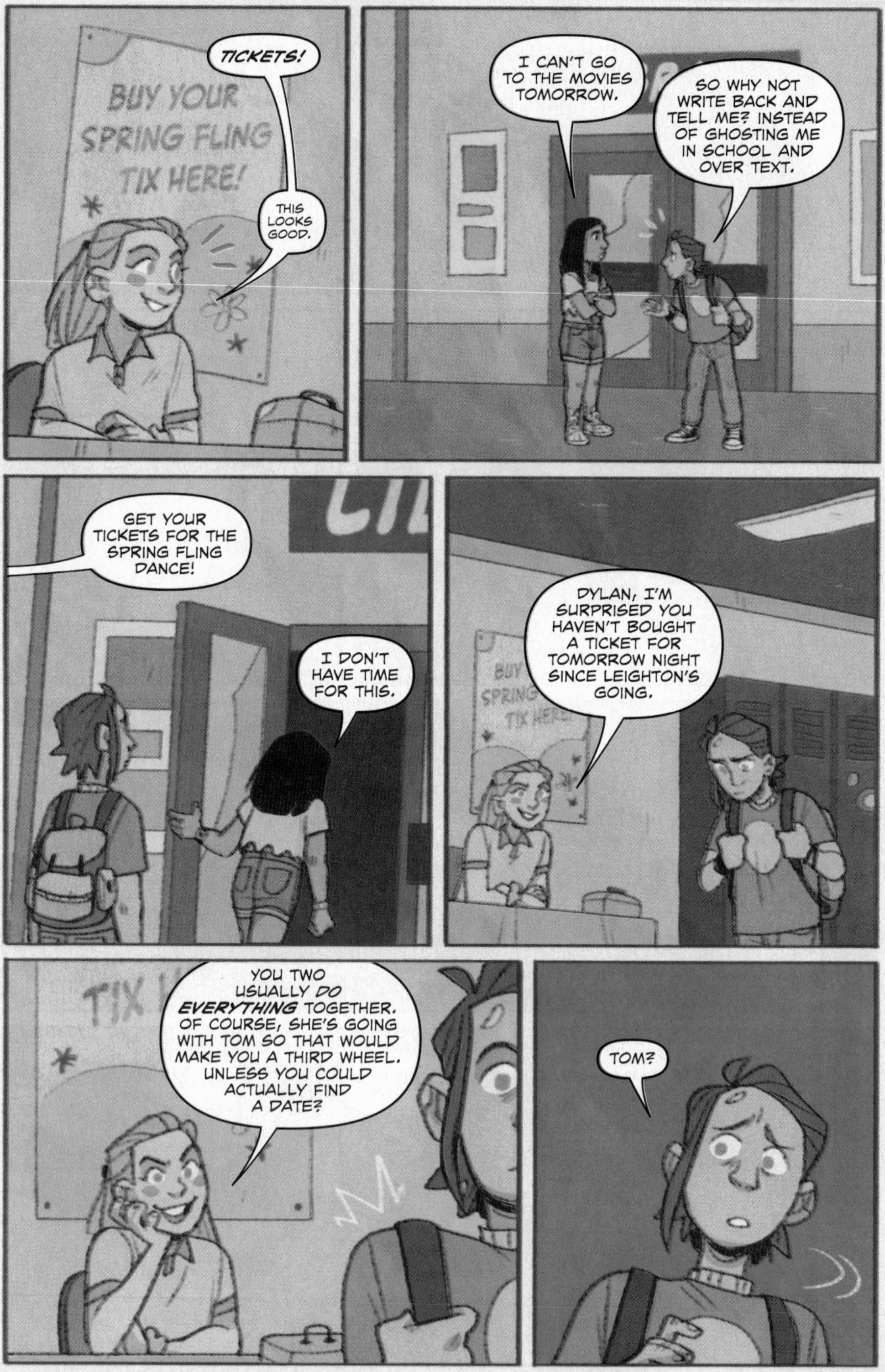

BUY YOUR SPRING FLING TIX HERE!
TICKETS!
THIS LOOKS GOOD.
I CAN'T GO TO THE MOVIES TOMORROW.
SO WHY NOT WRITE BACK AND TELL ME? INSTEAD OF GHOSTING ME IN SCHOOL AND OVER TEXT.
GET YOUR TICKETS FOR THE SPRING FLING DANCE!
I DON'T HAVE TIME FOR THIS.
DYLAN, I'M SURPRISED YOU HAVEN'T BOUGHT A TICKET FOR TOMORROW NIGHT SINCE LEIGHTON'S GOING.
YOU TWO USUALLY *DO* ***EVERYTHING*** TOGETHER. OF COURSE, SHE'S GOING WITH TOM SO THAT WOULD MAKE YOU A THIRD WHEEL. UNLESS YOU COULD ACTUALLY FIND A DATE?
TOM?

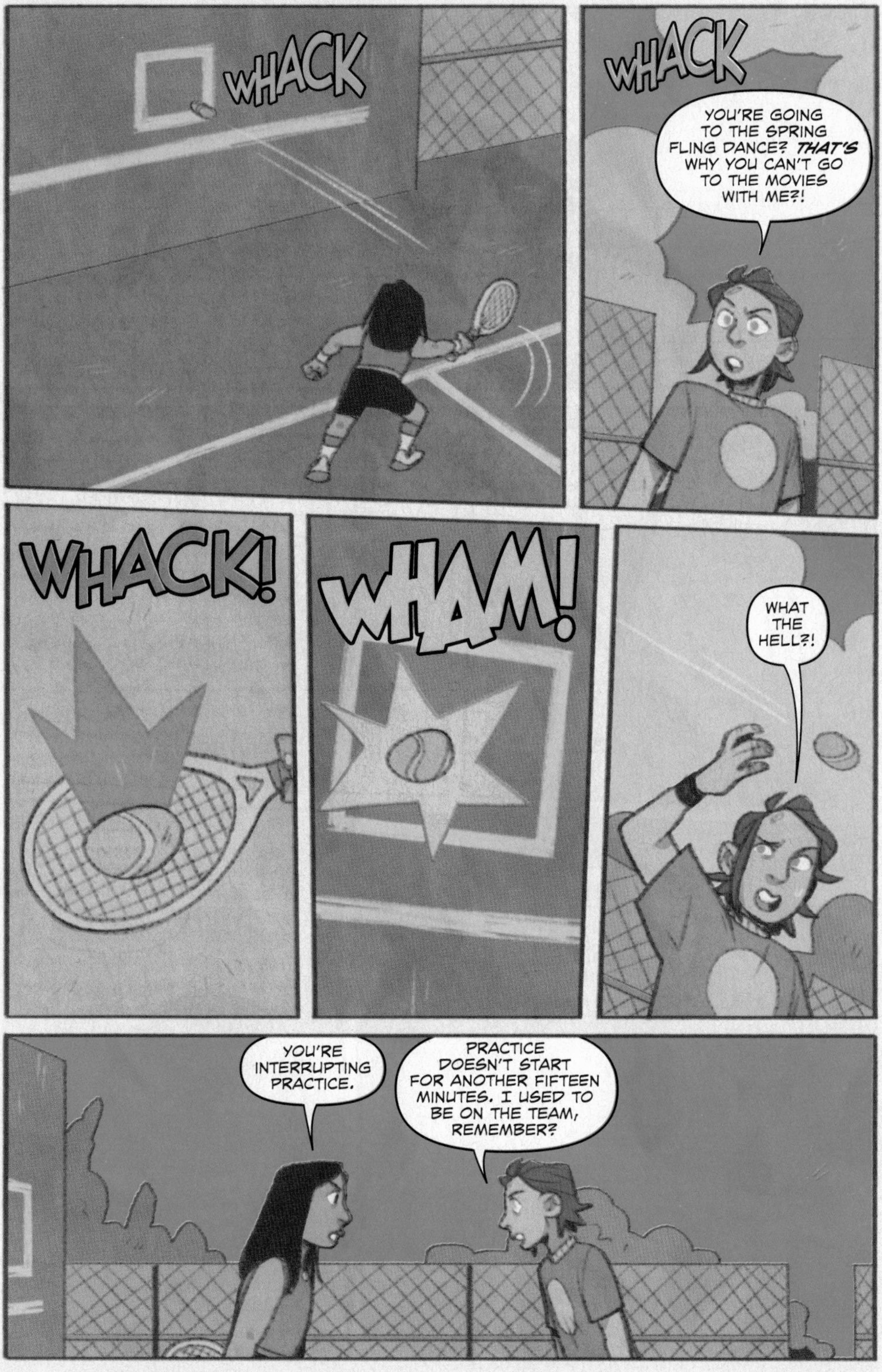
WHACK
WHACK
YOU'RE GOING TO THE SPRING FLING DANCE? THAT'S WHY YOU CAN'T GO TO THE MOVIES WITH ME?!
WHACK!
WHAM!
WHAT THE HELL?!
YOU'RE INTERRUPTING PRACTICE.
PRACTICE DOESN'T START FOR ANOTHER FIFTEEN MINUTES. I USED TO BE ON THE TEAM, REMEMBER?

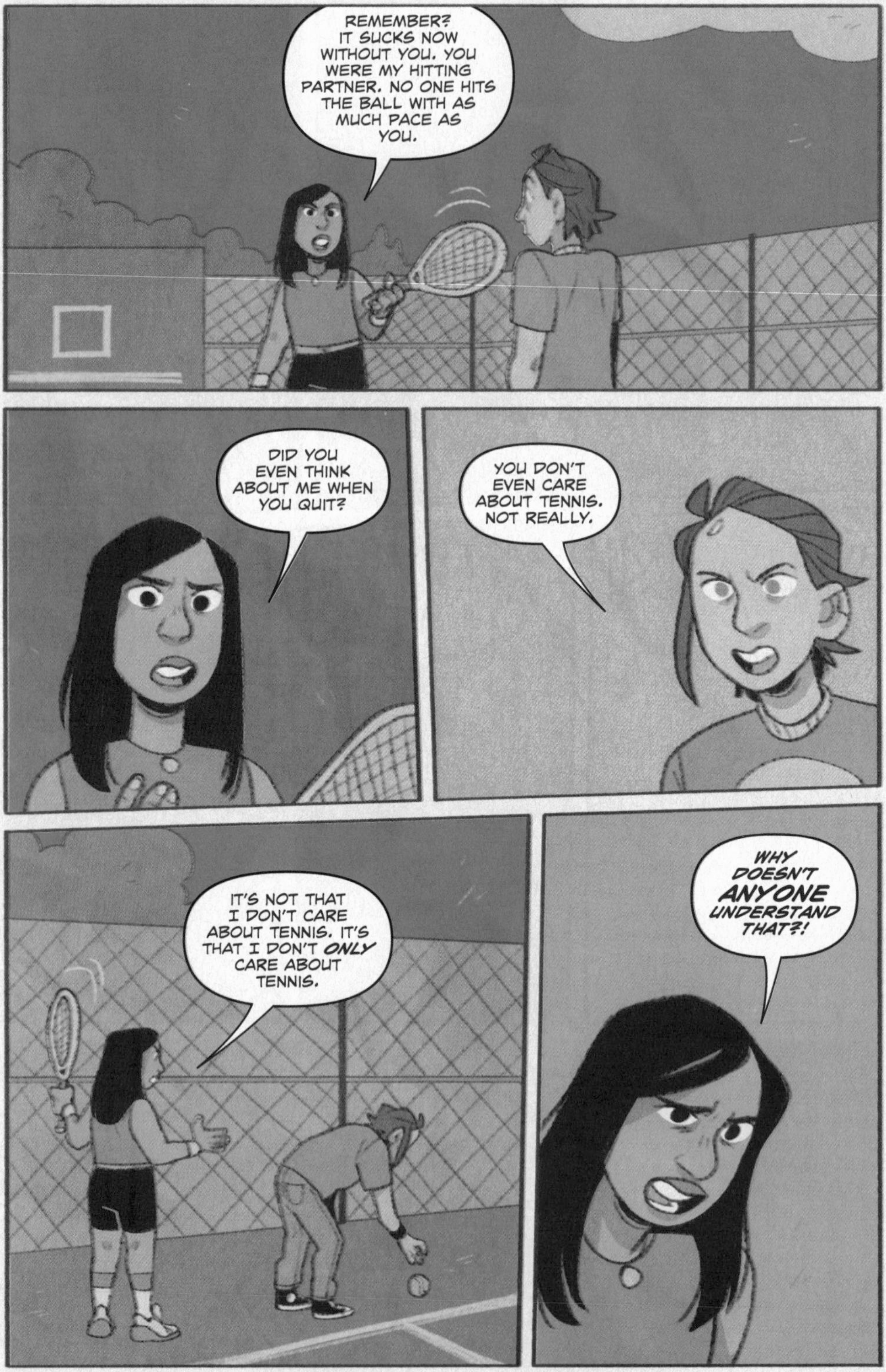
REMEMBER? IT SUCKS NOW WITHOUT YOU. YOU WERE MY HITTING PARTNER. NO ONE HITS THE BALL WITH AS MUCH PACE AS YOU.
DID YOU EVEN THINK ABOUT ME WHEN YOU QUIT?
YOU DON'T EVEN CARE ABOUT TENNIS. NOT REALLY.
IT'S NOT THAT I DON'T CARE ABOUT TENNIS. IT'S THAT I DON'T *ONLY* CARE ABOUT TENNIS.
WHY DOESN'T ***ANYONE*** *UNDERSTAND THAT?!*

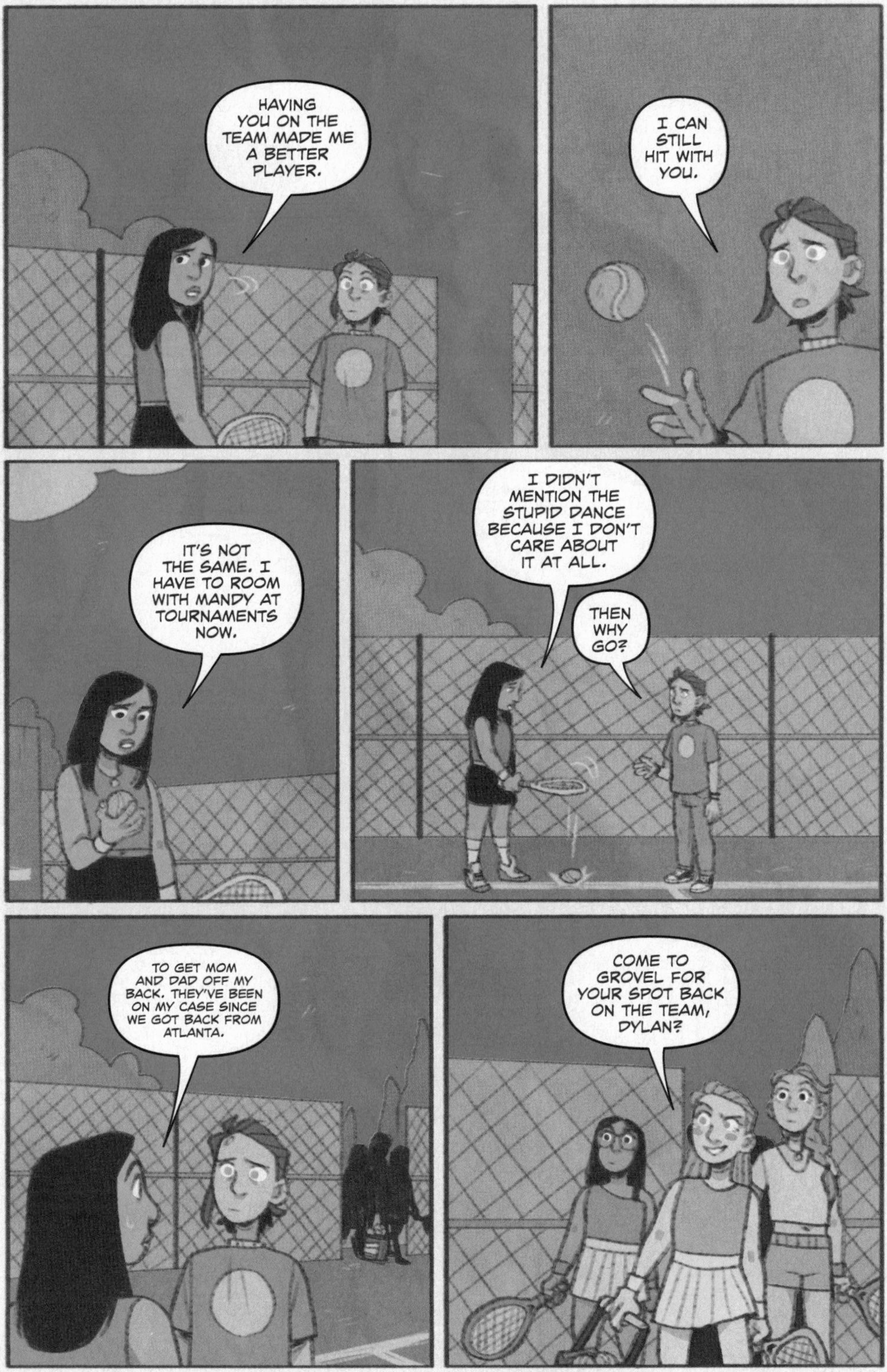
HAVING YOU ON THE TEAM MADE ME A BETTER PLAYER.
I CAN STILL HIT WITH YOU.
IT'S NOT THE SAME. I HAVE TO ROOM WITH MANDY AT TOURNAMENTS NOW.
I DIDN'T MENTION THE STUPID DANCE BECAUSE I DON'T CARE ABOUT IT AT ALL.
THEN WHY GO?
TO GET MOM AND DAD OFF MY BACK. THEY'VE BEEN ON MY CASE SINCE WE GOT BACK FROM ATLANTA.
COME TO GROVEL FOR YOUR SPOT BACK ON THE TEAM, DYLAN?

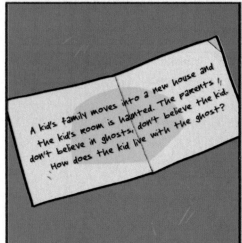

A kid's family moves into a new house and the kid's room is haunted. The parents don't believe in ghosts, don't believe the kid. How does the kid live with the ghost?

I'VE GOT IT. I'LL BE THE GHOST. YOU PLAY THE KID. WHO NEEDS THE PARENTS?!

SMACK

YES!

WE COULD TURN OUR STORY INTO A COMEDY, A FARCE.

NO. THE AUTHOR IS CLEARLY HURT. WE NEED TO HONOR THAT, NOT MAKE FUN OF IT.

LOVE MEANS

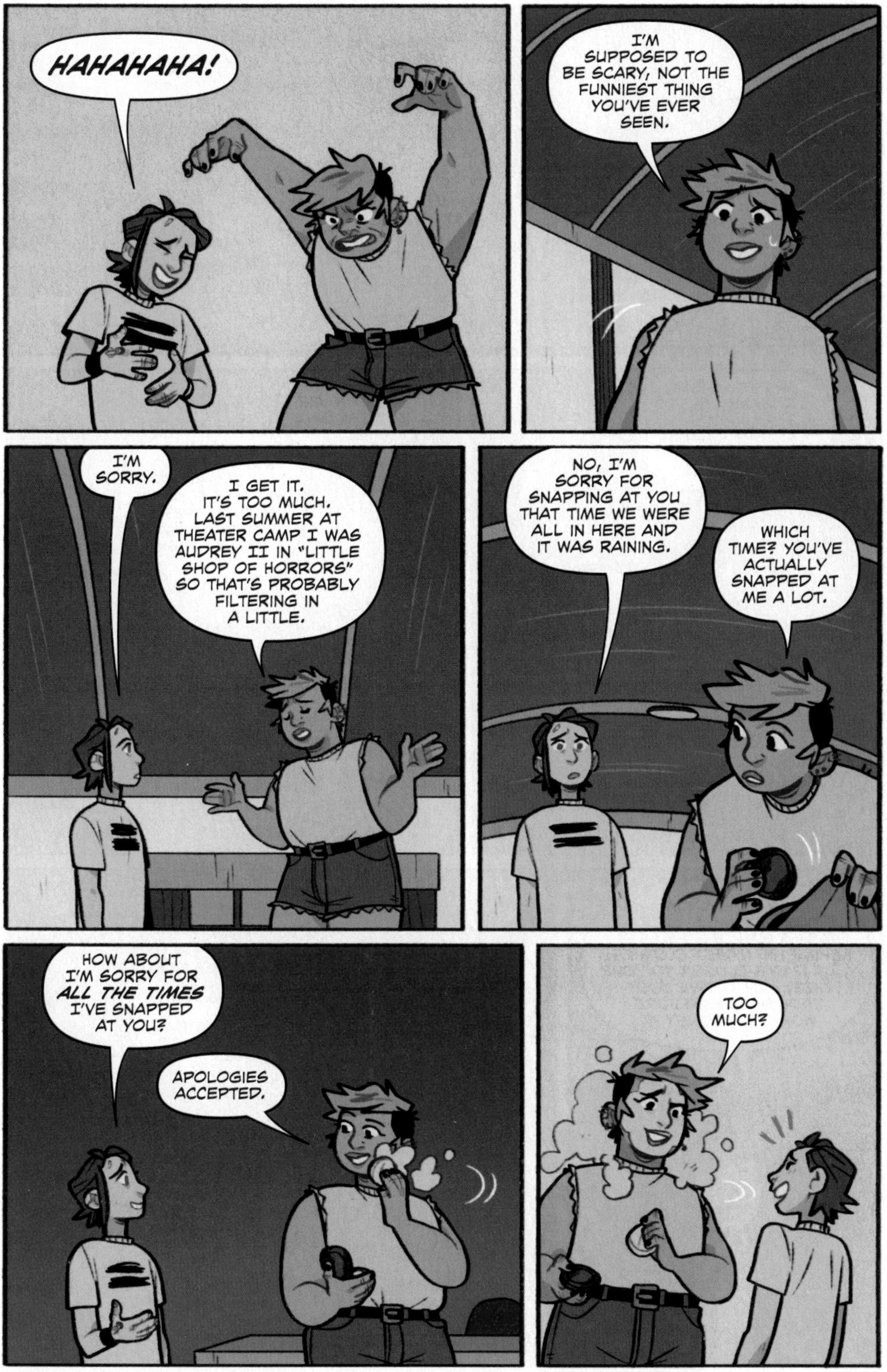
HAHAHAHA!
I'M SUPPOSED TO BE SCARY, NOT THE FUNNIEST THING YOU'VE EVER SEEN.
I'M SORRY.
I GET IT. IT'S TOO MUCH. LAST SUMMER AT THEATER CAMP I WAS AUDREY II IN "LITTLE SHOP OF HORRORS" SO THAT'S PROBABLY FILTERING IN A LITTLE.
NO, I'M SORRY FOR SNAPPING AT YOU THAT TIME WE WERE ALL IN HERE AND IT WAS RAINING.
WHICH TIME? YOU'VE ACTUALLY SNAPPED AT ME A LOT.
HOW ABOUT I'M SORRY FOR *ALL THE TIMES* I'VE SNAPPED AT YOU?
APOLOGIES ACCEPTED.
TOO MUCH?

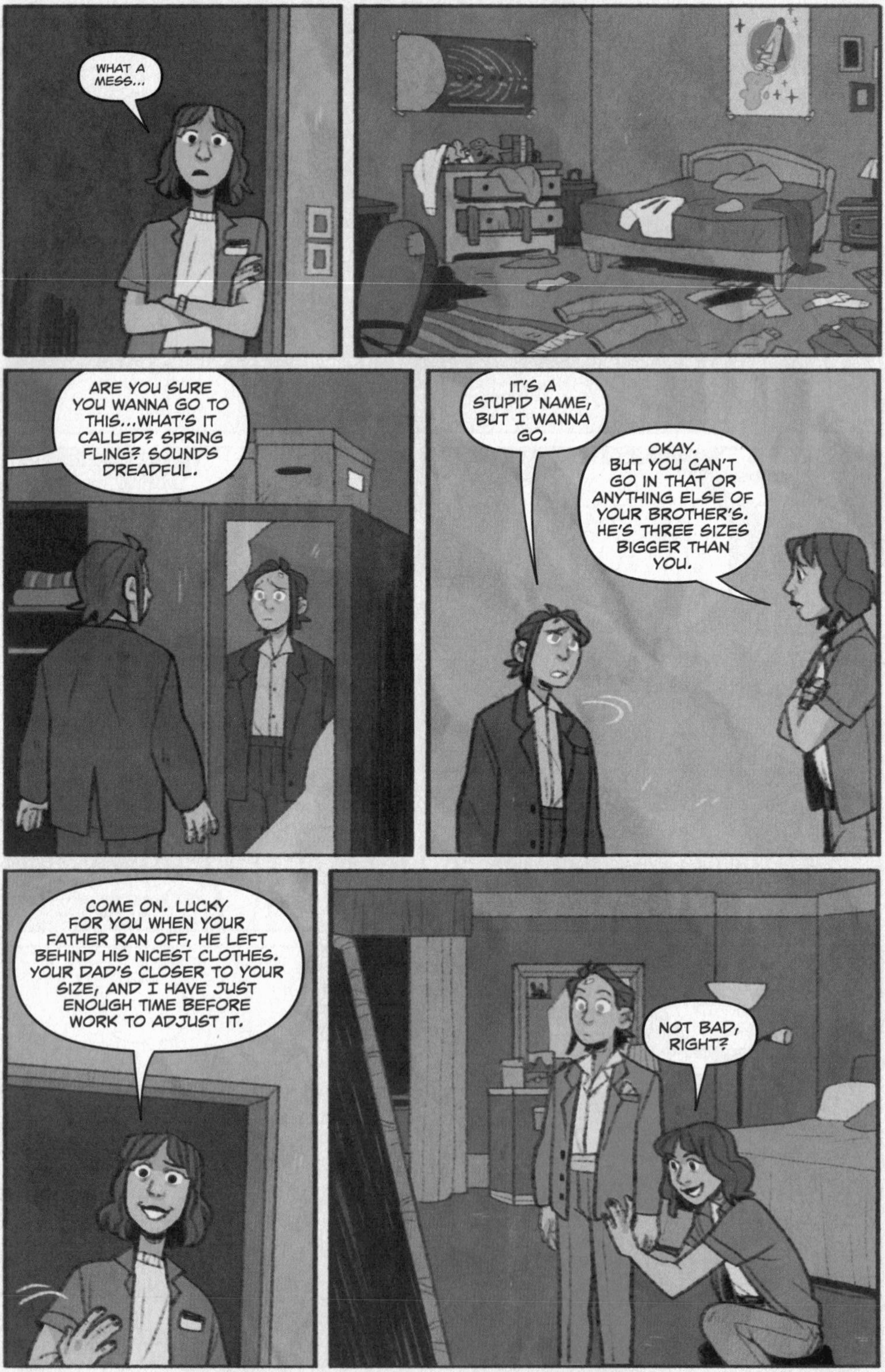
WHAT A MESS...
ARE YOU SURE YOU WANNA GO TO THIS...WHAT'S IT CALLED? SPRING FLING? SOUNDS DREADFUL.
IT'S A STUPID NAME, BUT I WANNA GO.
OKAY. BUT YOU CAN'T GO IN THAT OR ANYTHING ELSE OF YOUR BROTHER'S. HE'S THREE SIZES BIGGER THAN YOU.
COME ON. LUCKY FOR YOU WHEN YOUR FATHER RAN OFF, HE LEFT BEHIND HIS NICEST CLOTHES. YOUR DAD'S CLOSER TO YOUR SIZE, AND I HAVE JUST ENOUGH TIME BEFORE WORK TO ADJUST IT.
NOT BAD, RIGHT?

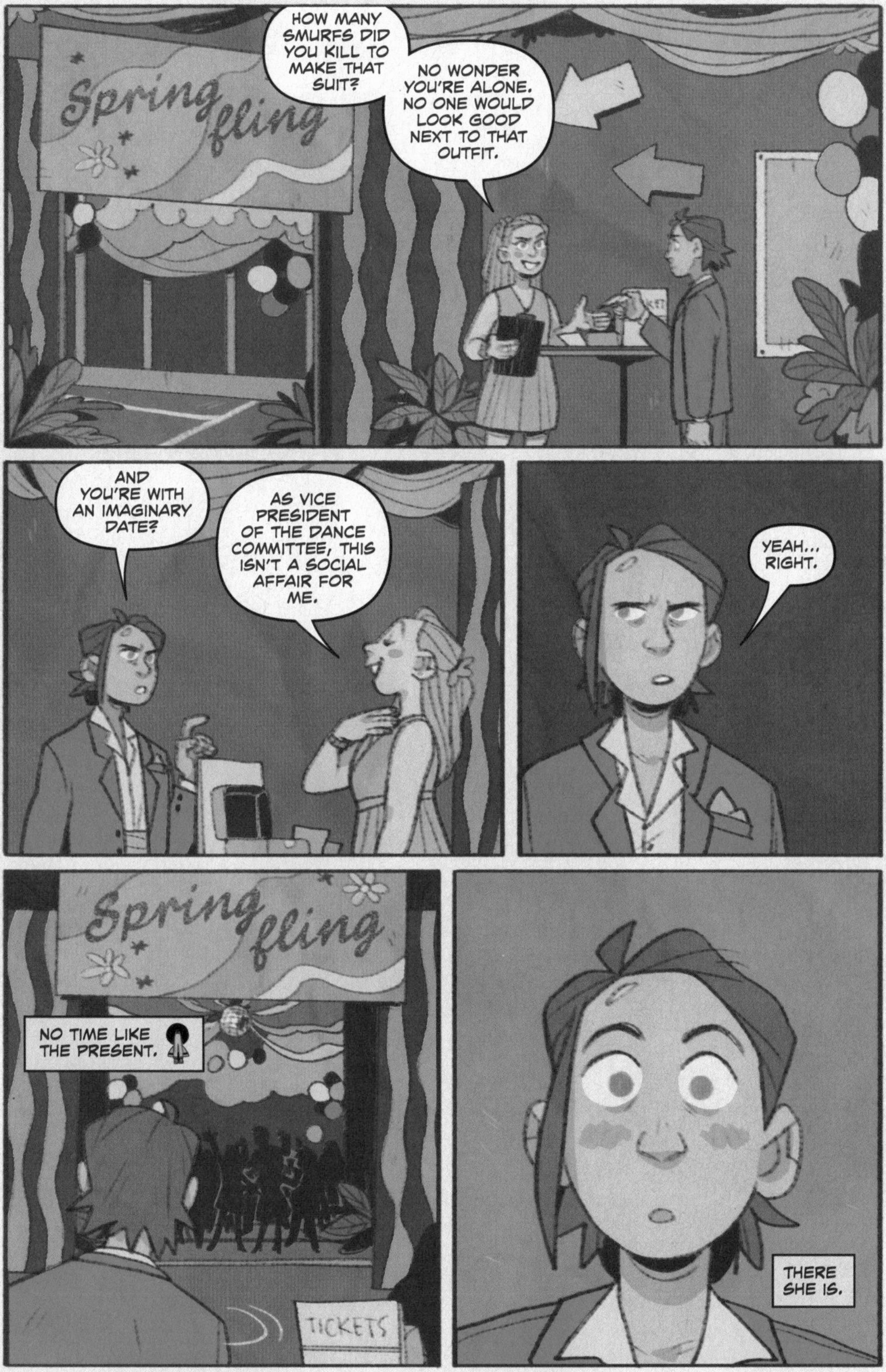
Spring fling
HOW MANY SMURFS DID YOU KILL TO MAKE THAT SUIT?
NO WONDER YOU'RE ALONE. NO ONE WOULD LOOK GOOD NEXT TO THAT OUTFIT.
AND YOU'RE WITH AN IMAGINARY DATE?
AS VICE PRESIDENT OF THE DANCE COMMITTEE, THIS ISN'T A SOCIAL AFFAIR FOR ME.
YEAH... RIGHT.
Spring fling
NO TIME LIKE THE PRESENT.
TICKETS
THERE SHE IS.

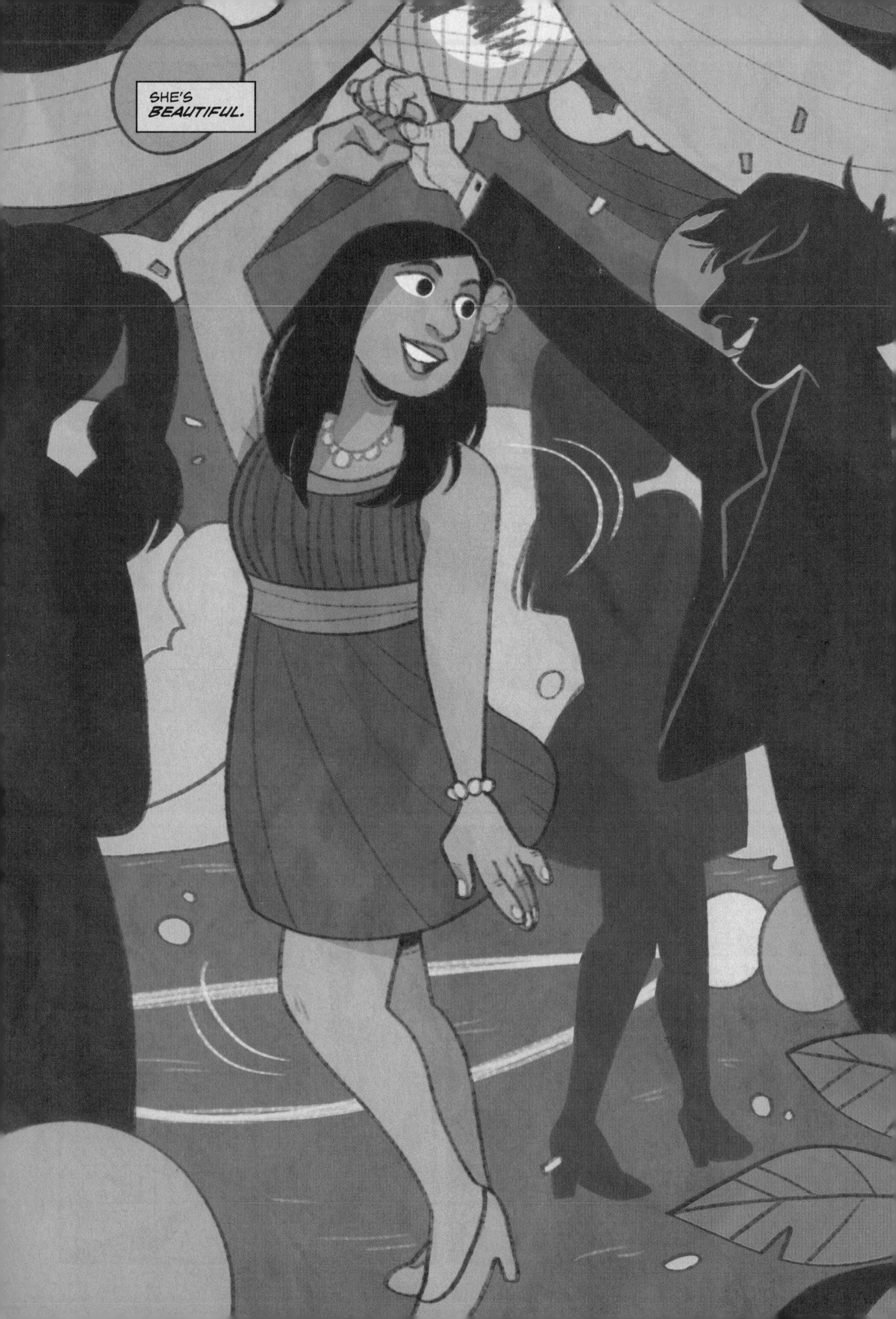
SHE'S BEAUTIFUL.

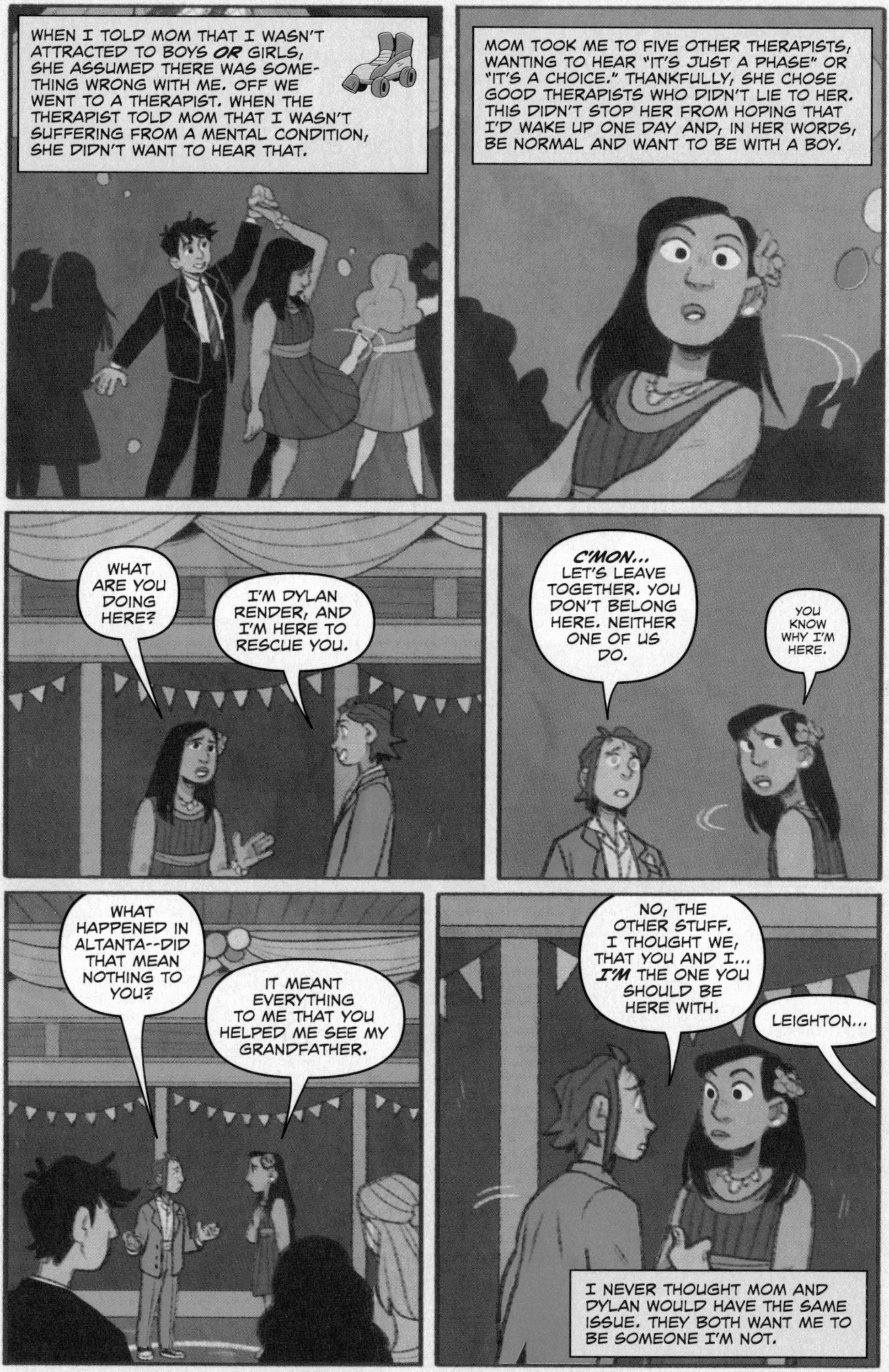

WHEN I TOLD MOM THAT I WASN'T ATTRACTED TO BOYS *OR* GIRLS, SHE ASSUMED THERE WAS SOMETHING WRONG WITH ME. OFF WE WENT TO A THERAPIST. WHEN THE THERAPIST TOLD MOM THAT I WASN'T SUFFERING FROM A MENTAL CONDITION, SHE DIDN'T WANT TO HEAR THAT.
MOM TOOK ME TO FIVE OTHER THERAPISTS, WANTING TO HEAR "IT'S JUST A PHASE" OR "IT'S A CHOICE." THANKFULLY, SHE CHOSE GOOD THERAPISTS WHO DIDN'T LIE TO HER. THIS DIDN'T STOP HER FROM HOPING THAT I'D WAKE UP ONE DAY AND, IN HER WORDS, BE NORMAL AND WANT TO BE WITH A BOY.
WHAT ARE YOU DOING HERE?
I'M DYLAN RENDER, AND I'M HERE TO RESCUE YOU.
C'MON... LET'S LEAVE TOGETHER. YOU DON'T BELONG HERE. NEITHER ONE OF US DO.
YOU KNOW WHY I'M HERE.
WHAT HAPPENED IN ALTANTA--DID THAT MEAN NOTHING TO YOU?
IT MEANT EVERYTHING TO ME THAT YOU HELPED ME SEE MY GRANDFATHER.
NO, THE OTHER STUFF. I THOUGHT WE, THAT YOU AND I... *I'M* THE ONE YOU SHOULD BE HERE WITH.
LEIGHTON...
I NEVER THOUGHT MOM AND DYLAN WOULD HAVE THE SAME ISSUE. THEY BOTH WANT ME TO BE SOMEONE I'M NOT.

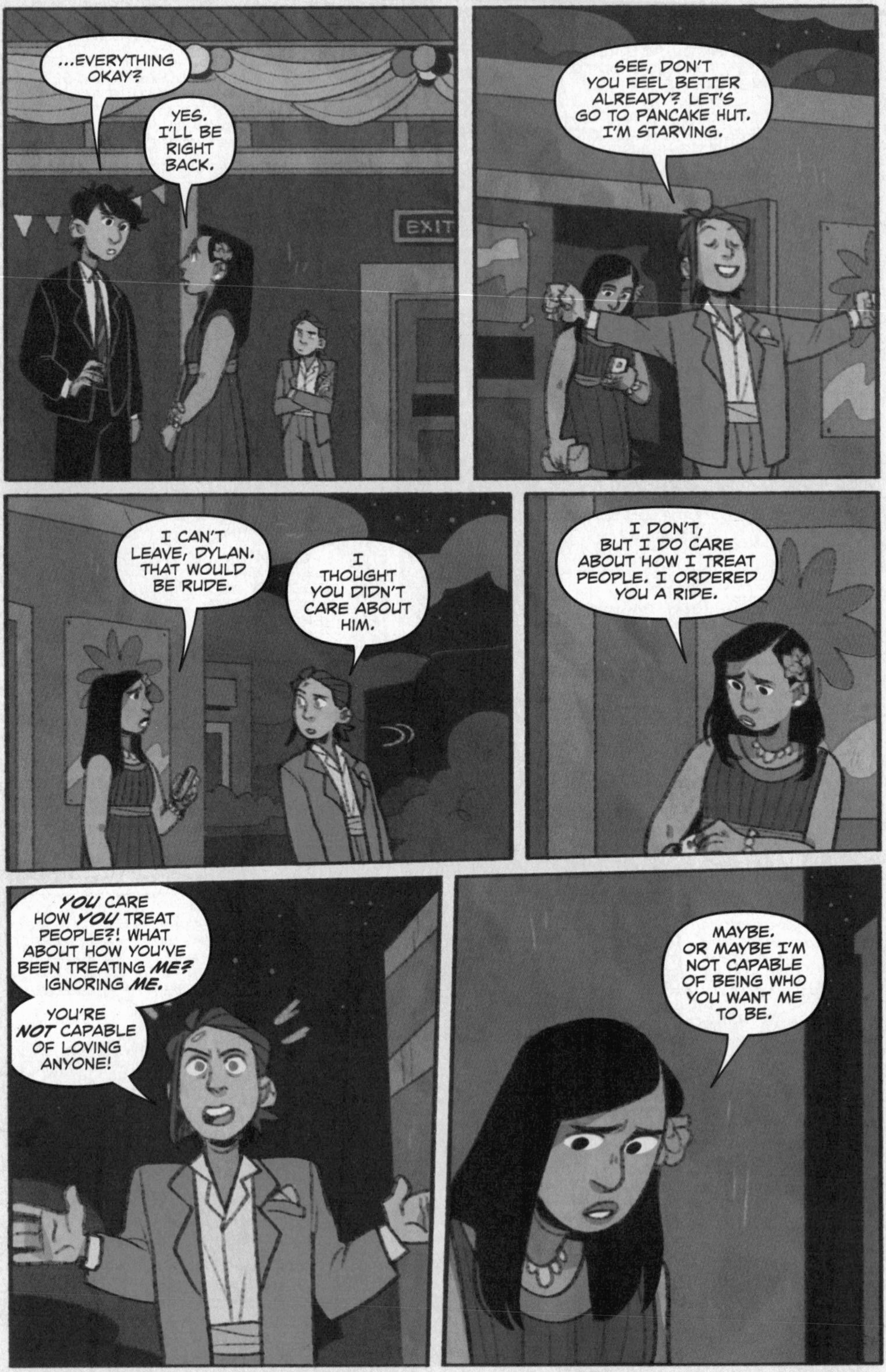
...EVERYTHING OKAY?
YES. I'LL BE RIGHT BACK.
EXIT
SEE, DON'T YOU FEEL BETTER ALREADY? LET'S GO TO PANCAKE HUT. I'M STARVING.
I CAN'T LEAVE, DYLAN. THAT WOULD BE RUDE.
I THOUGHT YOU DIDN'T CARE ABOUT HIM.
I DON'T, BUT I DO CARE ABOUT HOW I TREAT PEOPLE. I ORDERED YOU A RIDE.
YOU CARE HOW YOU TREAT PEOPLE?! WHAT ABOUT HOW YOU'VE BEEN TREATING ME? IGNORING ME.
YOU'RE NOT CAPABLE OF LOVING ANYONE!
MAYBE. OR MAYBE I'M NOT CAPABLE OF BEING WHO YOU WANT ME TO BE.

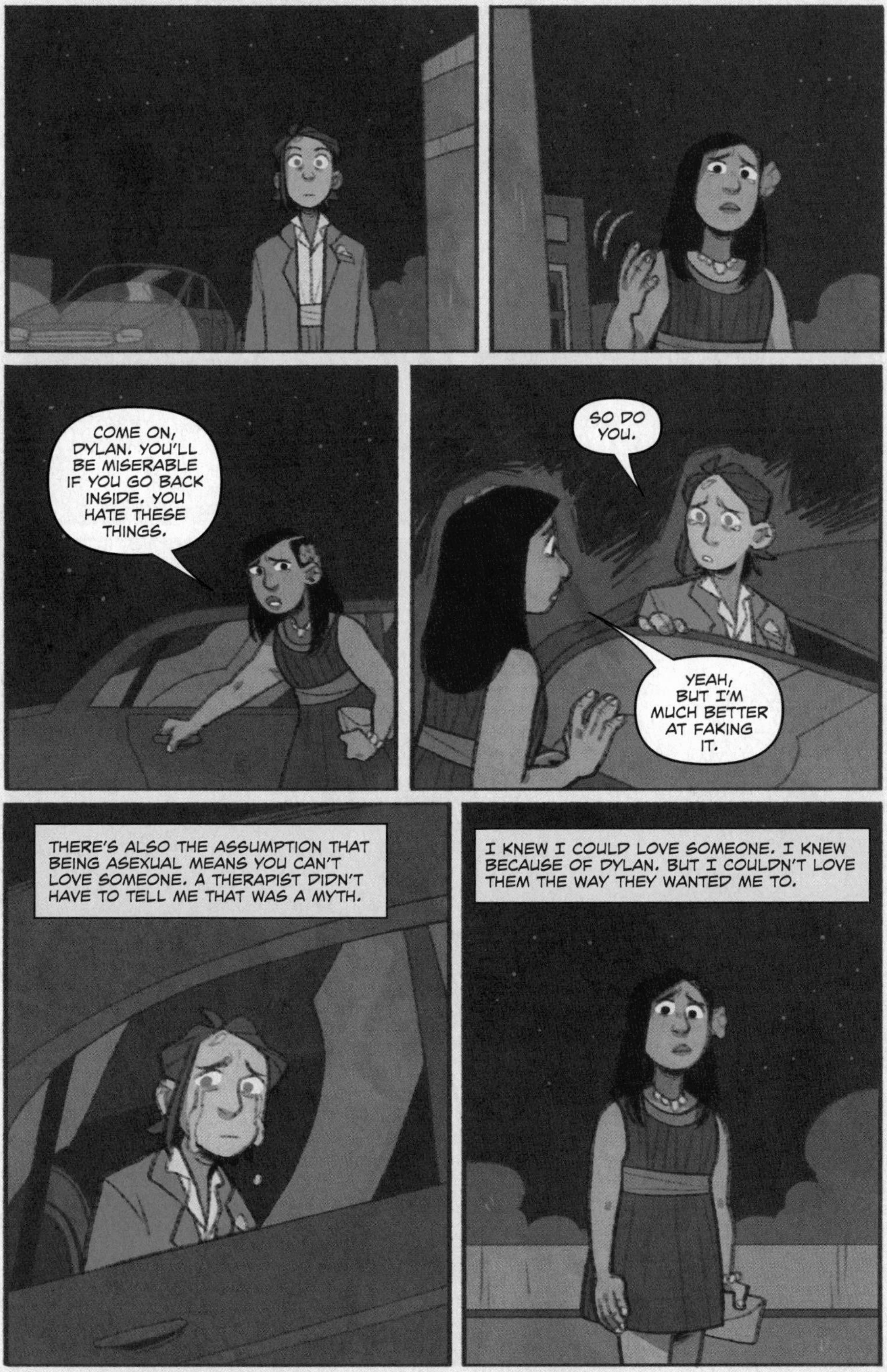
COME ON, DYLAN. YOU'LL BE MISERABLE IF YOU GO BACK INSIDE. YOU HATE THESE THINGS.
SO DO YOU.
YEAH, BUT I'M MUCH BETTER AT FAKING IT.
THERE'S ALSO THE ASSUMPTION THAT BEING ASEXUAL MEANS YOU CAN'T LOVE SOMEONE. A THERAPIST DIDN'T HAVE TO TELL ME THAT WAS A MYTH.
I KNEW I COULD LOVE SOMEONE. I KNEW BECAUSE OF DYLAN. BUT I COULDN'T LOVE THEM THE WAY THEY WANTED ME TO.

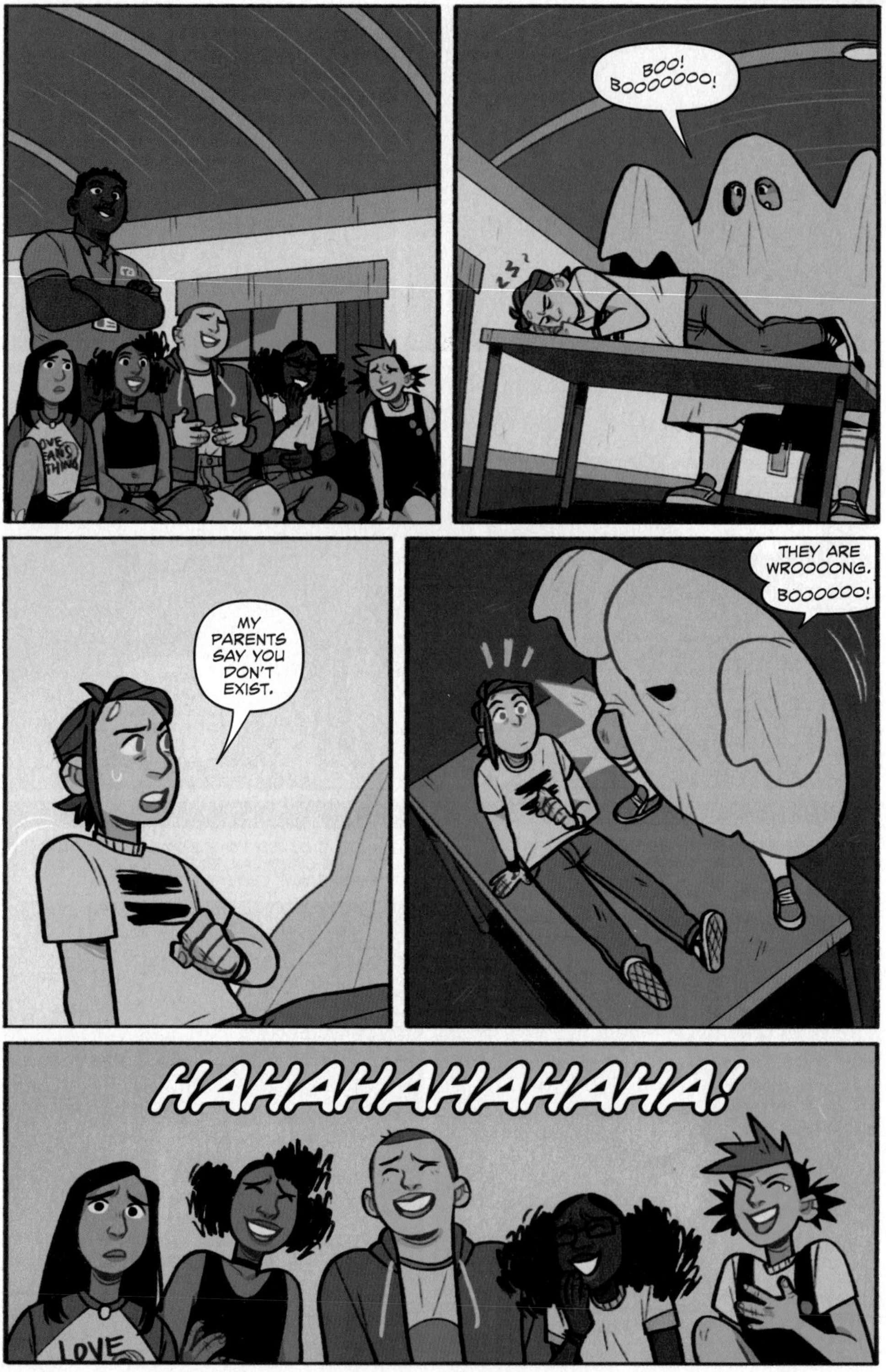
BOO! BOOOOOOO!
MY PARENTS SAY YOU DON'T EXIST.
THEY ARE WROOOONG. BOOOOOO!
HAHAHAHAHAHAHA!
LOVE

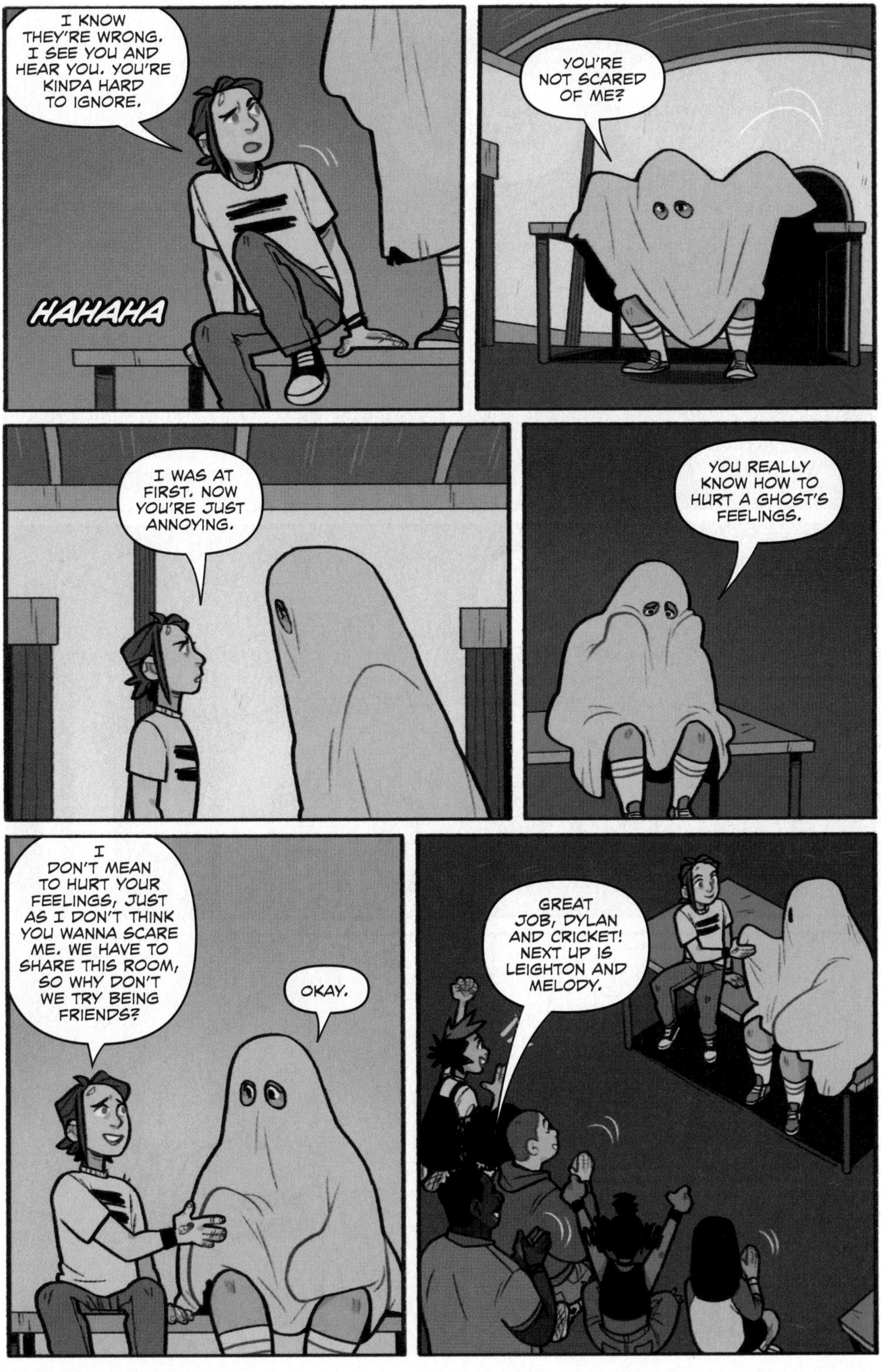
I KNOW THEY'RE WRONG. I SEE YOU AND HEAR YOU. YOU'RE KINDA HARD TO IGNORE.
HAHAHA
YOU'RE NOT SCARED OF ME?
I WAS AT FIRST. NOW YOU'RE JUST ANNOYING.
YOU REALLY KNOW HOW TO HURT A GHOST'S FEELINGS.
I DON'T MEAN TO HURT YOUR FEELINGS, JUST AS I DON'T THINK YOU WANNA SCARE ME. WE HAVE TO SHARE THIS ROOM, SO WHY DON'T WE TRY BEING FRIENDS?
OKAY.
GREAT JOB, DYLAN AND CRICKET! NEXT UP IS LEIGHTON AND MELODY.

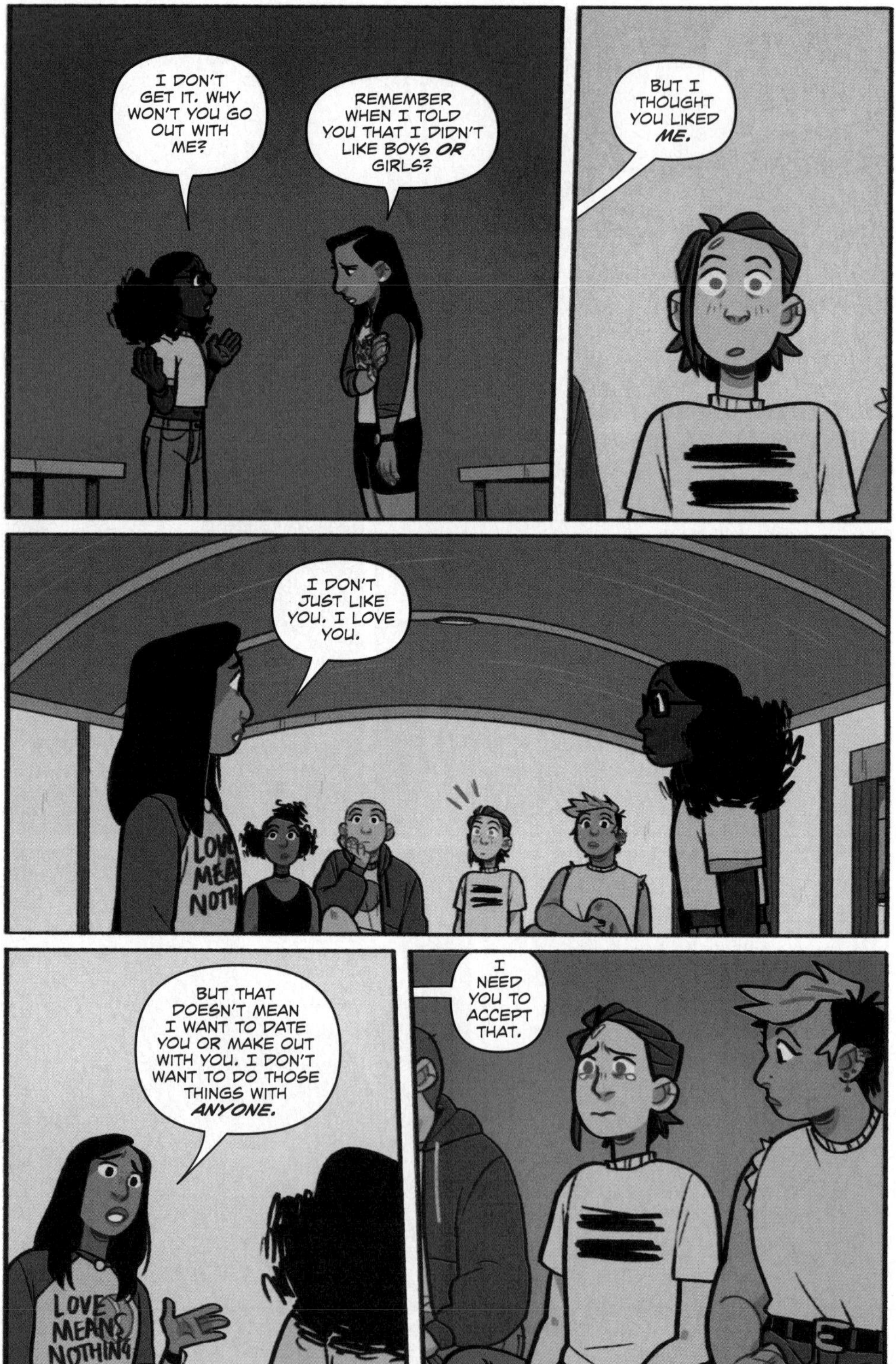
I DON'T GET IT. WHY WON'T YOU GO OUT WITH ME?
REMEMBER WHEN I TOLD YOU THAT I DIDN'T LIKE BOYS *OR* GIRLS?
BUT I THOUGHT YOU LIKED *ME.*
I DON'T JUST LIKE YOU. I LOVE YOU.
BUT THAT DOESN'T MEAN I WANT TO DATE YOU OR MAKE OUT WITH YOU. I DON'T WANT TO DO THOSE THINGS WITH *ANYONE.*
LOVE MEANS NOTHING
I NEED YOU TO ACCEPT THAT.

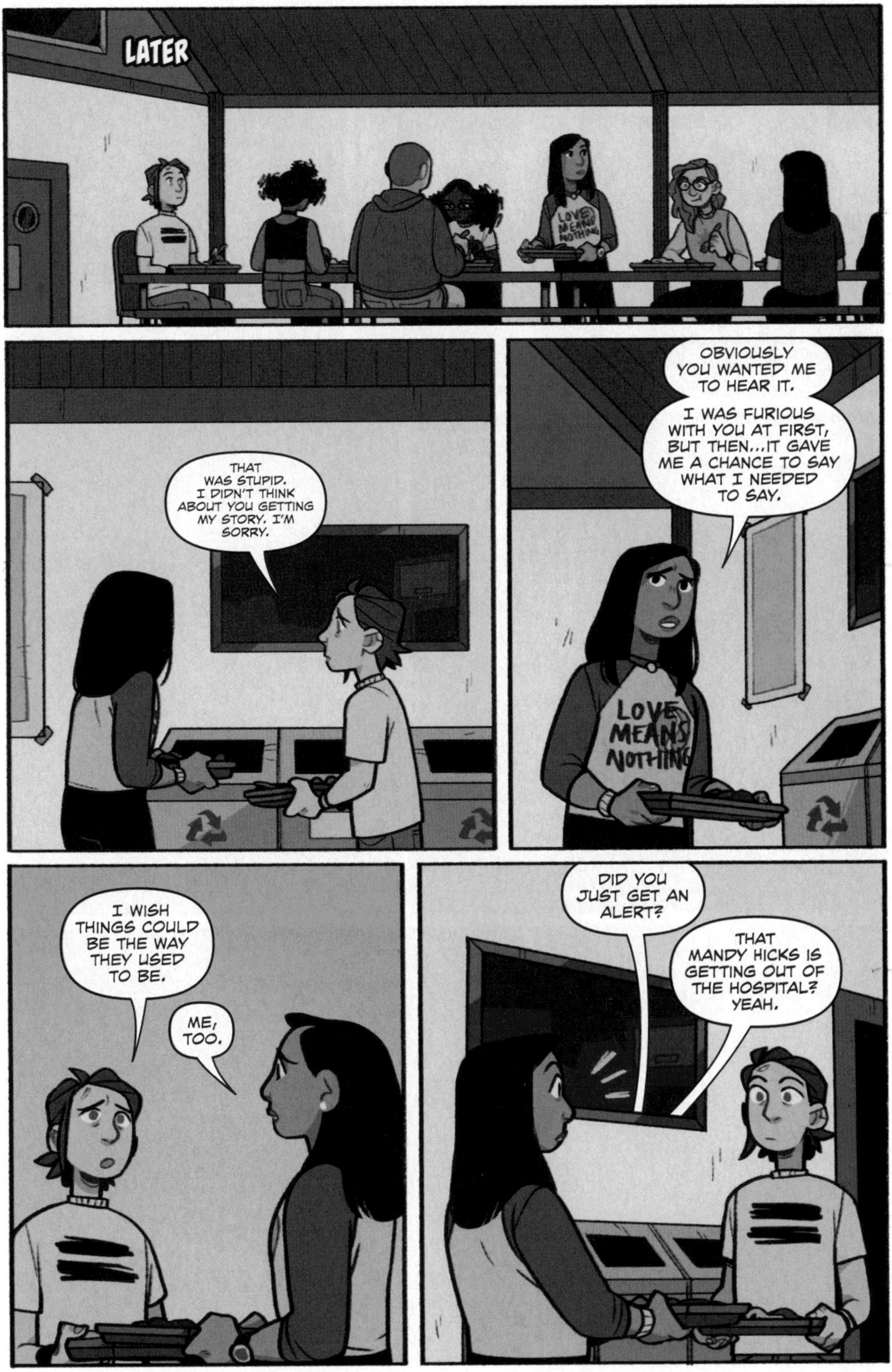
LATER
LOVE MEANS NOTHING
THAT WAS STUPID. I DIDN'T THINK ABOUT YOU GETTING MY STORY. I'M SORRY.
OBVIOUSLY YOU WANTED ME TO HEAR IT.
I WAS FURIOUS WITH YOU AT FIRST, BUT THEN...IT GAVE ME A CHANCE TO SAY WHAT I NEEDED TO SAY.
I WISH THINGS COULD BE THE WAY THEY USED TO BE.
ME, TOO.
DID YOU JUST GET AN ALERT?
THAT MANDY HICKS IS GETTING OUT OF THE HOSPITAL? YEAH.

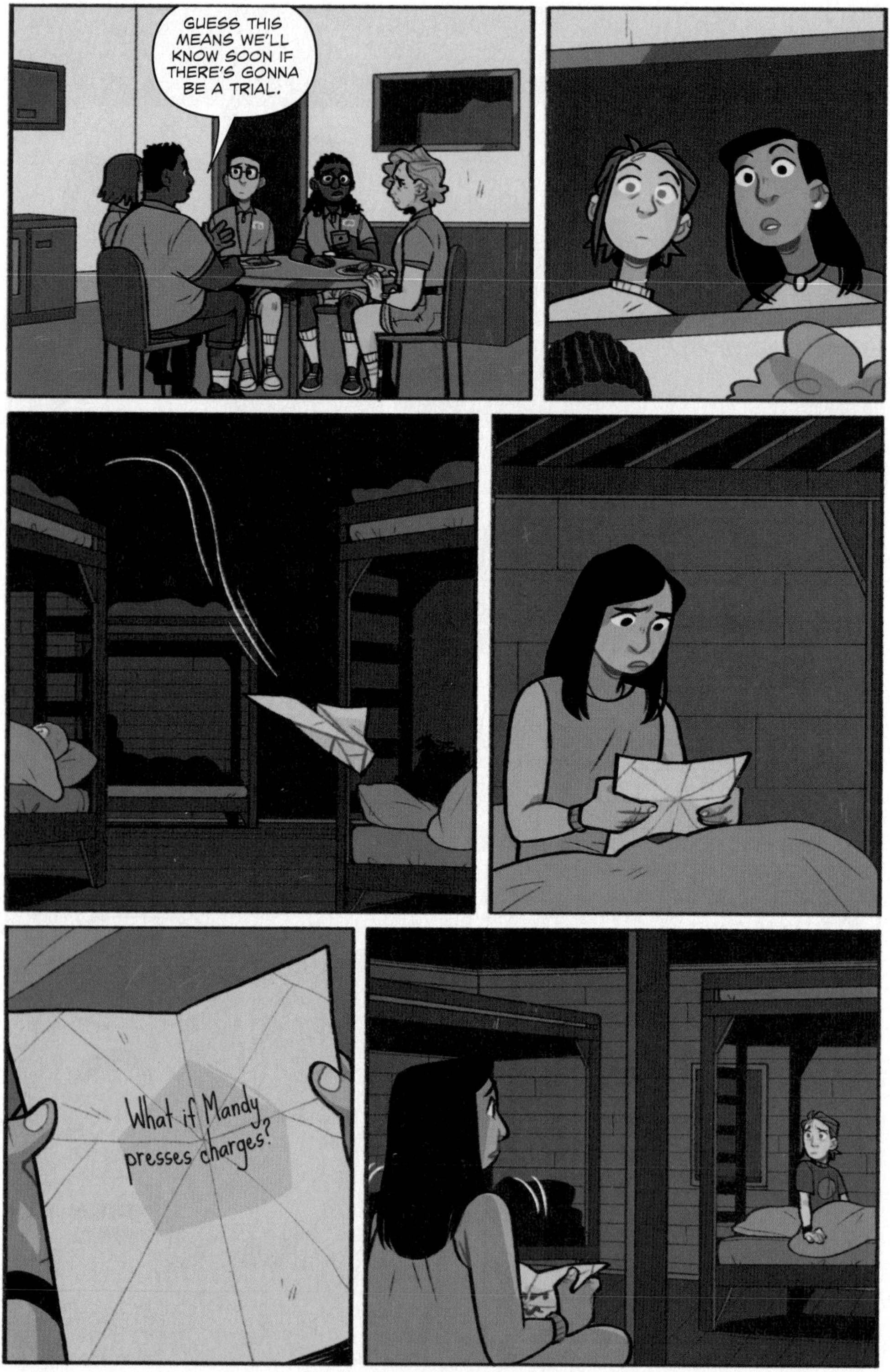
GUESS THIS MEANS WE'LL KNOW SOON IF THERE'S GONNA BE A TRIAL.
What if Mandy presses charges?

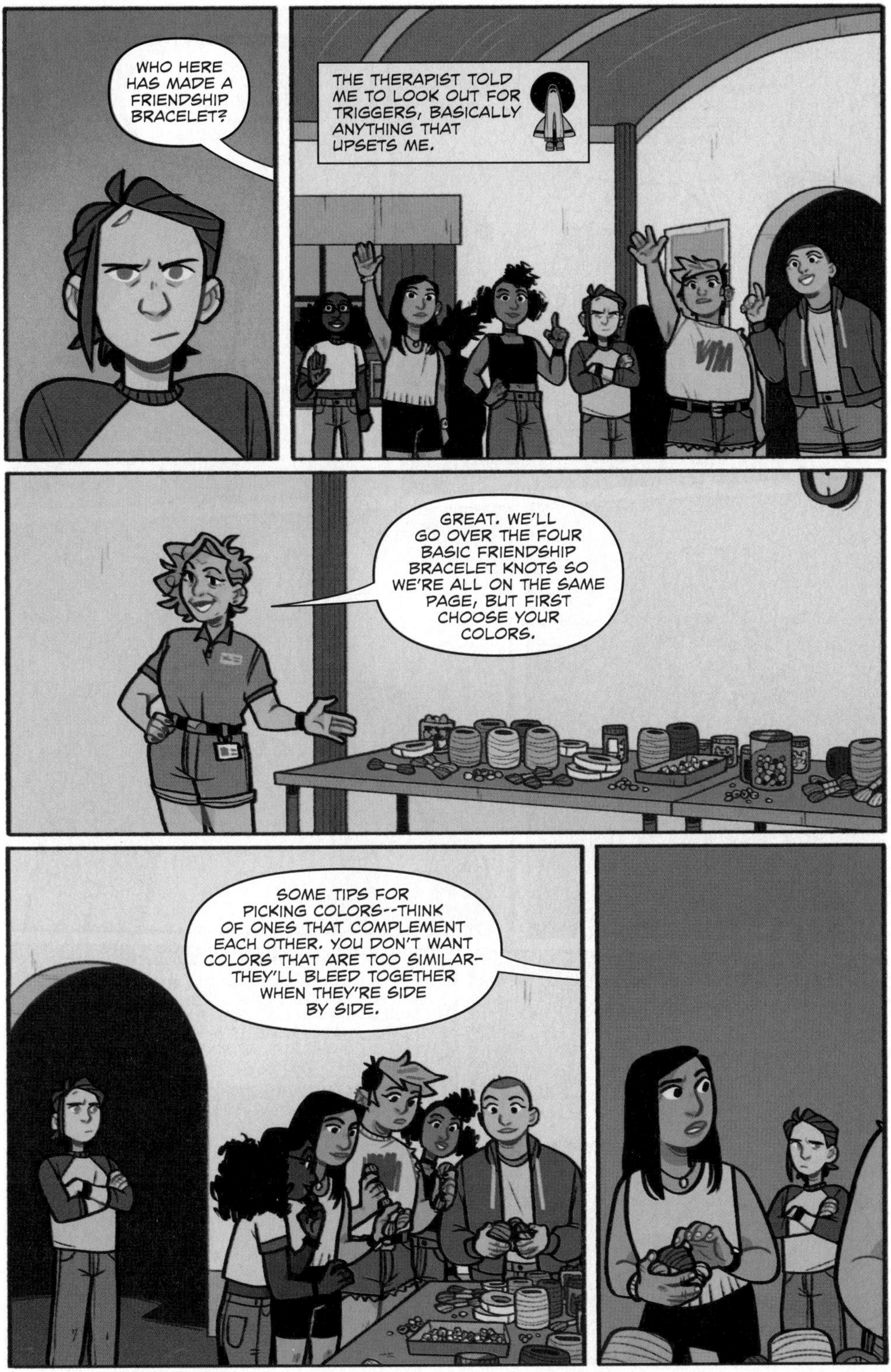
WHO HERE HAS MADE A FRIENDSHIP BRACELET?
THE THERAPIST TOLD ME TO LOOK OUT FOR TRIGGERS, BASICALLY ANYTHING THAT UPSETS ME.
GREAT. WE'LL GO OVER THE FOUR BASIC FRIENDSHIP BRACELET KNOTS SO WE'RE ALL ON THE SAME PAGE, BUT FIRST CHOOSE YOUR COLORS.
SOME TIPS FOR PICKING COLORS--THINK OF ONES THAT COMPLEMENT EACH OTHER. YOU DON'T WANT COLORS THAT ARE TOO SIMILAR- THEY'LL BLEED TOGETHER WHEN THEY'RE SIDE BY SIDE.

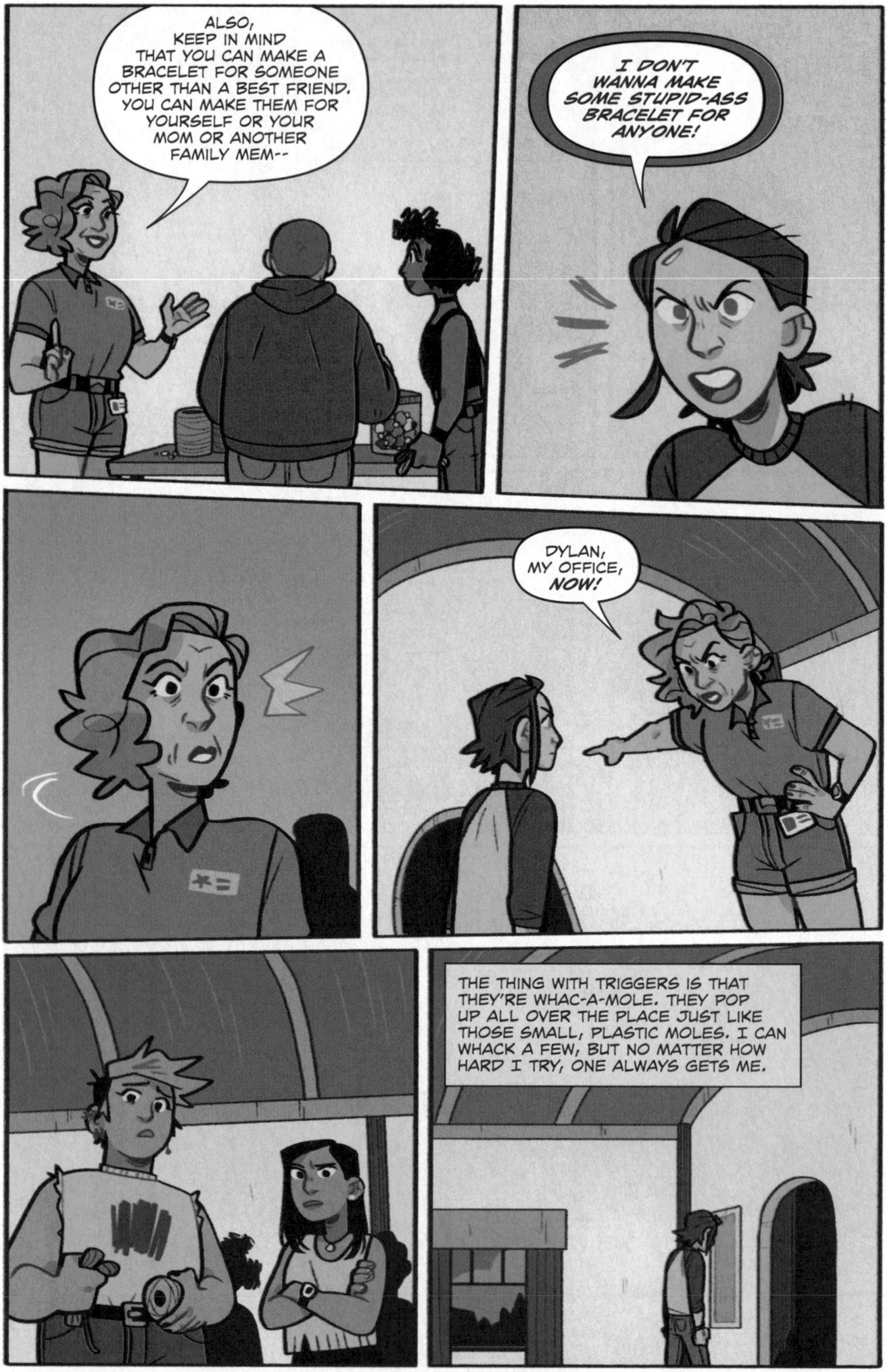
ALSO, KEEP IN MIND THAT YOU CAN MAKE A BRACELET FOR SOMEONE OTHER THAN A BEST FRIEND. YOU CAN MAKE THEM FOR YOURSELF OR YOUR MOM OR ANOTHER FAMILY MEM--
I DON'T WANNA MAKE SOME STUPID-ASS BRACELET FOR ANYONE!
DYLAN, MY OFFICE, NOW!
THE THING WITH TRIGGERS IS THAT THEY'RE WHAC-A-MOLE. THEY POP UP ALL OVER THE PLACE JUST LIKE THOSE SMALL, PLASTIC MOLES. I CAN WHACK A FEW, BUT NO MATTER HOW HARD I TRY, ONE ALWAYS GETS ME.

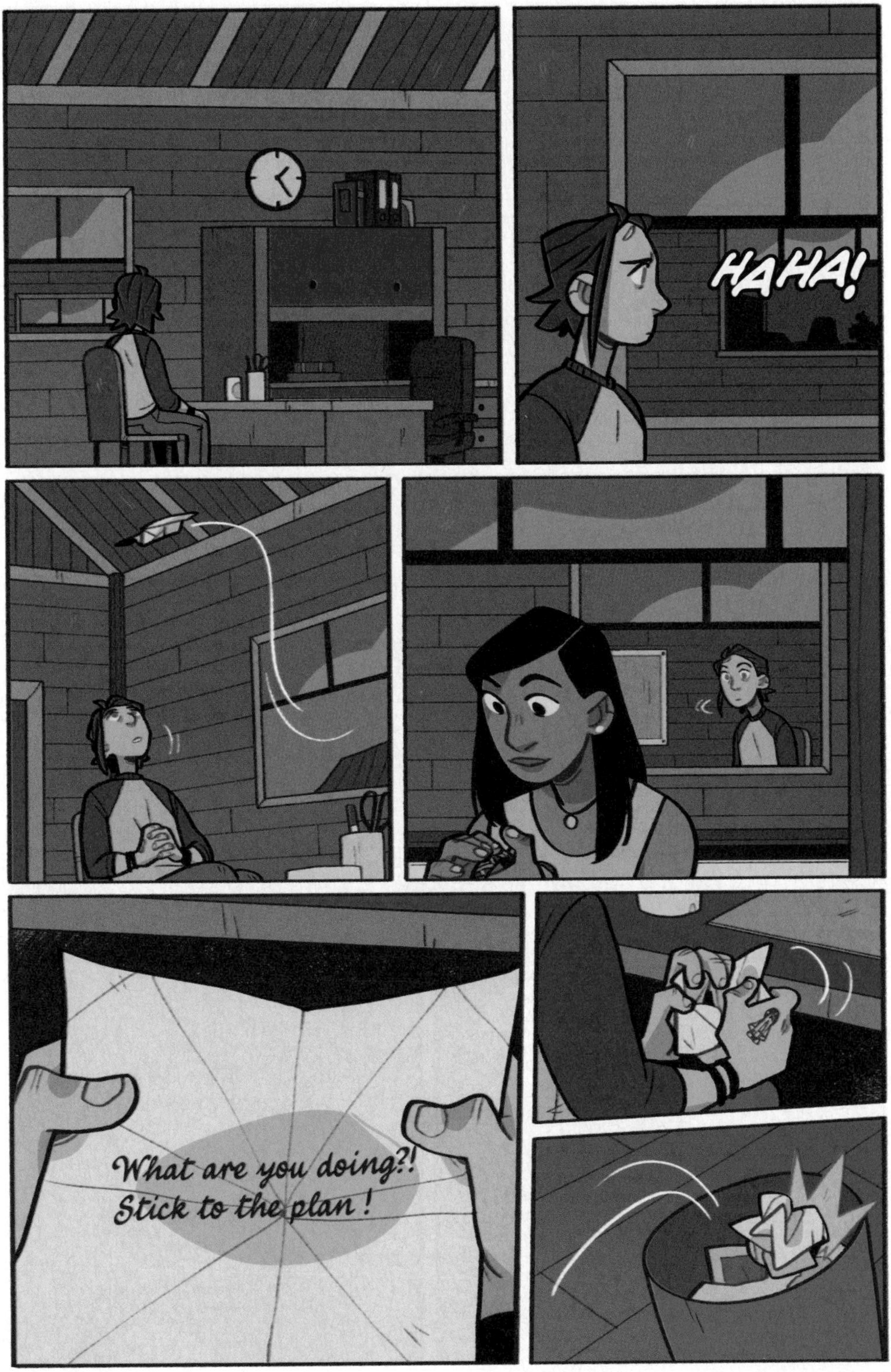
HAHA!
What are you doing?!
Stick to the plan!

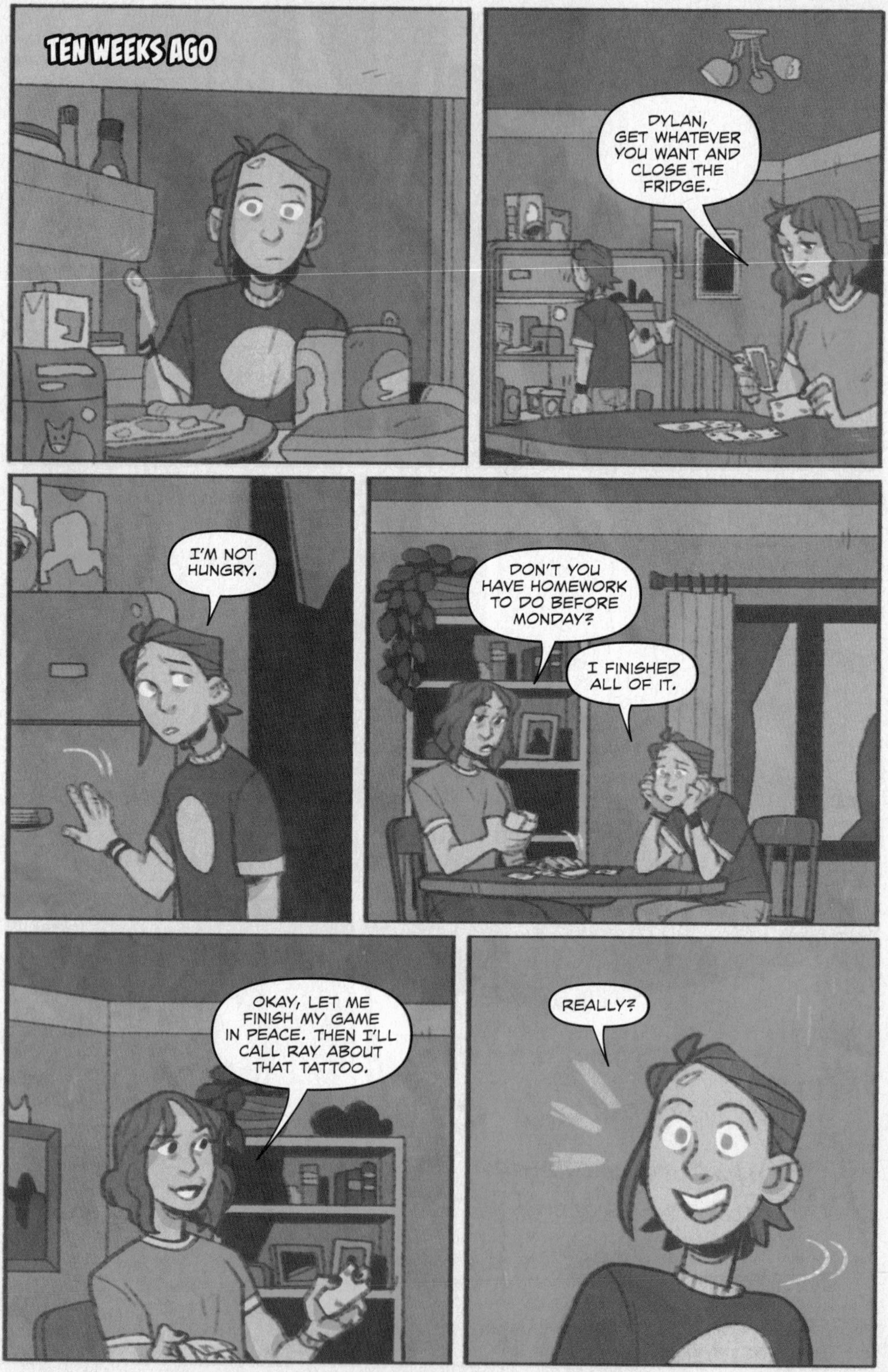
TEN WEEKS AGO
DYLAN, GET WHATEVER YOU WANT AND CLOSE THE FRIDGE.
I'M NOT HUNGRY.
DON'T YOU HAVE HOMEWORK TO DO BEFORE MONDAY?
I FINISHED ALL OF IT.
OKAY, LET ME FINISH MY GAME IN PEACE. THEN I'LL CALL RAY ABOUT THAT TATTOO.
REALLY?

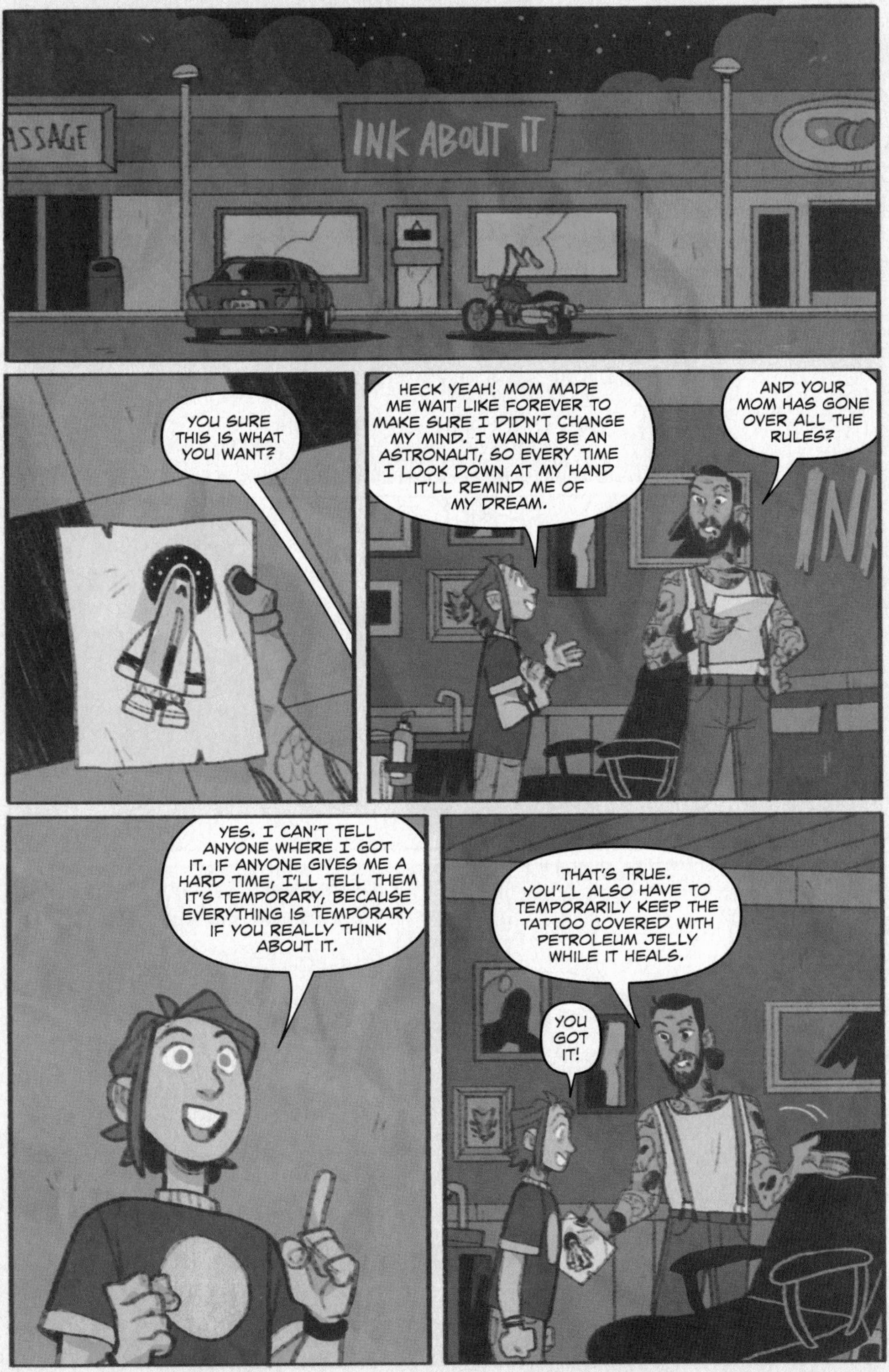
INK ABOUT IT
ASSAGE
YOU SURE THIS IS WHAT YOU WANT?
HECK YEAH! MOM MADE ME WAIT LIKE FOREVER TO MAKE SURE I DIDN'T CHANGE MY MIND. I WANNA BE AN ASTRONAUT, SO EVERY TIME I LOOK DOWN AT MY HAND IT'LL REMIND ME OF MY DREAM.
AND YOUR MOM HAS GONE OVER ALL THE RULES?
YES. I CAN'T TELL ANYONE WHERE I GOT IT. IF ANYONE GIVES ME A HARD TIME, I'LL TELL THEM IT'S TEMPORARY, BECAUSE EVERYTHING IS TEMPORARY IF YOU REALLY THINK ABOUT IT.
THAT'S TRUE. YOU'LL ALSO HAVE TO TEMPORARILY KEEP THE TATTOO COVERED WITH PETROLEUM JELLY WHILE IT HEALS.
YOU GOT IT!

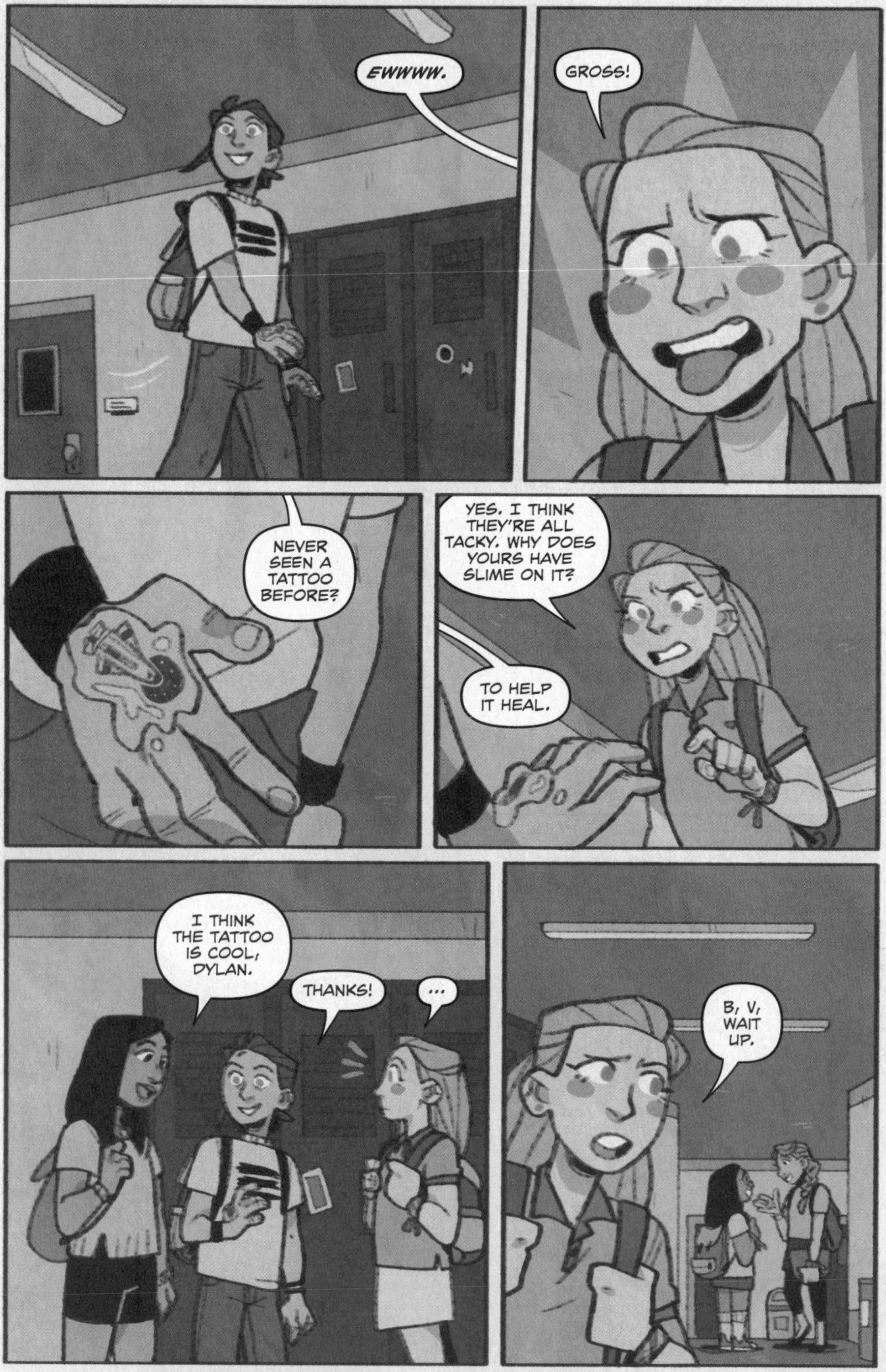
EWWWW.
GROSS!
NEVER SEEN A TATTOO BEFORE?
YES. I THINK THEY'RE ALL TACKY. WHY DOES YOURS HAVE SLIME ON IT?
TO HELP IT HEAL.
I THINK THE TATTOO IS COOL, DYLAN.
THANKS!
...
B, V, WAIT UP.

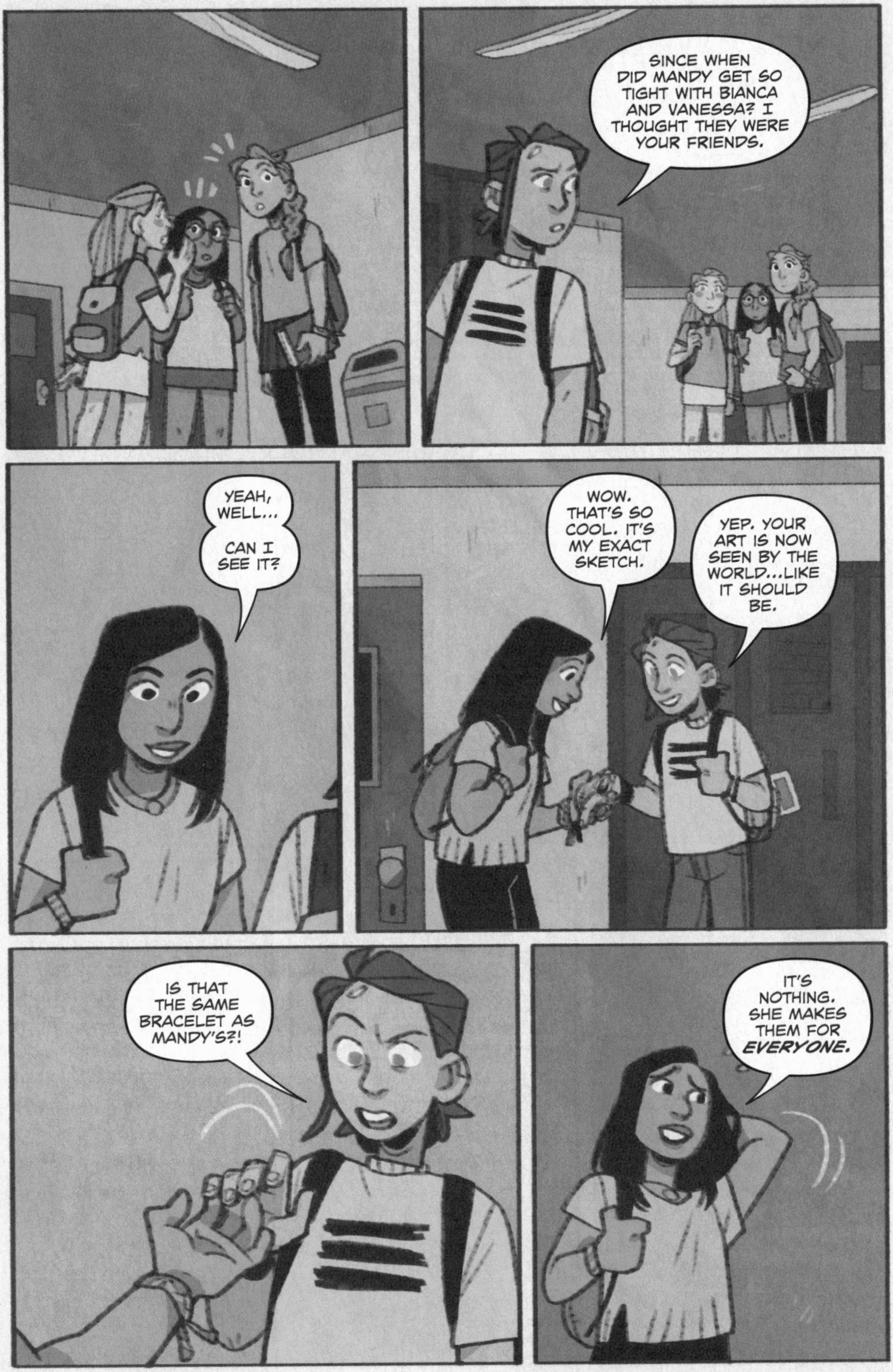
SINCE WHEN DID MANDY GET SO TIGHT WITH BIANCA AND VANESSA? I THOUGHT THEY WERE YOUR FRIENDS.
YEAH, WELL...
CAN I SEE IT?
WOW. THAT'S SO COOL. IT'S MY EXACT SKETCH.
YEP. YOUR ART IS NOW SEEN BY THE WORLD...LIKE IT SHOULD BE.
IS THAT THE SAME BRACELET AS MANDY'S?!
IT'S NOTHING. SHE MAKES THEM FOR *EVERYONE*.

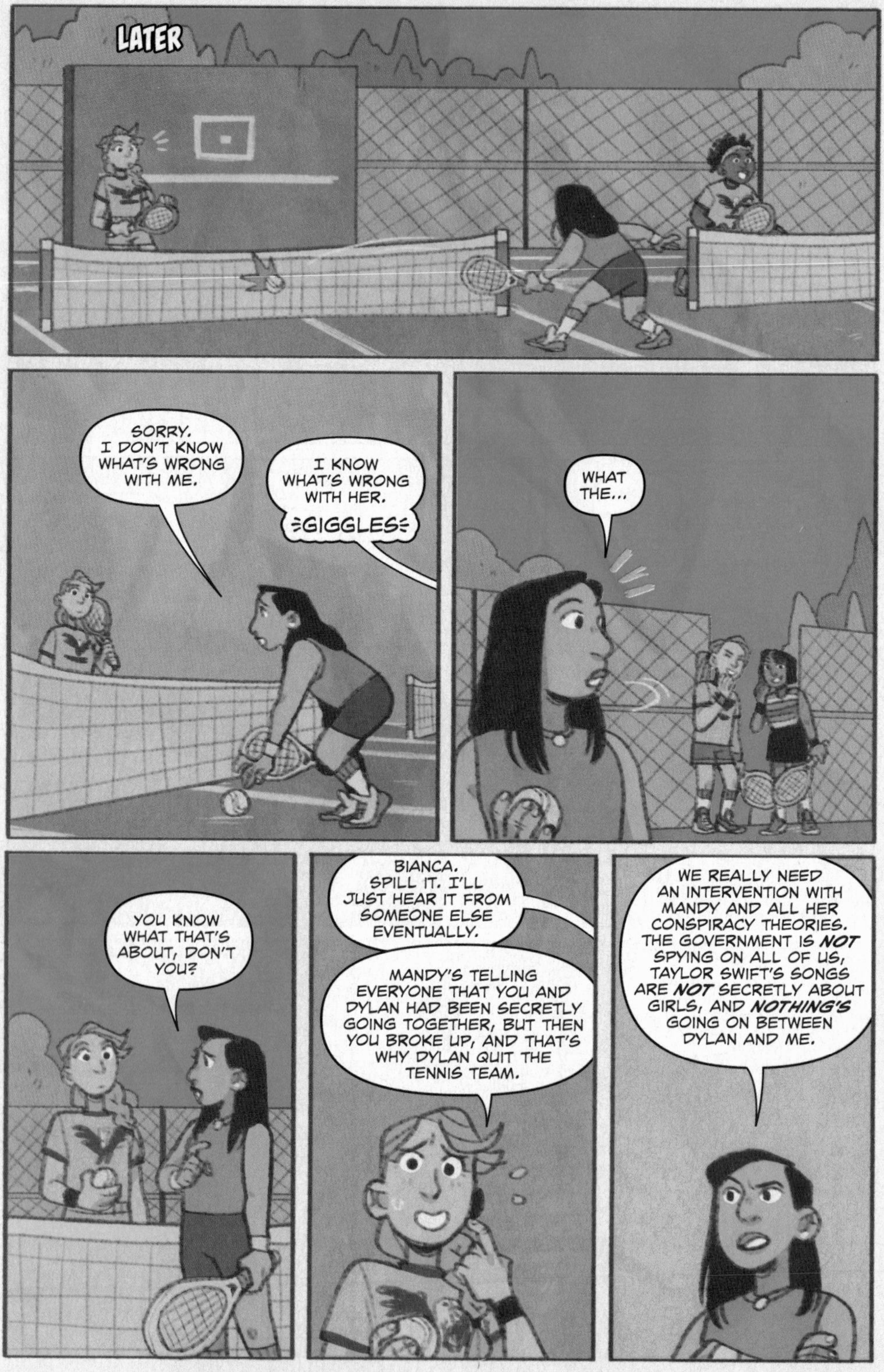
LATER
SORRY. I DON'T KNOW WHAT'S WRONG WITH ME.
I KNOW WHAT'S WRONG WITH HER.
GIGGLES
WHAT THE...
YOU KNOW WHAT THAT'S ABOUT, DON'T YOU?
BIANCA. SPILL IT. I'LL JUST HEAR IT FROM SOMEONE ELSE EVENTUALLY.
MANDY'S TELLING EVERYONE THAT YOU AND DYLAN HAD BEEN SECRETLY GOING TOGETHER, BUT THEN YOU BROKE UP, AND THAT'S WHY DYLAN QUIT THE TENNIS TEAM.
WE REALLY NEED AN INTERVENTION WITH MANDY AND ALL HER CONSPIRACY THEORIES. THE GOVERNMENT IS NOT SPYING ON ALL OF US, TAYLOR SWIFT'S SONGS ARE NOT SECRETLY ABOUT GIRLS, AND NOTHING'S GOING ON BETWEEN DYLAN AND ME.

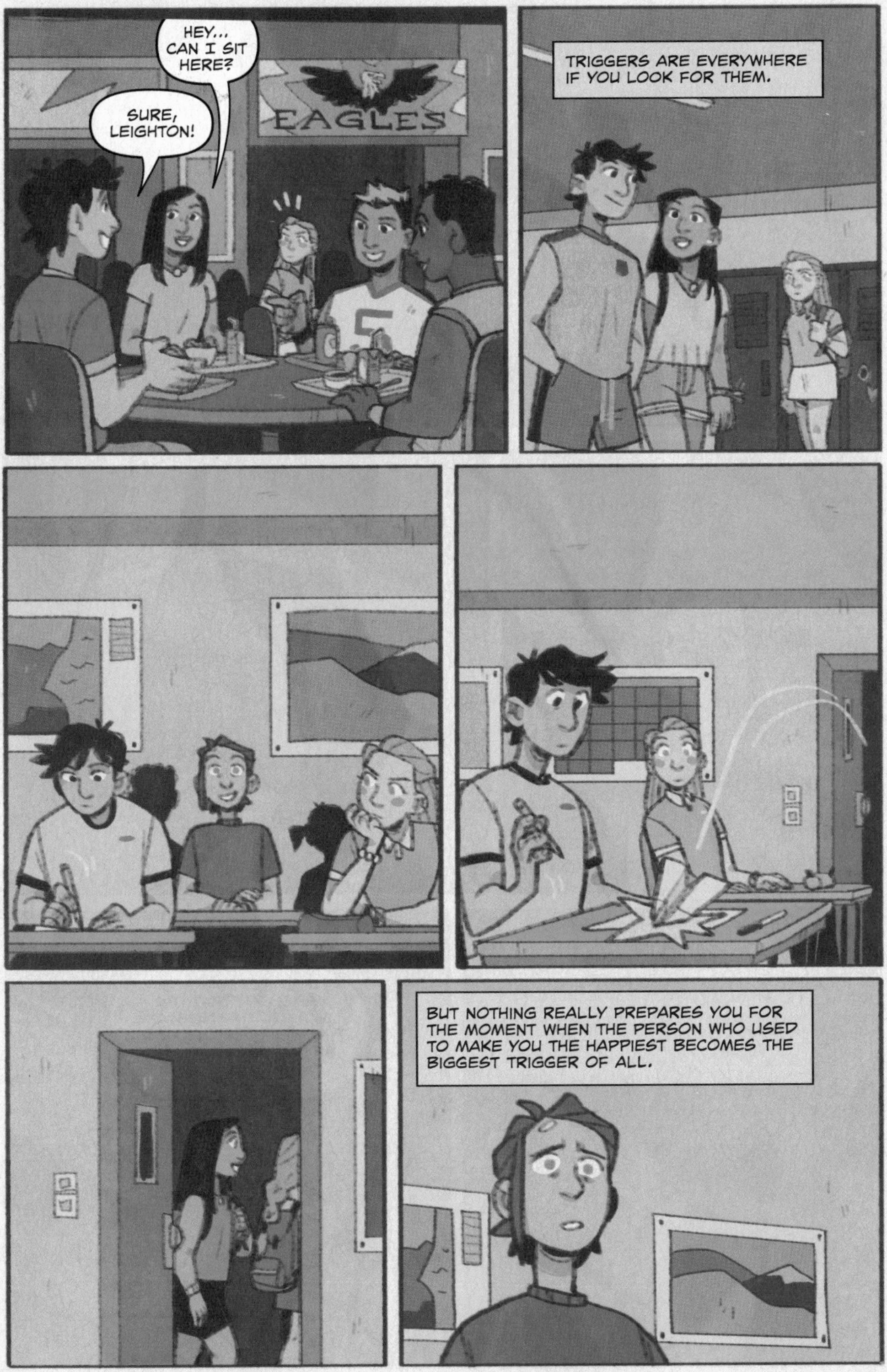
HEY... CAN I SIT HERE?
SURE, LEIGHTON!
EAGLES
TRIGGERS ARE EVERYWHERE IF YOU LOOK FOR THEM.
BUT NOTHING REALLY PREPARES YOU FOR THE MOMENT WHEN THE PERSON WHO USED TO MAKE YOU THE HAPPIEST BECOMES THE BIGGEST TRIGGER OF ALL.

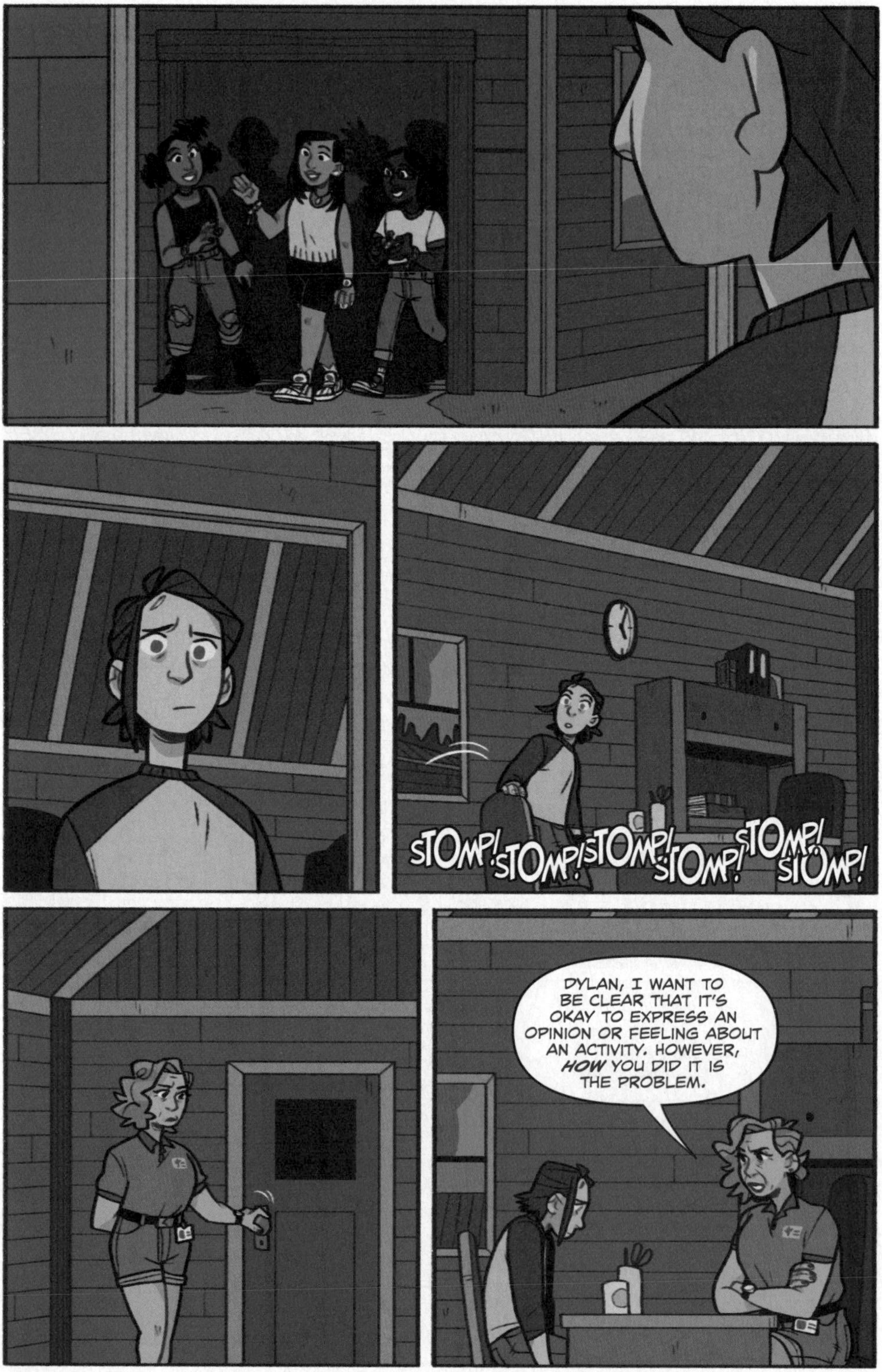
STOMP! STOMP! STOMP! STOMP! STOMP! STOMP!
DYLAN, I WANT TO BE CLEAR THAT IT'S OKAY TO EXPRESS AN OPINION OR FEELING ABOUT AN ACTIVITY. HOWEVER, *HOW* YOU DID IT IS THE PROBLEM.

THE LANGUAGE AND ANGRY TONE THAT YOU USED, AND INTERRUPTING ME-- IT'S NOT RESPECTFUL. THAT'S WHY I SENT YOU HERE. DO YOU UNDERSTAND?

YEAH... *UH,* YES, MA'AM.

NOW, AS I WAS SAYING WHEN YOU INTERRUPTED ME, FRIENDSHIP BRACELETS CAN BE MADE FOR A VARIETY OF PEOPLE AND REASONS.

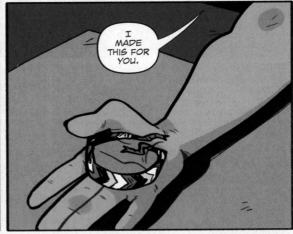

I MADE THIS FOR YOU.

NO ONE'S EVER GIVEN ME ONE BEFORE.

NOW SOMEONE HAS.

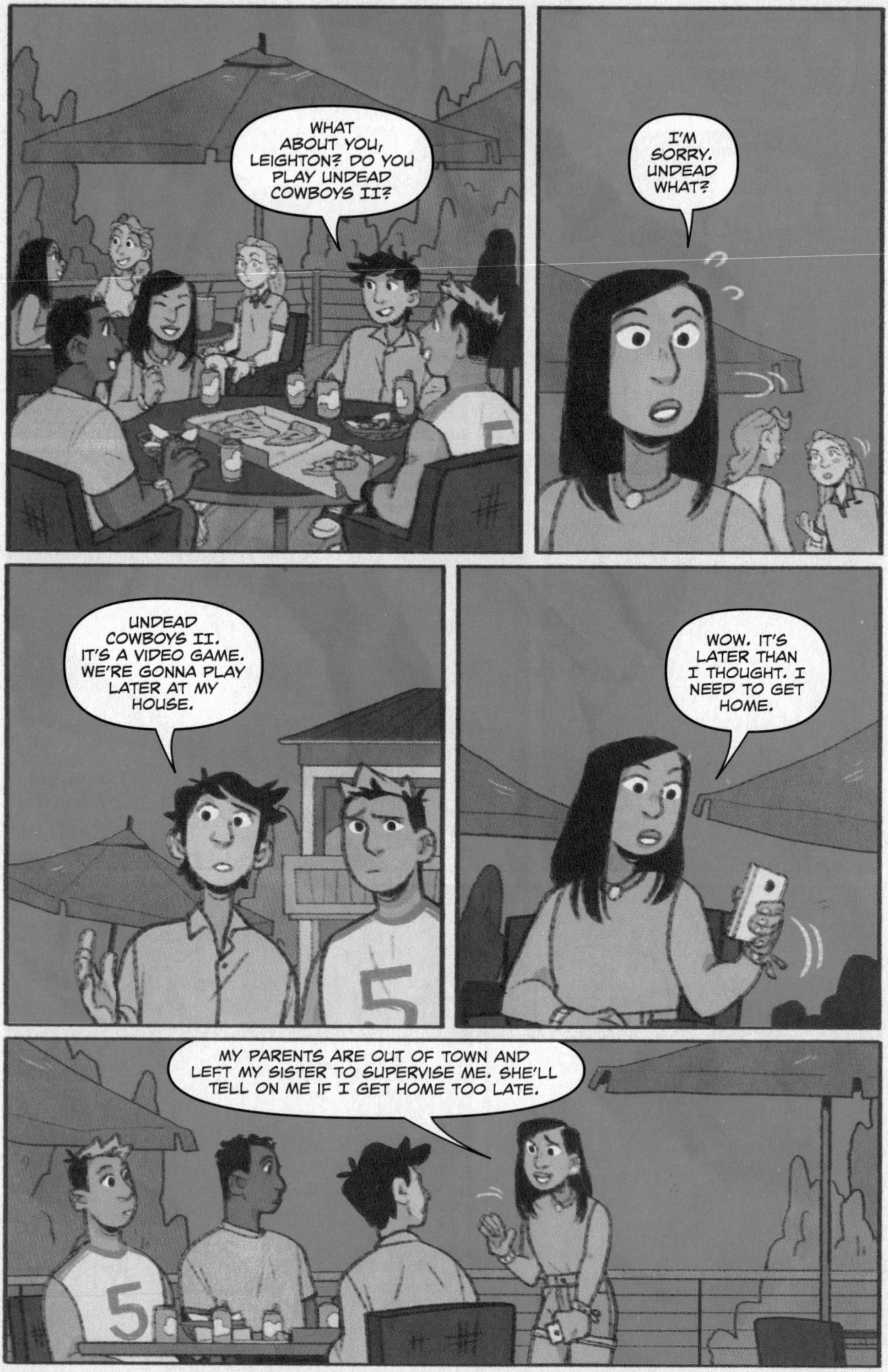
WHAT ABOUT YOU, LEIGHTON? DO YOU PLAY UNDEAD COWBOYS II?
I'M SORRY. UNDEAD WHAT?
UNDEAD COWBOYS II. IT'S A VIDEO GAME. WE'RE GONNA PLAY LATER AT MY HOUSE.
WOW. IT'S LATER THAN I THOUGHT. I NEED TO GET HOME.
MY PARENTS ARE OUT OF TOWN AND LEFT MY SISTER TO SUPERVISE ME. SHE'LL TELL ON ME IF I GET HOME TOO LATE.

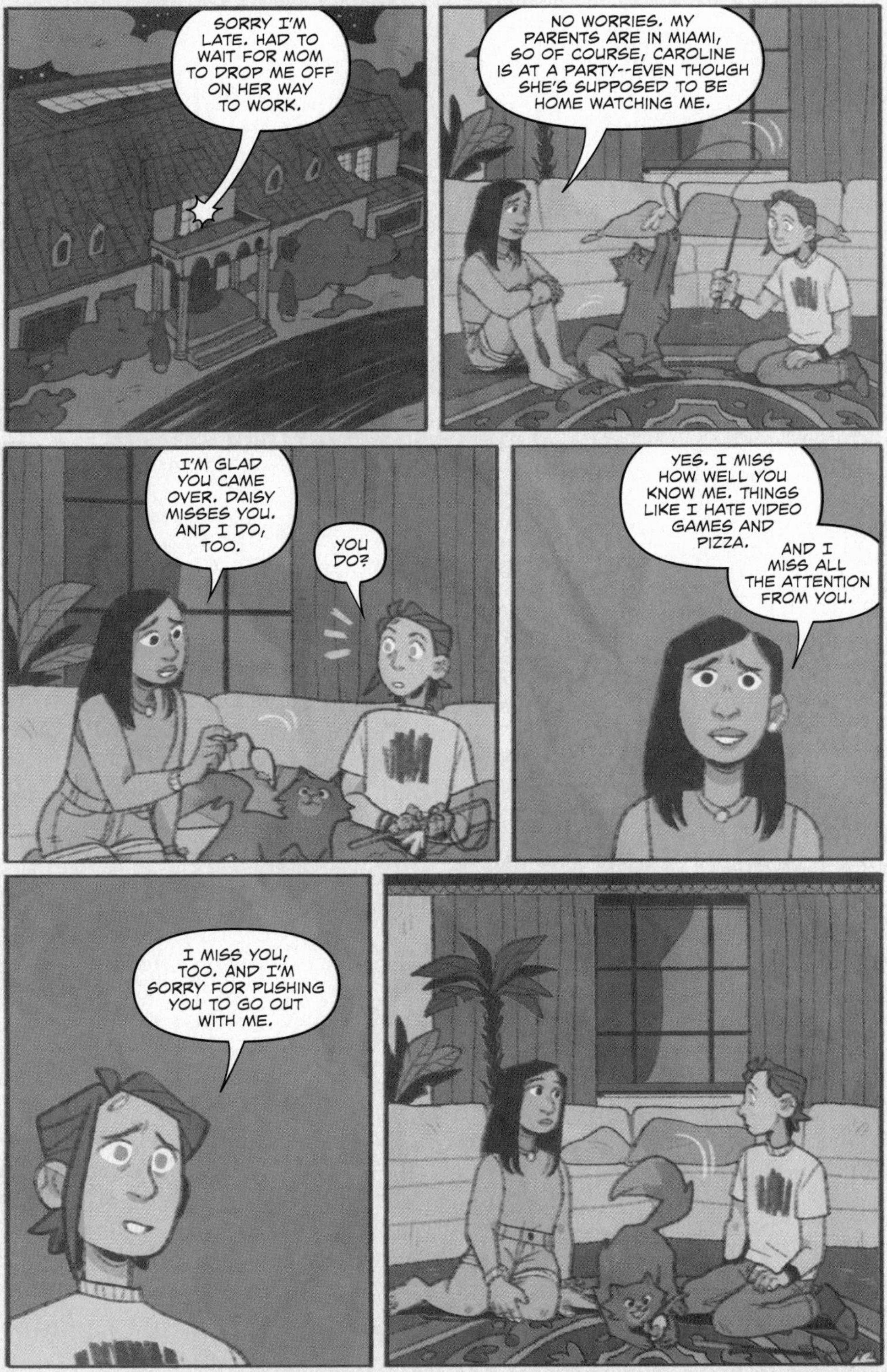
SORRY I'M LATE. HAD TO WAIT FOR MOM TO DROP ME OFF ON HER WAY TO WORK.
NO WORRIES. MY PARENTS ARE IN MIAMI, SO OF COURSE, CAROLINE IS AT A PARTY--EVEN THOUGH SHE'S SUPPOSED TO BE HOME WATCHING ME.
I'M GLAD YOU CAME OVER. DAISY MISSES YOU. AND I DO, TOO.
YOU DO?
YES. I MISS HOW WELL YOU KNOW ME. THINGS LIKE I HATE VIDEO GAMES AND PIZZA.
AND I MISS ALL THE ATTENTION FROM YOU.
I MISS YOU, TOO. AND I'M SORRY FOR PUSHING YOU TO GO OUT WITH ME.

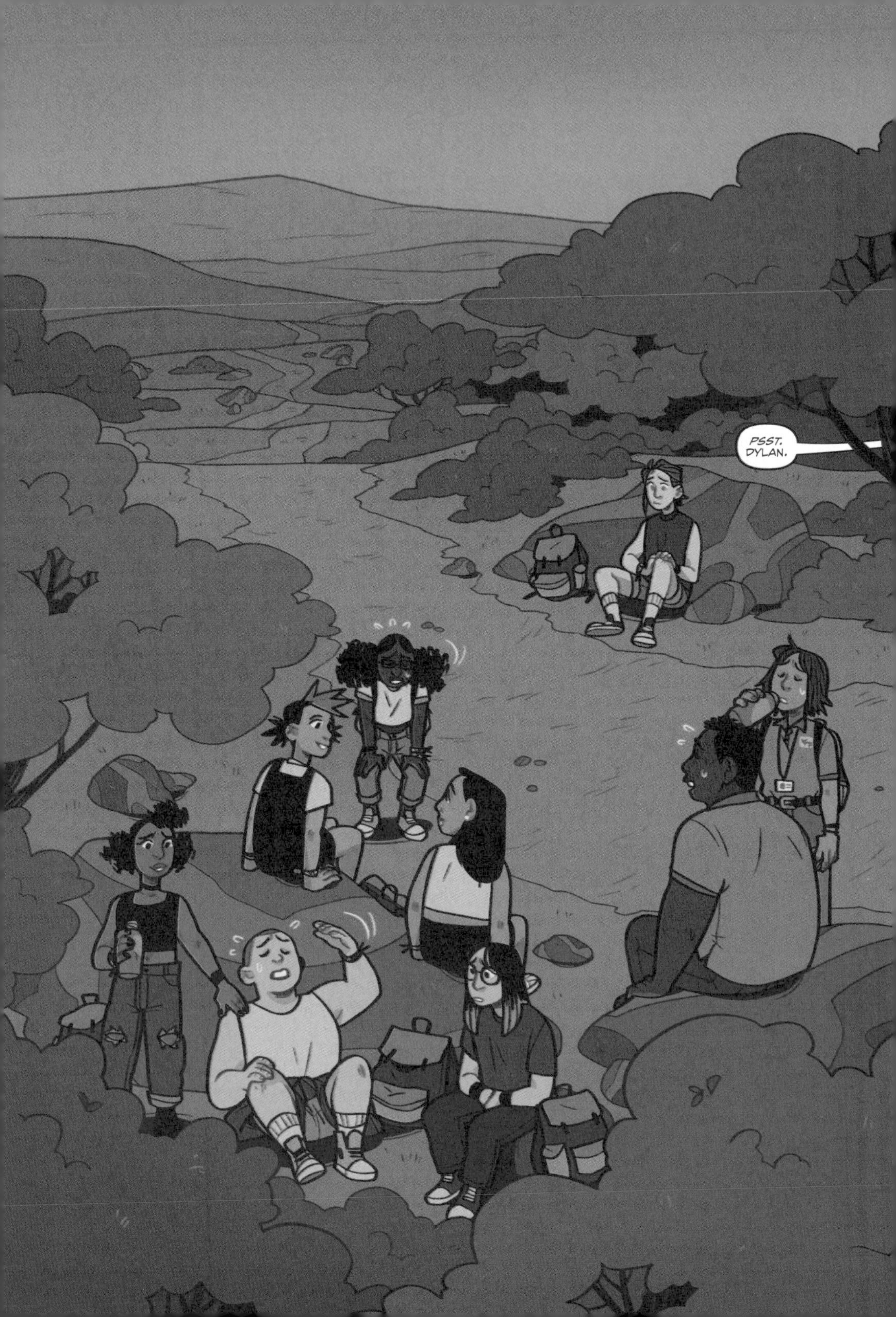
PSST. DYLAN.

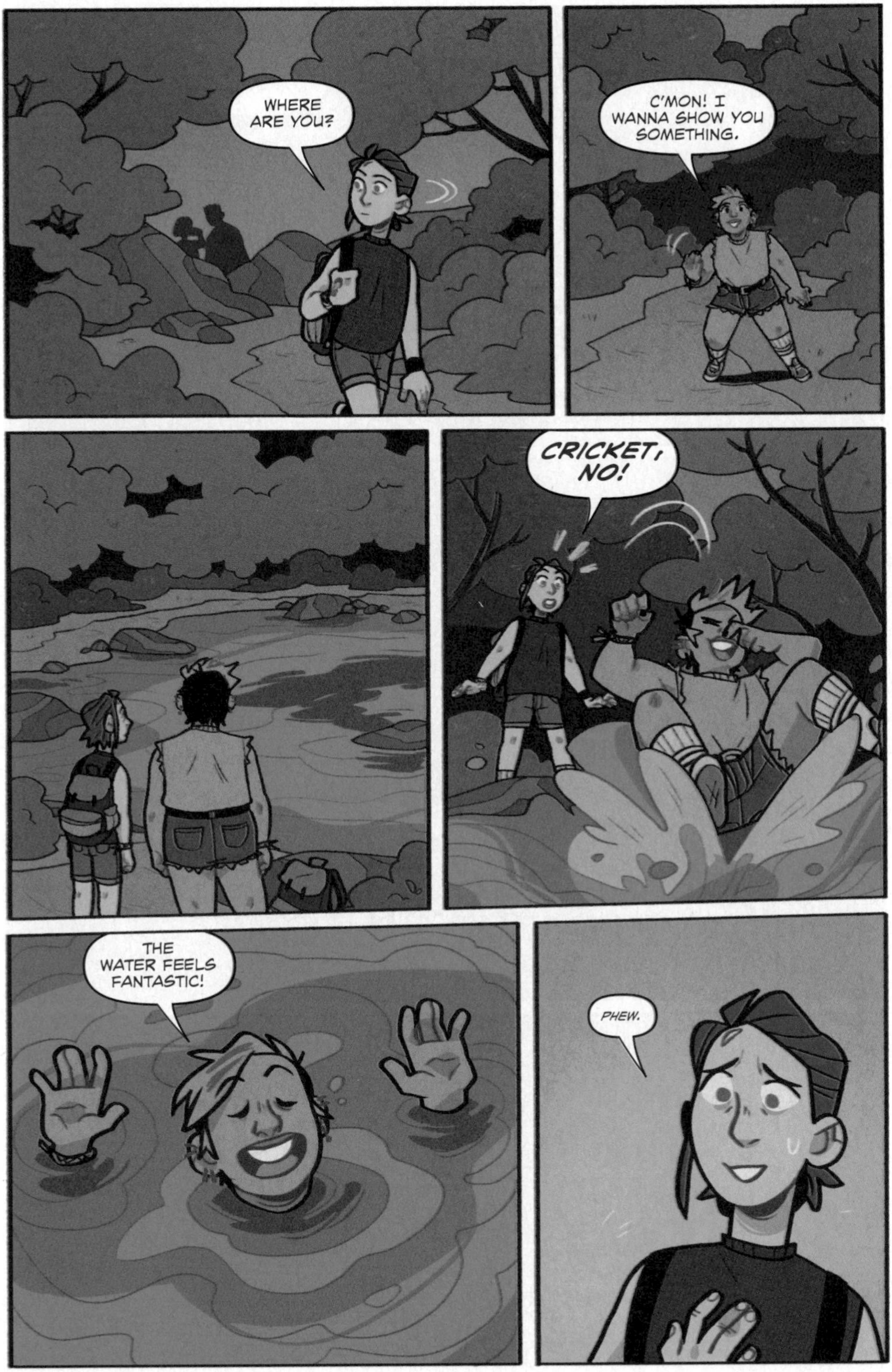
WHERE ARE YOU?
C'MON! I WANNA SHOW YOU SOMETHING.
CRICKET, NO!
THE WATER FEELS FANTASTIC!
PHEW.

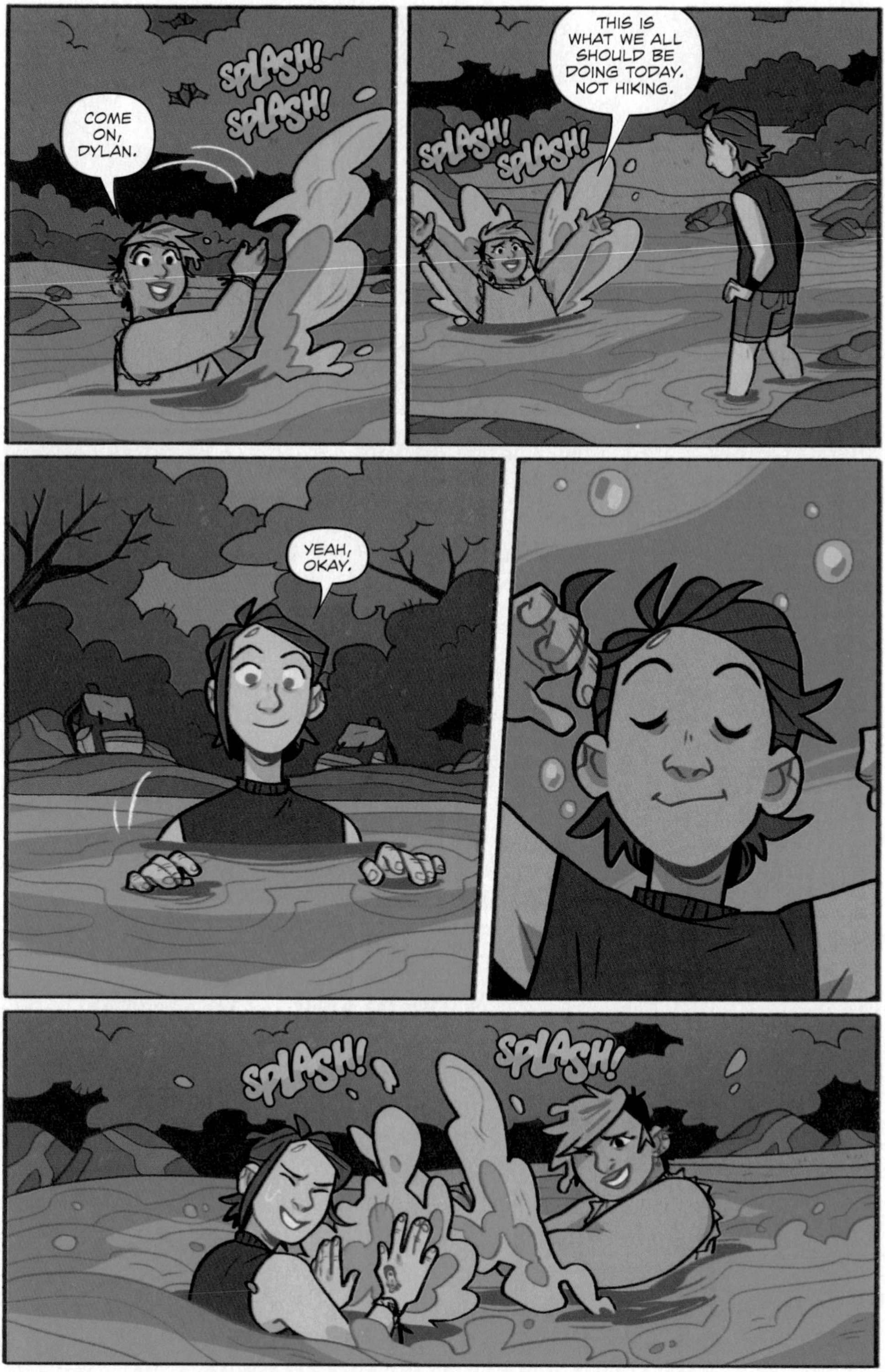
SPLASH!
SPLASH!
COME ON, DYLAN.
THIS IS WHAT WE ALL SHOULD BE DOING TODAY. NOT HIKING.
SPLASH!
SPLASH!
YEAH, OKAY.
SPLASH!
SPLASH!

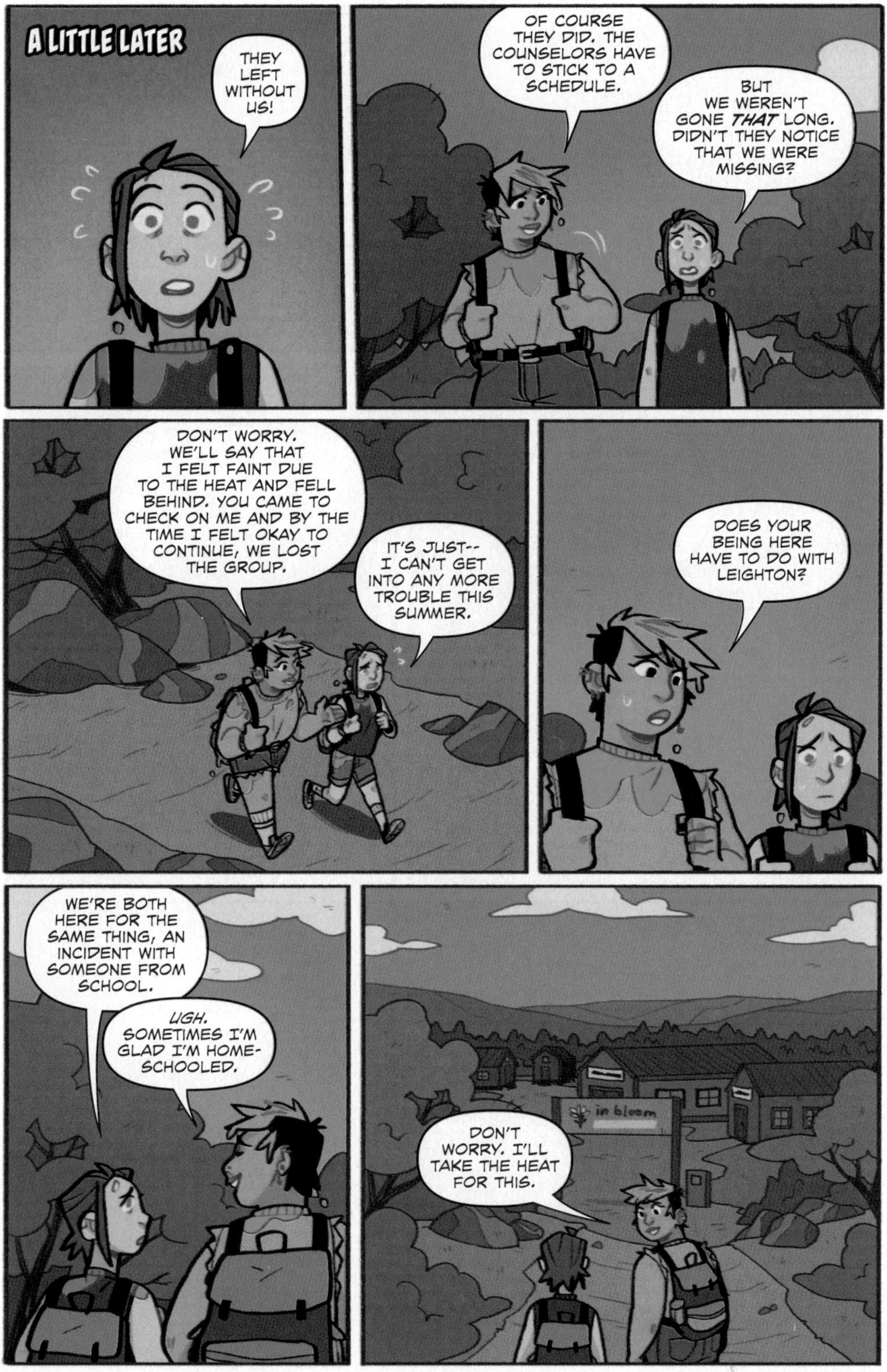
A LITTLE LATER
THEY LEFT WITHOUT US!
OF COURSE THEY DID. THE COUNSELORS HAVE TO STICK TO A SCHEDULE.
BUT WE WEREN'T GONE THAT LONG. DIDN'T THEY NOTICE THAT WE WERE MISSING?
DON'T WORRY. WE'LL SAY THAT I FELT FAINT DUE TO THE HEAT AND FELL BEHIND. YOU CAME TO CHECK ON ME AND BY THE TIME I FELT OKAY TO CONTINUE, WE LOST THE GROUP.
IT'S JUST-- I CAN'T GET INTO ANY MORE TROUBLE THIS SUMMER.
DOES YOUR BEING HERE HAVE TO DO WITH LEIGHTON?
WE'RE BOTH HERE FOR THE SAME THING, AN INCIDENT WITH SOMEONE FROM SCHOOL.
UGH. SOMETIMES I'M GLAD I'M HOME-SCHOOLED.
in bloom
DON'T WORRY. I'LL TAKE THE HEAT FOR THIS.

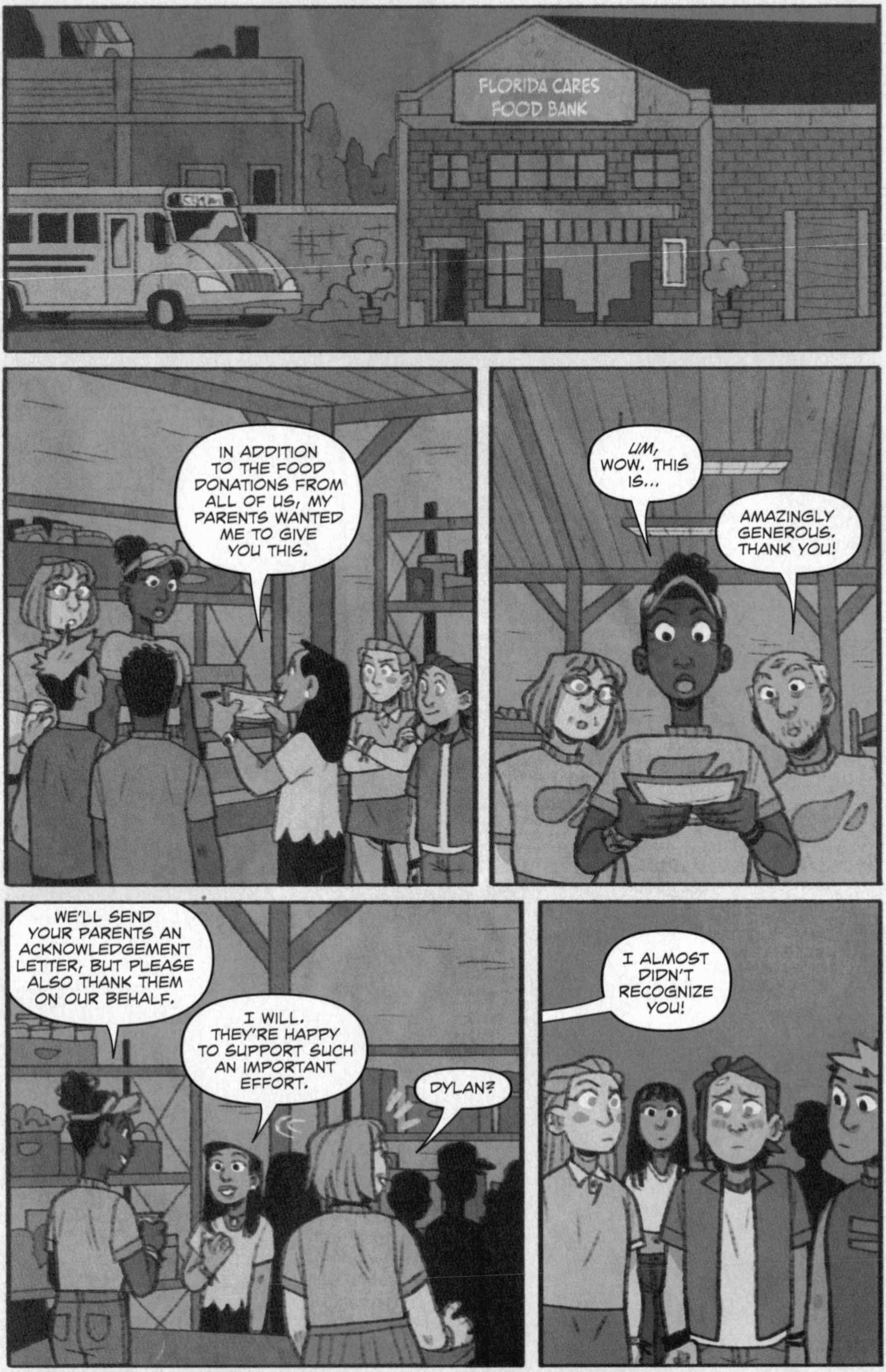
FLORIDA CARES FOOD BANK
IN ADDITION TO THE FOOD DONATIONS FROM ALL OF US, MY PARENTS WANTED ME TO GIVE YOU THIS.
UM, WOW. THIS IS...
AMAZINGLY GENEROUS. THANK YOU!
WE'LL SEND YOUR PARENTS AN ACKNOWLEDGEMENT LETTER, BUT PLEASE ALSO THANK THEM ON OUR BEHALF.
I WILL. THEY'RE HAPPY TO SUPPORT SUCH AN IMPORTANT EFFORT.
DYLAN?
I ALMOST DIDN'T RECOGNIZE YOU!

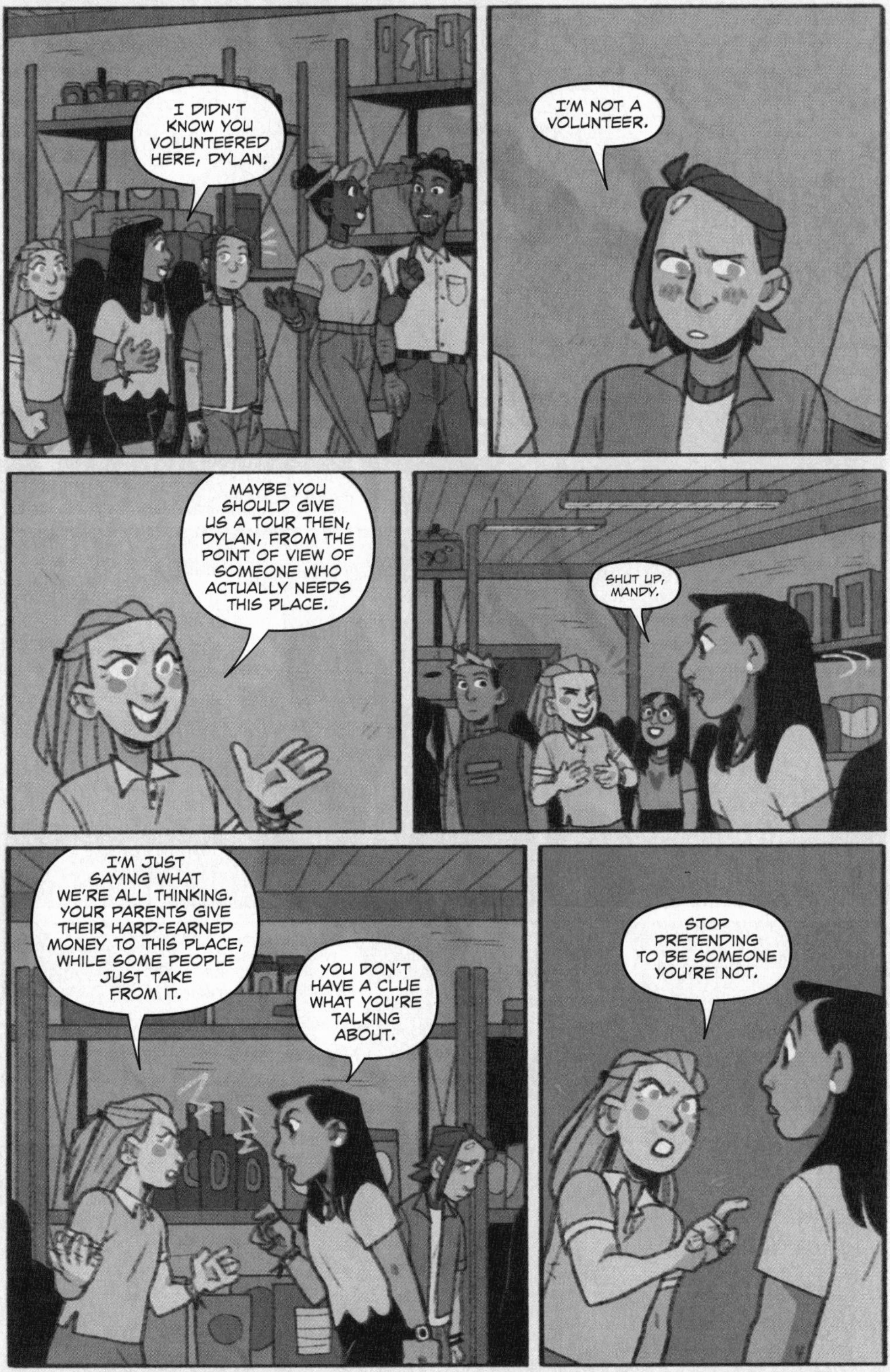
I DIDN'T KNOW YOU VOLUNTEERED HERE, DYLAN.
I'M NOT A VOLUNTEER.
MAYBE YOU SHOULD GIVE US A TOUR THEN, DYLAN, FROM THE POINT OF VIEW OF SOMEONE WHO ACTUALLY NEEDS THIS PLACE.
SHUT UP, MANDY.
I'M JUST SAYING WHAT WE'RE ALL THINKING. YOUR PARENTS GIVE THEIR HARD-EARNED MONEY TO THIS PLACE, WHILE SOME PEOPLE JUST TAKE FROM IT.
YOU DON'T HAVE A CLUE WHAT YOU'RE TALKING ABOUT.
STOP PRETENDING TO BE SOMEONE YOU'RE NOT.

HAD DYLAN NOT COME TO LOOK FOR ME, I MIGHT'VE FAINTED AND WOKEN UP HOURS LATER DEHYDRATED AND DISORIENTED. GOD KNOWS WHAT COULD'VE HAPPENED. IT'S TOO HOT TO BE HIKING.

DYLAN, NEXT TIME ALERT ONE OF THE COUNSELORS THAT CRICKET HAS FALLEN BEHIND, OKAY? YOU DID THE RIGHT THING BEING CONCERNED AND CHECKING ON HER, JUST DON'T DO IT ALONE.

YES, MA'AM.

SINCE YOU TWO ARE NOT GOING TO COMPLETE THE HIKE...

PICK ONE OF THE ACTIVITIES ON THIS LIST TO COMPLETE THIS AFTERNOON.

YOU'LL FIND WHAT YOU NEED FOR WHICHEVER ACTIVITY YOU CHOSE IN THE SUPPLY CLOSET OFF THE MAIN HALL.

VITIES

• go for a hike

• scavenger hunt

• build and launch an Antacid rocket

• outdoor treasure

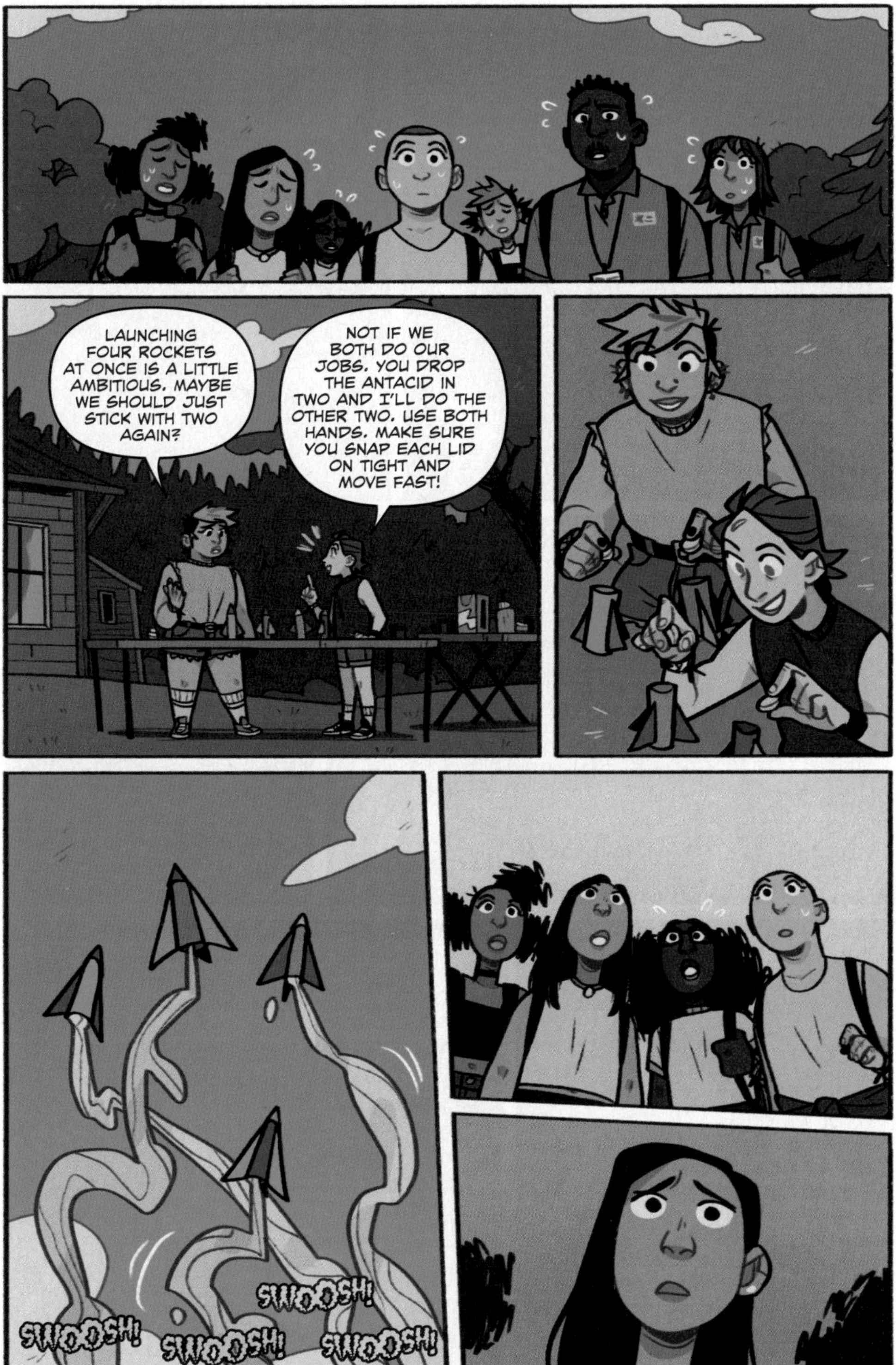
LAUNCHING FOUR ROCKETS AT ONCE IS A LITTLE AMBITIOUS. MAYBE WE SHOULD JUST STICK WITH TWO AGAIN?
NOT IF WE BOTH DO OUR JOBS. YOU DROP THE ANTACID IN TWO AND I'LL DO THE OTHER TWO. USE BOTH HANDS. MAKE SURE YOU SNAP EACH LID ON TIGHT AND MOVE FAST!
SWOOSH!
SWOOSH!
SWOOSH!
SWOOSH!

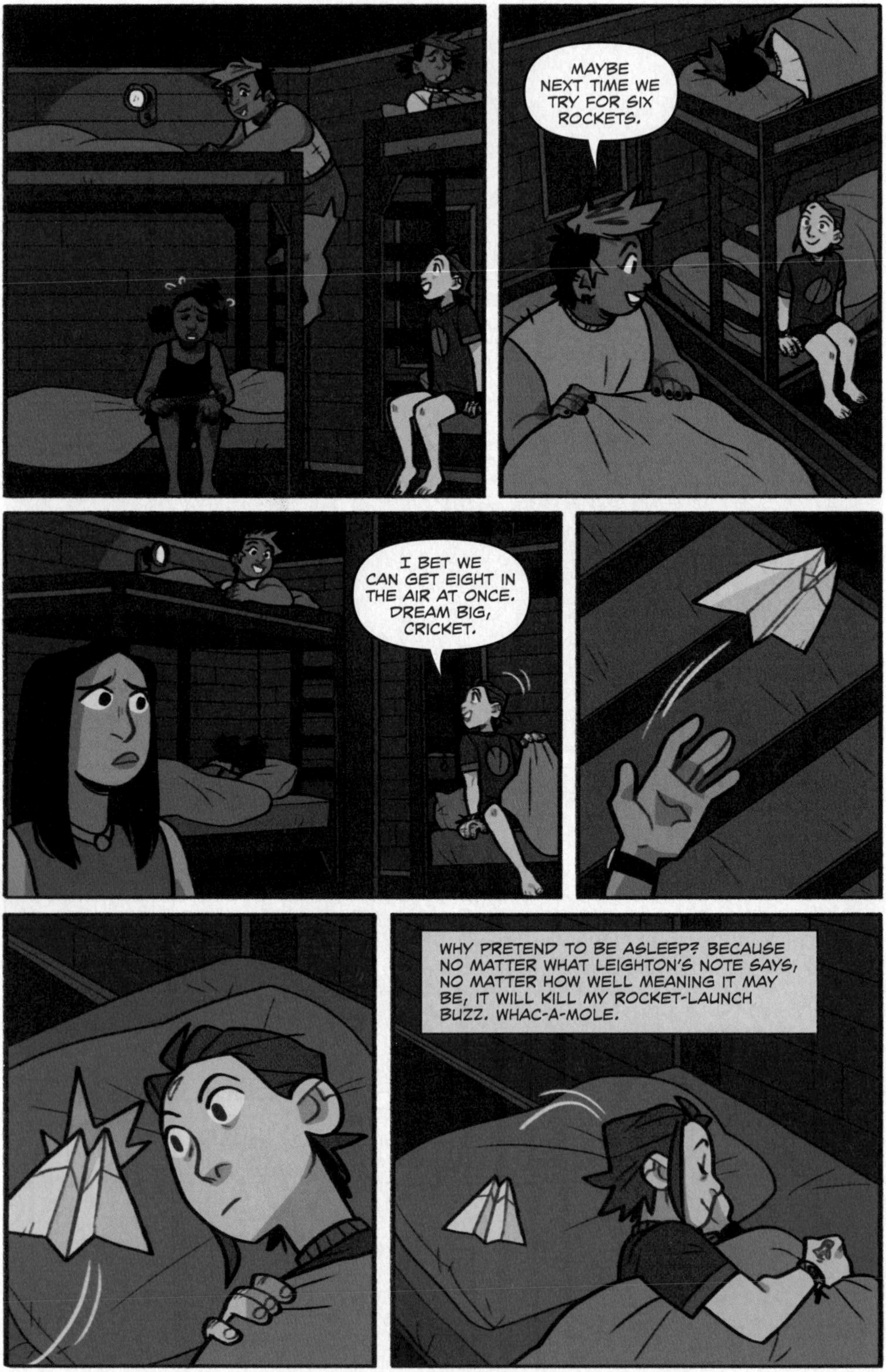
MAYBE NEXT TIME WE TRY FOR SIX ROCKETS.
I BET WE CAN GET EIGHT IN THE AIR AT ONCE. DREAM BIG, CRICKET.
WHY PRETEND TO BE ASLEEP? BECAUSE NO MATTER WHAT LEIGHTON'S NOTE SAYS, NO MATTER HOW WELL MEANING IT MAY BE, IT WILL KILL MY ROCKET-LAUNCH BUZZ. WHAC-A-MOLE.

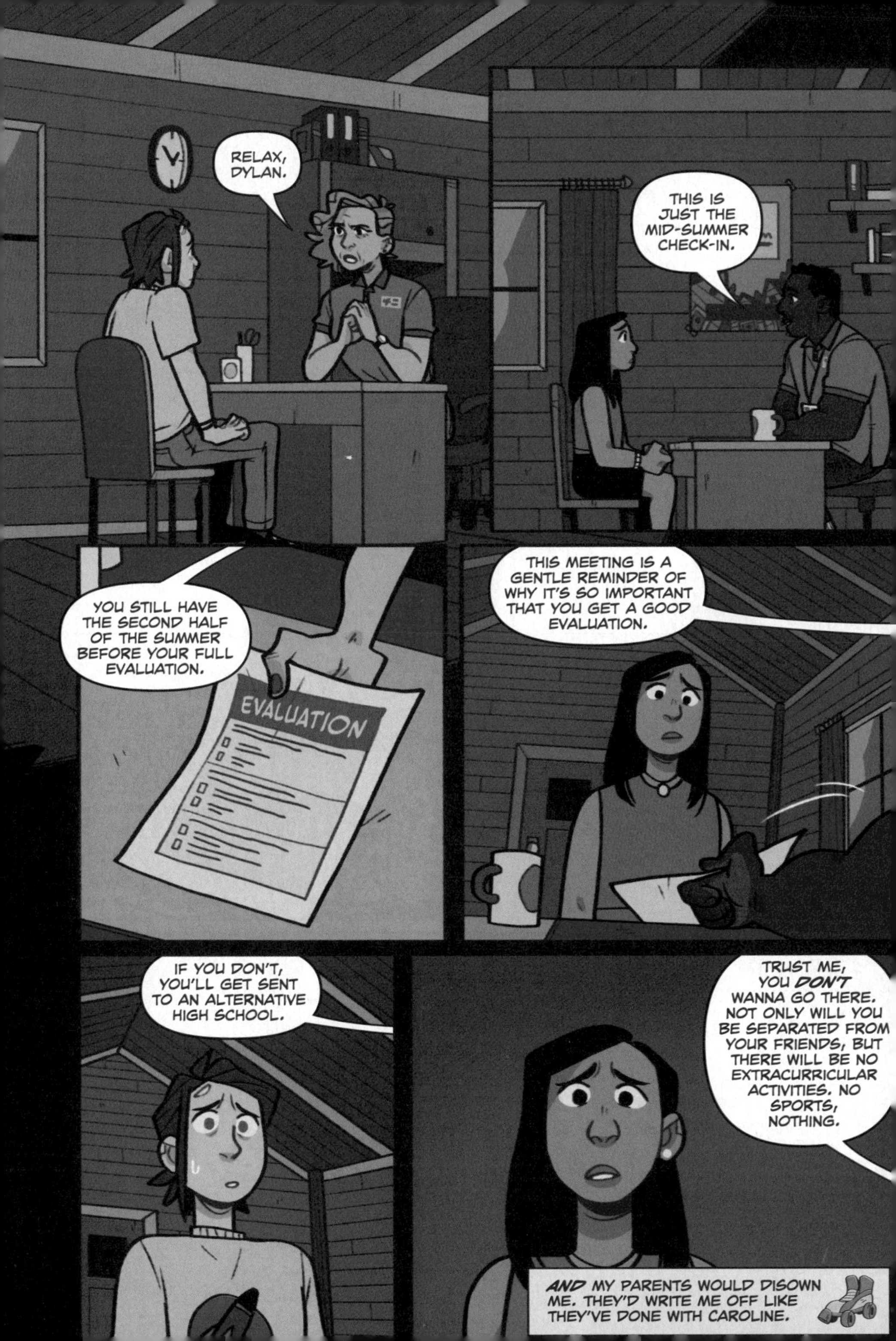
RELAX, DYLAN.
THIS IS JUST THE MID-SUMMER CHECK-IN.
YOU STILL HAVE THE SECOND HALF OF THE SUMMER BEFORE YOUR FULL EVALUATION.
EVALUATION
THIS MEETING IS A GENTLE REMINDER OF WHY IT'S SO IMPORTANT THAT YOU GET A GOOD EVALUATION.
IF YOU DON'T, YOU'LL GET SENT TO AN ALTERNATIVE HIGH SCHOOL.
TRUST ME, YOU *DON'T* WANNA GO THERE. NOT ONLY WILL YOU BE SEPARATED FROM YOUR FRIENDS, BUT THERE WILL BE NO EXTRACURRICULAR ACTIVITIES. NO SPORTS, NOTHING.
AND MY PARENTS WOULD DISOWN ME. THEY'D WRITE ME OFF LIKE THEY'VE DONE WITH CAROLINE.

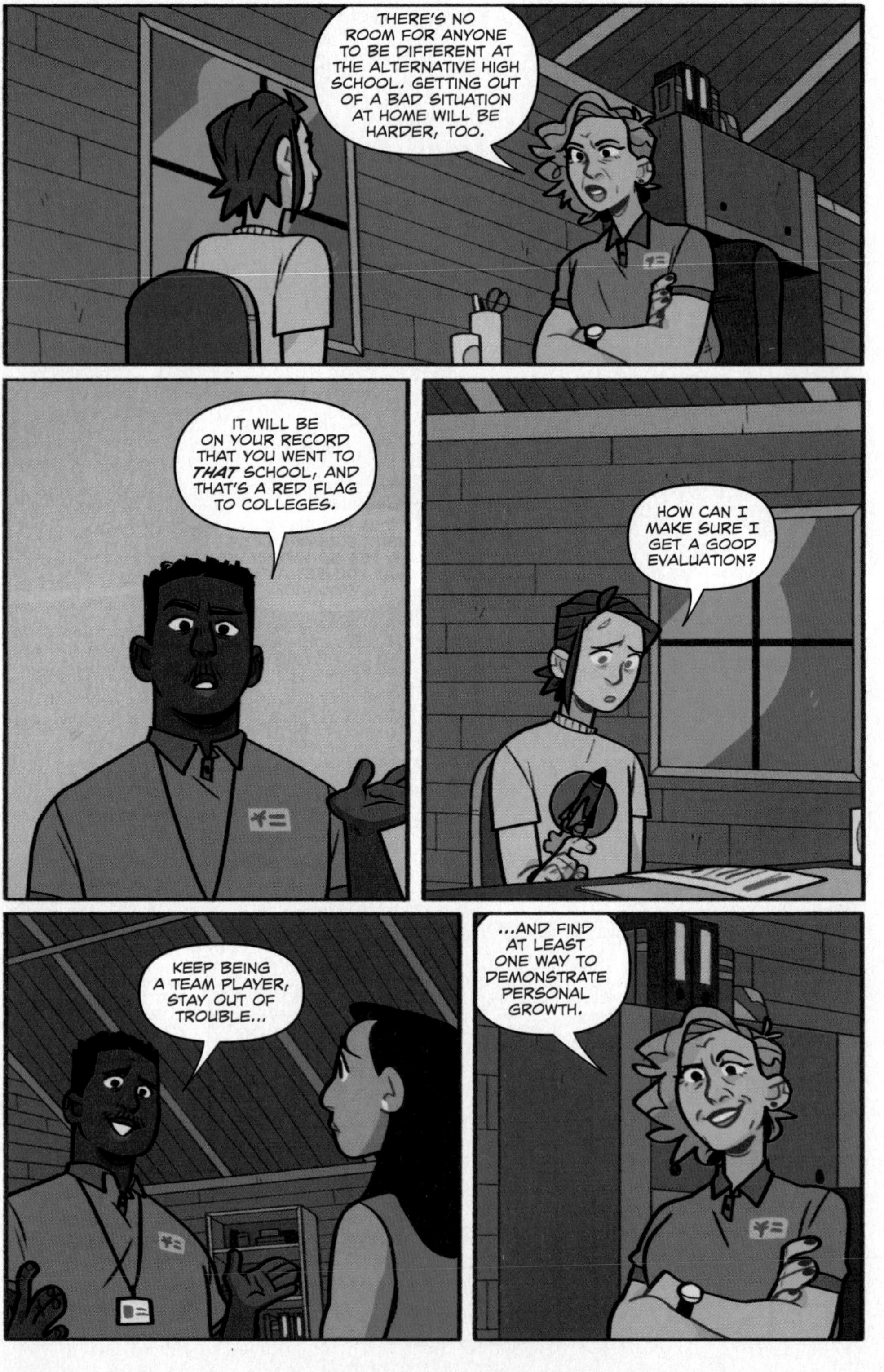
THERE'S NO ROOM FOR ANYONE TO BE DIFFERENT AT THE ALTERNATIVE HIGH SCHOOL. GETTING OUT OF A BAD SITUATION AT HOME WILL BE HARDER, TOO.
IT WILL BE ON YOUR RECORD THAT YOU WENT TO *THAT* SCHOOL, AND THAT'S A RED FLAG TO COLLEGES.
HOW CAN I MAKE SURE I GET A GOOD EVALUATION?
KEEP BEING A TEAM PLAYER, STAY OUT OF TROUBLE...
...AND FIND AT LEAST ONE WAY TO DEMONSTRATE PERSONAL GROWTH.

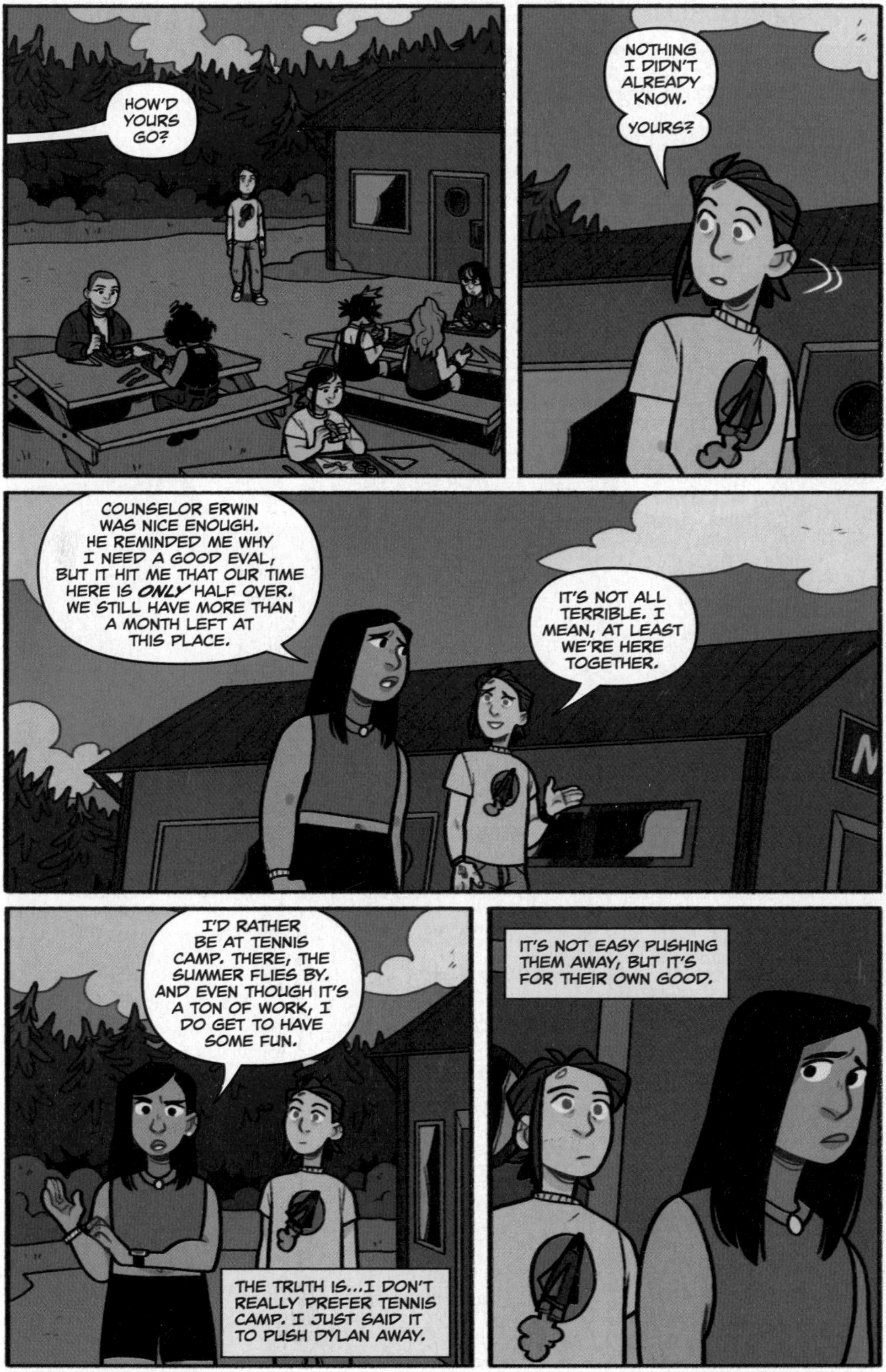
HOW'D YOURS GO?
NOTHING I DIDN'T ALREADY KNOW.
YOURS?
COUNSELOR ERWIN WAS NICE ENOUGH. HE REMINDED ME WHY I NEED A GOOD EVAL, BUT IT HIT ME THAT OUR TIME HERE IS *ONLY* HALF OVER. WE STILL HAVE MORE THAN A MONTH LEFT AT THIS PLACE.
IT'S NOT ALL TERRIBLE. I MEAN, AT LEAST WE'RE HERE TOGETHER.
I'D RATHER BE AT TENNIS CAMP. THERE, THE SUMMER FLIES BY. AND EVEN THOUGH IT'S A TON OF WORK, I DO GET TO HAVE SOME FUN.
THE TRUTH IS...I DON'T REALLY PREFER TENNIS CAMP. I JUST SAID IT TO PUSH DYLAN AWAY.
IT'S NOT EASY PUSHING THEM AWAY, BUT IT'S FOR THEIR OWN GOOD.

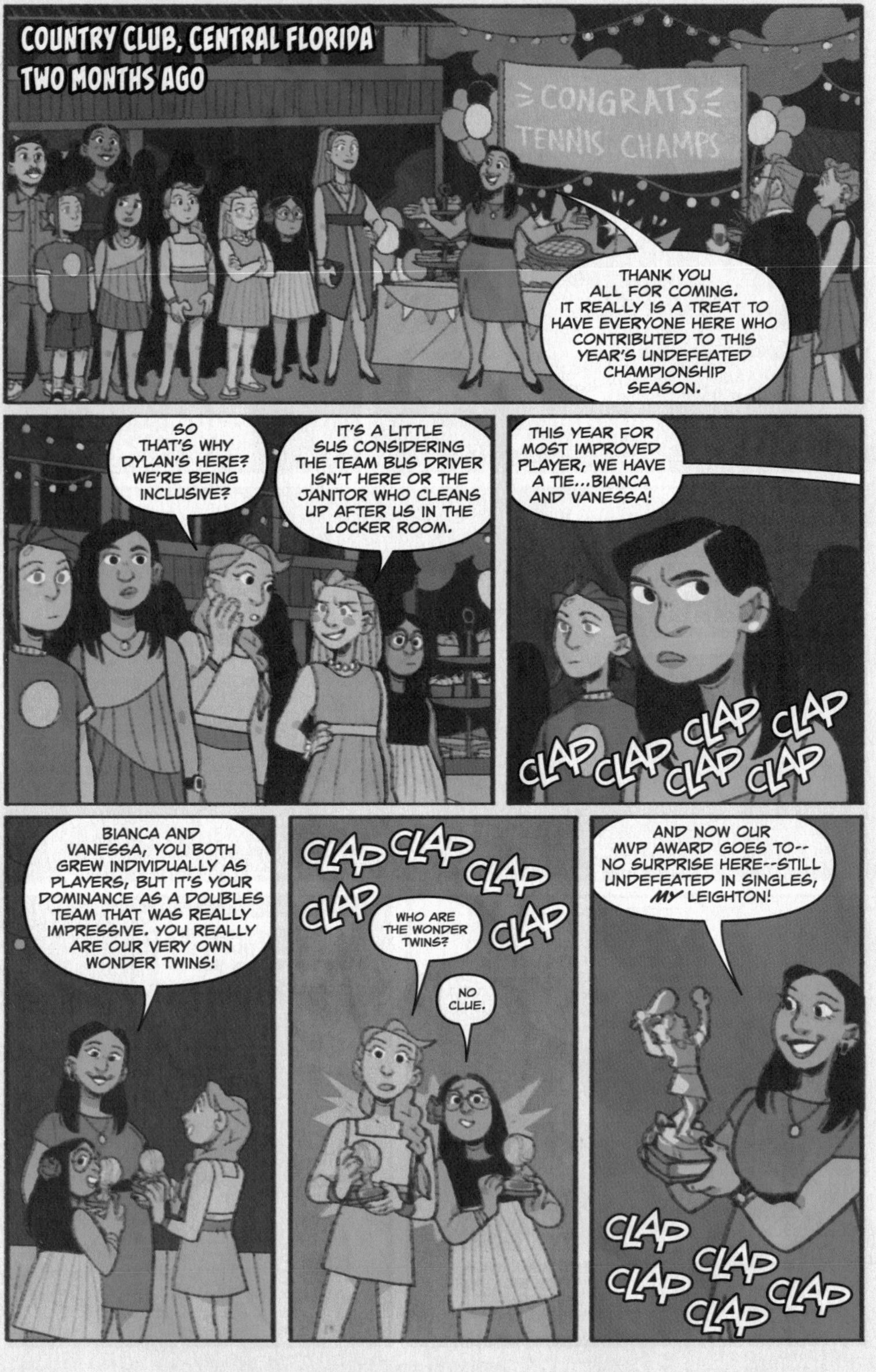
COUNTRY CLUB, CENTRAL FLORIDA TWO MONTHS AGO
CONGRATS TENNIS CHAMPS
THANK YOU ALL FOR COMING. IT REALLY IS A TREAT TO HAVE EVERYONE HERE WHO CONTRIBUTED TO THIS YEAR'S UNDEFEATED CHAMPIONSHIP SEASON.
SO THAT'S WHY DYLAN'S HERE? WE'RE BEING INCLUSIVE?
IT'S A LITTLE SUS CONSIDERING THE TEAM BUS DRIVER ISN'T HERE OR THE JANITOR WHO CLEANS UP AFTER US IN THE LOCKER ROOM.
THIS YEAR FOR MOST IMPROVED PLAYER, WE HAVE A TIE...BIANCA AND VANESSA!
CLAP CLAP CLAP CLAP CLAP CLAP CLAP
BIANCA AND VANESSA, YOU BOTH GREW INDIVIDUALLY AS PLAYERS, BUT IT'S YOUR DOMINANCE AS A DOUBLES TEAM THAT WAS REALLY IMPRESSIVE. YOU REALLY ARE OUR VERY OWN WONDER TWINS!
CLAP CLAP CLAP CLAP CLAP
WHO ARE THE WONDER TWINS?
NO CLUE.
AND NOW OUR MVP AWARD GOES TO-- NO SURPRISE HERE--STILL UNDEFEATED IN SINGLES, *MY* LEIGHTON!
CLAP CLAP CLAP CLAP CLAP CLAP

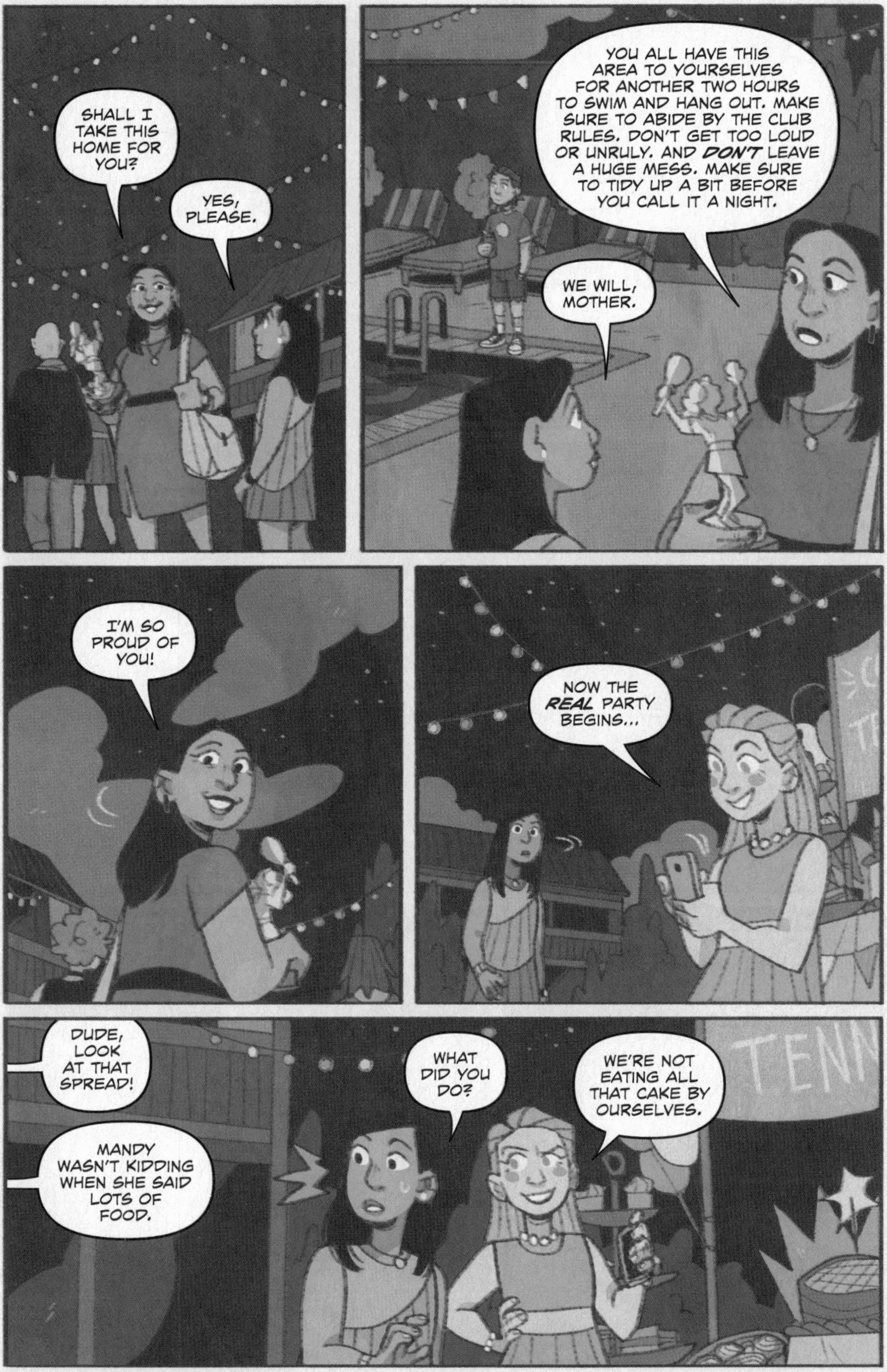

SHALL I TAKE THIS HOME FOR YOU?
YES, PLEASE.
YOU ALL HAVE THIS AREA TO YOURSELVES FOR ANOTHER TWO HOURS TO SWIM AND HANG OUT. MAKE SURE TO ABIDE BY THE CLUB RULES. DON'T GET TOO LOUD OR UNRULY. AND *DON'T* LEAVE A HUGE MESS. MAKE SURE TO TIDY UP A BIT BEFORE YOU CALL IT A NIGHT.
WE WILL, MOTHER.
I'M SO PROUD OF YOU!
NOW THE *REAL* PARTY BEGINS...
DUDE, LOOK AT THAT SPREAD!
MANDY WASN'T KIDDING WHEN SHE SAID LOTS OF FOOD.
WHAT DID YOU DO?
WE'RE NOT EATING ALL THAT CAKE BY OURSELVES.
TENN

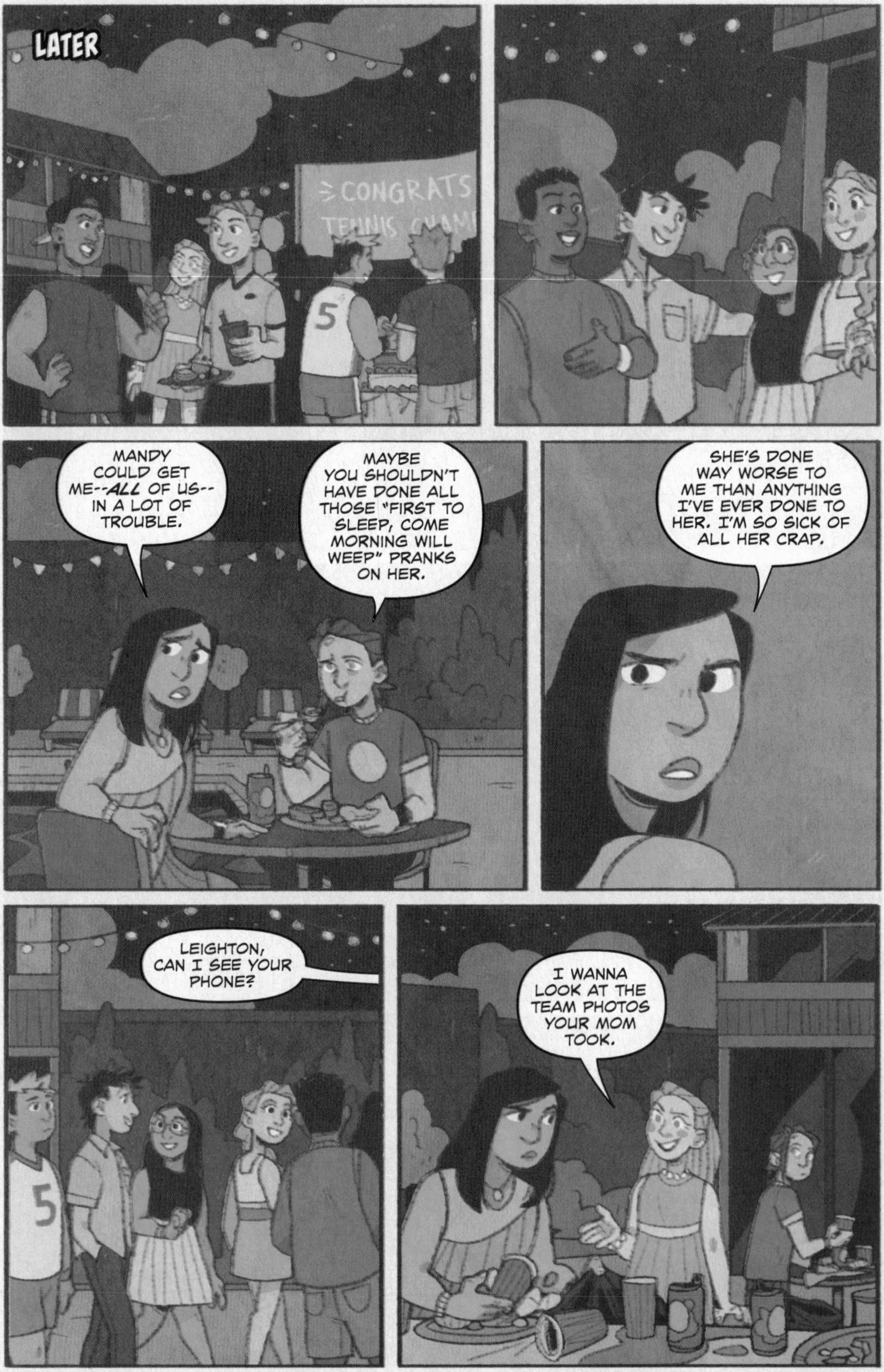
LATER
CONGRATS
TENNIS CHAMP
MANDY COULD GET ME--*ALL* OF US--IN A LOT OF TROUBLE.
MAYBE YOU SHOULDN'T HAVE DONE ALL THOSE "FIRST TO SLEEP, COME MORNING WILL WEEP" PRANKS ON HER.
SHE'S DONE WAY WORSE TO ME THAN ANYTHING I'VE EVER DONE TO HER. I'M SO SICK OF ALL HER CRAP.
LEIGHTON, CAN I SEE YOUR PHONE?
I WANNA LOOK AT THE TEAM PHOTOS YOUR MOM TOOK.

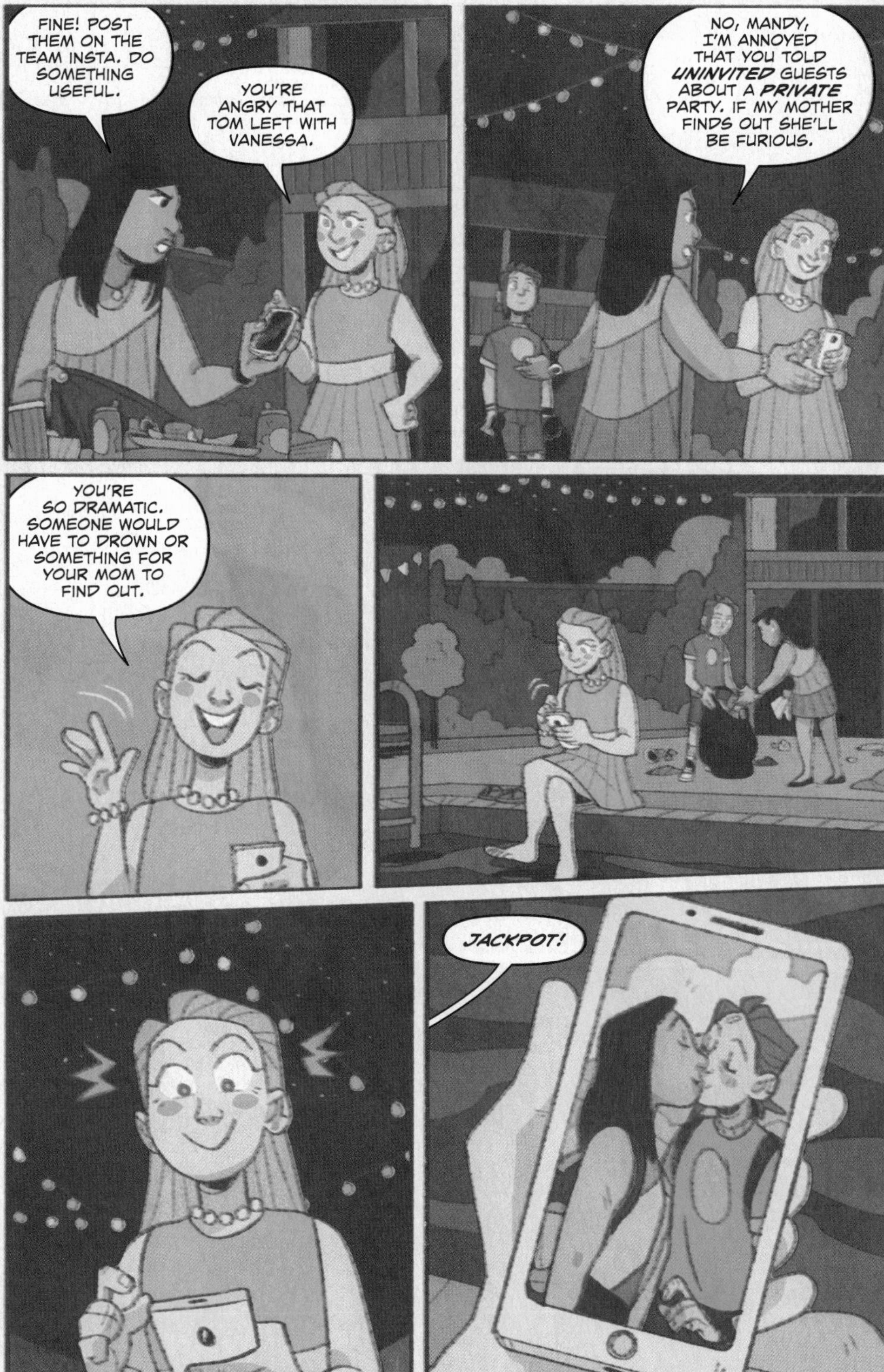
FINE! POST THEM ON THE TEAM INSTA. DO SOMETHING USEFUL.
YOU'RE ANGRY THAT TOM LEFT WITH VANESSA.
NO, MANDY, I'M ANNOYED THAT YOU TOLD *UNINVITED* GUESTS ABOUT A *PRIVATE* PARTY. IF MY MOTHER FINDS OUT SHE'LL BE FURIOUS.
YOU'RE SO DRAMATIC. SOMEONE WOULD HAVE TO DROWN OR SOMETHING FOR YOUR MOM TO FIND OUT.
JACKPOT!

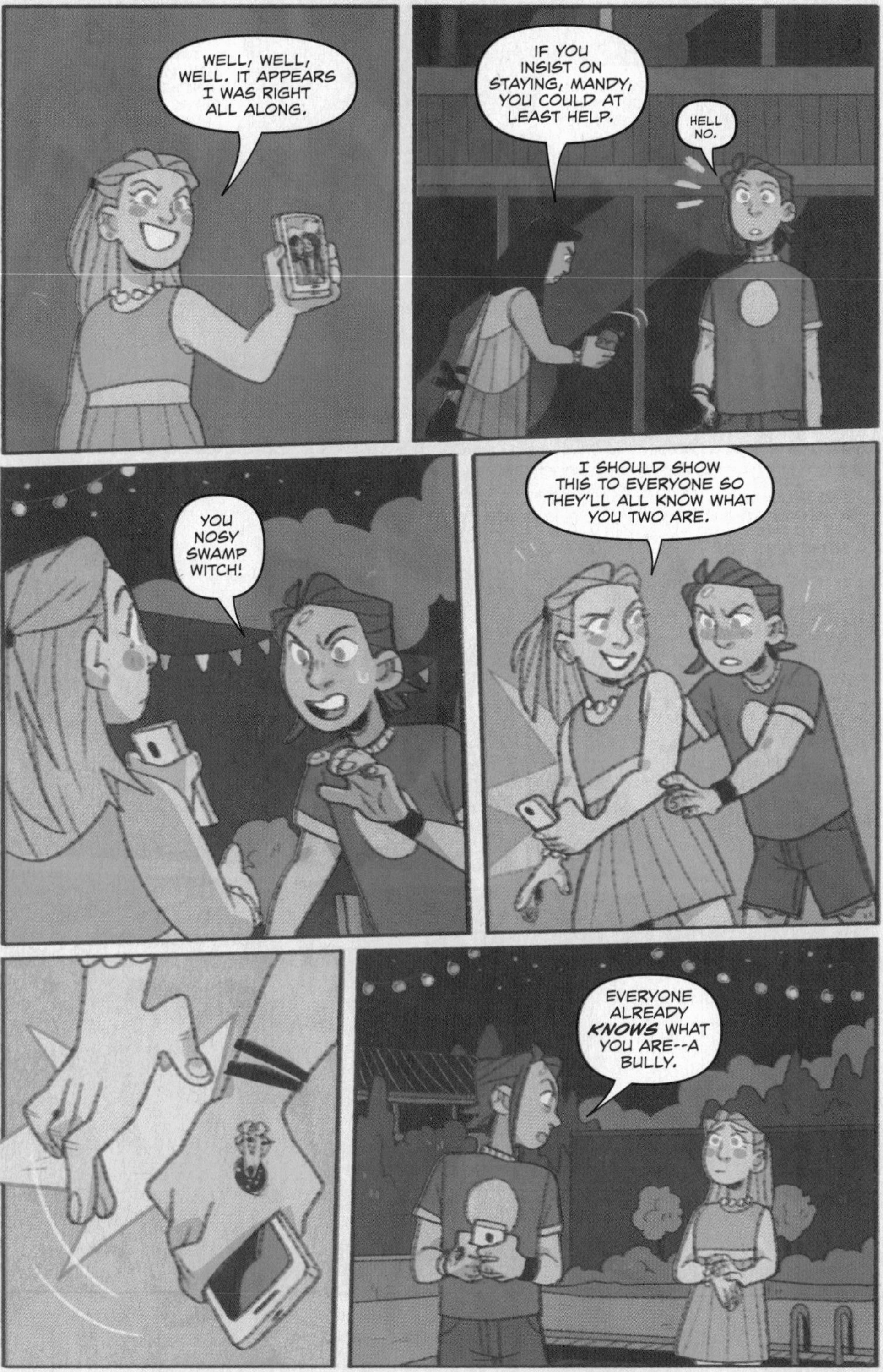
WELL, WELL, WELL. IT APPEARS I WAS RIGHT ALL ALONG.
IF YOU INSIST ON STAYING, MANDY, YOU COULD AT LEAST HELP.
HELL NO.
YOU NOSY SWAMP WITCH!
I SHOULD SHOW THIS TO EVERYONE SO THEY'LL ALL KNOW WHAT YOU TWO ARE.
EVERYONE ALREADY ***KNOWS*** WHAT YOU ARE--A BULLY.

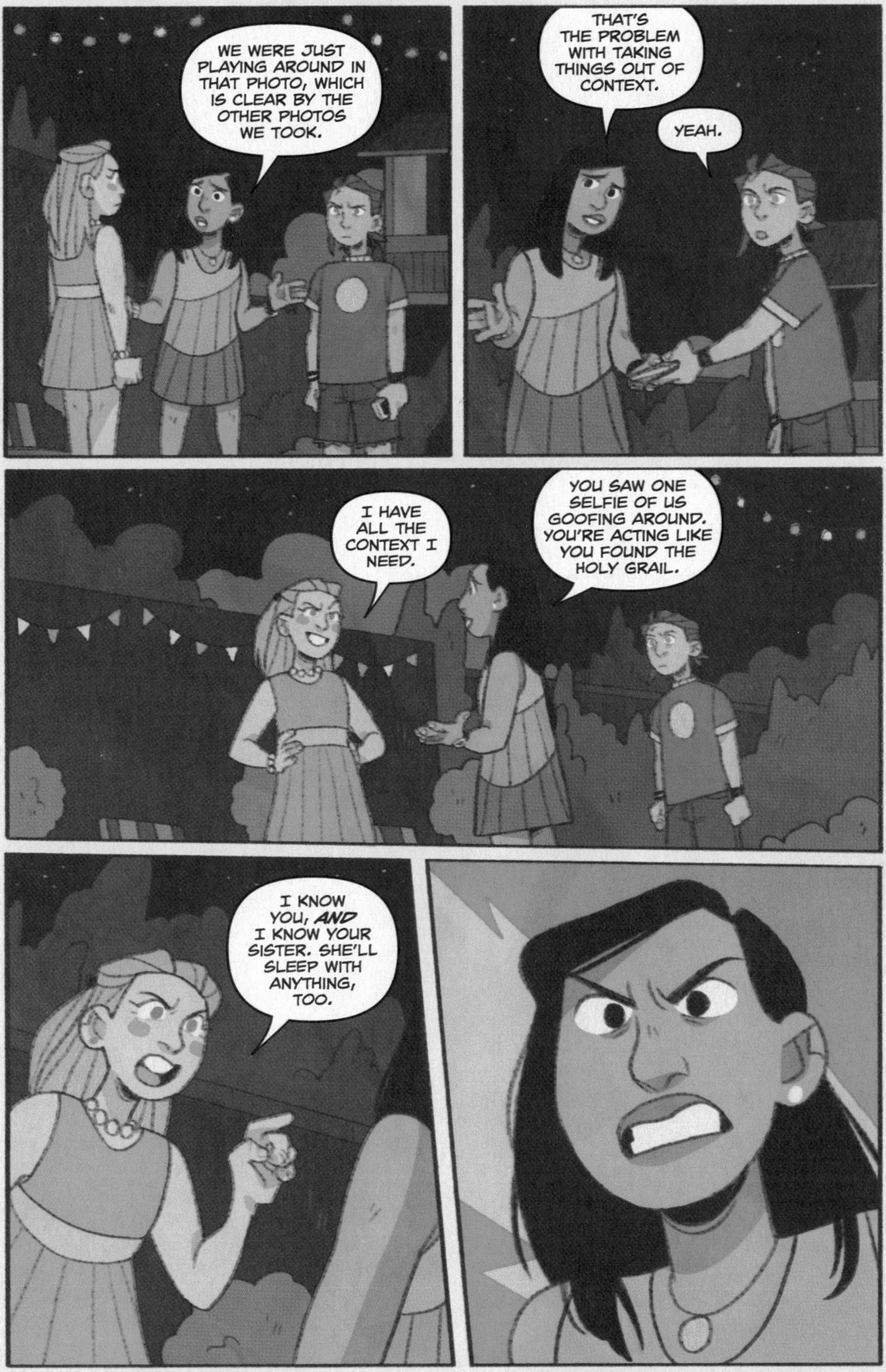
WE WERE JUST PLAYING AROUND IN THAT PHOTO, WHICH IS CLEAR BY THE OTHER PHOTOS WE TOOK.
THAT'S THE PROBLEM WITH TAKING THINGS OUT OF CONTEXT.
YEAH.
I HAVE ALL THE CONTEXT I NEED.
YOU SAW ONE SELFIE OF US GOOFING AROUND. YOU'RE ACTING LIKE YOU FOUND THE HOLY GRAIL.
I KNOW YOU, *AND* I KNOW YOUR SISTER. SHE'LL SLEEP WITH ANYTHING, TOO.

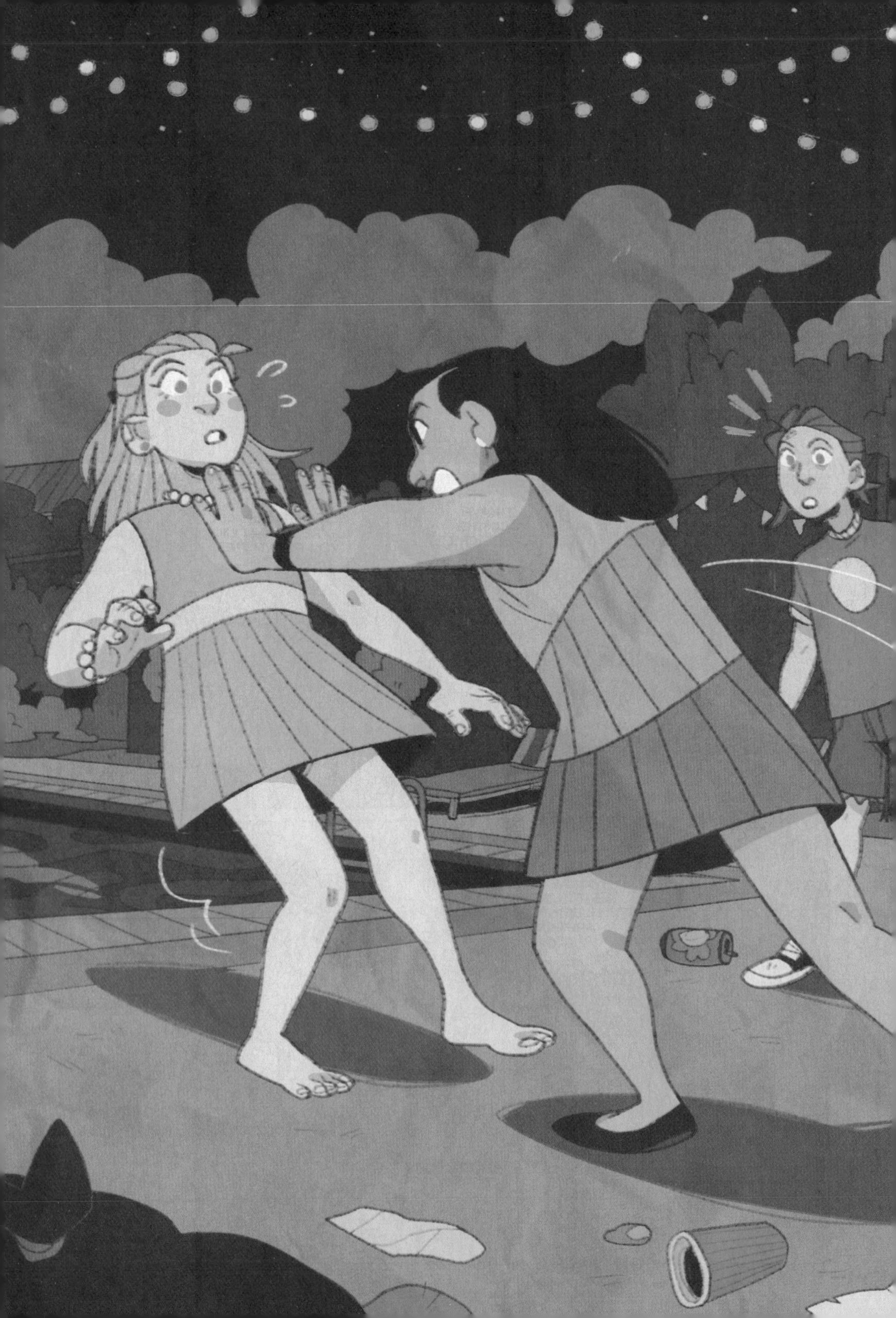

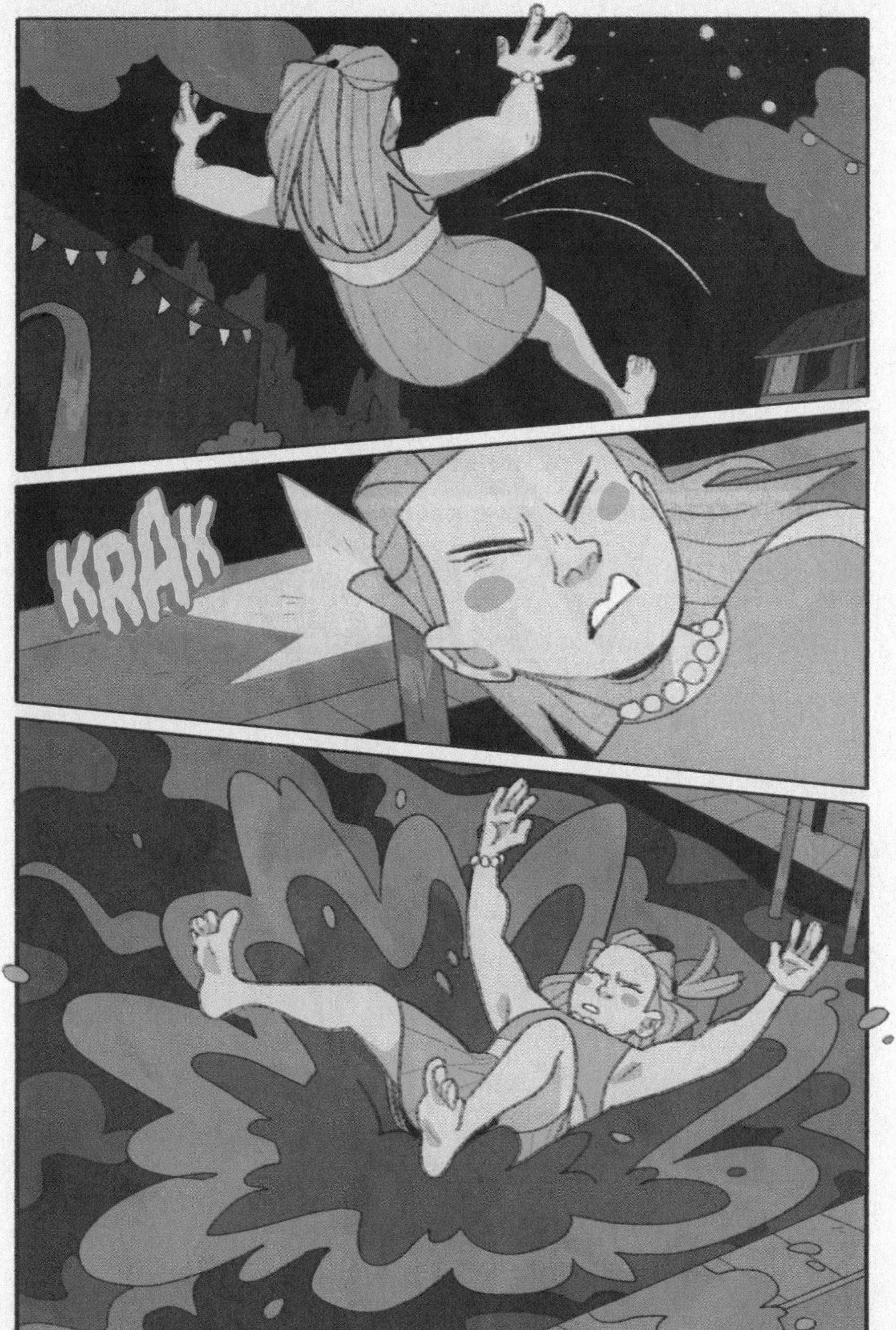
KRAK

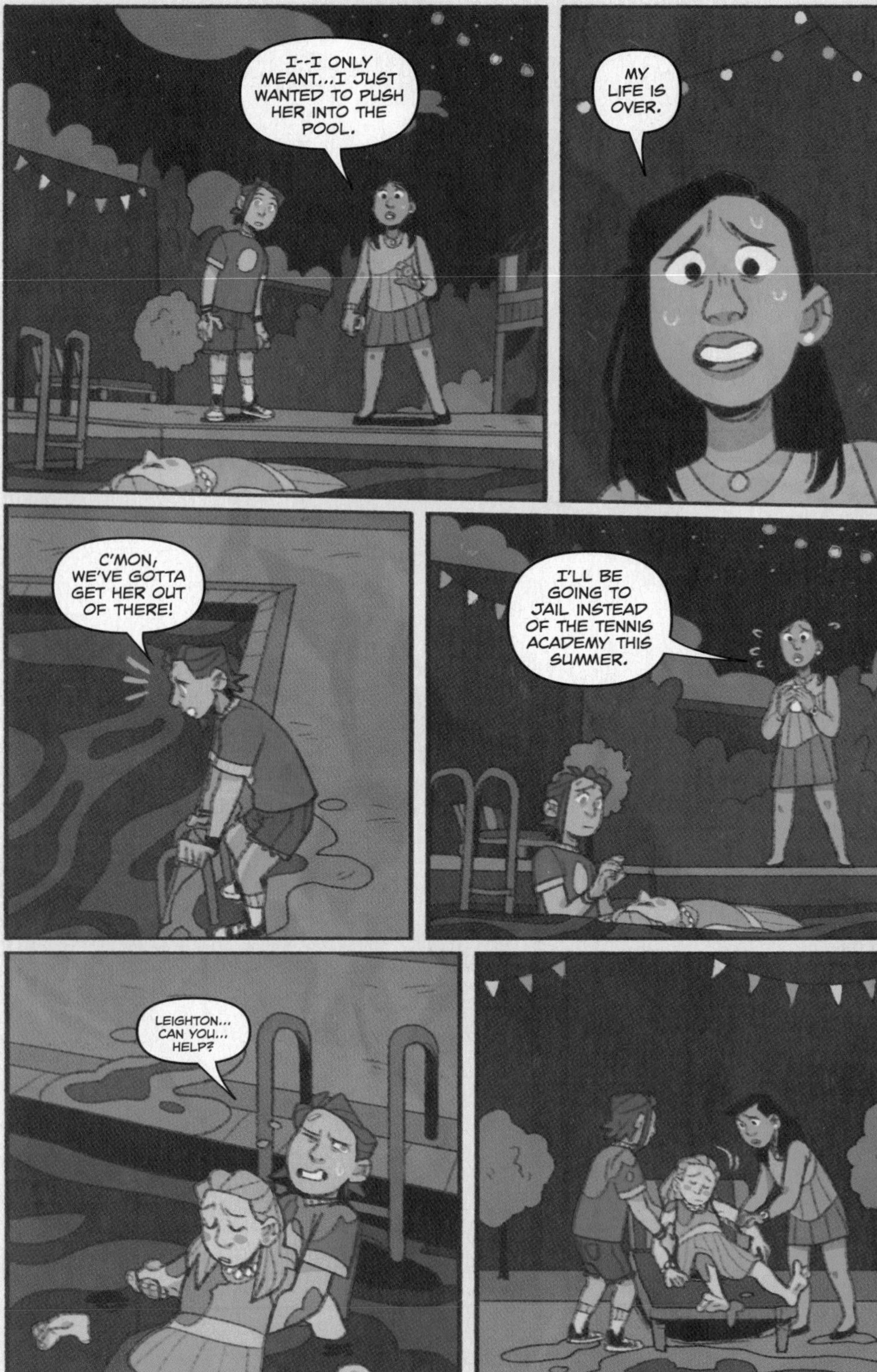
I--I ONLY MEANT...I JUST WANTED TO PUSH HER INTO THE POOL.
MY LIFE IS OVER.
C'MON, WE'VE GOTTA GET HER OUT OF THERE!
I'LL BE GOING TO JAIL INSTEAD OF THE TENNIS ACADEMY THIS SUMMER.
LEIGHTON... CAN YOU... HELP?

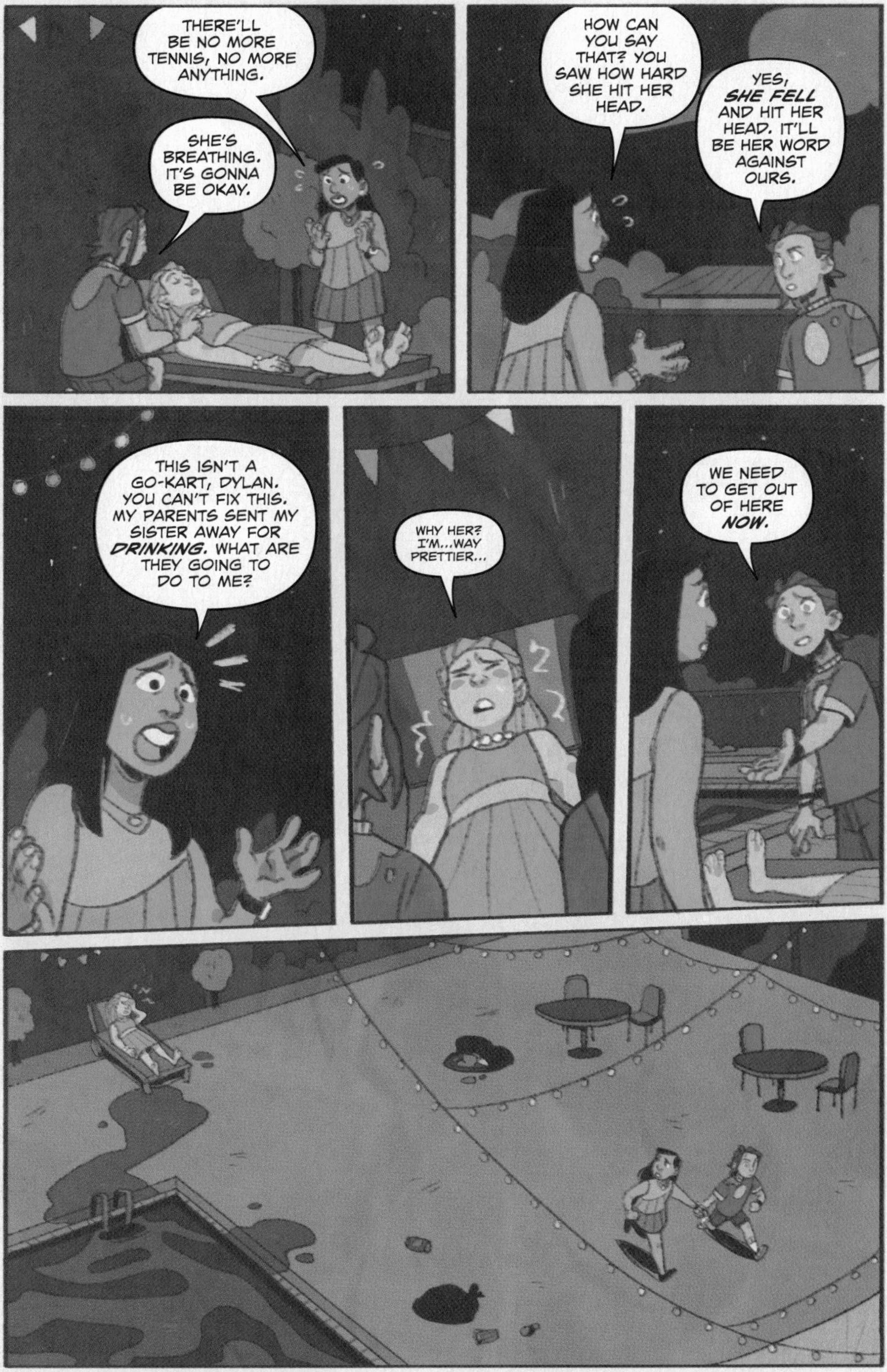
THERE'LL BE NO MORE TENNIS, NO MORE ANYTHING.
SHE'S BREATHING. IT'S GONNA BE OKAY.
HOW CAN YOU SAY THAT? YOU SAW HOW HARD SHE HIT HER HEAD.
YES, SHE FELL AND HIT HER HEAD. IT'LL BE HER WORD AGAINST OURS.
THIS ISN'T A GO-KART, DYLAN. YOU CAN'T FIX THIS. MY PARENTS SENT MY SISTER AWAY FOR DRINKING. WHAT ARE THEY GOING TO DO TO ME?
WHY HER? I'M...WAY PRETTIER...
WE NEED TO GET OUT OF HERE NOW.

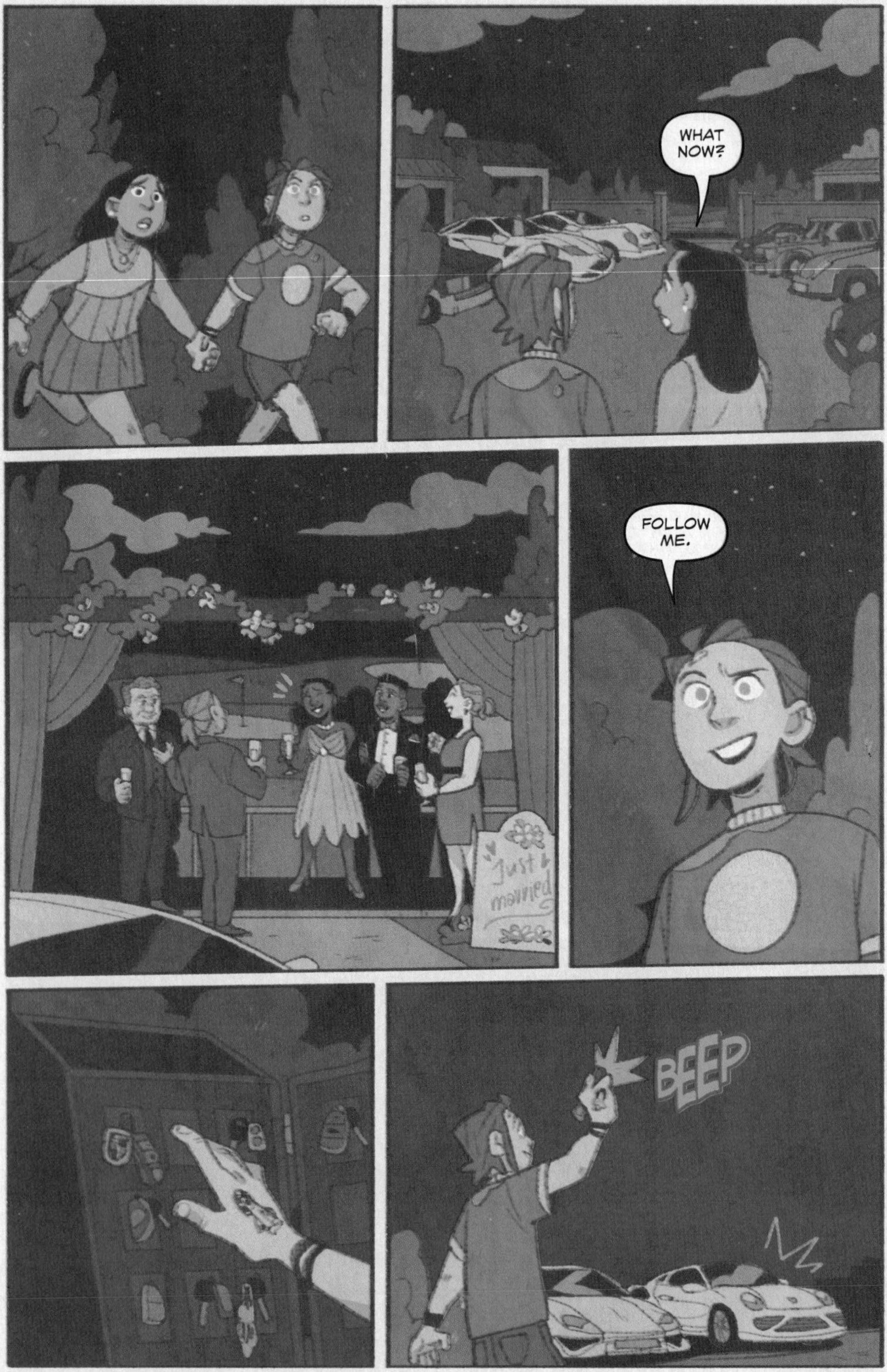
WHAT NOW?
FOLLOW ME.
Just married
BEEP

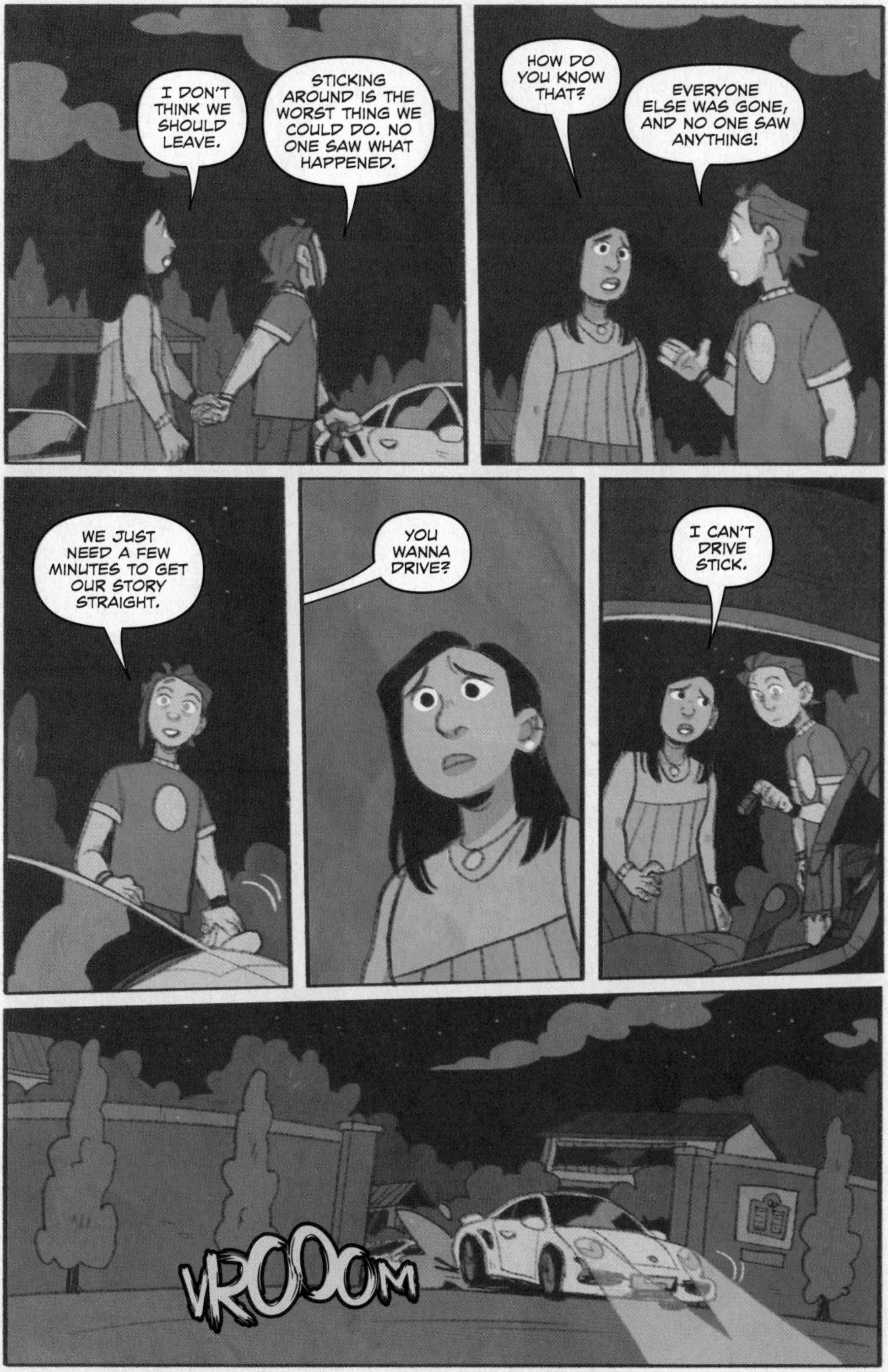

I DON'T THINK WE SHOULD LEAVE.
STICKING AROUND IS THE WORST THING WE COULD DO. NO ONE SAW WHAT HAPPENED.
HOW DO YOU KNOW THAT?
EVERYONE ELSE WAS GONE, AND NO ONE SAW ANYTHING!
WE JUST NEED A FEW MINUTES TO GET OUR STORY STRAIGHT.
YOU WANNA DRIVE?
I CAN'T DRIVE STICK.
VROOOOM

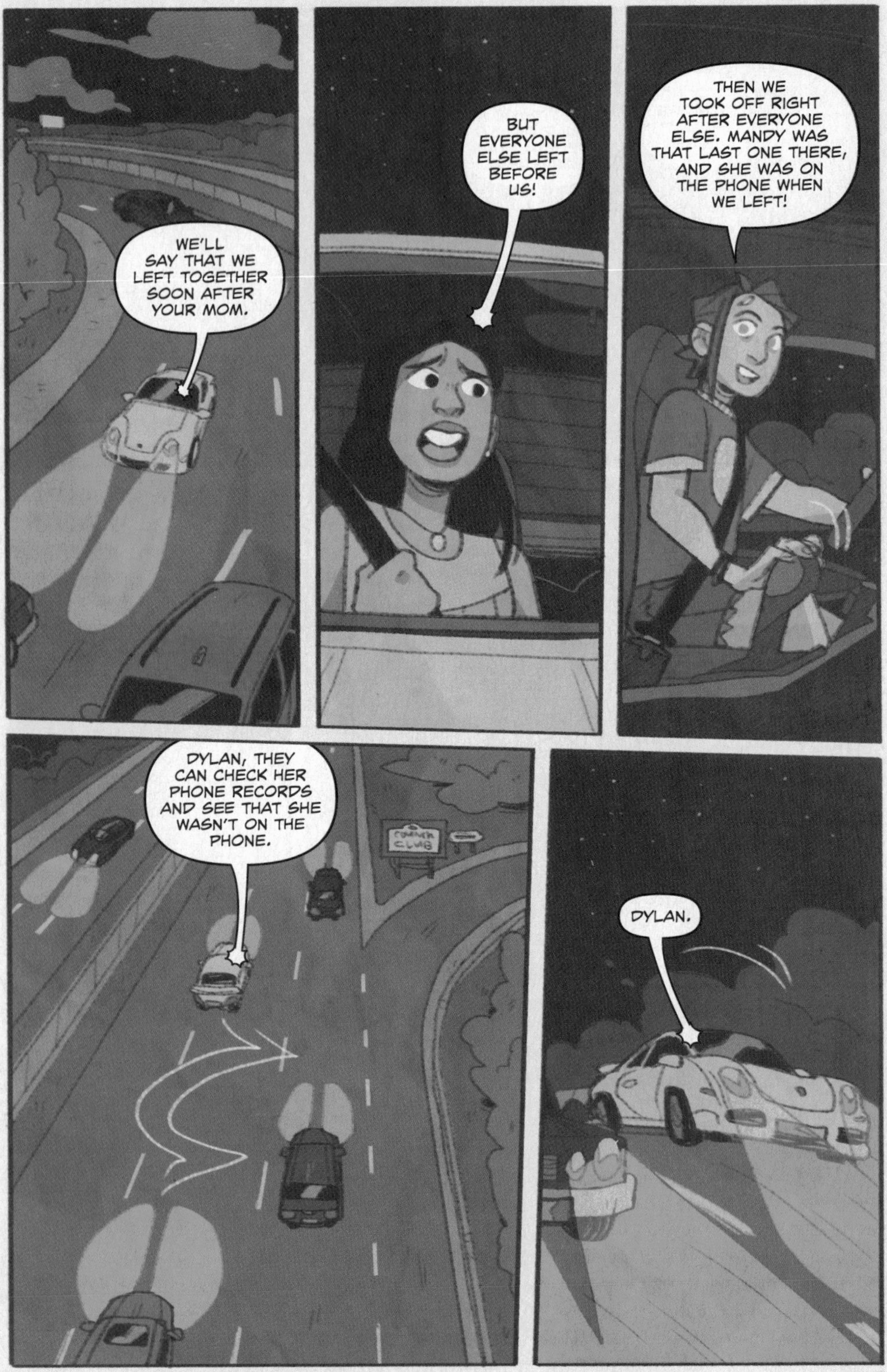
WE'LL SAY THAT WE LEFT TOGETHER SOON AFTER YOUR MOM.
BUT EVERYONE ELSE LEFT BEFORE US!
THEN WE TOOK OFF RIGHT AFTER EVERYONE ELSE. MANDY WAS THAT LAST ONE THERE, AND SHE WAS ON THE PHONE WHEN WE LEFT!
DYLAN, THEY CAN CHECK HER PHONE RECORDS AND SEE THAT SHE WASN'T ON THE PHONE.
DYLAN.

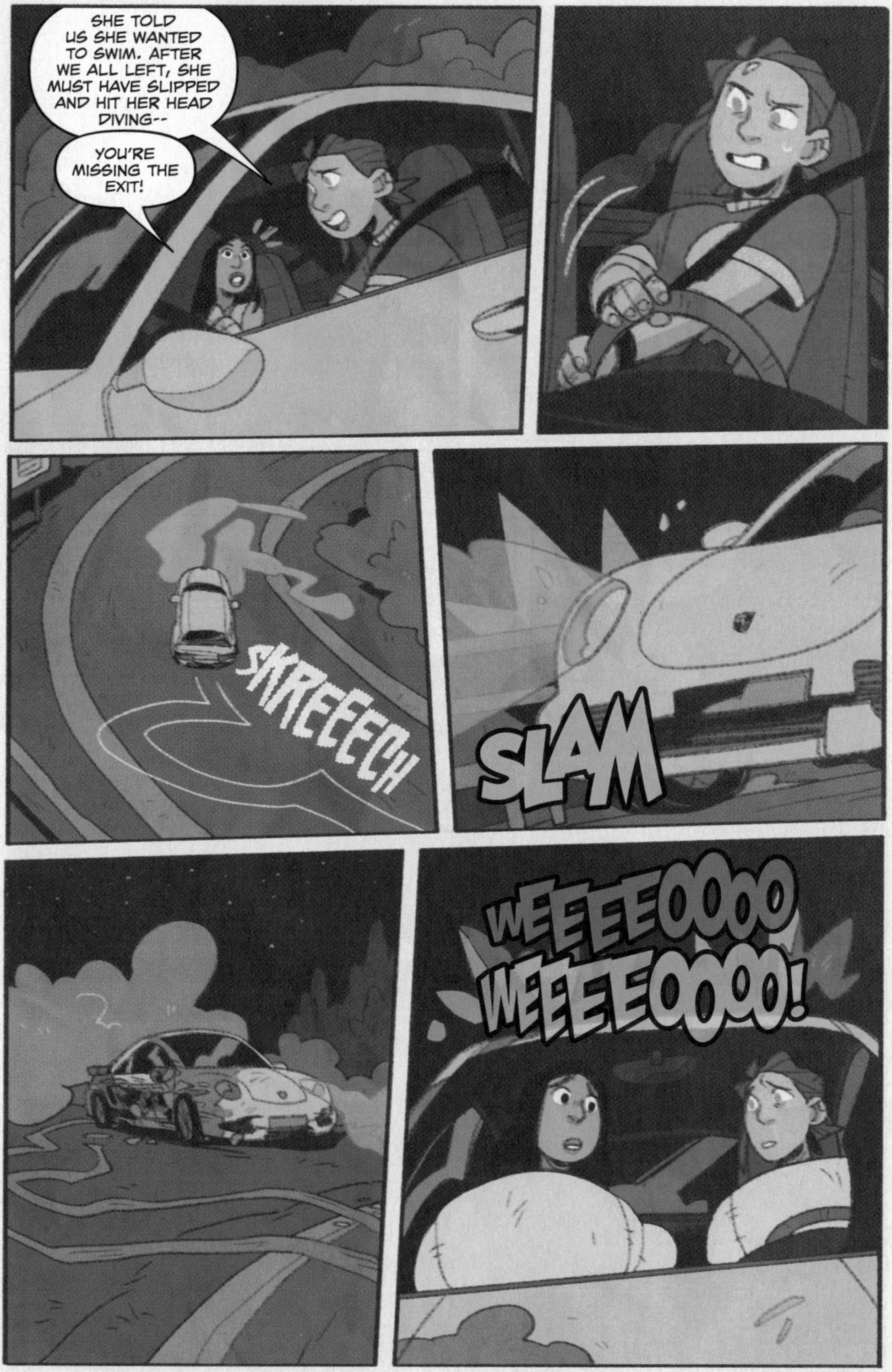
SHE TOLD US SHE WANTED TO SWIM. AFTER WE ALL LEFT, SHE MUST HAVE SLIPPED AND HIT HER HEAD DIVING--
YOU'RE MISSING THE EXIT!
SKREEECH
SLAM
WEEEEOOOO
WEEEEOOOO!

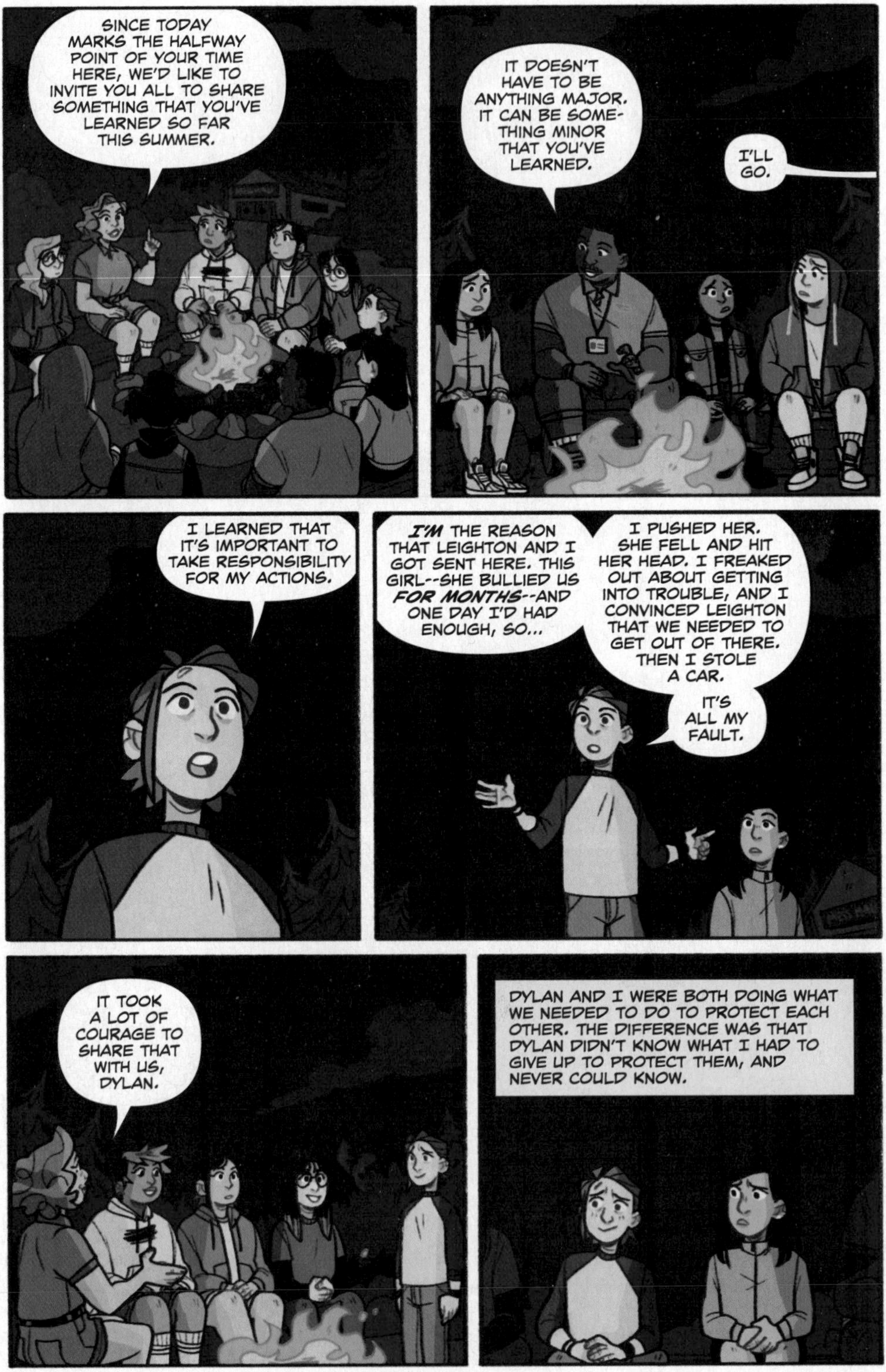
SINCE TODAY MARKS THE HALFWAY POINT OF YOUR TIME HERE, WE'D LIKE TO INVITE YOU ALL TO SHARE SOMETHING THAT YOU'VE LEARNED SO FAR THIS SUMMER.
IT DOESN'T HAVE TO BE ANYTHING MAJOR. IT CAN BE SOME-THING MINOR THAT YOU'VE LEARNED.
I'LL GO.
I LEARNED THAT IT'S IMPORTANT TO TAKE RESPONSIBILITY FOR MY ACTIONS.
I'M THE REASON THAT LEIGHTON AND I GOT SENT HERE. THIS GIRL--SHE BULLIED US *FOR MONTHS*--AND ONE DAY I'D HAD ENOUGH, SO...
I PUSHED HER. SHE FELL AND HIT HER HEAD. I FREAKED OUT ABOUT GETTING INTO TROUBLE, AND I CONVINCED LEIGHTON THAT WE NEEDED TO GET OUT OF THERE. THEN I STOLE A CAR.
IT'S ALL MY FAULT.
IT TOOK A LOT OF COURAGE TO SHARE THAT WITH US, DYLAN.
DYLAN AND I WERE BOTH DOING WHAT WE NEEDED TO DO TO PROTECT EACH OTHER. THE DIFFERENCE WAS THAT DYLAN DIDN'T KNOW WHAT I HAD TO GIVE UP TO PROTECT THEM, AND NEVER COULD KNOW.

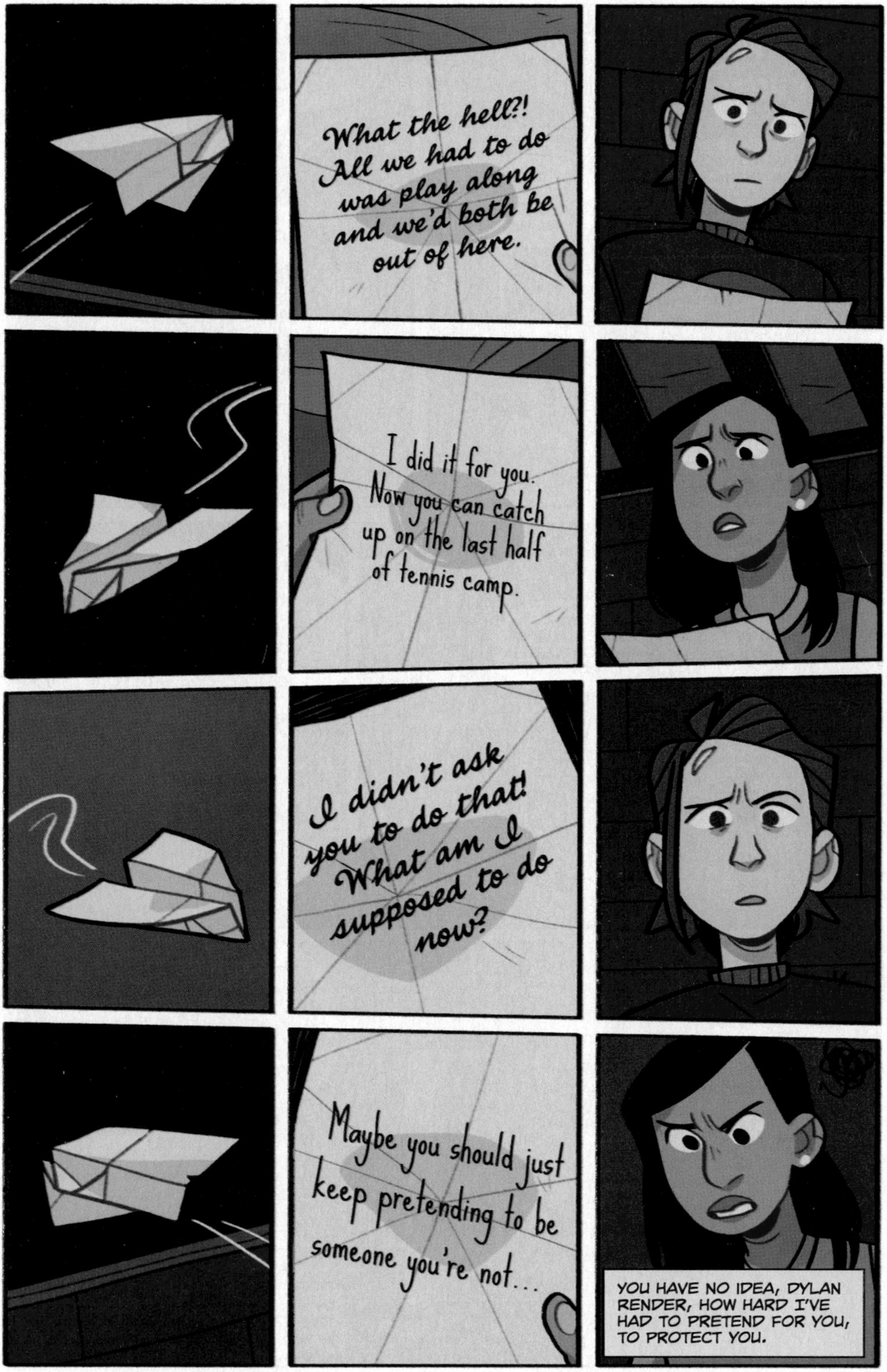
What the hell?! All we had to do was play along and we'd both be out of here.
I did it for you. Now you can catch up on the last half of tennis camp.
I didn't ask you to do that! What am I supposed to do now?
Maybe you should just keep pretending to be someone you're not...
YOU HAVE NO IDEA, DYLAN RENDER, HOW HARD I'VE HAD TO PRETEND FOR YOU, TO PROTECT YOU.

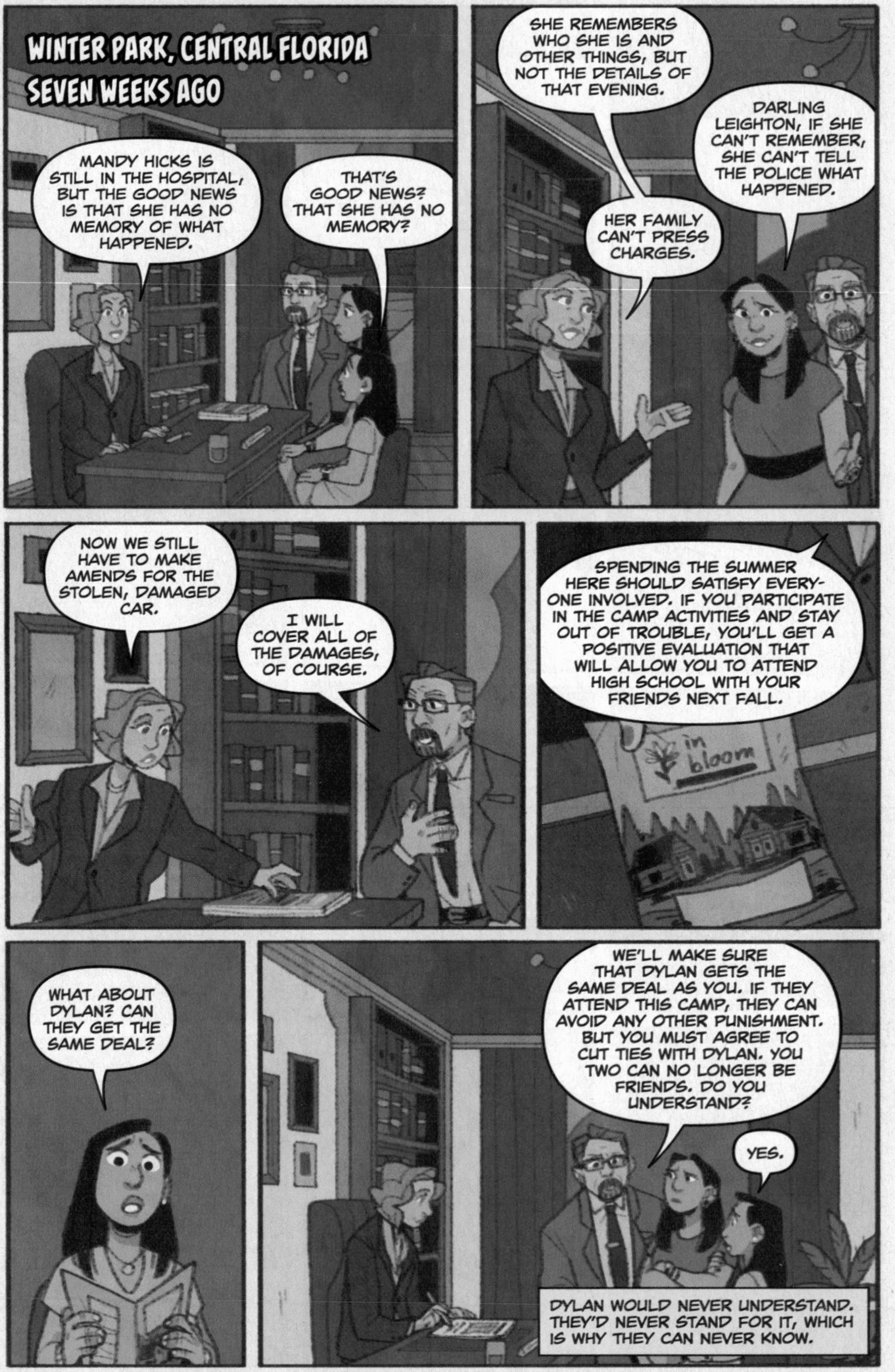
WINTER PARK, CENTRAL FLORIDA
SEVEN WEEKS AGO
MANDY HICKS IS STILL IN THE HOSPITAL, BUT THE GOOD NEWS IS THAT SHE HAS NO MEMORY OF WHAT HAPPENED.
THAT'S GOOD NEWS? THAT SHE HAS NO MEMORY?
SHE REMEMBERS WHO SHE IS AND OTHER THINGS, BUT NOT THE DETAILS OF THAT EVENING.
HER FAMILY CAN'T PRESS CHARGES.
DARLING LEIGHTON, IF SHE CAN'T REMEMBER, SHE CAN'T TELL THE POLICE WHAT HAPPENED.
NOW WE STILL HAVE TO MAKE AMENDS FOR THE STOLEN, DAMAGED CAR.
I WILL COVER ALL OF THE DAMAGES, OF COURSE.
SPENDING THE SUMMER HERE SHOULD SATISFY EVERY-ONE INVOLVED. IF YOU PARTICIPATE IN THE CAMP ACTIVITIES AND STAY OUT OF TROUBLE, YOU'LL GET A POSITIVE EVALUATION THAT WILL ALLOW YOU TO ATTEND HIGH SCHOOL WITH YOUR FRIENDS NEXT FALL.
in bloom
WHAT ABOUT DYLAN? CAN THEY GET THE SAME DEAL?
WE'LL MAKE SURE THAT DYLAN GETS THE SAME DEAL AS YOU. IF THEY ATTEND THIS CAMP, THEY CAN AVOID ANY OTHER PUNISHMENT. BUT YOU MUST AGREE TO CUT TIES WITH DYLAN. YOU TWO CAN NO LONGER BE FRIENDS. DO YOU UNDERSTAND?
YES.
DYLAN WOULD NEVER UNDERSTAND. THEY'D NEVER STAND FOR IT, WHICH IS WHY THEY CAN NEVER KNOW.

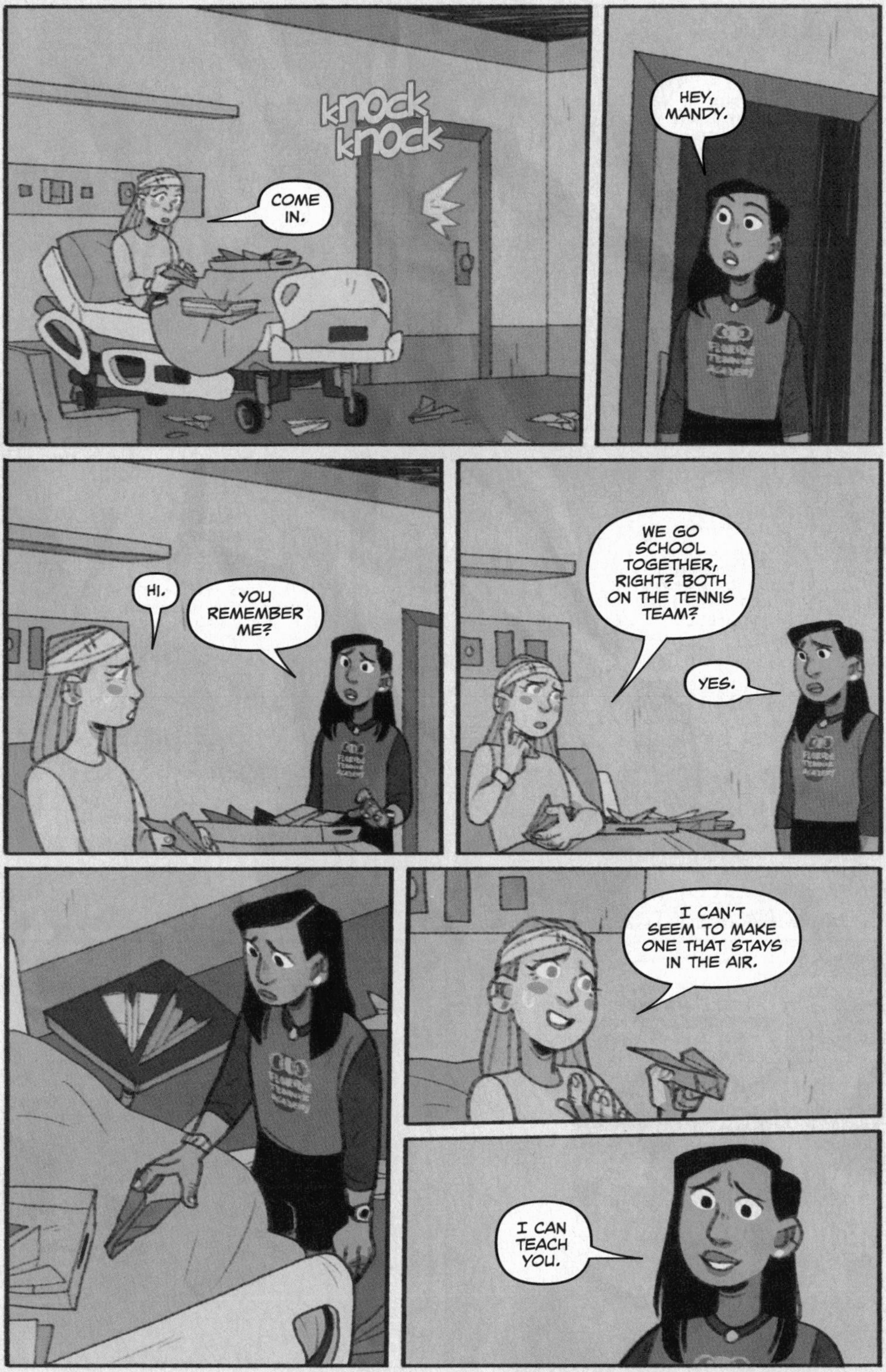
knock knock
COME IN.
HEY, MANDY.
HI.
YOU REMEMBER ME?
WE GO SCHOOL TOGETHER, RIGHT? BOTH ON THE TENNIS TEAM?
YES.
I CAN'T SEEM TO MAKE ONE THAT STAYS IN THE AIR.
I CAN TEACH YOU.

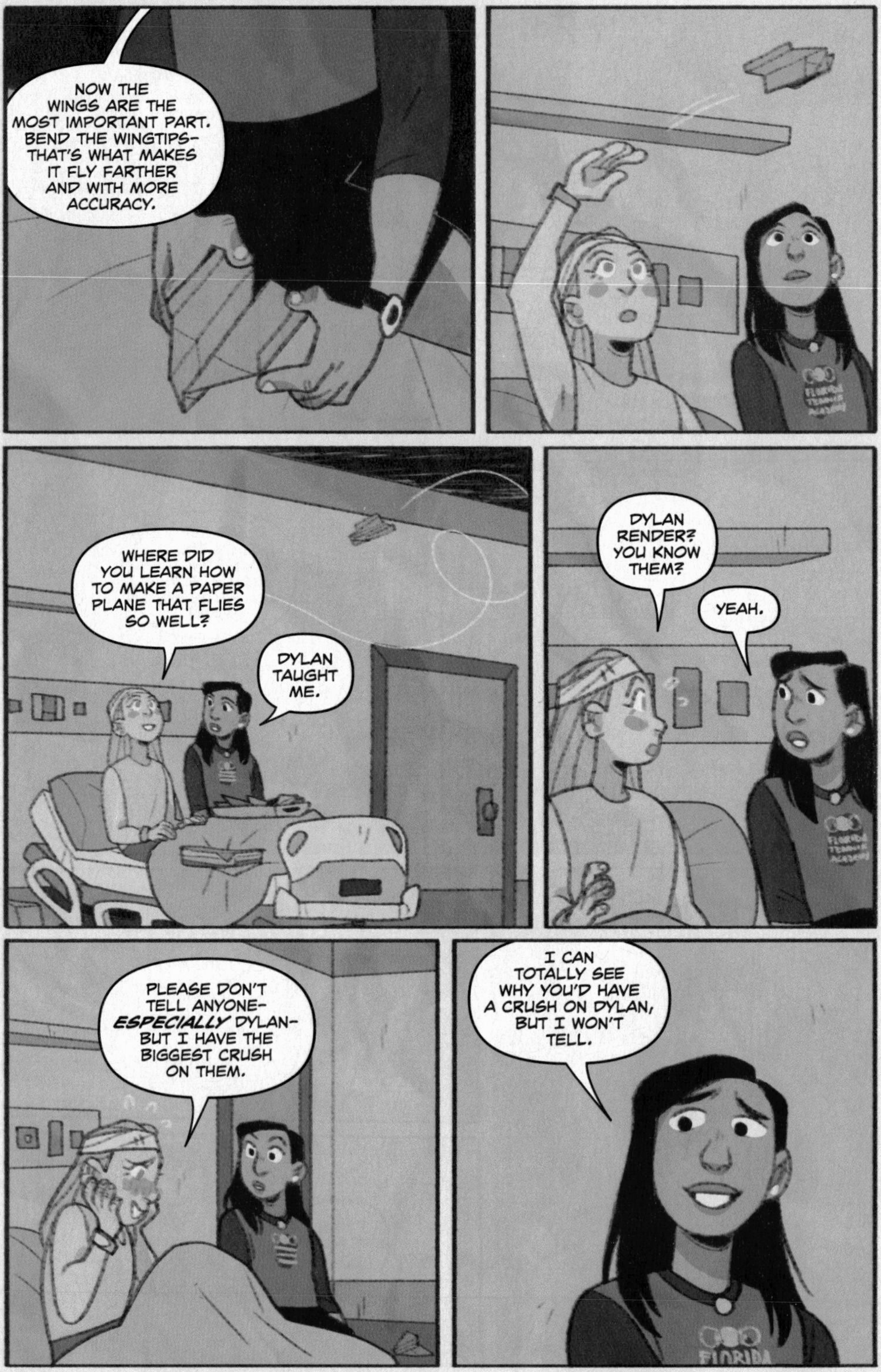
NOW THE WINGS ARE THE MOST IMPORTANT PART. BEND THE WINGTIPS– THAT'S WHAT MAKES IT FLY FARTHER AND WITH MORE ACCURACY.
WHERE DID YOU LEARN HOW TO MAKE A PAPER PLANE THAT FLIES SO WELL?
DYLAN TAUGHT ME.
DYLAN RENDER? YOU KNOW THEM?
YEAH.
PLEASE DON'T TELL ANYONE– *ESPECIALLY* DYLAN– BUT I HAVE THE BIGGEST CRUSH ON THEM.
I CAN TOTALLY SEE WHY YOU'D HAVE A CRUSH ON DYLAN, BUT I WON'T TELL.

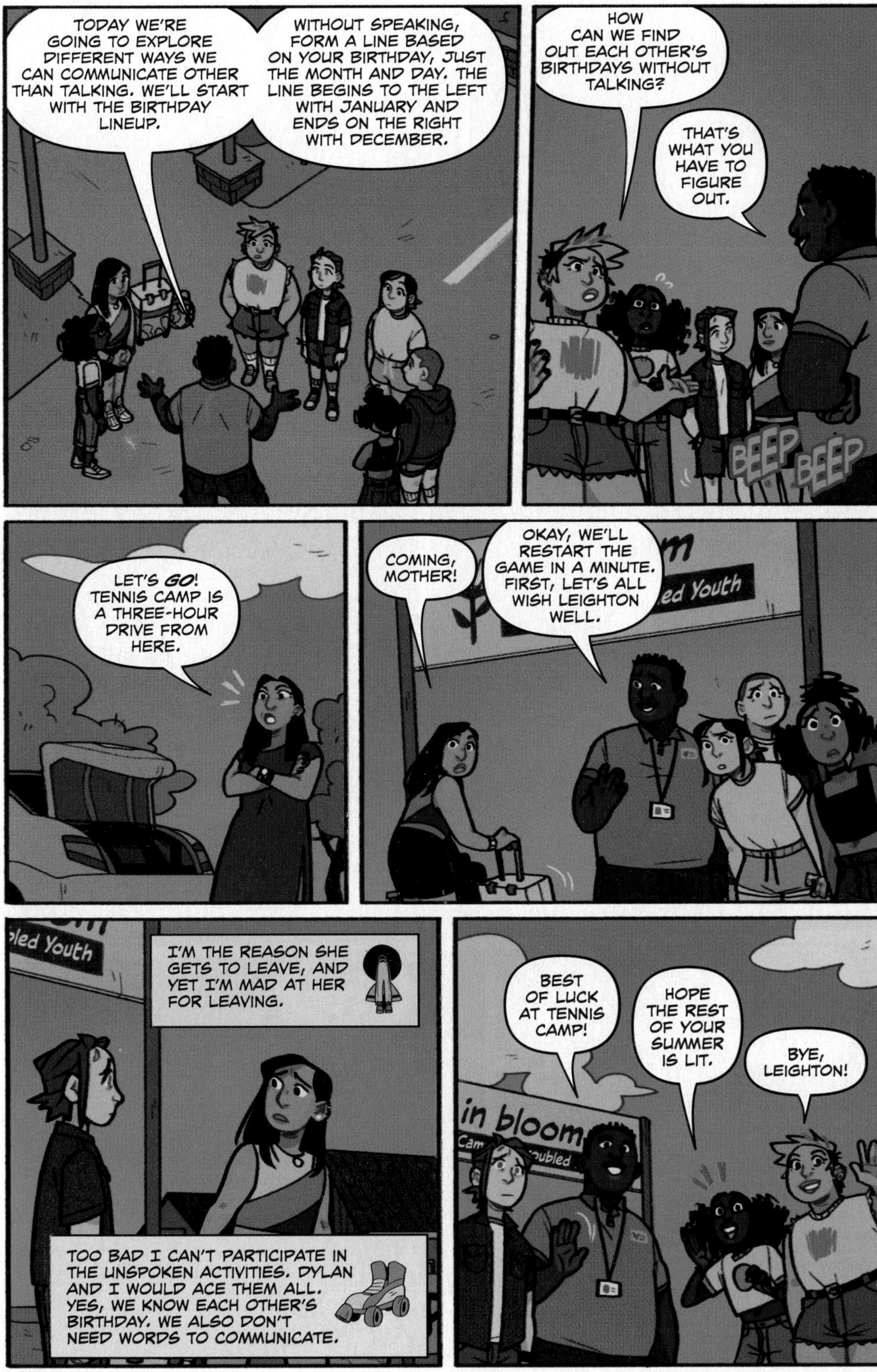
TODAY WE'RE GOING TO EXPLORE DIFFERENT WAYS WE CAN COMMUNICATE OTHER THAN TALKING. WE'LL START WITH THE BIRTHDAY LINEUP.
WITHOUT SPEAKING, FORM A LINE BASED ON YOUR BIRTHDAY, JUST THE MONTH AND DAY. THE LINE BEGINS TO THE LEFT WITH JANUARY AND ENDS ON THE RIGHT WITH DECEMBER.
HOW CAN WE FIND OUT EACH OTHER'S BIRTHDAYS WITHOUT TALKING?
THAT'S WHAT YOU HAVE TO FIGURE OUT.
BEEP BEEP
LET'S GO! TENNIS CAMP IS A THREE-HOUR DRIVE FROM HERE.
COMING, MOTHER!
OKAY, WE'LL RESTART THE GAME IN A MINUTE. FIRST, LET'S ALL WISH LEIGHTON WELL.
I'M THE REASON SHE GETS TO LEAVE, AND YET I'M MAD AT HER FOR LEAVING.
TOO BAD I CAN'T PARTICIPATE IN THE UNSPOKEN ACTIVITIES. DYLAN AND I WOULD ACE THEM ALL. YES, WE KNOW EACH OTHER'S BIRTHDAY. WE ALSO DON'T NEED WORDS TO COMMUNICATE.
BEST OF LUCK AT TENNIS CAMP!
HOPE THE REST OF YOUR SUMMER IS LIT.
BYE, LEIGHTON!
in bloom

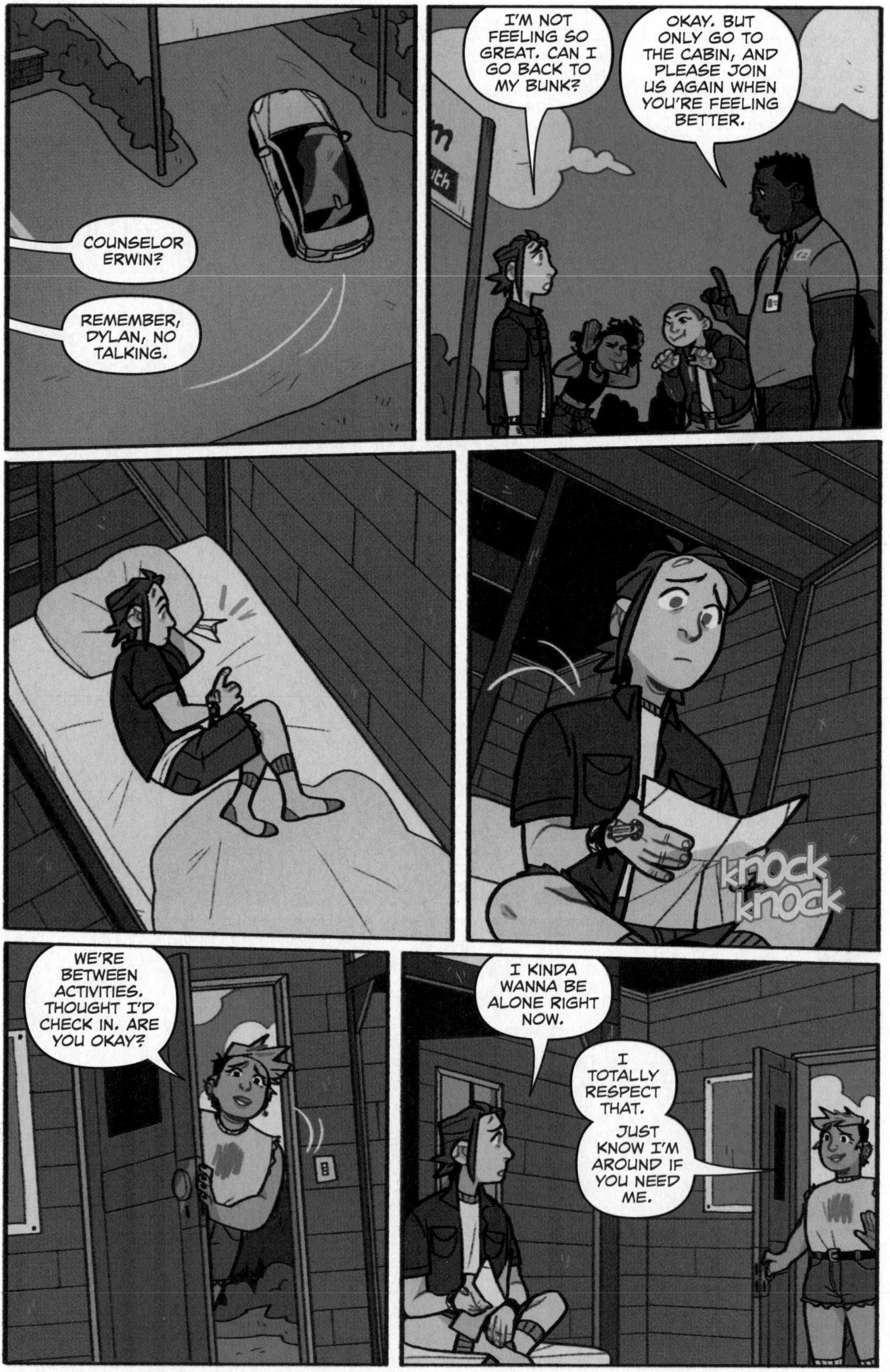
COUNSELOR ERWIN?
REMEMBER, DYLAN, NO TALKING.
I'M NOT FEELING SO GREAT. CAN I GO BACK TO MY BUNK?
OKAY. BUT ONLY GO TO THE CABIN, AND PLEASE JOIN US AGAIN WHEN YOU'RE FEELING BETTER.
knock knock
WE'RE BETWEEN ACTIVITIES. THOUGHT I'D CHECK IN. ARE YOU OKAY?
I KINDA WANNA BE ALONE RIGHT NOW.
I TOTALLY RESPECT THAT.
JUST KNOW I'M AROUND IF YOU NEED ME.

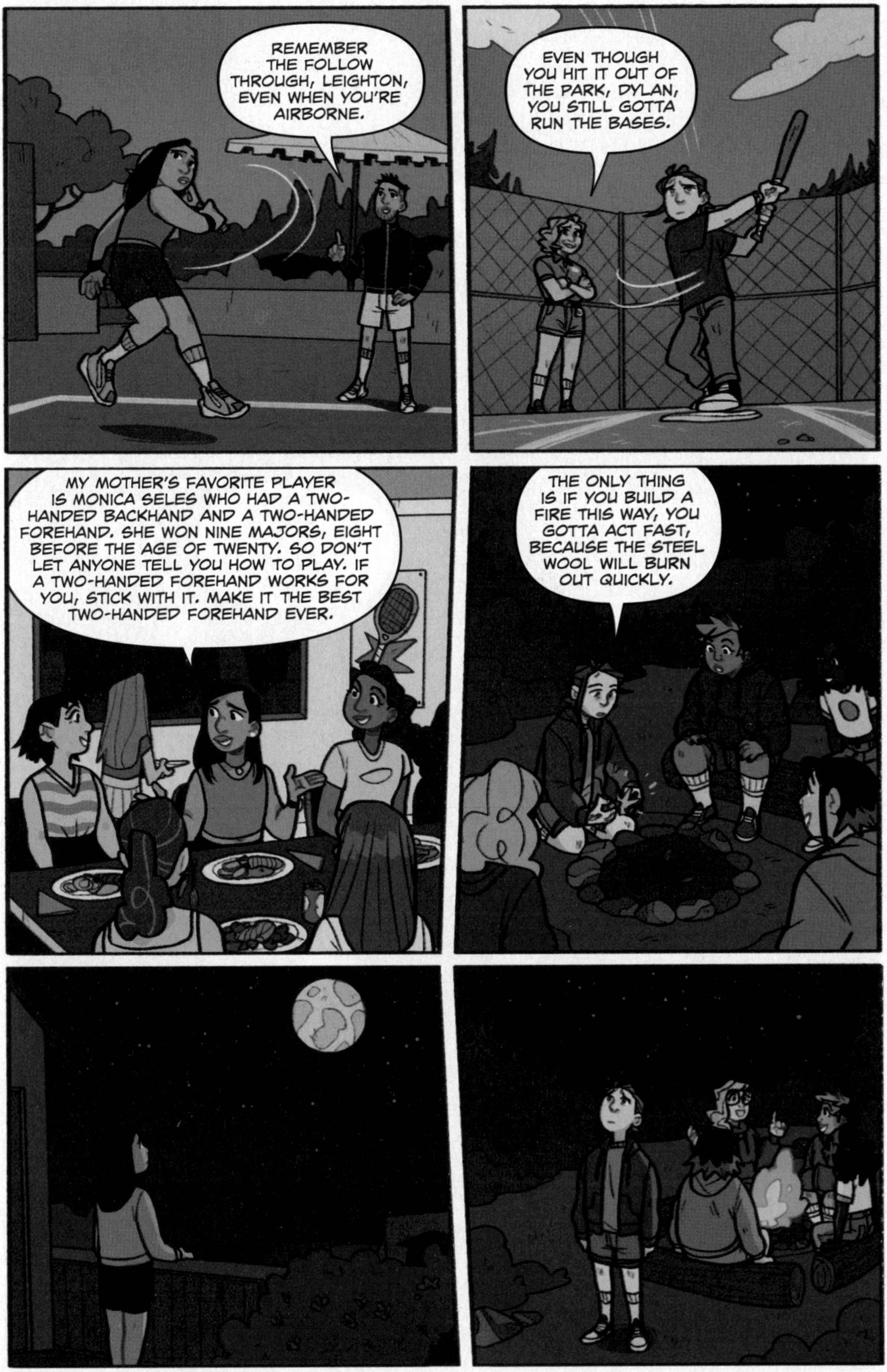

REMEMBER THE FOLLOW THROUGH, LEIGHTON, EVEN WHEN YOU'RE AIRBORNE.
EVEN THOUGH YOU HIT IT OUT OF THE PARK, DYLAN, YOU STILL GOTTA RUN THE BASES.
MY MOTHER'S FAVORITE PLAYER IS MONICA SELES WHO HAD A TWO-HANDED BACKHAND AND A TWO-HANDED FOREHAND. SHE WON NINE MAJORS, EIGHT BEFORE THE AGE OF TWENTY. SO DON'T LET ANYONE TELL YOU HOW TO PLAY. IF A TWO-HANDED FOREHAND WORKS FOR YOU, STICK WITH IT. MAKE IT THE BEST TWO-HANDED FOREHAND EVER.
THE ONLY THING IS IF YOU BUILD A FIRE THIS WAY, YOU GOTTA ACT FAST, BECAUSE THE STEEL WOOL WILL BURN OUT QUICKLY.

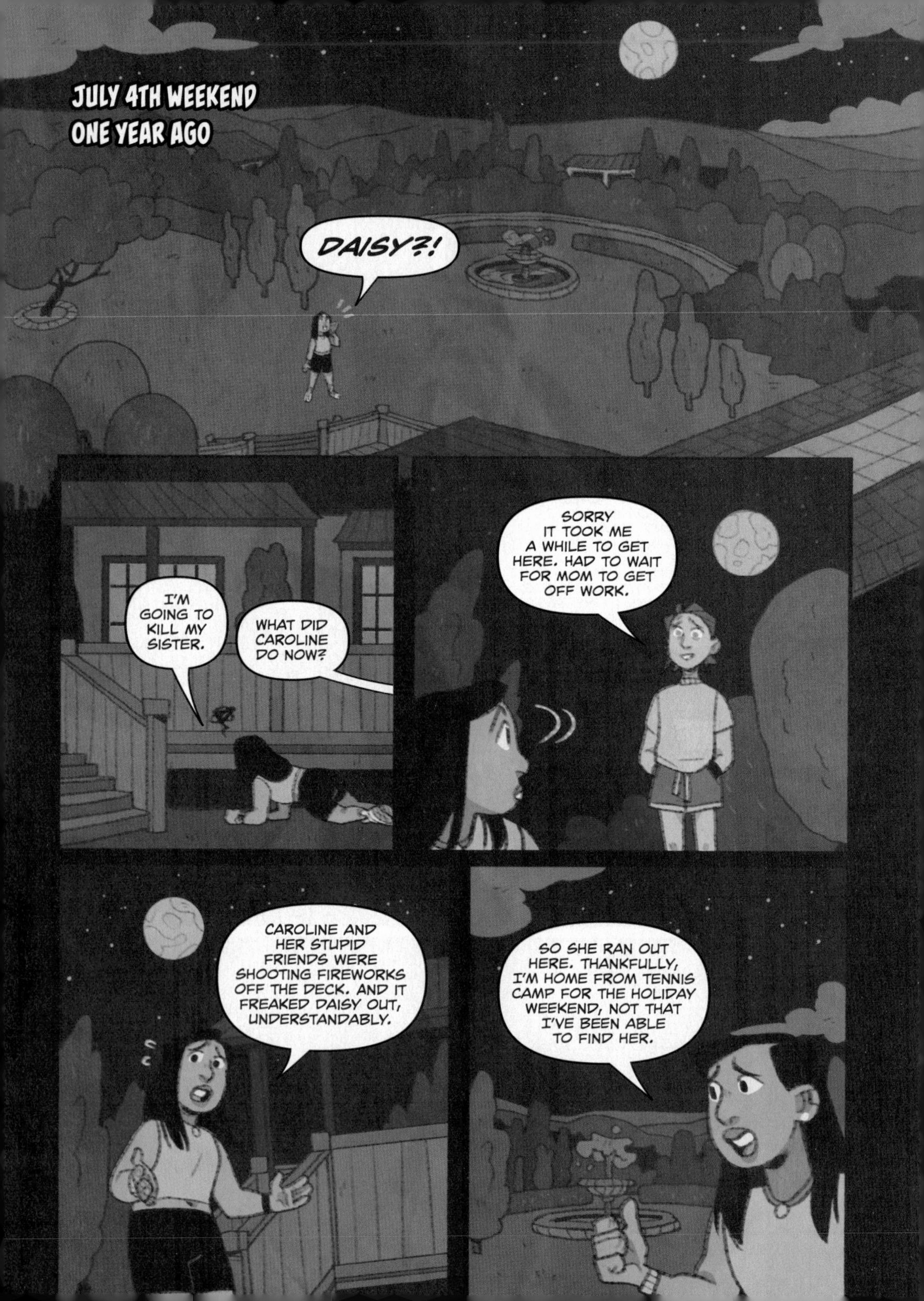
JULY 4TH WEEKEND
ONE YEAR AGO
DAISY?!
I'M GOING TO KILL MY SISTER.
WHAT DID CAROLINE DO NOW?
SORRY IT TOOK ME A WHILE TO GET HERE. HAD TO WAIT FOR MOM TO GET OFF WORK.
CAROLINE AND HER STUPID FRIENDS WERE SHOOTING FIREWORKS OFF THE DECK. AND IT FREAKED DAISY OUT, UNDERSTANDABLY.
SO SHE RAN OUT HERE. THANKFULLY, I'M HOME FROM TENNIS CAMP FOR THE HOLIDAY WEEKEND, NOT THAT I'VE BEEN ABLE TO FIND HER.

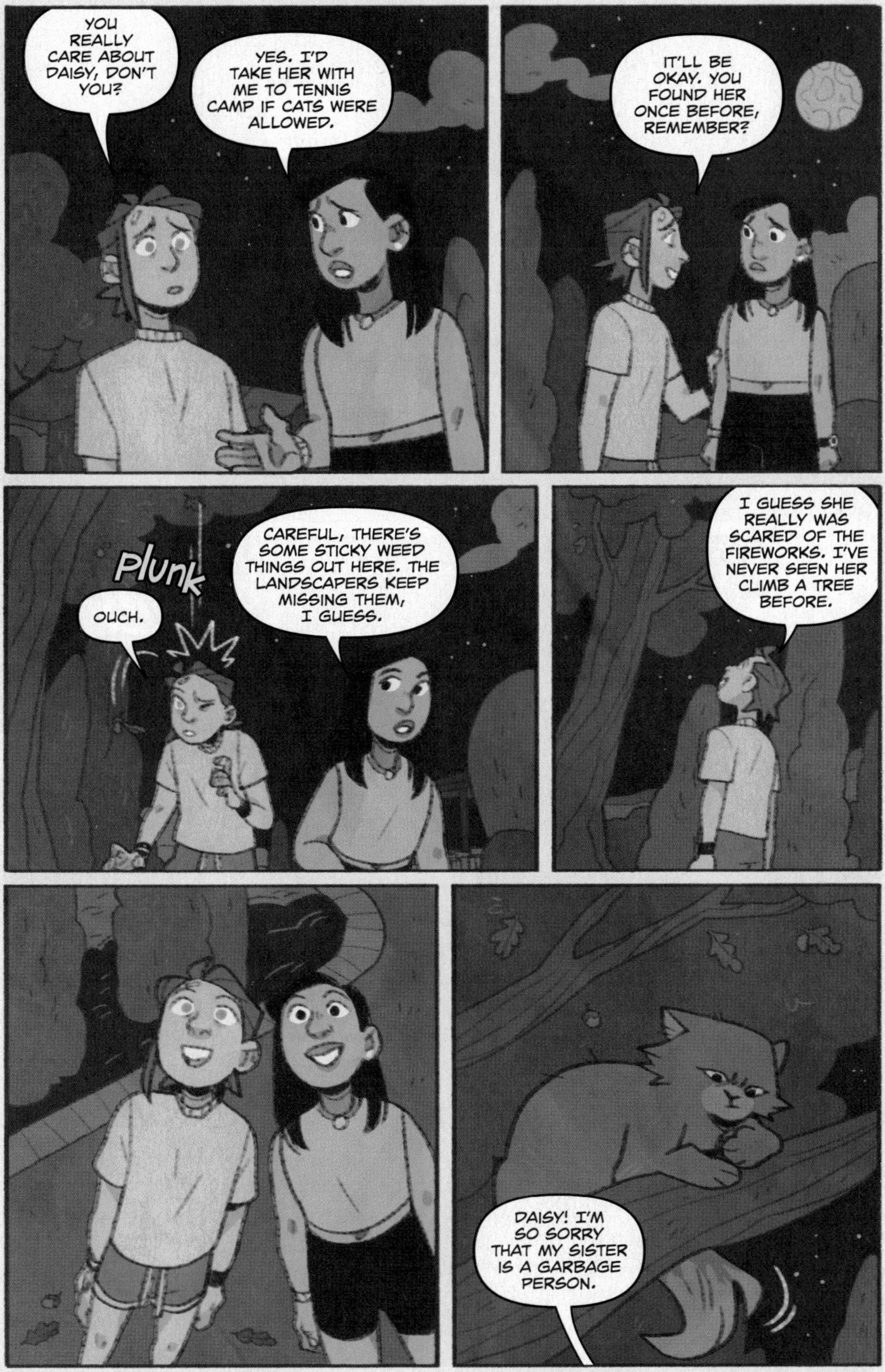
YOU REALLY CARE ABOUT DAISY, DON'T YOU?
YES. I'D TAKE HER WITH ME TO TENNIS CAMP IF CATS WERE ALLOWED.
IT'LL BE OKAY. YOU FOUND HER ONCE BEFORE, REMEMBER?
PLUNK
OUCH.
CAREFUL, THERE'S SOME STICKY WEED THINGS OUT HERE. THE LANDSCAPERS KEEP MISSING THEM, I GUESS.
I GUESS SHE REALLY WAS SCARED OF THE FIREWORKS. I'VE NEVER SEEN HER CLIMB A TREE BEFORE.
DAISY! I'M SO SORRY THAT MY SISTER IS A GARBAGE PERSON.

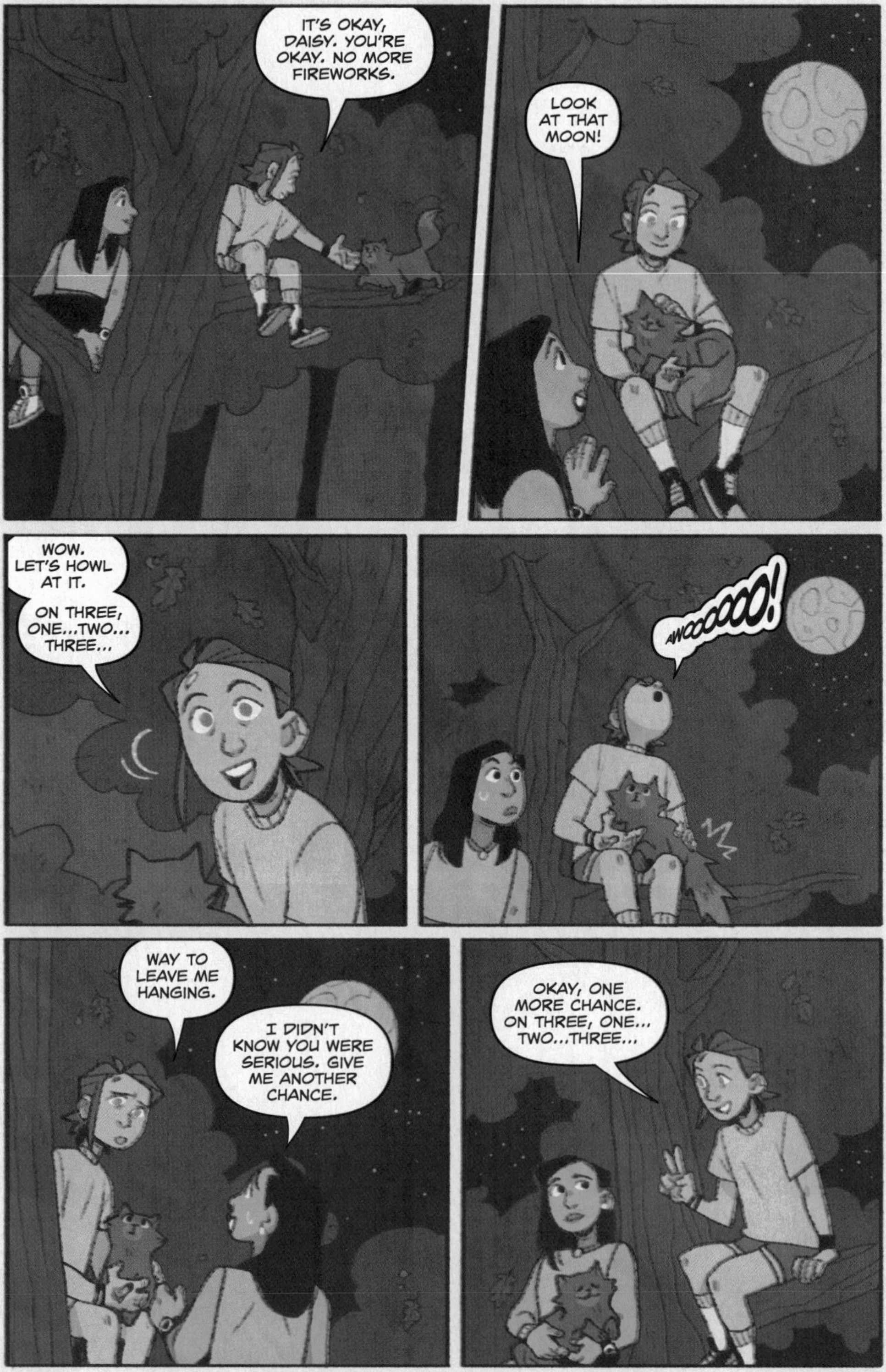
IT'S OKAY, DAISY. YOU'RE OKAY. NO MORE FIREWORKS.
LOOK AT THAT MOON!
WOW. LET'S HOWL AT IT.
ON THREE, ONE...TWO... THREE...
AWOOOOOO!
WAY TO LEAVE ME HANGING.
I DIDN'T KNOW YOU WERE SERIOUS. GIVE ME ANOTHER CHANCE.
OKAY, ONE MORE CHANCE. ON THREE, ONE... TWO...THREE...

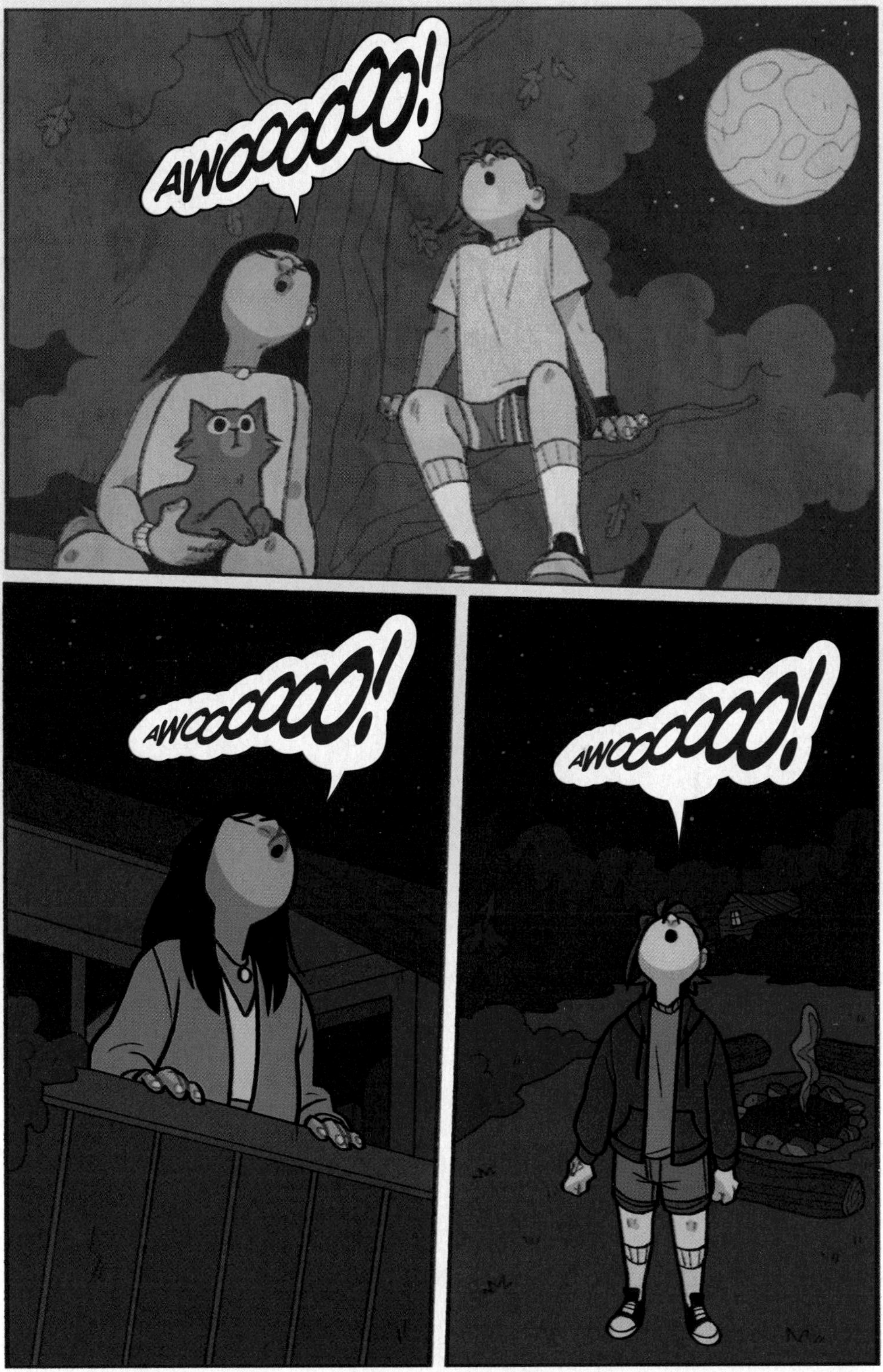
AWOOOOOO!
AWOOOOOO!
AWOOOOOO!

DYLAN, SO WE'RE CLEAR, THIS EVALUATION WILL DETERMINE WHERE YOU GO TO HIGH SCHOOL THIS FALL. DO YOU UNDERSTAND?

YES... YES, MA'AM.

WE'RE NOW GOING TO ASK YOU SOME QUESTIONS. THESE QUESTIONS ARE PART OF YOUR EVALUATION.

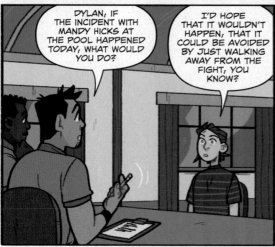

DYLAN, IF THE INCIDENT WITH MANDY HICKS AT THE POOL HAPPENED TODAY, WHAT WOULD YOU DO?

I'D HOPE THAT IT WOULDN'T HAPPEN, THAT IT COULD BE AVOIDED BY JUST WALKING AWAY FROM THE FIGHT, YOU KNOW?

BUT IF IT HAPPENED, I'D CALL 911 AS SOON AS MANDY HIT HER HEAD.

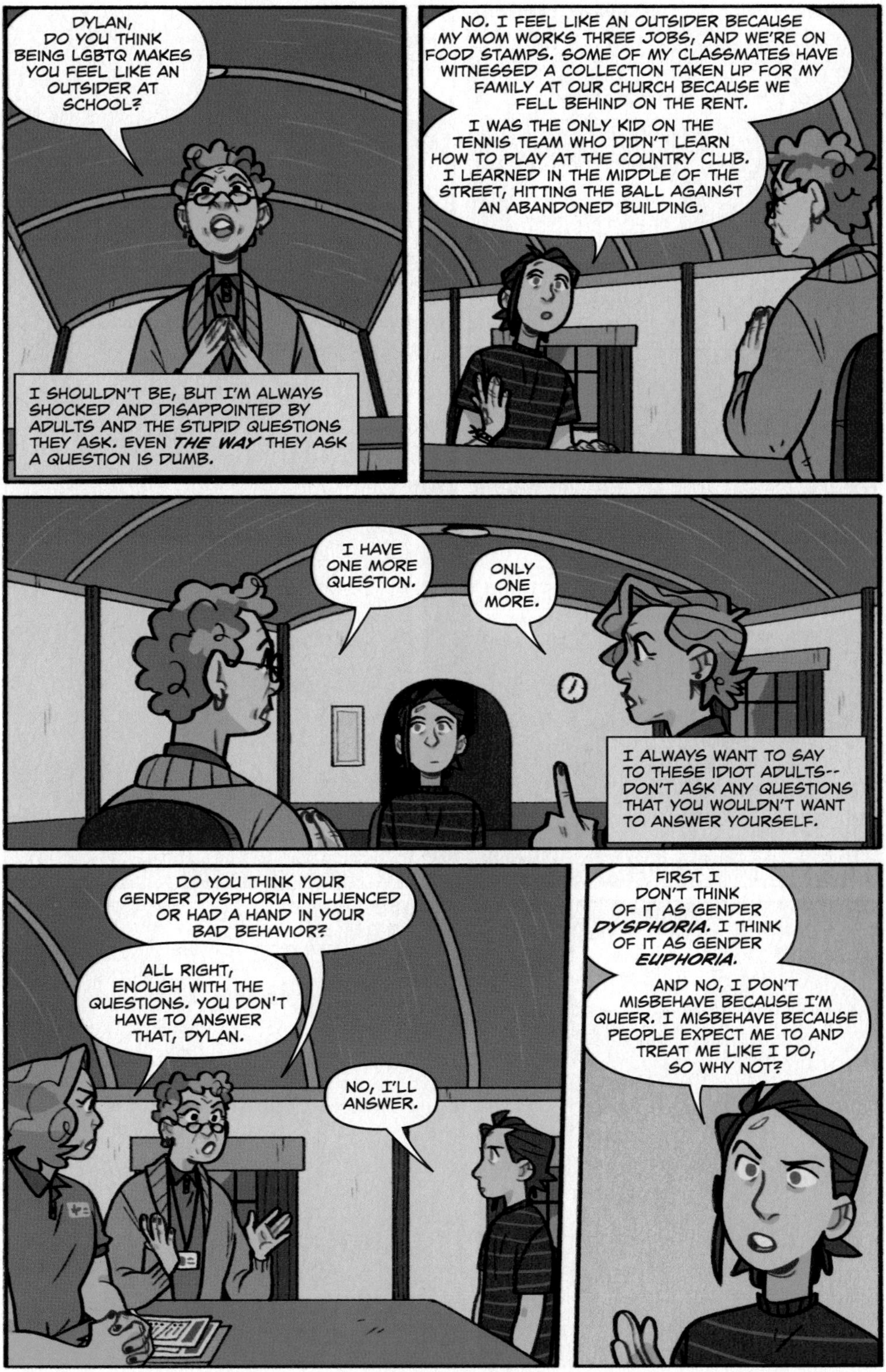

DYLAN, DO YOU THINK BEING LGBTQ MAKES YOU FEEL LIKE AN OUTSIDER AT SCHOOL?
I SHOULDN'T BE, BUT I'M ALWAYS SHOCKED AND DISAPPOINTED BY ADULTS AND THE STUPID QUESTIONS THEY ASK. EVEN *THE WAY* THEY ASK A QUESTION IS DUMB.
NO. I FEEL LIKE AN OUTSIDER BECAUSE MY MOM WORKS THREE JOBS, AND WE'RE ON FOOD STAMPS. SOME OF MY CLASSMATES HAVE WITNESSED A COLLECTION TAKEN UP FOR MY FAMILY AT OUR CHURCH BECAUSE WE FELL BEHIND ON THE RENT.
I WAS THE ONLY KID ON THE TENNIS TEAM WHO DIDN'T LEARN HOW TO PLAY AT THE COUNTRY CLUB. I LEARNED IN THE MIDDLE OF THE STREET, HITTING THE BALL AGAINST AN ABANDONED BUILDING.
I HAVE ONE MORE QUESTION.
ONLY ONE MORE.
I ALWAYS WANT TO SAY TO THESE IDIOT ADULTS-- DON'T ASK ANY QUESTIONS THAT YOU WOULDN'T WANT TO ANSWER YOURSELF.
DO YOU THINK YOUR GENDER DYSPHORIA INFLUENCED OR HAD A HAND IN YOUR BAD BEHAVIOR?
ALL RIGHT, ENOUGH WITH THE QUESTIONS. YOU DON'T HAVE TO ANSWER THAT, DYLAN.
NO, I'LL ANSWER.
FIRST I DON'T THINK OF IT AS GENDER *DYSPHORIA*. I THINK OF IT AS GENDER *EUPHORIA*.
AND NO, I DON'T MISBEHAVE BECAUSE I'M QUEER. I MISBEHAVE BECAUSE PEOPLE EXPECT ME TO AND TREAT ME LIKE I DO, SO WHY NOT?

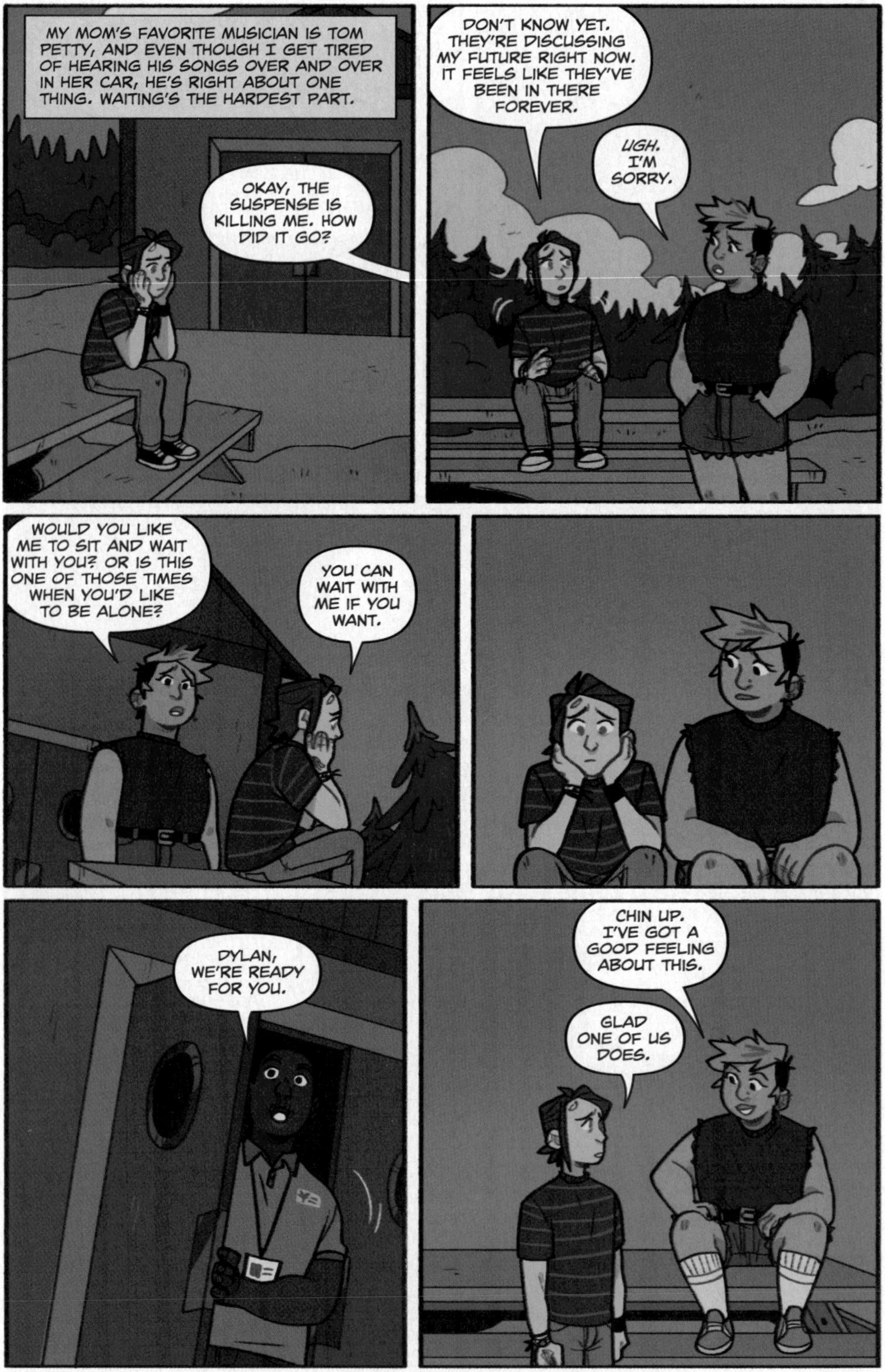

MY MOM'S FAVORITE MUSICIAN IS TOM PETTY, AND EVEN THOUGH I GET TIRED OF HEARING HIS SONGS OVER AND OVER IN HER CAR, HE'S RIGHT ABOUT ONE THING. WAITING'S THE HARDEST PART.
OKAY, THE SUSPENSE IS KILLING ME. HOW DID IT GO?
DON'T KNOW YET. THEY'RE DISCUSSING MY FUTURE RIGHT NOW. IT FEELS LIKE THEY'VE BEEN IN THERE FOREVER.
UGH. I'M SORRY.
WOULD YOU LIKE ME TO SIT AND WAIT WITH YOU? OR IS THIS ONE OF THOSE TIMES WHEN YOU'D LIKE TO BE ALONE?
YOU CAN WAIT WITH ME IF YOU WANT.
DYLAN, WE'RE READY FOR YOU.
CHIN UP. I'VE GOT A GOOD FEELING ABOUT THIS.
GLAD ONE OF US DOES.

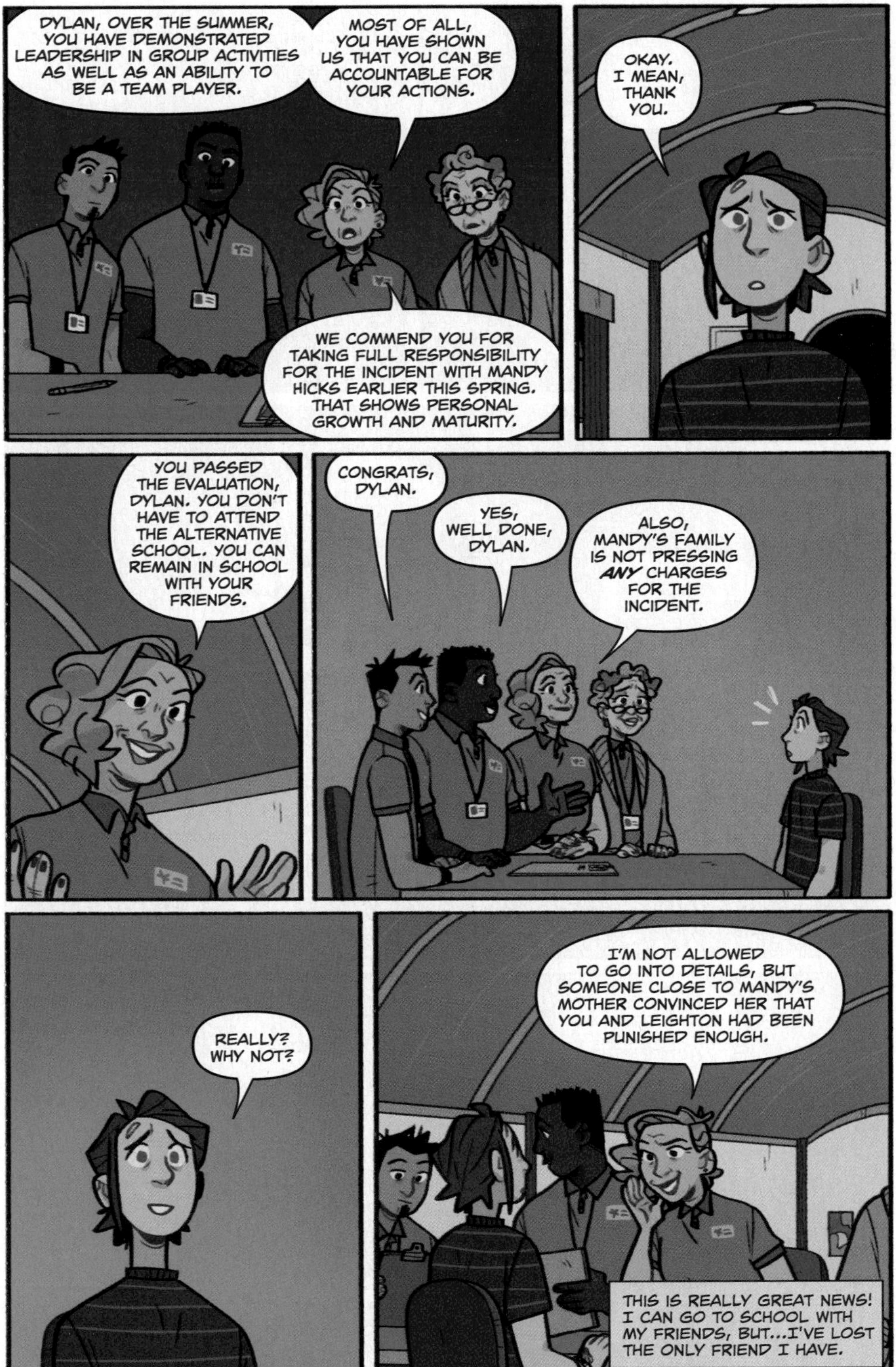
DYLAN, OVER THE SUMMER, YOU HAVE DEMONSTRATED LEADERSHIP IN GROUP ACTIVITIES AS WELL AS AN ABILITY TO BE A TEAM PLAYER.
MOST OF ALL, YOU HAVE SHOWN US THAT YOU CAN BE ACCOUNTABLE FOR YOUR ACTIONS.
WE COMMEND YOU FOR TAKING FULL RESPONSIBILITY FOR THE INCIDENT WITH MANDY HICKS EARLIER THIS SPRING. THAT SHOWS PERSONAL GROWTH AND MATURITY.
OKAY. I MEAN, THANK YOU.
YOU PASSED THE EVALUATION, DYLAN. YOU DON'T HAVE TO ATTEND THE ALTERNATIVE SCHOOL. YOU CAN REMAIN IN SCHOOL WITH YOUR FRIENDS.
CONGRATS, DYLAN.
YES, WELL DONE, DYLAN.
ALSO, MANDY'S FAMILY IS NOT PRESSING *ANY* CHARGES FOR THE INCIDENT.
REALLY? WHY NOT?
I'M NOT ALLOWED TO GO INTO DETAILS, BUT SOMEONE CLOSE TO MANDY'S MOTHER CONVINCED HER THAT YOU AND LEIGHTON HAD BEEN PUNISHED ENOUGH.
THIS IS REALLY GREAT NEWS! I CAN GO TO SCHOOL WITH MY FRIENDS, BUT...I'VE LOST THE ONLY FRIEND I HAVE.

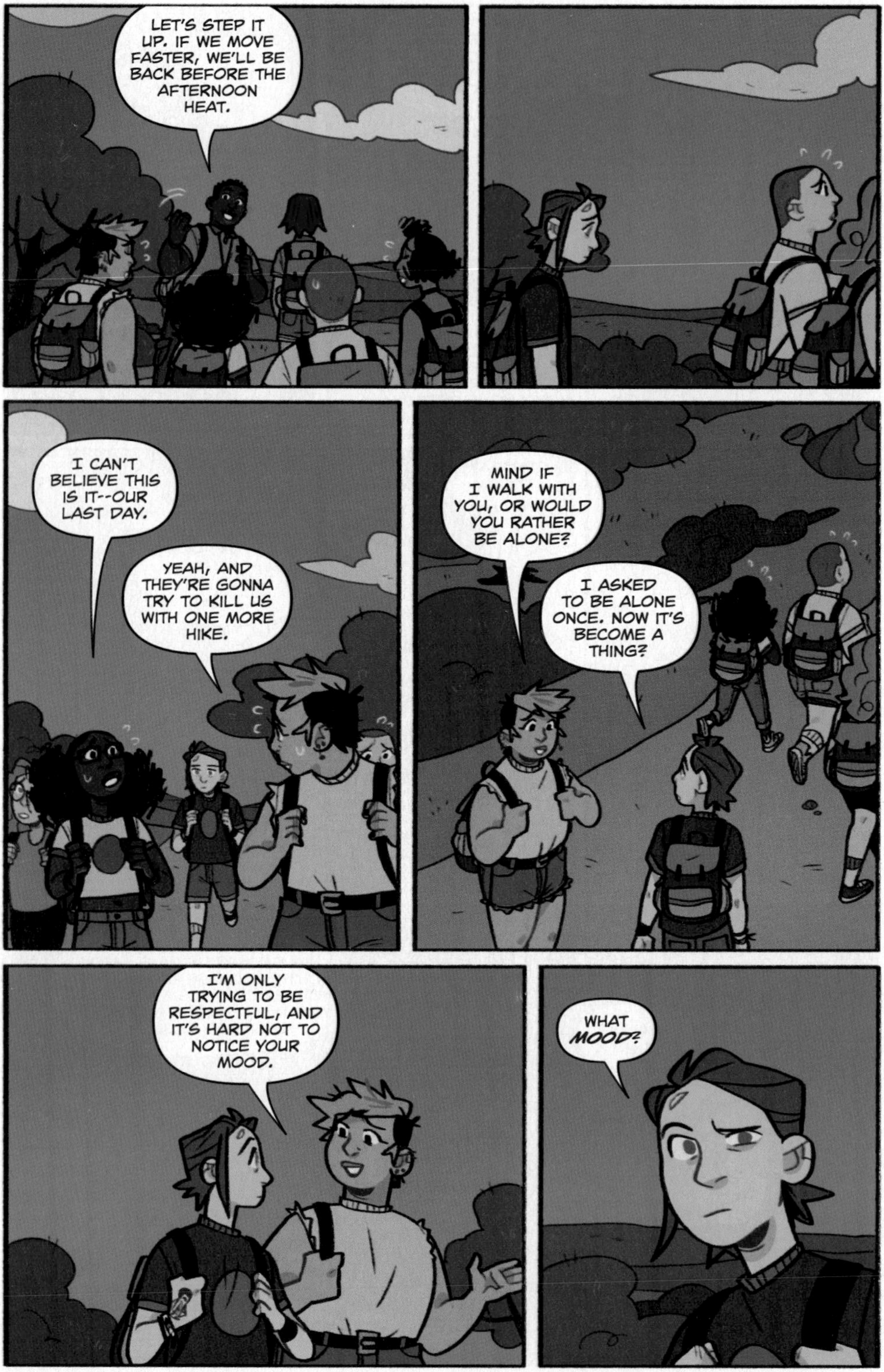
LET'S STEP IT UP. IF WE MOVE FASTER, WE'LL BE BACK BEFORE THE AFTERNOON HEAT.
I CAN'T BELIEVE THIS IS IT--OUR LAST DAY.
YEAH, AND THEY'RE GONNA TRY TO KILL US WITH ONE MORE HIKE.
MIND IF I WALK WITH YOU, OR WOULD YOU RATHER BE ALONE?
I ASKED TO BE ALONE ONCE. NOW IT'S BECOME A THING?
I'M ONLY TRYING TO BE RESPECTFUL, AND IT'S HARD NOT TO NOTICE YOUR MOOD.
WHAT *MOOD*?

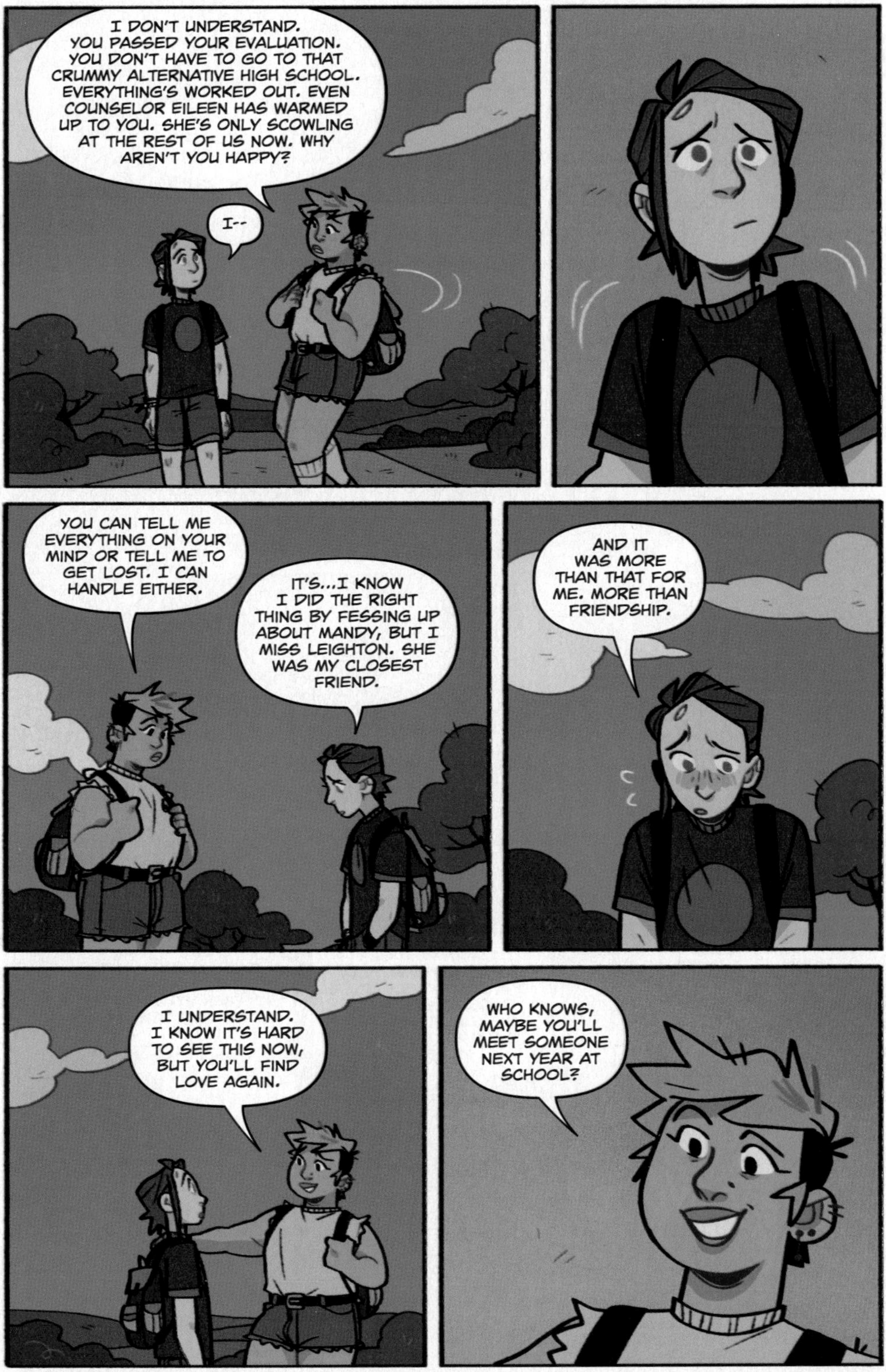
I DON'T UNDERSTAND. YOU PASSED YOUR EVALUATION. YOU DON'T HAVE TO GO TO THAT CRUMMY ALTERNATIVE HIGH SCHOOL. EVERYTHING'S WORKED OUT. EVEN COUNSELOR EILEEN HAS WARMED UP TO YOU. SHE'S ONLY SCOWLING AT THE REST OF US NOW. WHY AREN'T YOU HAPPY?
I--
YOU CAN TELL ME EVERYTHING ON YOUR MIND OR TELL ME TO GET LOST. I CAN HANDLE EITHER.
IT'S...I KNOW I DID THE RIGHT THING BY FESSING UP ABOUT MANDY, BUT I MISS LEIGHTON. SHE WAS MY CLOSEST FRIEND.
AND IT WAS MORE THAN THAT FOR ME. MORE THAN FRIENDSHIP.
I UNDERSTAND. I KNOW IT'S HARD TO SEE THIS NOW, BUT YOU'LL FIND LOVE AGAIN.
WHO KNOWS, MAYBE YOU'LL MEET SOMEONE NEXT YEAR AT SCHOOL?

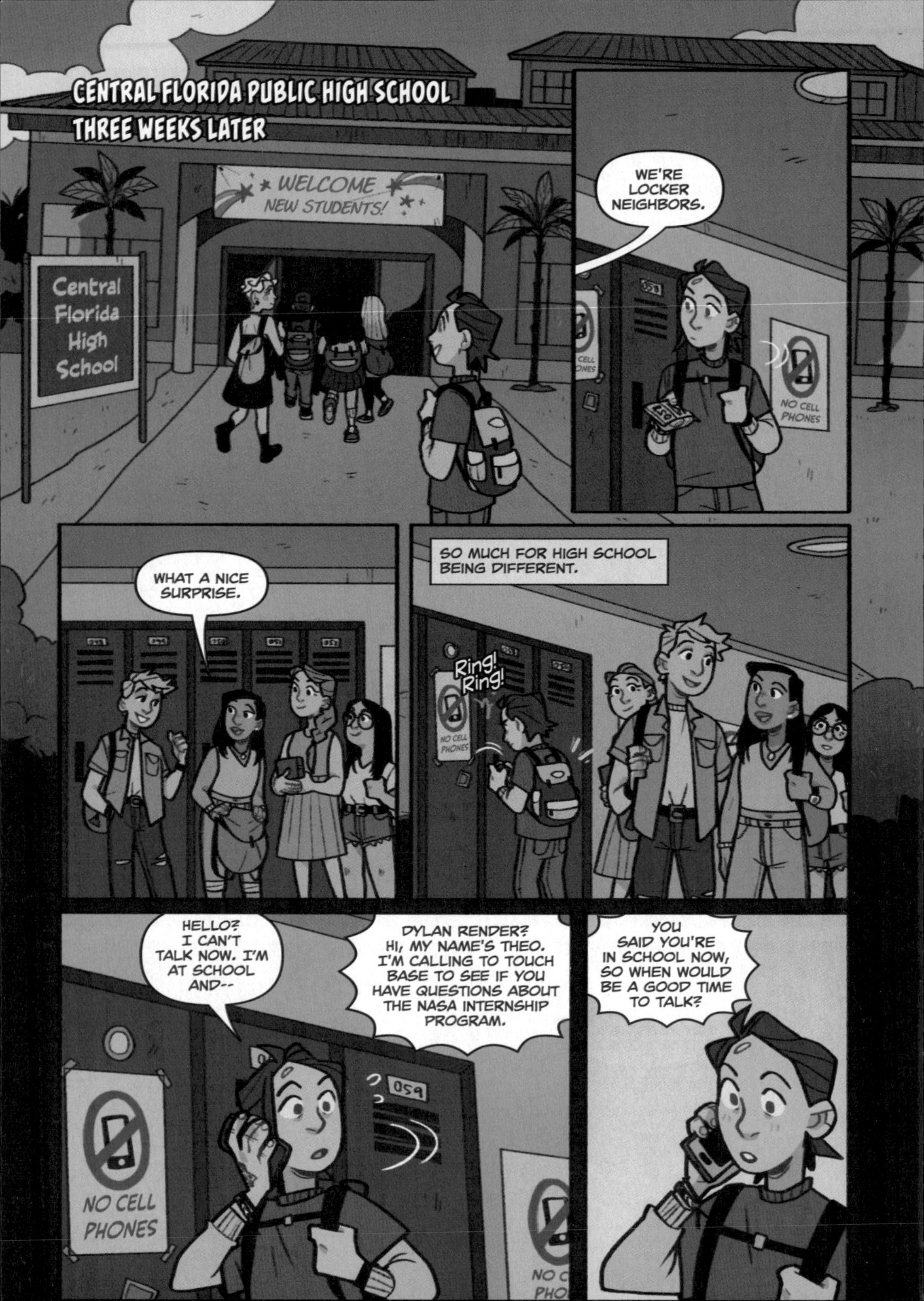

CENTRAL FLORIDA PUBLIC HIGH SCHOOL
THREE WEEKS LATER
WELCOME NEW STUDENTS!
Central Florida High School
WE'RE LOCKER NEIGHBORS.
NO CELL PHONES
WHAT A NICE SURPRISE.
SO MUCH FOR HIGH SCHOOL BEING DIFFERENT.
Ring! Ring!
NO CELL PHONES
HELLO? I CAN'T TALK NOW. I'M AT SCHOOL AND--
DYLAN RENDER? HI, MY NAME'S THEO. I'M CALLING TO TOUCH BASE TO SEE IF YOU HAVE QUESTIONS ABOUT THE NASA INTERNSHIP PROGRAM.
YOU SAID YOU'RE IN SCHOOL NOW, SO WHEN WOULD BE A GOOD TIME TO TALK?
NO CELL PHONES
059

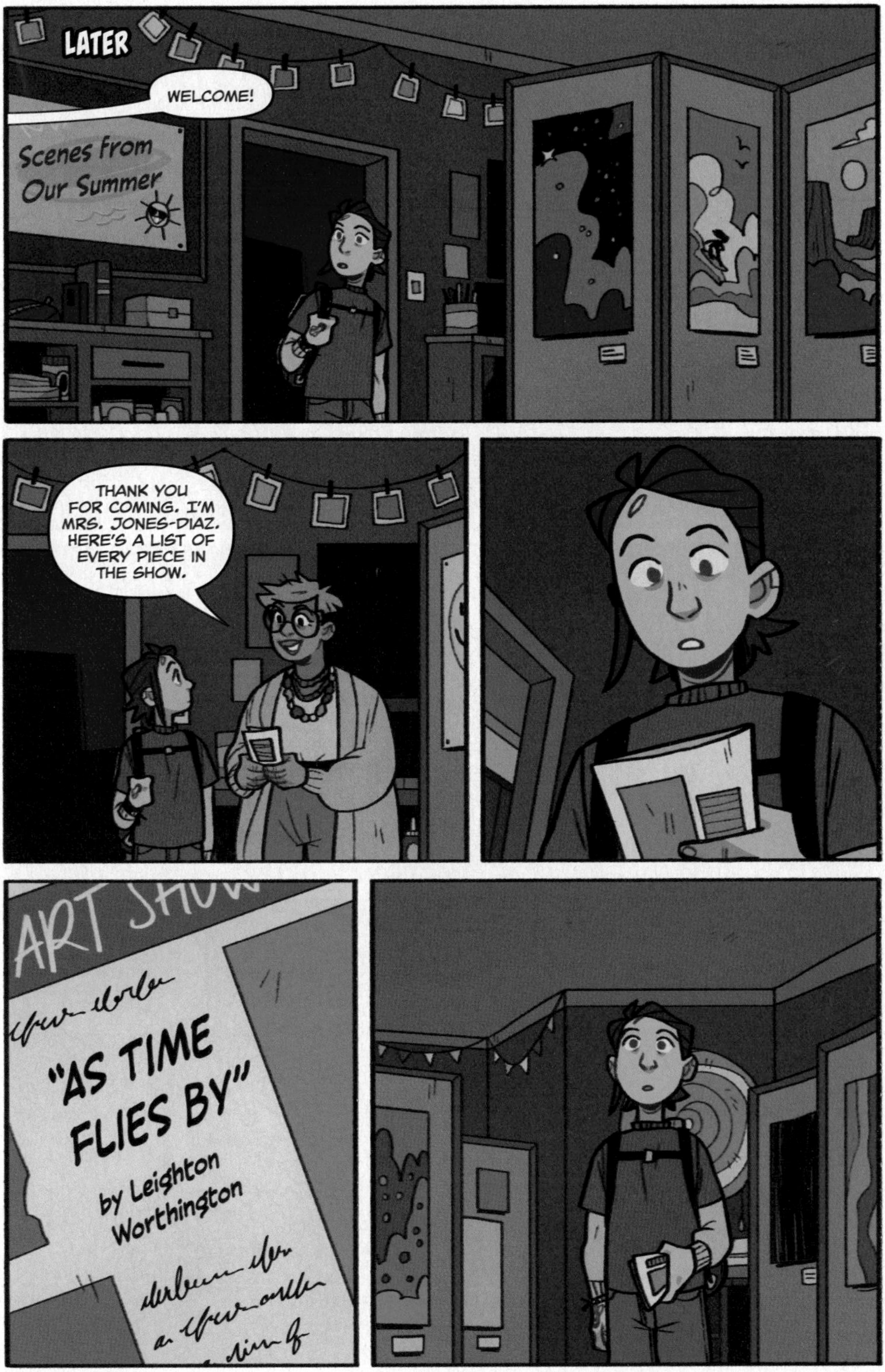
LATER
WELCOME!
Scenes from Our Summer
THANK YOU FOR COMING. I'M MRS. JONES-DIAZ. HERE'S A LIST OF EVERY PIECE IN THE SHOW.
ART SHOW
"AS TIME FLIES BY"
by Leighton Worthington

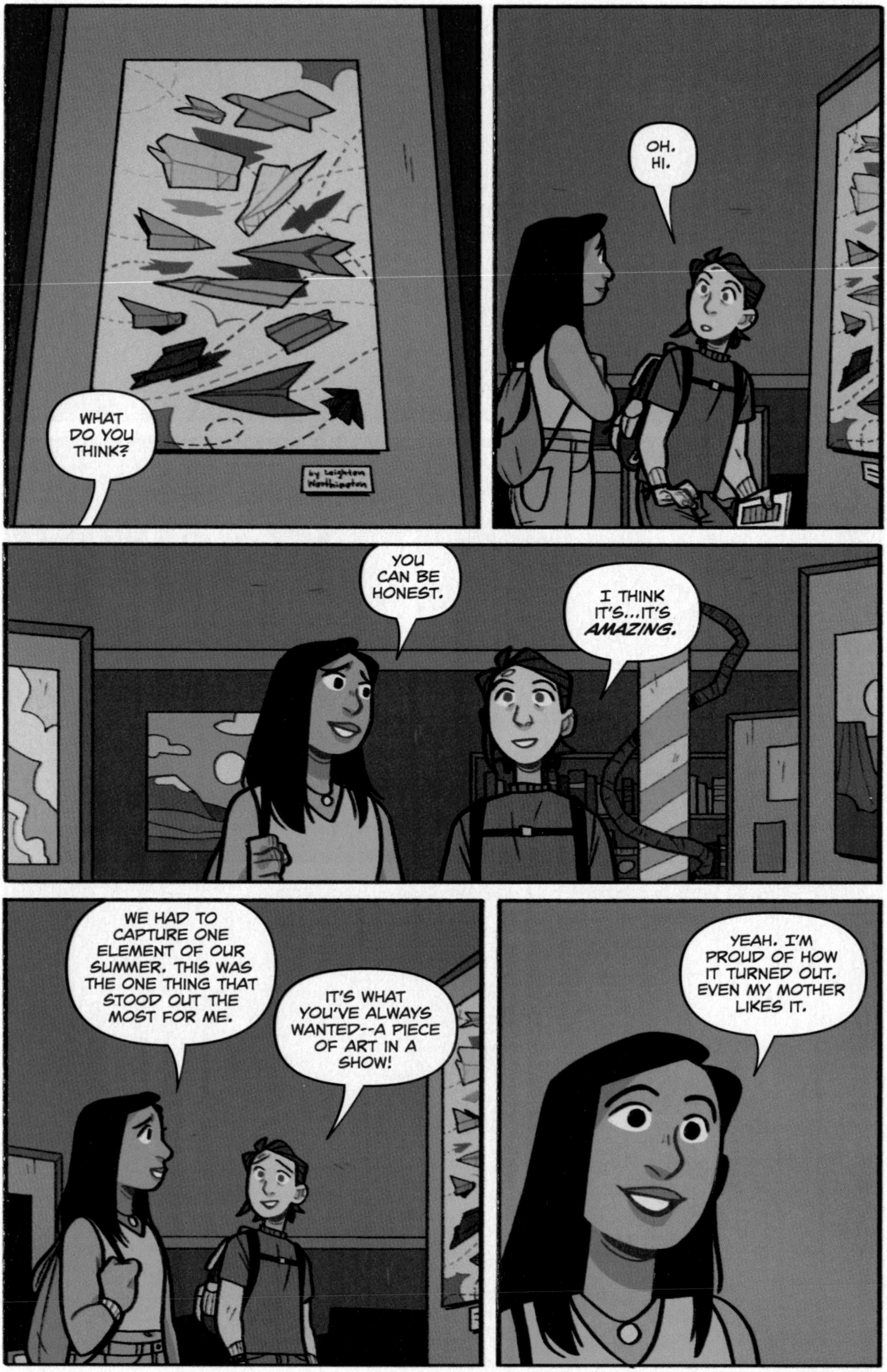
WHAT DO YOU THINK?
OH. HI.
YOU CAN BE HONEST.
I THINK IT'S...IT'S *AMAZING.*
WE HAD TO CAPTURE ONE ELEMENT OF OUR SUMMER. THIS WAS THE ONE THING THAT STOOD OUT THE MOST FOR ME.
IT'S WHAT YOU'VE ALWAYS WANTED--A PIECE OF ART IN A SHOW!
YEAH. I'M PROUD OF HOW IT TURNED OUT. EVEN MY MOTHER LIKES IT.

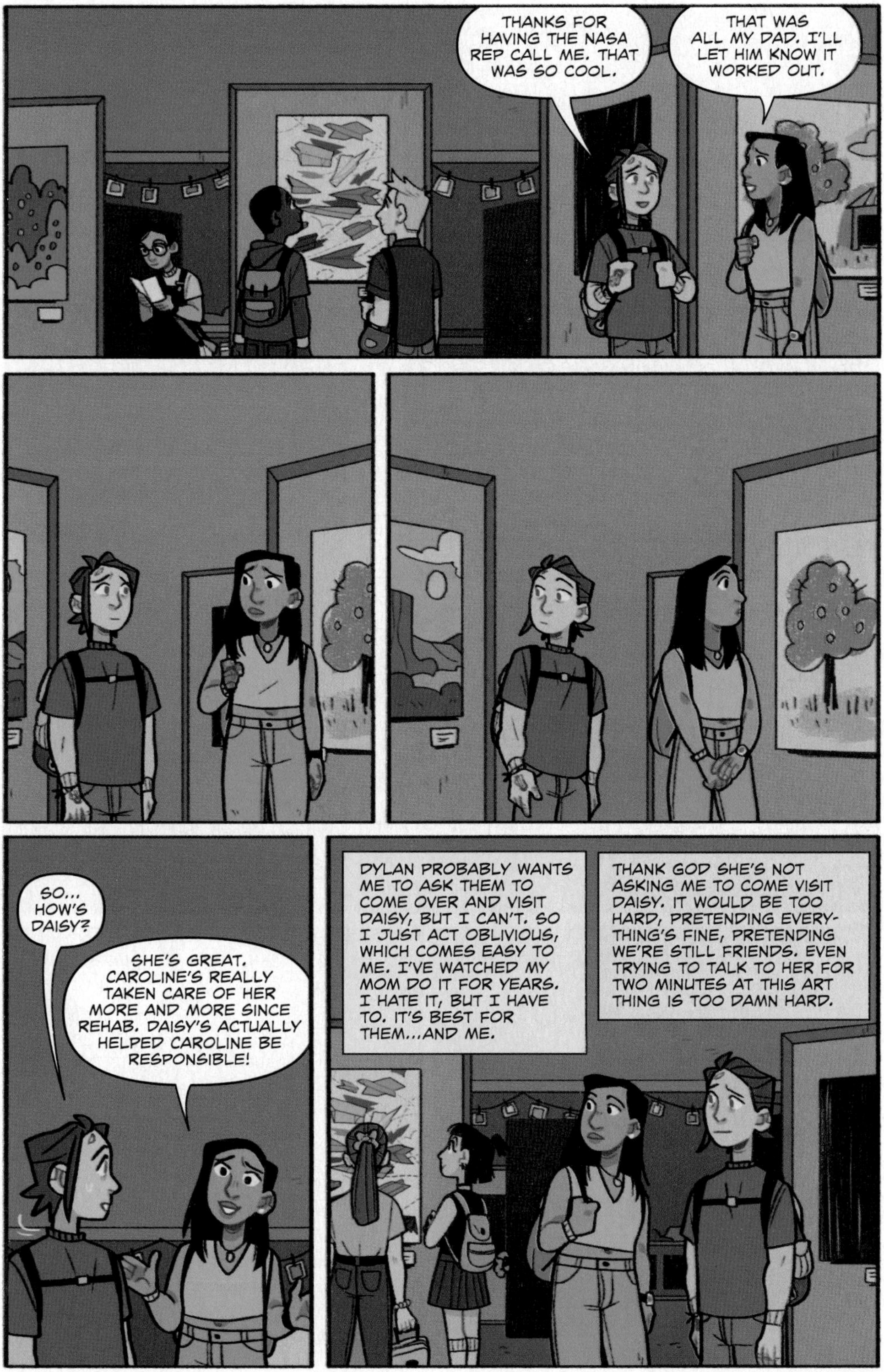
THANKS FOR HAVING THE NASA REP CALL ME. THAT WAS SO COOL.
THAT WAS ALL MY DAD. I'LL LET HIM KNOW IT WORKED OUT.
SO... HOW'S DAISY?
SHE'S GREAT. CAROLINE'S REALLY TAKEN CARE OF HER MORE AND MORE SINCE REHAB. DAISY'S ACTUALLY HELPED CAROLINE BE RESPONSIBLE!
DYLAN PROBABLY WANTS ME TO ASK THEM TO COME OVER AND VISIT DAISY, BUT I CAN'T. SO I JUST ACT OBLIVIOUS, WHICH COMES EASY TO ME. I'VE WATCHED MY MOM DO IT FOR YEARS. I HATE IT, BUT I HAVE TO. IT'S BEST FOR THEM...AND ME.
THANK GOD SHE'S NOT ASKING ME TO COME VISIT DAISY. IT WOULD BE TOO HARD, PRETENDING EVERY-THING'S FINE, PRETENDING WE'RE STILL FRIENDS. EVEN TRYING TO TALK TO HER FOR TWO MINUTES AT THIS ART THING IS TOO DAMN HARD.

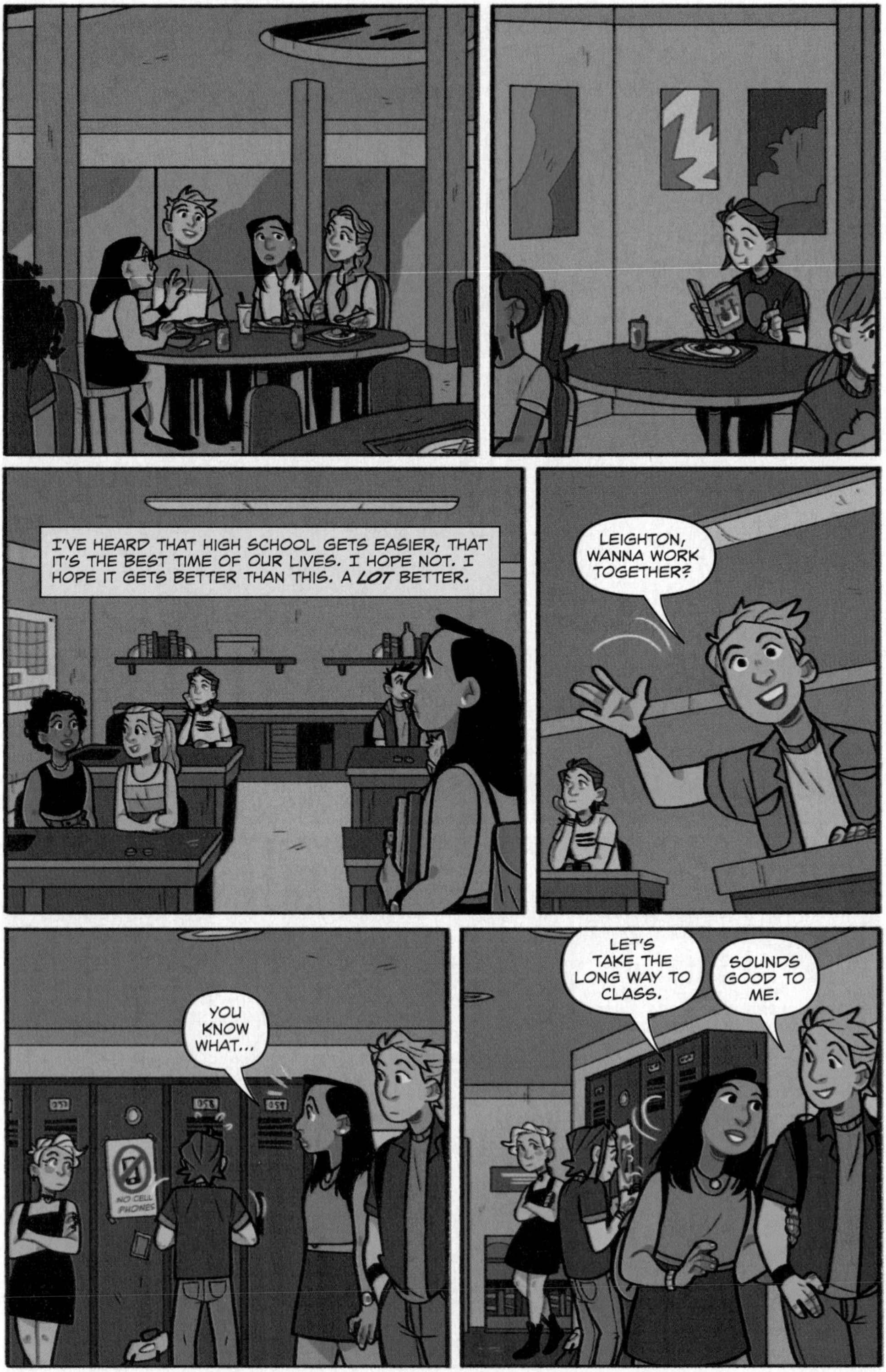
I'VE HEARD THAT HIGH SCHOOL GETS EASIER, THAT IT'S THE BEST TIME OF OUR LIVES. I HOPE NOT. I HOPE IT GETS BETTER THAN THIS. A *LOT* BETTER.
LEIGHTON, WANNA WORK TOGETHER?
YOU KNOW WHAT...
NO CELL PHONES
LET'S TAKE THE LONG WAY TO CLASS.
SOUNDS GOOD TO ME.

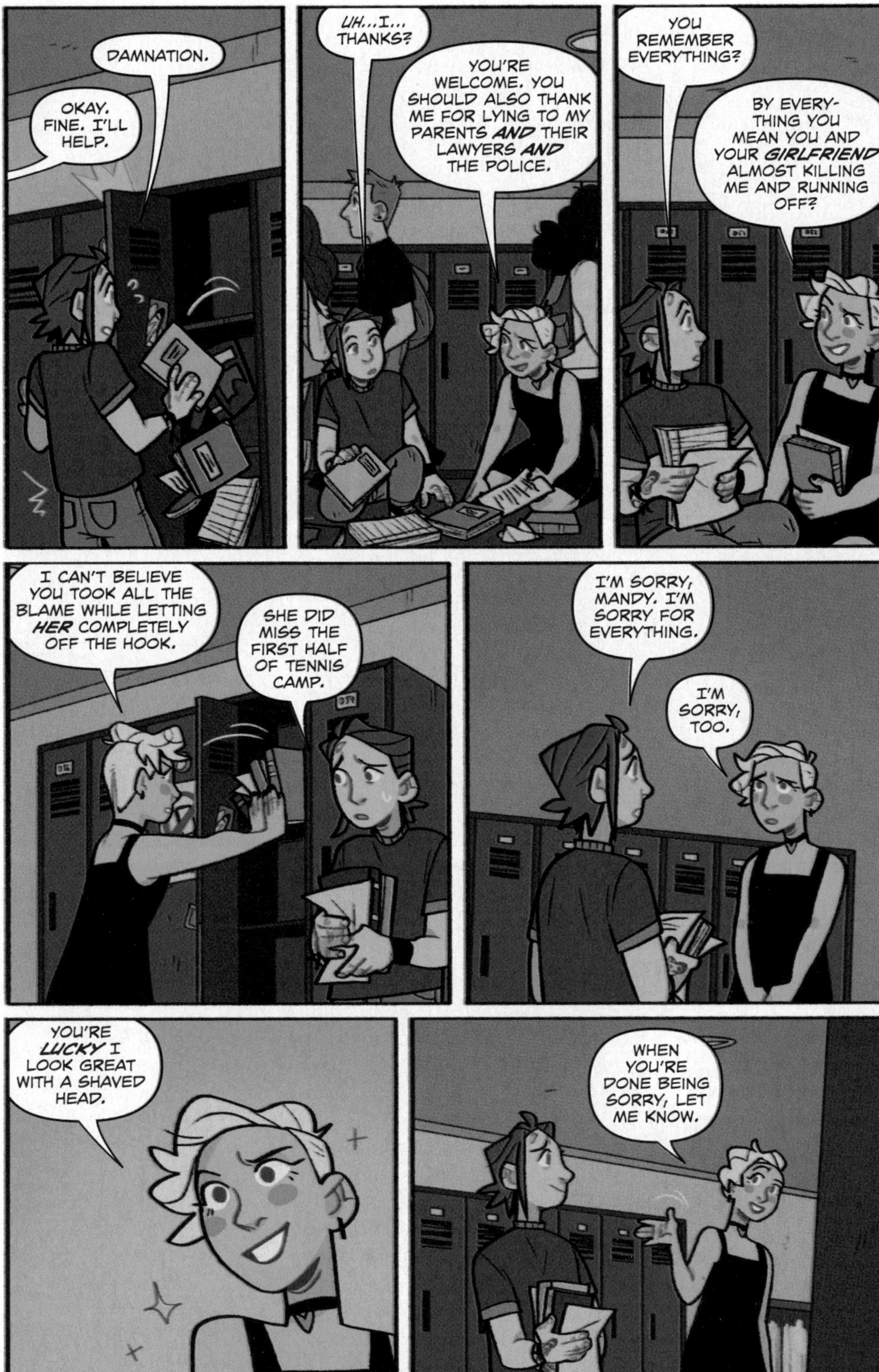
DAMNATION.
OKAY. FINE. I'LL HELP.
UH...I... THANKS?
YOU'RE WELCOME. YOU SHOULD ALSO THANK ME FOR LYING TO MY PARENTS AND THEIR LAWYERS AND THE POLICE.
YOU REMEMBER EVERYTHING?
BY EVERY-THING YOU MEAN YOU AND YOUR GIRLFRIEND ALMOST KILLING ME AND RUNNING OFF?
I CAN'T BELIEVE YOU TOOK ALL THE BLAME WHILE LETTING HER COMPLETELY OFF THE HOOK.
SHE DID MISS THE FIRST HALF OF TENNIS CAMP.
I'M SORRY, MANDY. I'M SORRY FOR EVERYTHING.
I'M SORRY, TOO.
YOU'RE LUCKY I LOOK GREAT WITH A SHAVED HEAD.
WHEN YOU'RE DONE BEING SORRY, LET ME KNOW.

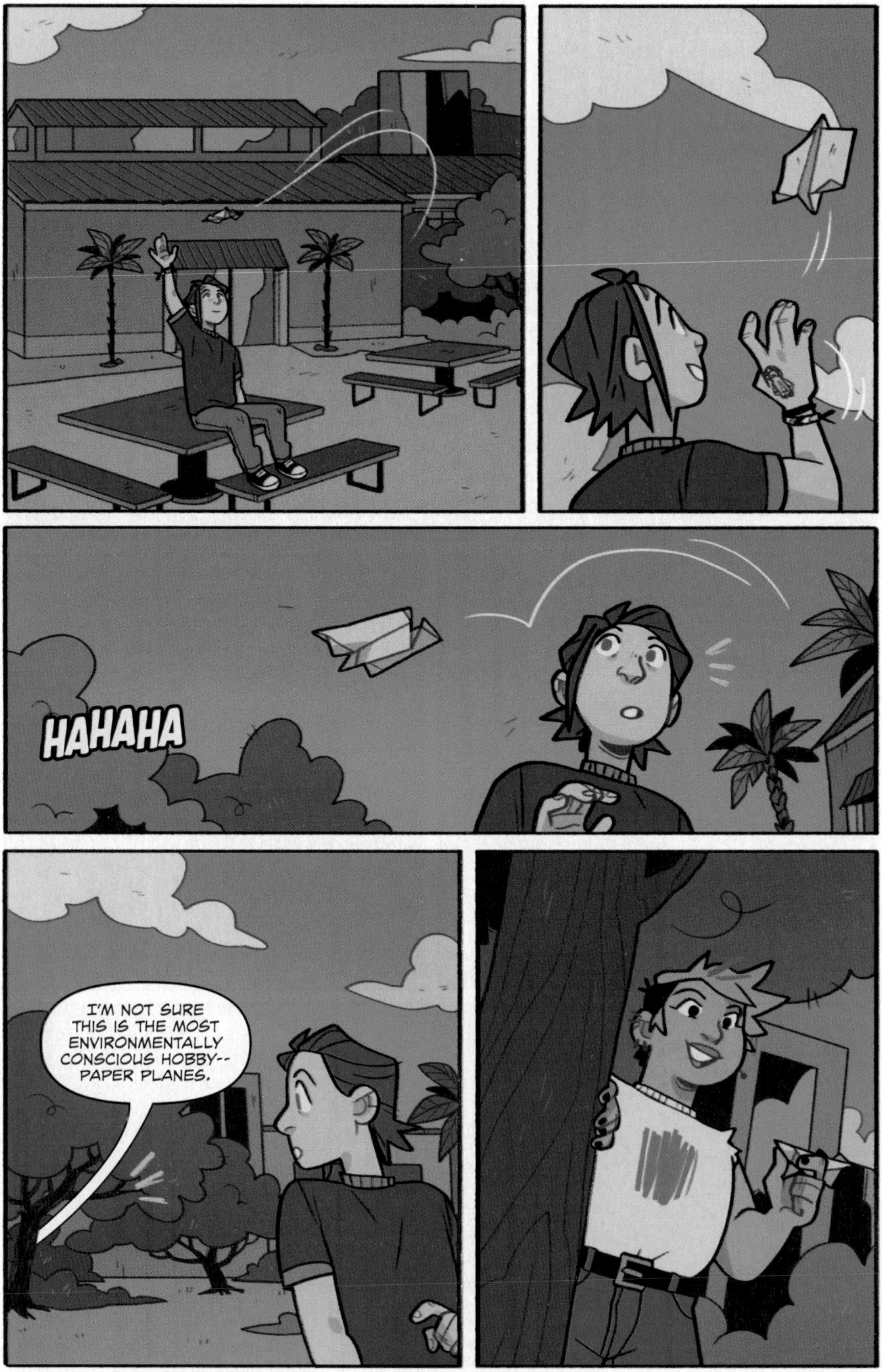
HAHAHA
I'M NOT SURE THIS IS THE MOST ENVIRONMENTALLY CONSCIOUS HOBBY-- PAPER PLANES.

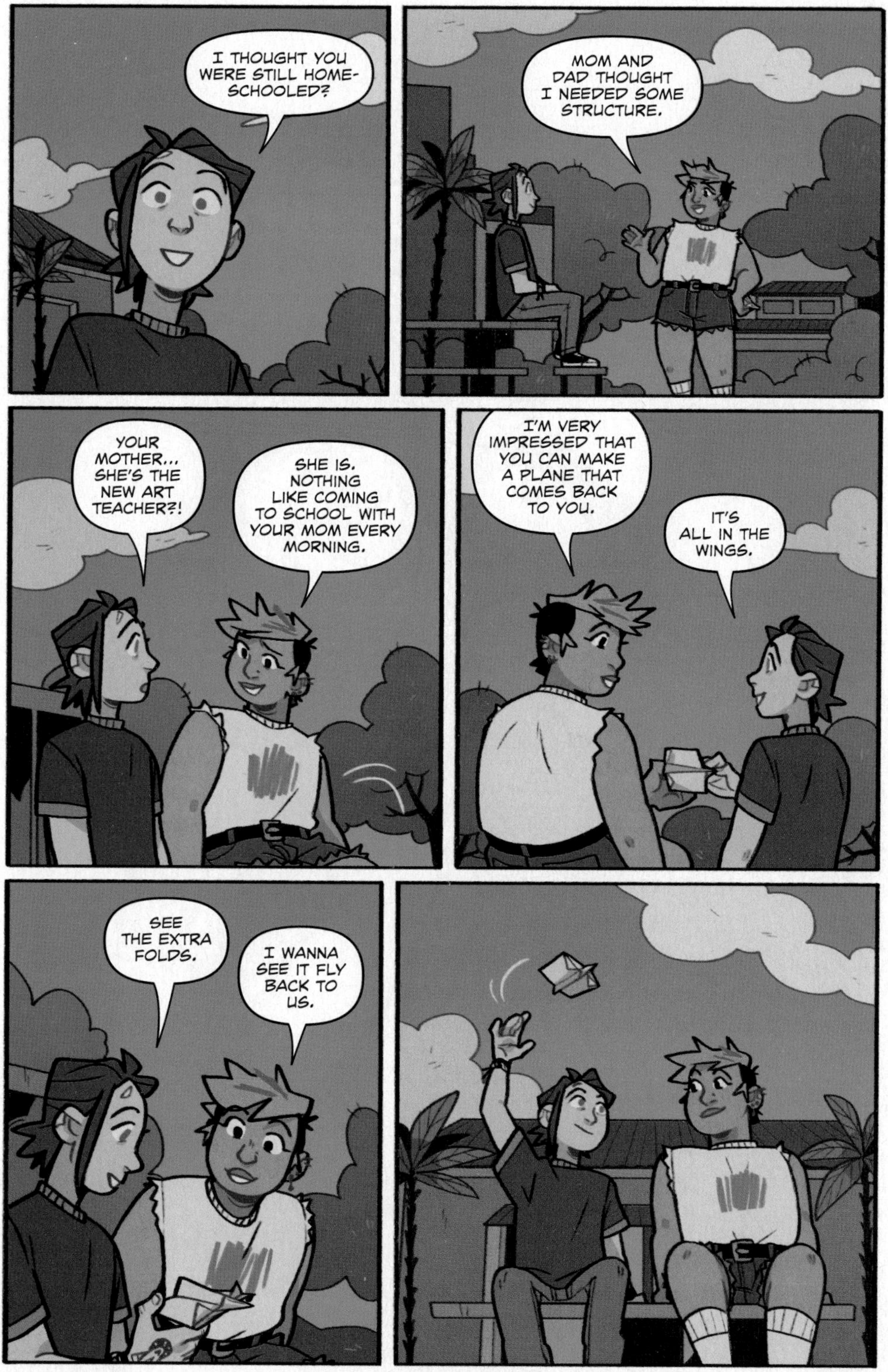
I THOUGHT YOU WERE STILL HOME-SCHOOLED?
MOM AND DAD THOUGHT I NEEDED SOME STRUCTURE.
YOUR MOTHER... SHE'S THE NEW ART TEACHER?!
SHE IS. NOTHING LIKE COMING TO SCHOOL WITH YOUR MOM EVERY MORNING.
I'M VERY IMPRESSED THAT YOU CAN MAKE A PLANE THAT COMES BACK TO YOU.
IT'S ALL IN THE WINGS.
SEE THE EXTRA FOLDS.
I WANNA SEE IT FLY BACK TO US.

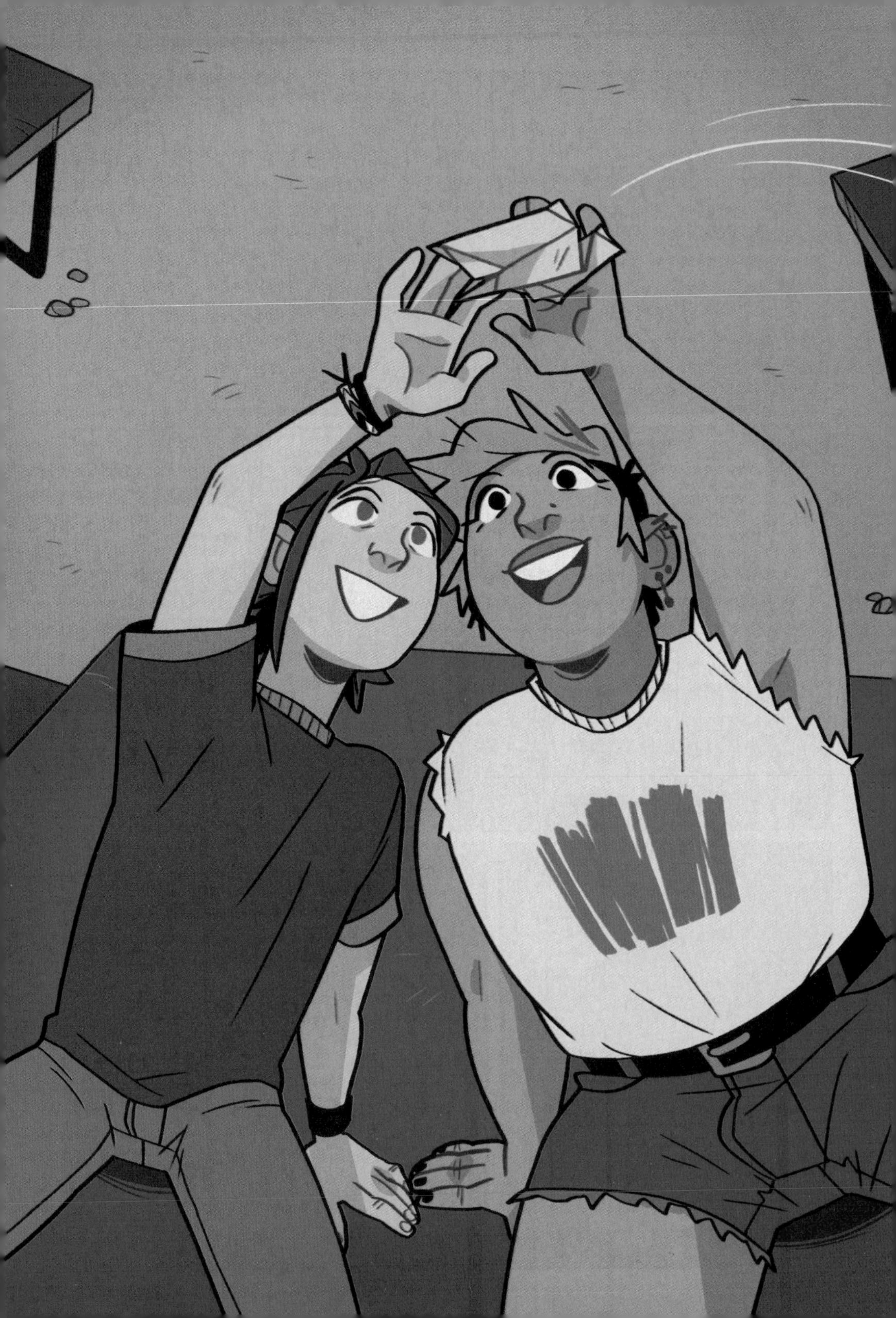

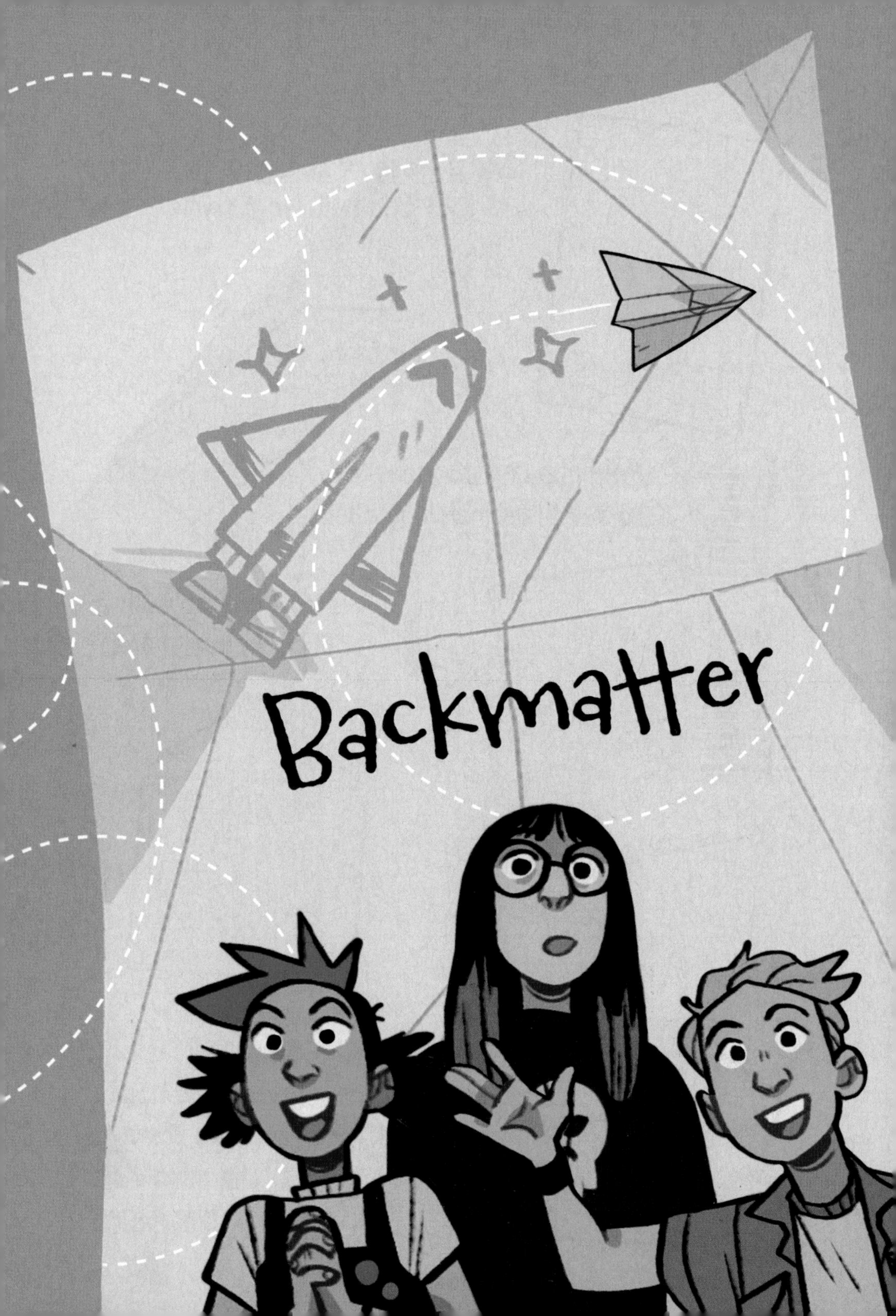
Backmatter

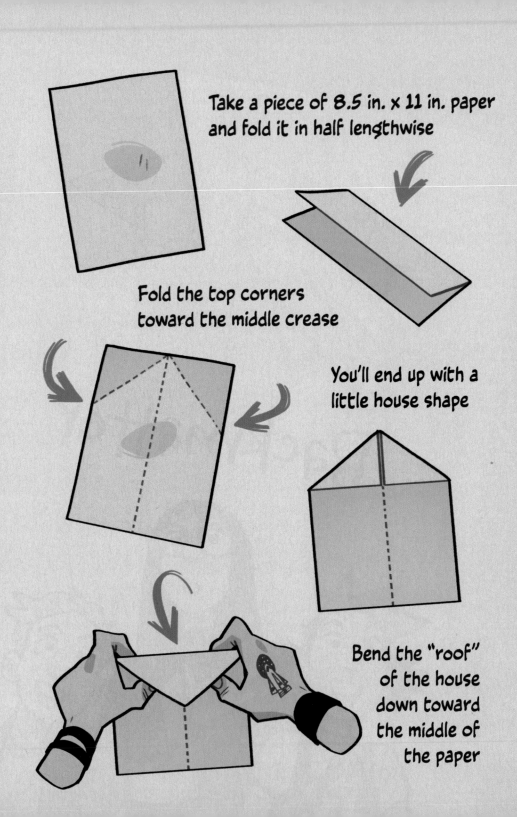

Take a piece of 8.5 in. x 11 in. paper and fold it in half lengthwise

Fold the top corners toward the middle crease

You'll end up with a little house shape

Bend the "roof" of the house down toward the middle of the paper

Fold the top corners down into
the middle so their tips touch
and create a little triangle

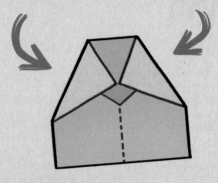

Bend the small triangle up to
secure your previous fold

Turn your plane and
fold it in half

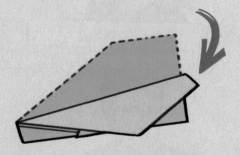

Create the wings by pushing
down both sides using the
secured fold as reference

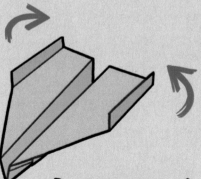

Bend the sides of
the wings up for
more air stability

DONE!

Creative Team

Jennie Wood

Jennie Wood is a nonbinary author and musician. They created the critically acclaimed, award-winning Flutter graphic novel series. Flutter has been named one of The Advocate's best LGBT graphic novels of the year, a Barnes & Noble book of the month, an INDIEFAB Book of the Year finalist, and a Virginia Library Association Diversity Honor Book. In 2018, Dark Horse published The Flutter Collection, the entire series in one book, which won the Next Generation Indie Book award for best graphic novel of the year. Jennie is also the author of the award-winning YA novel, A Boy Like Me. Their work can be seen in several anthologies, including The New York Times best-selling FUBAR, the Eisner award-winning anthology Love is Love, and John Carpenter's Tales For A HalloweeNight. Jennie lives in Boston with their partner Natalie and a supermutt named Moxie.

Dozerdraws

Dozerdraws Dozer is a nonbinary illustrator, comic artist and bird parent from Germany. They've done work on BOOM! Studios' Lumberjanes, several German TV and movie illustration and animation gigs, their own wrestling fan-comic and most recently illustrated Jasmine Walls' The Last Session for Mad Cave Studios. Teaming up with authors to bring new exciting stories with diverse characters to life is Dozer's passion!

Micah Myers

Micah Myers is a comic book letterer who has worked on comics for Image, Dark Horse, IDW, Heavy Metal, Mad Cave, Devil's Due, and many more. He also occasionally writes and has his own series about D-List supervillains, The Disasters.